# MURDER, SHE WROTE

# MURDER, SHE WROTE

---

- *The Murder of Sherlock Holmes*
- *Hooray for Homicide*
- *Lovers and Other Killers*

---

# BY JAMES ANDERSON

Based on the Universal Television series "Murder, She Wrote"
Created by Peter S. Fischer and Richard Levinson & William Link

Nelson Doubleday, Inc.
Garden City, New York

# CONTENTS

# MURDER, SHE WROTE

# THE MURDER OF
# SHERLOCK HOLMES

# Chapter One

"OF course, her uncle killed her," said Mrs. Fletcher.

Mrs. Thompson stared. "Oh, surely not!"

"Whatever makes you say that?" asked Mrs. Hoey.

"It just seems obvious. I mean, when the uncle showed up after the party wearing a different tie, he'd obviously changed it for a reason. And there was the phone call from the coroner—he couldn't have known about that unless he'd overheard the doctor talking to the priest."

Mrs. Thompson and Mrs. Hoey looked bemused. "Say that again," demanded Mrs. Hoey.

"Slowly," pleaded Mrs. Thompson.

"It's really quite simple." Mrs. Fletcher took a deep breath. Then she paused and frowned. "Or have I been completely bamboozled? Surely not . . ."

She stood up suddenly. "Well, there's one way to find out."

"Jessica, what are you going to do?"

"Ask the director."

Jessica Fletcher started to make her way down the aisle of the small theatre. Her friends followed her hastily.

"He'll never tell you," said Mrs. Thompson.

"Not perhaps in so many words," said Jessica placidly.

The director had risen from his seat in the first row of the otherwise empty auditorium. He was now haranguing some unhappy-looking actors who had formed a small group at the front of the stage. He made a gesture of dismissal and they shuffled off into the wings. The director turned and saw Jessica and her friends approaching. He scowled.

"Ladies, this is a private rehearsal. No outsiders."

Jessica raised her eyebrows. "Excuse me, Mr. Cellini, but you did ask us to meet you here."

He looked disbelieving. "Now, why would I do a thing like that? I don't even know you!"

"We're the refreshment committee," Mrs. Thompson explained.

"From the PTA," added Mrs. Hoey.

"Oh." This information did not seem to fill Mr. Cellini with intense delight. "The cookie ladies," he said wearily. "Look, see me after the rehearsal, will you? We've still got two acts to get through—and we open tomorrow night."

"Mr. Cellini, I just love the show," said Mrs. Thompson. "It's so . . . so mystifying."

"Yeah, well, that's the idea." Mr. Cellini looked at his watch.

"And so exciting to have a pre-Broadway premiere right here in a little place like Cabot Cove," added Mrs. Hoey.

"Well, there won't be any premiere, let alone a Broadway run, if I don't get the thing right. So if you'll excuse me . . ."

He moved away and started to climb the short flight of steps to the stage.

"And I'm sure no one will guess that the uncle is the killer," Jessica called after him.

Halfway up the steps Mr. Cellini froze. For a full five seconds he stood quite still. Jessica and her friends surveyed his back with interest. Then he turned slowly.

"*What* did you say?" exclaimed Mr. Cellini.

Lois Thompson gave a giggle. "Poor Mr. Cellini. I thought he was going to have a fit—once you'd convinced him you hadn't read the script, Jess."

"He can see his dreams of a Broadway run fading fast, I guess," said Eleanor Hoey.

Jessica gave a sigh. "Yes, I'm afraid that play's got about as much chance of a successful Broadway run as I have of swimming the English Channel. I felt a bit mean—but on the other hand, it's surely better that flaws be pointed out now, rather than have professional critics tear the play apart publicly."

"Well, I don't know," said Lois thoughtfully. "I enjoyed it. I think it might do quite well."

"And after all," said Eleanor, "neither Lois nor I guessed the end. It's just that you're so good at mysteries, Jessica. Even Agatha Christie and Ellery Queen didn't always fool you."

"A natural flair," said Lois. "Just like Miss Marple."

Jessica Fletcher was a widow in her mid-fifties. She was energetic, intelligent, intensely interested in people—and had the happy knack of being able to get on easily with folk of every age and social background. She had a strong sense of justice, a deep dislike of sham in any form, an ever-present urge to help those who needed it, and a belief in speaking her mind. Any tendency these characteristics might have had to give her the reputation of a do-gooding busybody was, however, offset by a wicked sense of fun and humor—which had once or twice come close to getting her into hot water. She was attractive, dressed smartly in a conservative manner—being much given to tweed suits and sweaters—and, when her services were required, worked as a substitute English teacher.

Her friends, Lois and Eleanor, were cheerful, friendly souls who admired Jessica and were, if truth were told, a little in awe of her. If their intelligence did not quite match up to hers, she at least never gave any indication of being aware of the fact.

Following their return from the theatre, the three ladies were drinking coffee in Jessica's home, a large Victorian house on a pleasant, tree-lined block in the small coastal town of Cabot Cove, Maine. In spite of many invitations from numerous relatives throughout the country for her to make her home with them, Jessica had lived alone since the death of her husband some years before. The house was too big for her, she knew. And every corner of it evoked poignant memories. But she did love the house, and the town, and by keeping every minute of her days occupied she was managing—now, at last—to hold the ache at bay.

"Say, Jessica." Eleanor put down her coffee cup suddenly. "Why don't you write a mystery?"

"Now that's an idea!" exclaimed Lois. "After all, you're a teacher of English, so you know all about literature and grammar and stuff."

Jessica gazed at them silently for a few seconds. Then she smiled. "Funny you should say that, girls."

For a moment they looked blank. Then Eleanor gave a squeal. "Jess—you mean you *have?*"

Jessica shrugged. "Well, sort of."

"My, how thrilling!" Lois' eyes were big. "Oh, Jess, you must let us read it."

"Certainly not," Jessica said firmly.

"But why?"

"Because it's simply not good enough."

"Oh, Jessica, nonsense! I'm sure it's just wonderful!"

"You can't possibly say that, Eleanor. You know nothing about the story."

"But we know *you,*" said Lois.

"You're sweet, girls, but I know *it.* In addition to writing it, I've read it. Which I think a lot of authors fail to do."

"At least tell us what it's called," said Eleanor.

"You'll laugh."

"No, we won't, honestly. Will we, Lois?"

"Cross our hearts."

"Well, it's called *The Corpse Danced at Midnight.* Just an old-fashioned whodunit."

"Oo." Lois gave a wriggle. "Thrilling!"

"Is it a *real* corpse? And does it *really* dance?"

"Eleanor, a real corpse could hardly *really* dance." Lois laughed. "It's
not a horror story."

"No, I suppose not," Eleanor admitted. "But, Jess, you mean you're
not going to try and get it published?"

"No way, my dear."

"Oh, Jess, I think you're so stupid. It might be a best seller."

Jessica laughed. "Not a chance, Eleanor."

"Oh, do let us read it," Lois pleaded. "Or just the first couple of
chapters. We'll tell you exactly what we think. Honestly. Won't we, Eleanor?"

"Cross our hearts."

Jessica hesitated. She was too kind to say it, but their opinion of her
book would be quite valueless to her. She was very fond of Lois and
Eleanor. But they were to literary criticism what John Wayne had been to
ballet dancing.

She gave a sigh. Oh well, perhaps it wouldn't do any harm to let them
read the first two chapters. At least, if they didn't like it (and whatever
they *said,* she'd know what they *thought),* it would tell her clearly that
the book was even worse than she suspected.

"All right," she said. "You win." She got to her feet.

"Oh, thanks, Jess."

"Have you got two copies?" Eleanor asked eagerly.

"Afraid not. You'll have to take turns. Toss a coin, or something." She
picked up her purse, rummaged in it, and drew out a small key.

"Isn't that a bit risky?" Eleanor said. "Not having a second copy, I
mean."

"Not at all—as I don't intend to send it away. I have my original
manuscript, of course."

Jessica crossed to a large, old-fashioned dark wood bureau in the corner of the room and unlocked one of the doors. She opened it, reached
inside, and then stood quite still. She bent down, peered into the cupboard, and started groping with both hands.

"What's the matter, Jess?" Eleanor spoke sharply.

Jessica slowly straightened up and turned to her friends. Her face was blank. "It's gone," she said. "The typescript of my book. Someone must have stolen it."

Fifteen minutes later Jessica sank back down into her chair. "Well," she said slowly, "there's certainly nothing else missing. That's one relief."

"You've checked in every room?" Lois queried.

Jessica nodded.

Eleanor was looking mystified. "But who on earth would break in and just steal a manuscript?"

Suddenly Lois' face lit up. "Another author, of course!" she said triumphantly. "He wants to steal your plot."

"Lois, until twenty minutes ago nobody in the world but myself knew the book existed."

Lois' face fell. "Oh."

"Hadn't you better call the police?" Eleanor asked.

"No."

"But Jessica, why not?"

"Because I know who's taken it. It just this moment hit me. It could only be one person."

In Grady Fletcher's Greenwich Village apartment the phone rang. Grady answered it. He was an eager, fresh-faced young man of twenty-seven, tall, slim, and nearly always smiling. Basically a romantic and idealist, his chosen profession of accounting forced him, perhaps fortunately, to bank down his natural exuberance. But it could do little to quench his considerable charm.

"Hullo?" he said.

He heard a familiar voice. "Grady?"

"Oh, hi, Aunt Jess. How are you?"

"Very well. Grady, I'll come straight to the point. Did you take the typescript of a novel with you last month when you left here?"

"Oh."

"I take it that means yes?"

"How did you guess it was me?"

"It couldn't have been anyone else. It had to be somebody staying in the house, not an ordinary thief. Grady, why did you do it?"

"I wanted to read it."

"Why didn't you ask?"

"I thought you'd say no. You remember, when I was staying with you, I came in one day just as you were putting the manuscript away?"

"Ah, I thought you caught a glimpse of it."

"I did. And for a moment you looked kind of embarrassed. I was intrigued—though I soon guessed those papers were a novel. I just had to read it. But knowing you, I was sure you wouldn't think it good enough to let anyone see it. So I realized I'd have to sneak it. Trouble was, you always kept the bureau locked. Until, that is, the very last day of my visit. You'd been to the bureau for something else and you left the key in. So when you went out of the room I grabbed the novel and slipped it in my case. I felt a bit awful at first. But after all, you *have* always told me to treat the house completely as my own, so . . ."

"Oh, don't be silly! I don't mind *that*. But all the same, it was very naughty of you to take the manuscript away."

Grady grinned. "You're the only person in the world who ever calls me naughty."

"More's the pity, probably. I could be very angry, Grady."

"Oh no, you couldn't, Aunt Jess—not with me. You know I'm your favorite relative."

"I know you're very conceited."

"Not at all. Just honest. Come on, now; it's true, isn't it?"

"Grady!"

"Will it help if I tell you it's mutual?"

"Flattery . . ."

"I know: is the sincerest form of imitation." The young man paused. "Hang on, there's something wrong there."

"Grady, you're . . ."

"Incorrigible?"

"I was going to say impossible."

"I like incorrigible better."

"This has gone on quite long enough," Jessica said firmly.

"Okay. Goodbye, Aunt Jess."

"Grady, don't hang up."

"Only kidding. Aunt Jess, I'm extremely sorry if I've upset you. I shouldn't have done it."

"Very well. We'll say no more about it—provided you return the manuscript at once. You have finished reading it, I suppose?"

"I have."

There was a pause. Then: "I see," said Jessica.

There was a longer pause. "You still there, Aunt Jess?"

"Er, yes."

"Something else you wanted to say?"

Jessica sighed. "You're waiting for me to ask how you liked it, aren't you?"

"If you really want to know . . ."

"All right, you'd better tell me."

Grady cleared his throat. "Well, to be absolutely frank . . ." He broke off, then laughed. "Aunt Jess, I think it's great."

"Really, Grady?"

"I couldn't put it down. I stayed up till three one morning finishing it."

"Well, that's very gratifying. Thank you. I value your opinion very much, Grady. But as you've finished it, I would like you to send it back now."

Grady sighed. "Afraid I can't do that. I loaned it to a friend."

"Oh, Grady, really!"

"It was so good, I just had to tell someone. And then this person naturally wanted to read it."

"Then ask for it back at once. If he hasn't finished it, you can *tell* him the end—if he's interested."

"It's a she, actually."

"Tell *her* the end, then."

"Oh, she's finished it."

"Then what *is* the problem?"

"Well, as a matter of fact, she's passed it on to her boss."

"Her boss? But why . . . I mean, who . . . ?"

"His name's Preston Giles."

"I don't care what his name is," Jessica said irritably. "I'm only interested in . . ." She broke off. "Preston Giles? That name seems to ring a bell."

"It should—for anyone interested in books. He's head of Coventry House."

"Coventry House? The publishers?"

"That's right. Now get hold of yourself, Aunt Jess, and listen. Kitt—oh, that's her name: Kitt Donovan—thought her firm might be interested in the book. Of course, Kitt doesn't pick books for publication herself; she's in the publicity department. So she took it straight to Mr. Giles. It's a terrific break. I mean, normally books have to go through the whole mill—readers, editors. But Giles promised Kitt that he would read *Corpse* personally."

"Read *what* personally?"

"*Corpse.* Oh, that's what Kitt and I have been calling it—sort of shorthand, you know. Where was I? Oh yes, he's promised to read it personally. Of course, he's very busy, so we don't know whether he's actually started it yet. Naturally she can't keep on pestering him about . . ."

"Grady, I'm not a writer. I've been filling in time since your uncle died. I wrote it to help keep my mind occupied, and as a sort of challenge —just to see if I could do it. I did think that if one day I wrote a book I could be proud of, I might send it to a publisher. But not this one. I want your friend to get it back."

Grady gave a groan. "I couldn't ask her to do that. Not after Giles agreed to read it personally. I couldn't do that to Kitt. It'd make her look a fool."

"But surely, when she explains that I simply don't want the book published . . ."

"That's just it. Giles doesn't know Kitt didn't have the author's permission to submit it. And *she* doesn't know, either. She thinks I have yours. She'd be terribly sore with me if she found out I didn't. And I'd hate to get Kitt sore with me. Oh, Aunt Jess, she's a wonderful girl."

"I'm sure she is, Grady. They always are."

"Oh, but she's different. She . . ."

"Her difference is not the point at issue." Jessica sighed. "Oh, I don't know. I suppose I'll *have* to leave the book with him now."

"That's great. I just knew you'd agree."

"Which is more than I knew. How long do you think before . . . ?"

"Oh, not more than a few weeks, I'm sure. We'll just have to hope Giles doesn't like it."

"I don't think I'd go that far. I'd like him to *like* it. That doesn't mean I have to let him publish it, does it?"

"No, I guess not. Okay, Aunt Jess, I'll get back to you the moment I hear anything."

"Grady, one more thing: this girl—Kitt—is it serious this time?"

Grady didn't answer for a moment. "Yes, it is. At least, it is with me."

"Good. I suggest you find out if it is with her. It's as well to have these matters quite clear. Goodbye, Grady."

"Goodbye, Aunt Jess."

# Chapter Two

FOR the next week or so Jessica's life proceeded on its usual busy but fairly unexciting course. She continued her work as substitute English teacher at Cabot Cove High School; she was active in the PTA; she bicycled and jogged and ran her house; she went out to eat with Lois and Eleanor.

But she didn't do any more writing.

It was ten days before Grady returned her call.

"Aunt Jess," he said when they'd exchanged greetings, "the news about *Corpse* is good and bad. Which do you want first?"

"The good."

"Well, Preston Giles enjoyed it very much and he'll be writing to tell you so."

"Oh, how nice," Jessica said. "I'll look forward to his letter. And I suppose the bad news is that nonetheless he doesn't want to publish it? But that's not bad news, Grady. I meant what I said: I don't *want* it published. So really . . ."

"You've got it wrong, Aunt Jessica. He does want to publish it. The bad news is that you're going to have quite a fight on your hands to stop him."

Jessica gave a gasp. "I don't believe it! He must be out of his mind."

"Not obviously so."

"You told him no, of course."

"I've told him nothing. I haven't seen him. He just today informed Kitt they were going to offer you a contract."

"Grady, you must . . ."

"It's out of my hands, Aunt Jess. You'll have to tell them yourself. Sorry and all that. Look, I must go: the Captain's just called a staff meeting. But congratulations—or commiserations. I don't know which. Bye."

He hung up.

\* \* \*

Jessica had genuinely intended to say no to Preston Giles. But the next day his letter arrived. It was very charming. And the advance he was offering—really, it was extremely generous. It would come in most useful. And, after all, she told herself, if Grady and Kitt Donovan *and* Mr. Giles all liked the book—well, she supposed it couldn't be too bad. Finally she succumbed and signed the contracts.

After that, rather surprisingly, nothing happened for a long time. Then one day, out of the blue, the proofs arrived. Jessica spent hours laboriously going over them for errors, and unnecessarily rechecking the spelling of dozens of words that in reality she knew perfectly how to spell.

A few months later the dust jacket turned up in the mail. To Jessica's relief it was in excellent taste, not at all like the lurid covers on some crime novels. In passing, it occurred to her that tasteful covers didn't necessarily help sales. But then, she reasoned, just because someone was publishing her book didn't mean that anyone would bother to read it. Every year hundreds of books died quietly and quickly, never to be heard of again.

She just hoped that Coventry House didn't actually lose money on it, that was all. . . .

Jessica stood outside the Cabot Cove Bookstore and stared disbelievingly at the window display. Copies of *The Corpse Danced at Midnight* by J. B. Fletcher filled all available space, while a huge, almost life-size picture of Jessica herself towered over them. Jessica squirmed inwardly. In the very center of the window was a placard that carried a photostat of the National Literary Circle best seller list. The eighth book, circled in red, was Jessica's. At the top of the placard was the legend in large type: NUMBER EIGHT BEST SELLER.

Jessica turned to see two of her students, a boy and a girl, standing beside her. She blushed slightly. They grinned at her.

"It's great, Mrs. Fletcher," said the boy.

The girl added: "Just terrific."

"Oh, thank you, Gail, Joe. But really, there must be some mistake."

At that moment the curtain at the rear of the window was pulled aside and the store owner appeared. He reached forward and removed the placard.

"There!" Jessica again swung around on the youngsters. "Didn't I tell you?" she asked triumphantly. "It *was* a mistake. All this fuss! I knew it didn't amount to anything."

But as she was speaking the bookseller reappeared. In his hand was a new placard. It read: THIS WEEK!! NUMBER TWO BEST SELLER. Jessica looked utterly dismayed. "Oh dear," she sighed.

Kitt Donovan stood in the reception area of McCallum Enterprises Inc. in New York City and critically surveyed a man's picture.

Kitt was a smart, strikingly attractive girl of twenty-four. If not actually beautiful, she had a freshness and vivacity that more than made up for it. Several years of working in the sophisticated world of New York publishing had done nothing to kill an innocence, spontaneity, and kindheartedness that were as refreshing as a spring day. She was very much in love with Grady Fletcher and he with her.

It was not, however, Grady's photograph that Kitt was studying at the moment, but a promotional poster advertising Cap'n Caleb's Chowder Houses. It had much the effect on her that the placard in the bookstore had had on Jessica.

The poster featured the face of Cap'n Caleb McCallum, a robust man in his early fifties, with white hair and flinty gray eyes. He was holding a bowl of chowder, and underneath was the slogan: OVER A BILLION BOWLS SOLD!

"Kitt, what a great surprise!"

She turned to see Grady Fletcher approaching from the direction of the elevator. He was conservatively dressed in a dark three-piece suit and looked every inch a successful CPA, which he wasn't—not just yet.

He took Kitt's hand. "I didn't expect to see you today."

"I know. But something's come up."

"About *Corpse?* To do with Aunt Jess?"

"Yes."

"Something bad?"

"She may think so. Though actually far from it."

"I don't follow."

"Patience. Look, can you manage lunch?"

"You bet." Grady told the receptionist he would return at two o'clock. Then he took Kitt by her arm. "Let's go."

As they were crossing the lobby, Kitt nodded toward the big poster. "Is that true?"

"What? Oh, the billion-bowls bit. I've no idea."

"I thought you were supposed to be his accountant."

They passed into the street. "One very lowly, fledgling member of his army of accountants," Grady said. "And with three new Chowder Houses opening every week somewhere in the country—to the horror of gourmets everywhere—he needs every one of us. Where do you want to eat?"

"Isn't there a Chowder House near here?" Kitt asked innocently.

Grady shuddered. "Thankfully, there's nothing in my contract of employment that says I have to eat the lousy stuff. Come on, I know a great little French restaurant just around the corner."

They started to walk. "What's he a captain of?" Kitt asked.

"Who—Caleb? Industry, I suppose. Certainly not of any known ship. Though now I come to think of it, he did buy himself a yacht recently—called, believe it or not, *Chowder King*. But he was calling himself Cap'n long ago. You know, I wouldn't object to Captain half as much."

"What's he like?"

"Well, as somebody said the other day, he's a man finely attuned to the product he sells: cold fish."

"Let's give the Cap'n his due," Kitt said. "If he and my boss weren't friends, you and I would never have met."

"Great thing, friendship," said Grady.

They entered the restaurant, ordered food and wine, then sat back and looked at each other with satisfaction.

"Now," Grady said, "what's all this about my revered aunt?"

"Do you think she'd come to New York for a week or so?"

"She might. What for?"

"Oh, just to autograph her book in a major Fifth Avenue store, be interviewed on the radio and by the press, and appear on several TV programs. Including the *Today* show."

Grady stared at her. "All that? You're not serious!"

She nodded.

"I can't believe it! *Your* doing?"

"Well . . ." She gave a little shrug and pursed her lips.

"Clever girl!"

"No, actually, I haven't had to hype her much at all. I mean, *Corpse* is at number two. Could go to the top. A first novel by a middle-aged widow lady in Maine! It makes your aunt of interest to a lot of people. Question is: will she play ball?"

"You leave her to me," Grady said. "Come back to the office with me after lunch and I'll call her—personal charge, of course. Can't have company accountants setting a bad example."

Back at MacCallum Enterprises an hour later, Grady and Kitt were waiting for an elevator. One arrived. The doors opened and a beautiful young woman emerged. She had jet-black hair, was immaculately turned out, and wore a dress that made Kitt's mouth water.

The young woman smiled intimately as she passed them. "Hullo, Grady," she murmured in a low and seductive voice. Then she was gone, leaving behind her the subtle aroma of expensive perfume.

Grady, looking embarrassed, replied, "Oh, er, good afternoon, er, Ashley," to her swayingly retreating back. He then ushered Kitt into the empty elevator. The doors closed and Grady pressed a button.

Kitt was round-eyed. *"Who* was that?"

"The girl? Oh, her name's Ashley Vickers."

"That outfit—oh boy! And what looks!"

"Oh, you think she's pretty?" Grady said casually.

In answer, Kitt kicked him sharply on the shin.

He gave a muted yell. "What's that for?"

"You know quite well. Pretending you've hardly noticed her!" She mimicked: *"Oh, you think she's pretty?* She's absolutely stunning, and you know it. What's she do here, anyway?"

"She's Caleb's personal assistant."

Kitt's eyebrows went up. "Real-ly?" she said slowly.

"Now, honey, don't get any ideas."

"You're telling *me* not to get ideas? You think the Cap'n hasn't had a few?"

"Whatever ideas he's had, there's not an iota of evidence he's put them into practice."

"Want to bet? You don't buy dresses like that on a PA's salary. There is a *Mrs.* McCallum, isn't there?"

"Yes, but"—he lowered his voice—"not another word. I've long suspected these elevators are bugged."

The elevator stopped and the doors opened. "Come on, let's call Aunt Jess."

"No, Grady, I can't," said Jessica.

"But it's all arranged. They've booked you on all these shows."

"They shouldn't have done so without my permission."

"But these publicity junkets come with the territory."

"What would I say on television? I'd make a fool of myself."

"Nonsense. They'll love you. Oh, come on, Aunt Jess, how about it?"

Jessica hesitated. She was facing an alarming prospect. But it *would* be an experience—not the sort of thing you ought to back away from just because you were scared of making a fool of yourself.

"Well," she said doubtfully, "I suppose I could come for a day or two."

"Terrific. Can you be here Monday? Around midday?"

"Well . . . yes."

"Okay. Let me know what time your train's arriving and I'll meet you at Grand Central. Must go. See you Monday." He hung up.

Jessica put the receiver down slowly and turned to confront the open-mouthed stares of Lois and Eleanor, who had been listening to her end of the conversation.

"Jessica," Eleanor asked excitedly, "are you really going to be on television?"

"I'm afraid I am."

Lois studied her critically from head to foot. Then she shook her head disapprovingly. "Not like *that,* you're not."

Jessica looked down at herself. She was wearing a tweed suit, with a white sweater and sensible shoes.

"Why, what's the matter?"

"Jessica, millions of people are going to be watching you. You have to look, er, *now—with it.*"

*"Au courant,"* said Eleanor smoothly.

"And those tweeds have got to go," said Lois.

The next day was one of the most miserable of Jessica's life. Eleanor and Lois took her on a round of local dress shops and boutiques, virtually forcing her to try on dozens of outfits, all of which, she was assured, reflected the latest big-city trends. Eventually, her resistance worn down, she found herself paying out good money for several positively bizarre creations, including one outlandish tentlike dress in gaudy red and white stripes, which she felt she ought to be saluting rather than wearing. But anything, Jessica thought, to get her two friends off her back.

However, the ordeal was far from over. Next it was to a beauty parlor, where the face was smeared with mud and her body pounded and pressed unmercifully and interminably.

Finally, her hair was shampooed, blown dry, brushed, and twisted. She left eventually, her head topped with a strange coiffure that the hairdresser promised was the latest rage in New York, and which Lois and Eleanor assured her did wonders for her.

By the end of the day Jessica was exhausted. As she staggered into her house and flopped onto a chair, she told herself that New York couldn't possibly be worse than this.

Jessica alighted from the train and the conductor handed down her one modest suitcase.

"Thank you, Daniel. Thanks for all your help." She fumbled in her purse for a dollar and held it out.

"Oh no, ma'am." He declined it firmly. "It's been my pleasure."

"Are you sure? Well, as you wish. Goodbye—and I do hope your boy gets that scholarship."

"Thank you, Mrs. Fletcher. You going to be all right now?"

"Oh yes. My nephew's meeting me." She turned. "Ah, there he is."

"Then have a nice stay, ma'am."

He tipped his cap and moved back into the train as Grady, followed by Kitt, came hurrying along the platform. Jessica put down her case and lifted her arms to Grady.

"Aunt Jess!" He gave her a hug. "It's great to see you."

"And you, my boy. Grady, I'm sorry if you don't like the way I'm dressed and how my hair is done, but nature never intended me to look like a barber pole or a kitchen mop."

He held her at arm's length and regarded her intently. "I don't know what you mean. You look just fine. Exactly the same as always."

"That's what I mean. I was very nearly modernized, but at the last moment I rebelled, so New York will have to take me as I am."

"That's all we want. Oh, Aunt Jess, this is Kitt Donovan."

Jessica smiled. "So you're the young lady I have to thank for all this."

"Guilty," said Kitt, with a grin.

"Nevertheless, I'm delighted to meet you." Jessica held out her hand.

"It's mutual, Mrs. Fletcher. Grady's told me so much about you."

"Well, he hasn't told me nearly enough about you, my dear. Only that you're wonderful and different."

"Quiet, please, Aunt Jess," Grady hissed. "You'll be giving her a swollen head. Now, let's not stand around here any longer." He picked up her case. "Where's the rest of your luggage?"

"That's all there is."

"Gee, you do travel light."

"Where's the first stop?" Jessica asked.

"Coventry House, if that's all right with you," Kitt told her. "Mr. Giles is looking forward to meeting you. Unless you'd like to check into your hotel first?"

Jessica shook her head. "By no means. Lead on to Coventry House. I'm very much looking forward to meeting Mr. Giles."

Preston Giles clasped Jessica warmly by the hand. "My dear Mrs. Fletcher, welcome to Manhattan. And to Coventry House. We're all delighted about *The Corpse Danced at Midnight.* It's going splendidly."

"Thank you," said Jessica, "it's very exciting for me."

"I do hope you're quite happy with the way everything's been handled?"

Jessica eyed him keenly, summing him up. He was a distinguished-looking man with a strong, rather handsome face, thick hair graying at the temples, and very deep-set eyes. She put his age at somewhere in the late fifties. He didn't look altogether well, being rather pale and having dark circles under his eyes. But his handshake was firm.

A workaholic, she decided. She had made a few inquiries and discovered that Coventry House was very much a one-man creation. Preston Giles had taken over a small run-down publishing house and, with a seemingly unerring instinct for popular taste, had produced a stream of best-selling books.

Now he gave a surreptitious glance at the clock on the wall of his office. Jessica got the impression that, for all his courtesy, he didn't really want to listen to her replies. His words appeared automatic, as though they'd been spoken many times before. He seemed under some pressure. He'd be relieved, she felt, to be done with her quickly. And she determined not to let *him* dismiss *her*.

She murmured that everything had been quite satisfactory.

"Fine, fine. And I'm sure I can leave you safely in Kitt's capable hands. I'm absolutely up to my ears in work or I'd be delighted to escort you myself. But I've had a dozen crises already this morning."

"Well, I certainly don't want to be number thirteen," Jessica remarked.

He smiled absently. "We must have dinner while you're in town and really get acquainted . . ."

"Do you eat apples?" Jessica interrupted.

"I beg your pardon?" He stared. For the first time she had his full attention.

"Apples. You really should, you know. The pectin. It's good for the complexion. You seem, if I may say so, very gray."

"Actually, I haven't been sleeping well . . ."

"Apples," said Jessica for the third time.

He gave a weak smile. "Yes. Thank you."

"And now," she said firmly, "you really must excuse me, Mr. Giles. I understand there are several engagements scheduled today, and I haven't even checked into my hotel yet. Goodbye for now."

She smiled demurely, and a moment later was outside.

"Well, that was short and sweet," said Grady, as they walked along the corridor.

Jessica nodded. "He was very charming. But definitely distrait."

Kitt said awkwardly, "I'm awfully sorry, Mrs. Fletcher. I'm sure if he were less busy . . ."

"Kitt, I'm certain it's far better to have a publisher who's too busy than one who doesn't have enough to do. Now I think perhaps you'd better take me to my hotel. I must prepare myself to meet the inquisitors."

The next few days were undoubtedly the most hectic that Jessica had ever spent. A harassed Kitt rushed her from one engagement to another.

There were not one, but two lengthy and tiring autographing sessions, at which most of the customers required long and involved inscriptions— or dedications to unknown people with names like Booboo, Attila, Big Chief, or Snuggles. One man purchased eight copies and, to Jessica's relief, demanded only her signature and the date on each.

"My, you must be a real book lover," she said as she started signing.

"Never open one. These are just an investment. If you turn out to be somebody, maybe they'll be worth somethin'. It's a long shot, though, I guess," he added as he staggered away under his load.

Jessica didn't know whether to laugh or cry.

She appeared on four TV shows. One interviewer was a supercilious highbrow critic who plainly regarded most detective fiction with contempt and used the occasion as a chance to air his views on Literature; another moderator was a severe and opinionated young woman who had convinced herself that *Corpse* was in fact a feminist tract and tried by every means at her disposal—though unsuccessfully—to make Jessica admit this. (She also, to Jessica's intense chagrin, gave away the identity of the murderer.)

Jessica appeared next in a discussion program—broadcast live at one a.m.—with three other writers, all experienced TV performers, who expatiated at inordinate length about authors and books she had never heard of. She hardly got a word in edgeways.

She was grilled by an abrasive and semiliterate radio talk show host who called her Jennifer and only seemed interested in finding out if she *(a)* was living in sin with anyone or *(b)* had a criminal record.

She was interviewed by three press reporters—one bored, one incredibly young and horribly nervous, and one drunk.

In four days she was asked about her favorite food, color, breed of dog; her star sign; and her opinion on capital punishment, drug abuse, environmental pollution, gun control, smoking, UFOs, the Olympic Games, and whole-grain bread. Nobody listened to her answers. Nobody asked her questions she'd prepared herself to answer: what were the most important qualities of a detective story? who were her favorite mystery writers? who had influenced her? and so on. None of her inquisitors, in fact, seemed very interested in mystery stories. And certainly none of them had read her book through from beginning to end.

Jessica also attended two cocktail parties and was joint guest of honor at a literary luncheon with an avant-garde Turkish poet who gave a forty-minute speech in his native language, which had to be translated sentence by sentence by someone who seemed fluent in neither English nor Turkish. Moreover, the food was horrible.

During all this time she saw hardly anything of Grady, wasn't able to catch any Broadway shows, see any sights, or do any shopping. And there was no word of any kind from Preston Giles. Kitt alone, always by her side and always cheerful, made everything just bearable.

Nevertheless, when Jessica was lying in bed on Thursday night, trying to decide which was aching worse, her feet or her head, she came to a firm decision.

First thing the next morning she tore into small fragments the list of engagements for the day, which Kitt had left with her the previous evening, and dropped them in the wastebasket. Then she phoned Coventry House.

"Miss Donovan, please," she said when the receptionist answered.

"I'm sorry, she's not in yet."

"Then will you please give her a message? You'd better take this down. Ready?"

"Yes, ma'am."

"This is Jessica Fletcher. Tell Miss Donovan I thank her for all her great personal kindnesses, and I hope she'll come visit with me at Cabot Cove one day soon. Got that?"

". . . one day soon. Yes, Mrs. Fletcher."

"And please tell her to cancel all my future engagements in New York. I'm going home today. All right?"

"Yes, but Mrs. Fletcher . . . ma'am . . . I really don't . . ."

"Thank you so much. Goodbye."

And with a sigh of relief Jessica hung up.


Jessica walked happily along the train platform, carrying her suitcase. She felt carefree for the first time in nearly a week. She was going home.

Then suddenly she heard a voice calling behind her.

"Aunt Jess—wait!"

She turned to see Grady sprinting along the platform toward her. A few yards behind him was Kitt. Jessica gave a sigh of resignation and put down her suitcase. "I might have guessed," she murmured to herself.

"Thank heavens we caught you," Grady gasped. "Why didn't you phone me before you left?"

"Well, it doesn't seem to have mattered, does it? Kitt obviously did. I'm sorry, Grady. I didn't realize you'd want so much to see me off."

"I don't want to see you off. I want you to stay."

"Why?"

"For one thing, I've barely set eyes on you since you've been here."

"That's hardly my fault, Grady."

"Nor mine."

"Quite true. But I think in the future it'll be much more satisfactory if we get together only in Cabot Cove. Now, honestly, don't you agree?"

Pleadingly, Kitt said: "Oh, Mrs. Fletcher, please don't go yet. I have several more things arranged with media people. They'll be mad with Coventry House if you don't show, and Mr. Giles will blame me."

"Kitt, my dear, he won't be able to. I shall write to him, praising you to the skies and telling him that *nobody* could have stopped me from leaving. Four days in the Big Apple have been quite enough for me, thank you."

Grady cleared his throat. "I think you can tell him now to his face, Aunt Jess." He jerked his head.

Jessica looked along the platform and saw Preston Giles hurrying toward them. In his hands was a big bunch of long-stemmed red roses. He came up and, almost diffidently, handed them to her.

"Mrs. Fletcher," he said quietly. "I'm mortified by my behavior. I've come to beg your forgiveness."

"Mr. Giles," said Jessica, "I'm sure you're a charming man, but for several days I have been insulted, browbeaten, and patronized, and I say no, thank you. Back in Cabot Cove the only things with claws are the lobsters. And we eat them."

"I know how you feel, believe me," he said. "It took me years to get used to this town."

He smiled gently. "Look, I'm having a few houseguests at my place in the country this weekend. And tomorrow night I'm throwing quite a big party. I'd like you to join me." He looked at Kitt and Grady. "All of you," he added. He turned back to Jessica. "You'll meet some real people —not critics and columnists, but my friends. Drive up with me tomorrow morning. And then on Monday, if you still want to go back home, I'll put you on this train personally. Fair enough?"

Jessica looked down at the flowers, then back up at him. "We'd better get these in water," she said, "before they wilt."

# Chapter Three

THE big Mercedes sedan sped along the elm-lined country road in up-state New York and whipped around a bend. Behind the wheel, Preston Giles looked more relaxed than Jessica had yet seen him.

"I suppose we get used to these self-important media types," he was saying. "We live with them because we have to."

"Why do you have to?" Jessica asked.

"Why? Well, because we . . ." He broke off and chuckled. "You know, I'm not sure I know why. I'll tell you something, though, Mrs. J. B. Fletcher: you could become a very disruptive influence in my life."

"Mr. Giles, only my students call me Mrs. Fletcher."

"And Mr. Giles is that stuffed shirt in the three-piece suit I left back in Manhattan."

They smiled at each other.

"I don't know about you, Jessica," Preston said, "but I'm glad we let your nephew and Kitt find their own way out here."

A few minutes later the car passed an old-fashioned road sign, which carried the words: ENTERING NEW HOLVANG. DRIVE CARE-FULLY.

"Oh, are we there?" Jessica asked.

"Just about."

Preston braked and turned off the road into a long driveway. They swept along it, to pull up eventually in front of an enormous and very attractive house.

Jessica looked around her. "My, isn't it all lovely!"

"Well, I like it here."

A butler had emerged from the house, and he opened the passenger door for Jessica to alight.

"Good afternoon, madam."

"Good afternoon." She got out. "Thank you."

Preston came around from the driver's side. "Davis, this is Mrs. Fletcher. Is her room ready?"

"Yes, sir."

"Fine. Her luggage is in the trunk."

Preston took Jessica's arm and they went through the front door into a large, elegantly furnished foyer.

"This is delightful, Preston," Jessica said with genuine admiration.

"Thank you. I hope you'll make yourself completely at home. Now, would you care for a drink, some tea . . . ?"

"Not just yet. I'd prefer to go straight to my room and freshen up, if I may."

Jessica found she had been allocated an airy, beautifully proportioned room overlooking the swimming pool. Davis put down her luggage.

"Will there be anything more, madam?"

"No, thank you."

He turned to leave. "I shall send a maid to unpack and assist you."

"Oh, mercy, no!" Jessica said hastily. "I've done my own packing and unpacking for a good few years."

"Just as you wish, madam." He made for the door.

"You know something, Davis?"

He turned back. "What, madam?"

Jessica surveyed him thoughtfully. "I don't think I've ever seen a real live butler before."

"Indeed, madam?"

"Indeed. I've seen them in the movies—though they're only actors, of course. I've read about butlers; I've even written about one. But until now I've never met one."

"We are a dying breed, madam."

"Oh, I do hope not. Rare perhaps, endangered maybe. But not dying."

He smiled. "Thank you, Mrs. Fletcher."

"Well, I just wanted to say that if you see me watching you closely over the weekend, please don't take it amiss. It'll just be research. *My* butler was based too much on *other* writers' butlers. I want my next one to be grounded in real life."

"I'll be honored to be a model, madam. But may I ask: will your next story be one in which the butler did it?"

"Wait and see, Davis; wait and see."

Jessica had taken time before leaving the city to buy some new clothes. She had just finished changing into a casual outfit and was seated at the dressing table fixing her face, when there was a tap on her door.

It was Grady.

"Hullo, dear," she said. "Sit down. Where's Kitt?"

"Taking a shower." He perched on the edge of her bed. "Well, what do you think of everything?" he asked.

"Very impressive. I had no idea Preston lived in such style."

"Oh, it's Preston now, is it?"

"Why not?"

"No reason at all. I'm delighted you've been reconciled to everything and you've stopped talking of running back to Cabot Cove."

"I still could. I'm far from sure the high life is for me. But tell me, Grady, about this weekend. Who's going to be here, exactly? Do you know?"

"Not really. But I just caught a glimpse of my revered boss—and his wife."

"Captain McCallum?"

"Yep. Giles is an old friend of them both."

"I see. It'll be interesting to meet your boss at last."

"You have a treat in store, Aunt Jess," he said sardonically.

"You know, Grady, he ought to do something about the food he serves at those Chowder Houses. I took the girls to one a while back—just out of loyalty to you, really—and honestly, it wasn't very good."

"I'm just an accountant, Aunt Jess, not the cook."

"But there are so many little ways in which things could be made better, at very little extra cost . . ."

"Well, you'll have plenty of opportunity to suggest them to him yourself. But if you're talking about extra cost, you can forget it."

"You don't make him sound very nice, Grady. He looks so cheerful on those posters."

"I figure it was an effort for him to hold that grin for the one-hundredth of a second it took to snap the picture."

"Don't you think you might be a little prejudiced, Grady?"

"Perhaps. I only see him at the office. There, he's a . . . well, a *driven* man. Maybe socially he's a different character." He stood up. "Ready to go down?"

Jessica picked up her purse and checked its contents. "You say Mrs. McCallum is here? What's she like?"

"Louise? I've never spoken to her. Seems a bit sour—hardly surprisingly. They say she hits the bottle more than she should."

"Oh, how sad."

"Well, at least she can afford it." He opened the door. "Come along, Aunt Jess, and judge them yourself—as you will do anyway, whatever I say."

They went downstairs. On the terrace they found Preston seated, sipping long, cool drinks with an attractive woman in her mid-forties.

Preston stood up as they approached. "Jessica, you look charming." He introduced Louise McCallum.

Louise held out her hand. "I'm delighted to know you, Mrs. Fletcher. I just loved your book."

"Why, thank you," Jessica said.

Preston continued the introductions. "Louise, I expect you know Grady Fletcher, Jessica's nephew."

"Well, we've never been formally introduced," Louise said. "Though I've seen you at the office, Mr. Fletcher, of course. Caleb talks of you as one of his most promising young men."

Grady look amazed—and a little embarrassed. "That's very kind of him. I thought he'd hardly noticed me."

"Oh, he's noticed you."

Jessica smiled to herself. "Where *is* the Captain?" she asked.

Louise jerked her head. "You can hear him."

Jessica had been vaguely conscious for some time of gunshots coming from an area out of sight at the other side of the pool.

"Oh, is that Captain McCallum?"

"That's Caleb, all right," Louise said dryly. "Terminating skeets with extreme prejudice."

"Is he a keen marksman?" Jessica inquired politely.

"I think he just likes smashing things," said Louise.

Grady gave a muffled snort and hastily turned it into a cough. Fortunately, at that moment Kitt, looking fresh and cool, emerged from the house. Preston introduced her to Louise.

Just as they were shaking hands, the air was suddenly shattered by a gigantic bang.

Everyone gave a start and most of those present instinctively, but far too late, raised their hands to their ears.

"What was *that?*" Jessica asked a little shakily.

"Sonic boom, I'm afraid," Preston said in an apologetic tone. "We've got an airport down the road. One of the few drawbacks about this place."

"What with that and my husband," said Louise, "we're not likely to have a very peaceful weekend."

"Actually, I think he's stopped," said Preston.

Sure enough, the gun seemed to have fallen silent, and a few seconds later they saw Caleb McCallum approaching. There was a shotgun crooked in his arm, and accompanying him was a beautiful young woman.

As the pair got closer, Kitt drew her breath in sharply and dug Grady in the ribs. McCallum's companion was Ashley Vickers.

As they approached, and before anyone else could speak, Louise called in a bright voice: "Good shooting, darling."

"How would you know?" he asked shortly.

"I could hear the skeets shattering from here. Besides, I'm sure the presence of Miss Vickers always spurs you to the peak of performance—whatever you're doing. Tell me, Miss Vickers, did you try your hand?"

Ashley gave a tight-lipped smile. "Oh no, I'm hopeless with guns."

"Never mind, dear. We can't all be good at *everything.*"

"Why don't you come and give it a try, Louise?" her husband asked. Then he added pointedly: "All it requires is a clear eye and a steady hand."

"I don't think so, Caleb, thanks. I might miss the skeet and hit a person. And the steadier my hand, the more likely I'd be to do it."

Preston hurriedly performed general introductions.

After McCallum and Ashley had been presented to Jessica and Kitt, Davis arrived, apparently unbidden, with more drinks.

When they were all settled, a few seconds of awkward silence ensued.

Then McCallum turned to Grady. "Oh, Fletcher, I've been figuring out a way we might get an additional tax concession on the . . ."

Preston interrupted with a mock groan. "Caleb, please! No work this weekend. It's supposed to be a rest, for all of us. That includes you. Give the boy a break."

Caleb grunted. "Oh, all right." He looked at Grady. "Talk to you about it Monday."

"Okay, sir."

Louise said: "Press, you don't know what you've done."

"What do you mean, Louise?" He sounded a trifle apprehensive.

"If you're not going to let Caleb work at all over the weekend, poor Miss Vickers will have nothing to do. You know Caleb only invited her along to help him in business matters. The child will be bored to tears."

"Oh, don't worry about me, Mrs. McCallum," Ashley said. "I could never be bored in a heavenly place like this. I'm just so grateful to Mr. Giles for inviting me."

McCallum got abruptly to his feet. "Give it a break, Louise, will you? I'm going indoors to change. 'Scuse me." He strode off.

There was another pause and then Grady rose. "Kitt, how about a walk around the grounds?"

"Yes, love it." She jumped up.

"Oh, do you mind if I come along?" Ashley asked. She, too, got to her feet.

Grady looked a bit disconcerted. But Kitt said quickly: "No, we'd be delighted, wouldn't we, Grady?"

"Oh yes, of course."

"Excuse us," said Kitt.

Grady, Kitt, and Ashley walked off together. As soon as they'd gotten out of sight of the three people they'd left behind, Ashley said: "All right, you two, don't worry. I only wanted an excuse to get away from that . . . that *dear* lady. I'm going to change and have a swim. Cool off. See you."

She hurried away. Grady stared after her.

"I think I'm beginning to like that girl," he said.

Kitt took his arm. "No, you're not. You can't stand her. Come on, I thought you wanted a walk."

Back on the terrace, Preston was saying: "Louise, I want you to know that in spite of what Ashley said, I *didn't* invite her. Well, I suppose I did. What I mean is, Caleb asked if he could bring her. I just said okay."

"That's all right, Press. I realize you couldn't say no."

She turned to Jessica. "Tell me, my dear, who are you coming as tonight? We don't want to duplicate."

Jessica looked puzzled. "Coming as? I'm afraid I don't follow."

"Oh, don't say he hasn't told you! Really, Press, that wasn't very fair on the poor woman."

"I'm sorry!" He threw his hands up in despair. "Believe it or not, I just clean forgot."

"I'm still not in the picture," said Jessica.

"Well, I was talked into making tonight's party a fancy dress affair. Everyone's to come as his favorite fictional character."

Jessica pursed her lips. "Oh, I see."

"I know, and you haven't got a thing to wear."

"Well, actually," Jessica said slowly, "that doesn't really matter."

"Oh?"

They both stared at her.

"You see, my favorite character—female character, that is—has always been Lady Godiva."

Giles and Louise both burst out laughing. Then Jessica snapped her fingers in vexation. "Oh, dear!"

"What's the matter?" Louise asked.

"I've just remembered Lady Godiva's not fictional. So I am in trouble."

Louise put her hand on Jessica's and chuckled. "Anyway, Jessica, wherever would you get all that hair?" She stood up. "Come and see me later. I'm sure between us we can work something out."

She left them and went indoors. Jessica stared after her thoughtfully.

"Penny for them," Preston said.

"I was only thinking how different she seemed just at the end again. Quite pleasant."

"She always used to be like that. She and Caleb both did. One of the nicest couples you could imagine. But then . . ." He shrugged.

"What a shame. Was it when he became rich?"

"I don't think it was *being* that spoiled things. It was the getting of it. I hope before you leave you see Caleb as he once was. Otherwise, you're going to think my friends no better than all those people you fled New York to get away from."

# Chapter Four

THE party was in full swing and Preston Giles' house swarmed with characters from what seemed to Jessica every play, book, and film ever written: Hamlet to Rooster Cogburn; Eliza Doolittle to Modesty Blaise. Many people enacted characters from children's stories, nursery rhymes, or comic strips. There was a Superman, a Batman, and a Little Orphan Annie. There were Jacks and Jills and Little Bo-Peeps, Humpty Dumpty, and a Peter Pan (female) escorted by a villainous Captain Hook. A plethora of Disney creations roamed the premises.

Jessica stood near the foot of the stairs, surveying the crowd. She herself was simply but effectively attired in a white evening dress with a tiara, and she carried a silver wand topped with a star.

Intriguing, she thought, the characters people admitted to being their favorites. That young man at the piano, for instance. He was wearing a black and threadbare early Victorian suit and was improvising a song, the refrain of which was based on the words *Bah—humbug*. Ebenezer Scrooge, of course. But could Scrooge be anyone's favorite character? A handsome young man, too, though with a somewhat sardonic expression.

Jessica let her eyes wander on around the room. There was Ashley, looking darkly beautiful as the wicked witch from "Snow White." And there, Caleb McCallum, wearing the familiar cloak and deerstalker hat of Sherlock Holmes and puffing on a meerschaum. He was standing with a group of people and next to a very pretty Little Red Riding Hood. As Jessica watched, McCallum's arm encircled the girl's waist. The girl moved slightly nearer him. Jessica realized that she wasn't the only one who had noticed the incident. Ashley was also watching, and Jessica saw her eyes narrow coldly. Then she turned hastily and made her way across to the piano. Jessica followed unobtrusively.

The sardonic young man was now singing some lines about delighting in sleet and ice. Ashley leaned up against the piano and listened for a moment before interrupting.

"Aren't you a little out of season, Peter? It's not Christmas."

"Wrong, Ashley," he answered curtly. "It's never inappropriate to wish the world a little ill will."

He broke off and looked around the small group who had been listening to him.

"Well, folks, any requests?" With no immediate response forthcoming, he addressed a middle-aged man who was there with his wife. "How about you, Doctor? A medley of my hit from yesteryear, perhaps?"

The doctor spread his hands. "Whatever you like, Peter. Your stuff's all terrific."

Peter smiled icily. "Your taste is impeccable, Doctor. I may get deathly ill, just to cement our relationship."

The doctor said hastily: "What's this I hear about your putting together a new Broadway show?"

"*Off*-Broadway, my friend. The fringes of the civilized world. To be specific—Seventeenth Street."

He smashed his hands down onto the keys in a sudden, jarring discord. Then he seemed to collect himself and started to play normally again.

A voice spoke softly in Jessica's ear. "I'm flabbergasted. Is this what you improvised from odds and ends?"

Jessica turned. It was Preston. She smiled. "With a little help from Louise," she said. "And before you ask—I'm Cinderella's fairy godmother. Would you care to make a wish?"

He took her hand and kissed her fingers. "I wish for a dozen more books by J. B. Fletcher."

"Oh, books aren't produced by magic. Only by hard work."

"Then suppose I just settle for the pleasure of her company."

"That's an easy wish to grant, especially to someone looking as dashing as you. Excuse my ignorance, but who precisely are you?"

He stepped back and struck a pose. "Guess."

Jessica regarded him with her head to one side. "Let me see. Nineteenth century."

"Correct."

"And obviously from the very cream of society. A nobleman."

"*Mais oui, madame.*"

"Ah—French. Someone from Dumas?"

"Bravo."

"Edmond Dantes?"

"Well done. I must admit I'm relieved I look the part. After all, if the host can't manage to get himself in character . . ." He lowered his voice. "Some of them are rather unimaginative, don't you think?"

"Yes, and some rather strange. That young man at the piano, now. Who is he, by the way?"

"That's Peter Brill. He's a composer and songwriter."

"So I gathered."

"He had several hits on Broadway a few years back, but he's been going through a lean period, poor fellow. He's scared his talents have gone for good."

"So, he sees himself as a notorious miser, hoarding what he's got and rather hating the world. I see . . ."

"Aren't you being rather Freudian, Jessica? People might come as a particular character for any reason. Maybe just convenience."

"Perhaps you're right."

"And, incidentally, I'm particularly disappointed in Grady and Kitt. They're dressed in perfectly standard evening clothes. Definitely cheating."

"That's what I said. But Grady pointed out that his favorite characters are detectives or secret agents—all of whom dress quite normally."

Preston chuckled. "Where *are* those two, anyway? I haven't seen them around for a long time."

"Nor have I," replied Jessica.

"I expect they've found something better to do."

At that moment Grady and Kitt were in fact locked in a close embrace in the near darkness outside the house. Eventually, however, they drew apart.

"Look," Grady said, "what d'you say we duck out?"

"We can't yet." She took his hand, felt for his watch, and pressed the button that lit up the dial. "It's only nine-fifteen."

"I hate parties," he said.

"Look, *my* boss is giving it; *your* boss is a guest. At least pretend you enjoy their company."

"I like yours better," Grady said with a grin.

"Besides, I'm freezing."

"Oh well, in that case . . ."

He took her in his arms and held her close. As he did so, he happened to glance up at the great mass of the house, and he suddenly stiffened.

"What's the matter?" she asked.

"Look! I think somebody's searching one of the rooms."

She turned and stared. The upper stories were all in darkness. But through one window she could see the faint, jerky movements of a flashlight.

She drew her breath in. "A thief!"

"Got to be. And hang on . . ."

He broke off and appeared to be making some rapid calculations. Then he gasped. "It's *my* room!"

He suddenly broke away from her and started to sprint to the house.

Kitt ran after him. "Grady—be careful!"

Grady rushed past the open french doors into the noisy living room. He pushed his way roughly through the crowd and started up the stairs two at a time.

Jessica and Preston, still standing talking, stared at him in amazement.

"What on earth . . . ?" Preston began.

"Grady!" Jessica called.

He shouted some reply, which they couldn't catch, but didn't pause.

At that moment Kitt came stumbling into the room. She glanced around, disoriented for a moment, then spotted Preston and Jessica and hurried across to them.

"Grady thinks there's a thief in his room," she panted. "Someone with a flashlight—searching."

Without a word, Preston put down his glass, strode to the stairs, and started rapidly up them. Jessica and Kitt followed.

Every eye in the room was on them, and there was a hush until Brill, at the piano, broke into some unmistakable cowboy chase music. Without pausing, he called across the room to McCallum: "Looks like you may be needed, Sherlock."

In the corridor leading to his room Grady stopped. Little point in hurrying now. No one could get out without being seen. He stood still for a few seconds, catching his breath, then tiptoed to his bedroom door and put his ear against it. He could hear nothing. He only hoped he had the right room.

Grady put his hand on the knob, then threw the door open and stepped into the room.

He'd made no mistake. A shadowy figure near the window swung around as he entered.

"Don't move!" Grady groped for the light switch.

But he wasn't familiar with its exact position, and as he fumbled, he was suddenly blinded by the flashlight shining directly into his eyes.

The intruder was coming straight at him, as if intending to brush him aside by sheer brute force.

Grady braced himself, raised his fists, and then at the last moment stepped aside and ducked. Instantly he was out of the beam of light, and behind the hand that held the flashlight he was able to discern the dim outline of the intruder.

Grady straightened and delivered a powerful left jab at the man's midriff. It brought him up short with a gasp and Grady aimed a right at his jaw.

The man jerked his head back, and this time Grady's fist caught him only a glancing blow. However, it was enough to send him staggering backward through the open doorway into the corridor—where he cannoned violently into Preston, who was just arriving.

Both men went sprawling, with Preston underneath. The unknown man, though, was quickly on his feet and, before Grady could reach the doorway, was off like a jackrabbit.

Grady charged to the door and saw the man's back disappearing along the corridor. Ahead of him, frozen in the center of the passage, were Jessica and Kitt.

Grady gave a yell. "Get out of his way!"

In a flash Jessica jumped to one side, grabbing Kitt by the arm as she did so. They flattened themselves against the wall.

As the man approached them he raised his arm as if to cover his face. Then he was level with them, still sprinting at full speed.

The next second there was a sudden flash of silver across the corridor, and the man went sprawling. He lay dazed as Jessica calmly bent down and picked up her wand, now broken in the middle, with which she'd deftly tripped him.

Grady came running up. "Well done, Aunt Jess!"

He bent down, grabbed the man by the back of his jacket, and hauled him unceremoniously to his feet.

At that moment Preston, obviously none the worse for his tumble, came hurrying up. At the same time there could be heard, from the direction of the stairs, a rising buzz of conversation, as of the sound of approaching locusts, together with the muffled tramp of many feet on deep-pile carpet. It was clear that all the other guests had decided to investigate the mysterious and noisy happenings aloft.

Preston shot a glance at Kitt. "Kitt, tell them everything's under control, nothing to worry about. Take 'em back downstairs and make sure they stay there. Get 'em playing blindman's buff, if necessary."

"Right, Mr. Giles."

Kitt turned to Jessica and gave a little grimace. She muttered, "Who'd be in PR work?" and hurried off.

Preston directed his attention to the intruder, still tightly held in

Grady's grip. Having apparently recovered his breath, the man spoke for the first time. And he spoke with surprising dignity.

"All right, young man, that's enough. You can release me. There's no need to be boorish."

Preston and Jessica stared at him in surprise. Grady grinned.

"Nothing doing, pal. Not until I know what you were up to in my room."

"Jessica," Preston said, "would you be so kind as to call the police? The nearest phone is in my bedroom. Fourth door on the right."

"Certainly."

Jessica moved off, only to stop as the man barked sharply. "Wait!"

He addressed Preston. "Before you take so irremediable a step, you would be well advised to listen to what I have to say."

Preston hesitated, then, to Jessica's surprise, glanced at her and raised his eyebrows, as if asking her advice.

She said slowly: "I suppose it would do no harm."

The man gave her a little bow. "Thank you, madam."

"Very well," Preston said. "We'll *all* go to my bedroom. Can you manage him, Grady?"

"I think so, sir." He gave the intruder a shove. "Move."

"Really, this manhandling is totally unnecessary," the newcomer said stiffly.

"We'll decide that," Preston told him.

They reached Preston's bedroom. He opened the door, switched on the light, and then stood back to allow Grady to march the intruder in. Jessica followed. Finally, Preston himself went in. He closed the door, turned the key in the lock, pocketed it, then walked across to the intruder and rapidly frisked him.

"I am not armed," the man said coldly.

"So I see." Preston stepped back. "Grady, I think you can release the . . . er, gentleman now."

"Thank you at least for the courtesy of that word," the man said, as Grady released him and stepped away.

In the brighter light of Preston's bedroom they were able for the first time to get a good look at the intruder. He was of middle age and, in spite of his somewhat disheveled appearance, had an indefinably elegant air about him. He was wearing a three-piece suit, which he was in the act of brushing down with his hands, and a slightly askew silk tie. He certainly did not fit Jessica's mental image of an average burglar.

"Well," Preston snapped after a few seconds, "we're waiting."

"A moment."

The man took from his pocket a silk handkerchief and with it gently dabbed at a cut on his lip. He regarded the small spot of blood left on the handkerchief, sighed, and returned it to his pocket.

"My name," he responded at last, "is Dexter Baxendale. I am a private detective."

"A *what?*" Preston exclaimed.

"I believe I made myself quite clear."

"You're kidding," Grady said incredulously.

Baxendale turned a supercilious gaze on him. "Not everyone in my profession sports a broken nose and dirty fingernails, my pubescent friend. When society seeks confidential assistance, it does not necessarily hire Mike Hammer."

He reached into his vest pocket, produced a business card, and handed it to Preston.

Preston gave it a cursory glance. "This does not explain what you are doing here."

"I have been retained by a very influential individual to conduct a discreet investigation. With Dexter Baxendale, discretion is a way of life."

"You still haven't answered my question," Preston said. "What are you doing *here?*"

"I'm not at liberty to say."

Preston gave a sigh. He crossed to the telephone, lifted the receiver, and started to dial.

Baxendale said sharply: "You may turn me over to the local authorities, Mr. Giles, but no amount of coercion will force me to break a trust. On the other hand, when the newspapers latch onto this story, a finger of suspicion will point equally at each of your guests. Which one is under investigation? Need I warn you, the *Enquirer* will have a field day?"

Preston hesitated, then lowered the receiver. He stood in thought for a moment before reaching a decision. "Grady," he said, "will you do me a favor? Escort Mr. Baxendale to his car."

"Sure thing, Mr. Giles."

"And out the *back* way, please. I'd rather not disturb our guests any further." He went to the door, unlocked and opened it.

Baxendale turned to Jessica and again gave his little bow. "A pleasure meeting you, Mrs. Fletcher, even though our conversation has been somewhat limited. You have a rare gift for murder. Continued success."

"Thank you," Jessica said. Then she added: "I think."

Grady tapped Baxendale's arm. "Let's go."

Baxendale started for the door, then stopped. His eye fell upon a small statuette, about a foot high, standing on a shelf. He went toward it and inspected it more closely. In brass, it represented Blind Justice, her scale unevenly balanced. A smile suddenly crossed Baxendale's lips and he looked again at Preston.

"Forgive me, Mr. Giles," he said, "but since I first entered this room, I've been trying to deduce who you're dressed as, and I think I have it. Edmond Dantes, isn't it? Otherwise known as the Count of Monte Cristo?"

Preston raised his eyebrows. "Very good, Mr. Baxendale. I'm almost sorry I'm throwing you out. You might have made a charming guest."

Baxendale smiled again, then he and Grady went out. As Grady turned to close the door behind him, Preston called out, "Grady, thanks a lot. Very well done."

Grady grinned. "Any time, Mr. Giles, any time." He closed the door.

Preston turned to Jessica. "I think, in fact, that all this has made your nephew's day."

"I wouldn't be at all surprised."

"What did I promise you? A quiet weekend?"

"I get plenty of quiet back in Cabot Cove. I won't say the incident has made *my* day, but it's certainly presented something to think about."

"Jessica, don't tell me that fiendishly clever brain of yours is beginning to feel the stirrings of a new plot?"

"Too soon to say. But isn't that what you want?"

"Yes, but I'm not sure *I* want to be a character in your next book."

"Do you realize," Grady said, "that guy was a private detective?"

"So you just told me," said Kitt. She and Grady were in the living room, standing slightly apart from the other party guests.

"A P.I. A gumshoe. Like Philip Marlowe, Sam Spade, Dick Tracy."

"So?"

"So, *I* flattened him. And I'm just an accountant."

"I know, darling, terrific."

"Yes, but don't you see: it opens up the possibility of a whole new fiction genre. There have never been any thrillers with an accountant as hero. Imagine a TV series: *The Fighting CPA.* Or how about *The Fastest Auditor in the West?* Every week there's an uppity young punk accountant who tries to take his title away. Imagine the drama as they battle against each other and the clock. Sensation: our hero loses. But wait—the punk's figures don't balance. One cent is unaccounted for. The good triumphs. Or . . ."

"Grady."

"Yes, Kitt?"

"Shut up."

"Yes, Kitt."

"You were great. I'm very proud of you. But the fact is, you still don't know why that man was in *your* room."

"Probably doing the rounds of all the bedrooms. I just happened to spot him when he'd reached mine."

"Could be, I suppose."

But Kitt sounded doubtful.

"Oh, there's Mr. Giles and Aunt Jess," Grady observed. "I'd better go and report that Baxendale's gone. 'Scuse me a moment."

He crossed the room and engaged Preston in conversation. While they were talking, Jessica heard her name called. She turned and saw Caleb McCallum beckoning her. He was standing with Ashley, the doctor, and one or two other people she didn't know. She went across.

"Mrs. Fletcher," McCallum said loudly, "the doc here's been saying there's things I could do to make my Chowder Houses better. But if there's one thing I know, it's the public taste bud. They want their food fast and cheap. Now, you're from Maine. You know fish. You ever eaten at a Cap'n Caleb's?"

"I have indeed, Captain," said Jessica. "And I must say it was an experience I shall never forget."

McCallum looked pleased. "I rest my case."

The doctor gave Jessica the ghost of a wink and Jessica smiled back. Would this be a good chance to support the doctor and give Cap'n Caleb *her* suggestions for improvements?

She opened her mouth to disabuse him as to her meaning. But she never got the words out, for suddenly McCallum's expression of satisfaction was replaced by one of extreme irritation. However, his look was not directed at Jessica, but over her shoulder.

Jessica looked behind her. Approaching them with a very unsteady gait was Louise.

She reached the group, leaned on a table for support, and stared at her husband.

"The party's beginning to pall, Caleb," she said loudly, her words slightly slurred. "Let's go home."

McCallum regarded his wife coldly. "Get yourself some coffee, Louise."

"I don't want coffee. I want to go home."

"I don't," he said fiercely.

The other guests in the immediate vicinity had all been looking slightly embarrassed and edging away. Now only Jessica was nearby.

Louise smiled sweetly at Caleb. "Fine, darling, you stay. I'll trot off like a civilized wife and let you and Ashley do whatever it is you do."

She turned and lurched away. Jessica hesitated for a few moments, glanced at McCallum, who had dismissively turned his back, then went after Louise herself.

Just inside the front door, Louise stopped and began fumbling in her purse. As Jessica came up to her, she produced her car key.

Jessica put a hand on her arm. "Louise, please don't go," she said gently. "Not just yet."

Louise pulled away, zigzagged to the door, opened it, and went out into the darkness.

Jessica sighed. "Oh, dear."

She looked around helplessly. Then her eye alighted on Grady, who was making his way back to Kitt. Jessica hurried across to him.

"Grady, be a good boy and help Mrs. McCallum home."

He looked a little disgruntled and glanced toward Kitt. "But . . ."

"I know we're all using you tonight," Jessica said hastily, "but this is important. In her condition, Louise really shouldn't drive. She won't take any notice of me—and you're one of the few completely sober people here."

He nodded. "I see. Sure." He turned and hurried out.

In the open air he paused, peering around. There seemed to be dozens of cars parked on the circular driveway, and the only light came from the windows of the house behind him. Then he spotted Louise's figure weaving through the cars, and he started forward.

By the time he caught up with her, she had reached a Cadillac sedan. She placed her hand on the catch of the driver's door.

"Hi, Mrs. McCallum," he called cheerfully.

She peered suspiciously at him. "Who's that?"

"Me. Grady Fletcher." He went closer. "How about letting me drive you home?"

She shook her head dazedly. "Do I know you?"

"Sure you do. I work for the firm. The promising young man, remember?"

"Promising? Well, promise me something now, eh?"

"What's that?"

"To clear off and leave me alone."

"But it'll be no trouble. Just let me have the key."

He leaned forward, but she suddenly screamed at him hysterically. "I said, leave me alone!"

At the same time, she swung open the car door so violently that he had to step clear hastily. While he was still off-balance, she shoved him in the chest with both hands. He staggered backward and sat down hard on the gravel.

Before he could recover, she jumped into the Cadillac and started the engine. As he scrambled to his feet, the car shot away in a cascade of spraying gravel and spinning tires.

Grady stared after it and swore under his breath.

"Grady, are you all right?"

Jessica trotted solicitously up to him. Kitt was a few steps behind her.

"Yes, fine," he said. "It's her I'm worried about. She's crazy. Did you hear how she yelled at me?"

"I did. I'm sorry to have let you in for all that. Perhaps I shouldn't have interfered. However, I *am* going to tell her husband what's happened. After that, there's nothing more I can do." She started back toward the house.

Kitt edged up to Grady and took him by the arm. "Sure you're all right?"

"Yes, of course."

They started off after Jessica. "I've been thinking," Kitt said. "This TV series—*The Fighting CPA*—will there be an episode in which *he's* flattened by a middle-aged female drunk?"

"Aw, I hate a smart-aleck broad," said Grady.

# Chapter Five

ON entering the house, Jessica located Caleb McCallum in a side room, where he was exerting all his not overabundant charm on Little Red Riding Hood. Jessica told him of Louise's departure. He thanked her perfunctorily, but clearly couldn't care less.

Jessica sighed and returned to the party. It was still going with a swing. More and more people seemed to be learning of her identity, and she found herself quite a center of attraction. This was not greatly to her taste, and—after having been asked for the eighth time in a little over half an hour, "How on earth did you think up the plot?"—was soon seeking a means of escape from the limelight. It was just after ten-thirty and the revelry was plainly going on for hours yet.

Then she noticed that Peter Brill had again been persuaded, not with great difficulty, to return to the piano. More from a desire to fade into the background than from any intense wish to hear him perform, Jessica joined the small crowd that had gathered around him.

"Thirty dollars a ticket?" the man dressed as Humpty Dumpty was declaiming. "I'm sorry, Peter, at those prices, off Broadway is beyond my budget."

"And you know what it takes to mount a new production?" Brill said bitterly. "A quarter million barely gets you started. Ah well, if this new show fails, I can always write for Nashville."

Half on key, he started to sing in an exaggerated country and western style:

> She was Queen of office sweethearts,
> He was the King that brought her to ruin,
> He gave her dictation and a place to stay,
> Then he gave her a royal . . .

At that point he noticed Ashley, who had come from the bar. "Oops," he said, "sorry, Ashley, no offense intended."

"None taken," she said coolly. "For the past several months my relationship with the Captain has been strictly business."

Jessica eyed her thoughtfully. Brill shrugged and played two other tunes. Then he took another drink and surveyed the room. "By the way, where *is* Sherlock? I haven't seen him for quite a while."

"You haven't seen Little Red Riding Hood either, I'll be bound," said Ashley. "Maybe she's taken him to investigate the murder at Grandmother's house." She raised her glass. "Here's to crime."

Just as she was about to drink, someone passing behind jostled her, and most of the contents of the glass cascaded down the front of her dress.

She gave an exclamation of annoyance.

Jessica bustled forward. "Quickly, my dear, we'd better get that out before it stains."

"Oh, forget it," said Ashley.

"Nonsense, that's much too good a dress to ruin. Come with me."

She took Ashley firmly by the wrist and led her in the direction of the kitchen.

In the kitchen they found Preston. He was on the phone. As they entered, he was saying: ". . . please, I don't want Mrs. Fletcher bothered."

He turned, saw Jessica and Ashley, and made a wry grimace before saying into the phone: "All right, then, I'll see you." He listened for a few seconds, then added: "Very well," and hung up.

As he came away from the phone, he noticed the state of Ashley's dress. "An accident?"

"Nothing serious," Jessica told him. "Was that about me?"

"Yes—a very persistent reporter from the *New York Times*. Name of Chris Landon. He wants to interview you on Monday."

"What did you tell him?"

"Well, knowing how you felt about the press, I explained that you'd left for Pago Pago and weren't expected back until the turn of the century. Unfortunately, he didn't believe me. I've arranged to see him, but I don't think that'll satisfy him."

"The *New York Times,* after all," said Jessica, *"is* in a somewhat different league from some of the others."

While speaking, she had gone across to the cabinets and started rummaging through them. "Hope you don't mind," she said, retrieving a large mixing bowl and a box of baking soda.

"Be my guest."

He and Ashley watched fascinated as she went to the fridge, gradually unearthing two eggs and a quart of milk.

"I don't know what that's going to be," said Preston, "but I'm not eating any."

"It's an old Fletcher recipe," she explained, piling the ingredients into the bowl. "Guaranteed to take the spots off a leopard. Come on, Ashley, we'll go upstairs."

"Jessica, really," Ashley insisted, "it isn't worth the trouble."

"I'm a frugal Yankee. Humor me."

She led Ashley out of the kitchen. Really, Jessica thought, what with one thing and another, this is an extremely busy evening. But interesting. Yes, undeniably so . . .

Although she was very late getting to sleep that night, Jessica nevertheless woke early. Feeling surprisingly fresh, she got up and pulled back the curtains. It was another glorious day.

Much too glorious, in fact, to go back to bed. How fortunate that she'd brought her jogging outfit with her.

Ten minutes later Jessica went downstairs. She could hear one of the servants clearing up the horrible detritus left by the party, but everybody else was clearly still in bed.

Resisting the impulse to go in and offer to help with the clearing up (whatever would Davis think?), Jessica let herself out and started off down the drive. She jogged about a mile, enjoying the freshness of the air in her lungs and on her cheeks, and then turned and made her way back toward the house.

When she was halfway up the drive again, she heard behind her the sound of a car. She looked over her shoulder and saw that it was the McCallum Cadillac. Louise was at the wheel. She pulled up alongside Jessica and let down the window. She was wearing the same clothes as the previous night. She looked terrible—with hair awry, makeup smeared, eyes bleary, and complexion gray.

"Good morning, Louise," Jessica said. "You . . ."

Louise raised a hand. "Don't say it. However dismal I look, I assure you I feel a hundred times worse. Get in, Jessica, will you?"

Jessica opened the door and scrambled in beside her. Louise surveyed her without enthusiasm. Jessica smiled. "We were very worried about you last night."

"*We?*"

"Grady and Kitt and I. And Preston when I told him later."

"Tell me, Jessica: did I behave very badly?"

"I wouldn't say so. A lot of people had too much to drink and became a little obstreperous."

Louise gave a harsh laugh. "That's a nice way to put it. What about your nephew? Did I knock him down, or something?"

"There was a slight accident with the car door, that's all. He just stumbled. No harm done."

Louise rested her head on her hands, which were crossed on the wheel. "No, that's not true. I pushed him over. I remember. I screamed at him. And I made a fool of myself indoors, about Caleb and that girl."

"Look, let's go up to the house and have some coffee."

Louise shook her head. "Oh no, I don't want to hang around any longer than I have to. I just wanted to see Caleb, and I thought perhaps at this hour everyone else would still be in bed. Caleb did sleep here last night, didn't he?"

"Well, I don't know," Jessica said a little awkwardly. "After you left I rather lost track of him."

"He went off somewhere?"

"Not necessarily. And if he did, he may have come back after I went to bed. Perhaps he borrowed a car and went looking for you."

"Don't try and kid me, Jessica. I was the last person he wanted to see."

"Maybe he's gone home. Have you been there?"

"No. At least, I'm pretty sure I haven't. The last thing I remember is driving away from here. This morning I woke just before sunup behind the wheel of the car. On the beach."

"Let's see if he is at the house now. If not, you can phone home. Or I will for you, if you like."

Louise rubbed her eyes. "Very well. And thanks, Jessica. It's a waste of time, though. He's with some floozie. I don't know why I expected to find him here. Still a bit fuddled, I guess."

They drove up the rest of the driveway and got out of the car. Before they reached the front door, utterly without warning, from somewhere came a nerve-shattering, piercing scream.

The two women froze. "Who the . . ." Louise asked shakily.

Jessica thought a second. "That seemed to come from the pool." She turned and ran in the direction of the sound. Louise stared after her.

Approaching the pool area, Jessica rounded a corner of the house, where she ran full tilt into Kitt. The girl was wearing a swimsuit—and sobbing hysterically.

"Kitt, my dear! What on earth's the matter?" Jessica took her by the shoulders.

"The pool," Kitt gasped, "the pool."

"What about it?"

"He's . . . he's . . . Oh no! It's horrible!"

She shook Jessica off, covered her face with her hands, and leaned up against the wall, sobbing.

Jessica eyed her for a second, then took a deep breath. She walked resolutely up to the edge of the pool and looked in.

Floating on the surface of the water was a man. And his face . . .

Jessica turned her head aside with a shudder. Where his face had been there was now . . . nothing. Nothing but . . .

Jessica somehow managed to fight down her nausea and forced herself to take another look.

Spread out like a water mattress under the man's body was a grimly familiar Victorian cloak. And on his head—what was left of his head—was a deerstalker hat.

Again Jessica averted her eyes. She had seen all she needed.

She became aware of a patch of red near her feet and looked down. It was blood. She stepped hastily away from it. And her foot came in contact with an object she had half noticed before, but which had barely registered on her mind. It was the skeet gun.

At that moment she heard running footsteps behind her. She spun to see Louise approaching. Jessica stepped toward her, throwing up her arms.

"No, Louise!"

But it was no use. Louise ignored her and half stumbled up to the edge of the pool. She looked in and gave a choking gasp of revulsion.

Then she screamed just one word:

"Caleb!"

# Chapter Six

POLICE Chief Roy Gunderson was a cigar-smoking, gray-haired man in his early fifties. The main impression he made on Preston Giles was of a man intensely irritated at having been called to investigate an early Sunday morning crime. The police chief, Preston felt, resented his thoughtlessness in hosting a party on Saturday rather than Sunday. Otherwise, when guests began knocking one another off, the chief could have commenced his murder investigation in the proper and tidy way, on Monday morning.

"It *is* murder, then—quite definitely?" Preston asked him, trying to ignore the impression.

They were in Preston's study. The photographers and fingerprint experts had done their work. The body had been briefly examined and taken away. The routine of criminal investigation was well under way. And it was still not nine a.m.

Gunderson took a much-chewed cigar from his mouth. "Nobody, but nobody, blows his own face to pulp with a twelve-gauge shotgun, Mr. Giles."

Preston winced. "Perhaps not, but an accident . . . ?"

"Difficult to make those guns go off by accident. You can drop 'em, throw 'em down even. Besides."

As Preston waited, Gunderson deliberately relit his cigar, then brought out his *pièce de résistance.* "There's no prints on the gun. It's been wiped clean."

Preston said: "Oh."

"Now, maybe Captain McCallum and somebody else were foolin' around and the other person picked up the gun and pulled the trigger, not knowing it was loaded. And then panicked. Or maybe McCallum attacked someone who shot him in self-defense. That could make it manslaughter or justifiable homicide. That's for the courts to decide. Somebody did it, and they're concealing the fact. In my book, that makes it a murder inquiry. No matter the reason it happened."

Preston shrugged. "As you say, Chief."

Gunderson took out his notebook. "Now, I want to get clear who's who in this place. Seems the first three people to see the body—within a couple of minutes of each other—were all da . . . er, ladies. Right?"

"I believe so."

"A Miss Kitt Donovan, a Mrs. Jessica Fletcher, and the dead man's wife—widow—Louise. That was shortly after six a.m. Kind of early to be up on a Sunday morning, wasn't it? Especially after a late-night party?"

"You'll have to ask them about that."

"Oh, I will, Mr. Giles. I've seen your doctor friend, who first examined the body, and he says I can't speak to Miss Donovan or the widow yet. They had bad shocks and he insisted they go and lie down. But it seems this Mrs. Fletcher's made of sterner stuff."

"Well, she is J. B. Fletcher, you know—the author of *The Corpse Danced at Midnight*. My firm published it."

An expression of disgust came over Gunderson's face. "Aw, mystery writers! They make me sick! Thinking up these impossible, crazy crimes, and making the police out a lot of dopes."

He stubbed out his cigar viciously. "Where is she, anyway? I want to see her."

"She was in the living room with my other guests. Shall we go in?"

In the living room they found Grady, Peter Brill, Ashley Vickers, and the doctor. There was no sign of Jessica, but Davis was serving coffee.

Preston looked around. "Where's your aunt gone, Grady?"

"I think she's outside."

"Thanks. Want to come and find her, Chief?"

But Gunderson's eyes were on the steaming liquid being dispensed by Davis. Preston spotted this.

"Coffee, Chief?"

Gunderson glanced at his watch. "Yeah, thanks. I could use some. Guess Mrs. Fletcher will keep."

Davis handed him a cup and he sipped with relish, while Preston performed introductions.

"Doc," Gunderson said, "I know you're not the coroner, but you did look at the body. How long d'you figure he'd been dead?"

The doctor pursed his lips. "Hard to say accurately without a proper examination. But several hours, at least."

"In other words, he was probably killed while your party was going on, Mr. Giles. Yet nobody heard a shot. From a twelve-gauge shotgun?"

Preston said: "You have to remember, Chief, the party was noisy. It gets chilly at night, so the windows were closed. And the pool *is* some distance from the house."

Gunderson grunted. "What's the last time any of you saw him?"

They looked at each other. At last Ashley broke the silence. "I was talking to him and several other people about ten before ten. Then Louise came up and said she wanted to go home. You were there, Doctor."

The doctor nodded.

Ashley went on: "Louise was somewhat the worse for drink. Caleb—Captain McCallum—told her to go and get some coffee. She stormed off on her own. A minute or so later the Captain drifted away. I didn't see him after that."

"Did anybody else?" Gunderson studied their faces. There was a general shaking of heads. "What happened to Mrs. McCallum?"

Grady supplied the answer. "She drove off almost at once."

"Somewhat the worse for drink?"

Grady shrugged. "We tried to stop her, but it was no use."

"And," Preston said, "she didn't get back here until a few minutes before the body was found."

Gunderson rounded on him. "You know that for a fact, Mr. Giles?"

"Well, not exactly, but Mrs. Fletcher told me, just before you arrived . . ."

Gunderson interrupted. "Never mind what Mrs. Fletcher told you. I'll be talking to her. And to all the guests, I suppose." He cast his eyes upward. "Gee, what a job! Nine out of ten of 'em will have been halfsoused . . ."

He wandered over to the window and put his cup on the ledge. "Okay, we'll leave opportunity for the moment. What about motive? Somebody got any preliminary ideas about that?"

Peter Brill spoke for the first time. "A motive for killing Caleb McCallum? Surely you jest, sir. Half the country had reason to kill the man, and the other half didn't know him."

Gunderson scowled at him. "Not funny, friend."

"But accurate," Ashley said calmly. "The Captain was not particularly well loved, though I doubt if any of us despised him enough to kill him."

"Except for me, of course."

The voice came from the door. They all jerked around to face Louise. She was deathly pale.

The doctor got to his feet and hurried toward her. "Mrs. McCallum, you ought to be resting. You should have let me give you a sedative."

She waved him away. "I'm all right, Doctor, thank you."

She came fully into the room. "Did I shock you? But it's what you're all thinking, isn't it?"

"Louise," Preston said gently, "I was just telling Chief Gunderson that you left here alone last night and didn't get back until six this morning."

"That right, Mrs. McCallum?" Gunderson asked.

"Frankly, I don't know."

"You don't?"

"No. I'm being quite candid, you see. I don't think I came back, but I don't really remember anything between leaving here and waking up in my car on the beach this morning. But I did not kill my husband, Mr. Gunderson."

"But if you don't remember anything that happened between . . ."

"Well, I do think, don't you, that however drunk I was, I would remember a thing like that?"

Gunderson stared intently at her for a moment without speaking before turning to pick up his coffee cup. As he did so, he happened to glance out of the window.

A woman was walking along, staring intently up toward the top of the house, shading her eyes with her hand. Gunderson beckoned to Preston, who joined him at the window.

"Would that be Mrs. Fletcher, by any chance?"

"Yes, that's Jessica."

As they were speaking, Jessica moved to a small flower bed. She got down on her hands and knees, peered closely at the bed, and then gently poked at the soil with her finger.

"What's she up to?" Preston muttered.

Gunderson gave a muted exclamation. "Starting her own private investigation, is my guess. That's all I need! Amateurs!"

He faced the occupants of the room again. "We'll be taking statements from all of you. So keep yourselves available." He made for the door.

Brill said hurriedly, "Chief, I'm holding auditions for a new show. I must be back in town by this evening."

Gunderson stopped and looked at him hard. "You will leave when I say so, Mr. Brill. Not before."

He went out.

Against the wall of the house near the flower bed was some lattice-work. After rising to her feet, Jessica surveyed it. Then she moved forward, took hold of it, shook it, and started to climb. It supported her weight quite well.

However, she had only gone a couple of feet off the ground, when behind her she heard the sound of throat-clearing. She looked over her shoulder. A gray-haired man was standing a few feet away, staring at her calmly.

"Morning," he said.

"Oh, good morning." Hastily, Jessica climbed down. She felt rather foolish.

"Mrs. Fletcher?"

"That's right."

"Roy Gunderson. Police chief."

"Oh, how do you do, Chief Gunderson." Jessica held out her hand. "Look, I do beg your pardon, but I was just checking something out. I probably should have asked you first. I didn't disturb any evidence, believe me."

Gunderson deliberately took a cigar from his pocket and lit it. "I read your book," he said.

"Oh, did you really? How nice."

"Said I read it. Didn't say I liked it."

"Oh."

"I been talking to some of the others inside. None of them saw McCallum last night after the spat with his wife. Did you?"

"Just immediately after. I told him that she'd left. That was shortly before ten, I think. He wasn't very concerned. After that he disappeared."

"So, what do you think?"

"I beg your pardon?"

"You know people, ma'am. You spot the little things, the inconsistencies. So, what do you think about Mrs. McCallum?"

"Surely she's not a suspect?"

"At the moment she's *the* suspect."

"My goodness."

Jessica started to walk slowly and thoughtfully across the grass, away from the house. Gunderson fell in beside her. She stopped and looked at him. "Chief, did Mr. Giles tell you about the intruder we had here last night?"

"That New York private eye? You think *he* killed the Captain?"

"No, not at all. But I'm sure you noticed the shoes on the body floating in the pool."

"Shoes?"

"They were brown—casual—with soft rubber soles. At the party, the Captain was wearing black patent leather—highly polished."

"That so?"

"The private detective was wearing brown shoes. I noticed them when I tripped him in the corridor. Now, I'm pretty sure he got in through that window."

She pointed upward to a partially opened second-story window. He followed her gaze, then looked down again, as she moved back a few steps to the flower bed.

"Now, look: you see these broken flowers—and over there, that footprint? In order to make the climb to that window, the detective would have had to wear soft, rubber-soled shoes."

Gunderson stared at her. "Mrs. Fletcher, just what are you telling me?"

"Oh, I wouldn't presume to tell you anything, Mr. Gunderson. But, as the face of the man in the pool was not identifiable, it did occur to me that perhaps we were all a little hasty in assuming . . ." She trailed off.

Gunderson's eyes bulged. "You mean . . . the guy in the pool wasn't McCallum?"

"No, he damn well wasn't!"

The voice was stentorian, and they both swung toward it.

Standing alongside the house, accompanied by a young deputy, was Captain Caleb McCallum.

"Well," Roy Gunderson gasped, "I'll be a son of a . . ."

McCallum strode forward, interrupting him rudely.

"You *are,* Chief. You always have been. And you're a stupid one, to boot."

Gunderson glowered at him. It was clear that at this moment he was sorry the body was *not* that of Caleb McCallum.

"Is that so?" he snapped. "All right, McCallum, suppose you show how bright you are and tell me who that corpse is, and how come he was wearing your costume."

"I haven't the faintest idea," McCallum said calmly.

"You know all about it, though?"

"Your deputy's just told me."

Before Gunderson could speak again there was an interruption.

*"Caleb!"*

The voice held a mixture of disbelief and joy. Louise was standing quite still, staring at her husband, her face stained with tears. The next moment she was running toward him. She threw herself against him and flung her arms around his neck.

"Oh, Caleb! Thank God!"

McCallum, looking somewhat embarrassed, gave her a perfunctory embrace.

"It's all right, Louise," he muttered. "I'm fine, just fine."

She drew back and stared up into his face. Then she glanced sideways at Jessica and Gunderson. Her expression was changing. Already, it was possible to believe, she was feeling slightly ashamed of her display of emotion. She looked at her husband again.

"You're really all right?"

"I've said so, haven't I?"

He looked and sounded irritated. And this fact suddenly sank in on Louise. She flushed.

"Is that so?" she said harshly. "Well, I've news for you, Caleb: *I'm not!*"

Without warning, she drew back her arm and dealt him a stinging blow across the cheek.

McCallum stumbled back. "What's that for?" he roared.

"That's for last night. And all the other last nights you've put me through."

Louise turned on her heel and strode away.

Gunderson emitted a muffled snort, heard only by Jessica, and which she was quite sure was suppressed laughter. However, his demeanor was grave as he stepped forward.

"Let's go indoors," he said. "It's time you and I had a serious talk, McCallum."

McCallum hesitated, then gave a curt nod. They started toward the house. Jessica, her face pensive, fell in behind.

Gunderson kept the Captain waiting for a minute or so while he conferred earnestly with the young deputy. Then he accompanied McCallum into the house.

The news of Caleb's resurrection had preceded him—doubtless by way of Louise—and a crowd was waiting to greet him. Of Louise herself there was now no sign.

Preston stepped forward with outstretched hand and beaming face. "Caleb, my dear fellow, this is wonderful! I can hardly believe it."

McCallum took his hand a shade unwillingly. "Thanks, Press."

Ashley approached him. "Good to have you back among the living, Captain McCallum."

"Well, Ashley, actually I'd never left, as you can see."

Brill came toward him and laid a hand affectionately on his shoulder. "Caleb," he said in a voice charged with emotion, "I can't tell you how much this means to me—to be able to see you again, touch you, to know that you're going to be around." He gulped. "I can hardly keep back my tears. Tears of joy, of course."

McCallum glared at him suspiciously, but Brill's face was perfectly straight.

Gunderson said: "Mr. Giles, do you mind if I use your study for a bit?"

"No, go right ahead," Preston said.

"Thanks. Come along, Mr. McCallum."

In the study, Gunderson seated himself behind Preston's desk and had McCallum sit facing him. He relit his cigar, gazing at McCallum as he did so. "What do you know about a guy called Dexter Baxendale?"

McCallum gave a start. "Baxendale? Well, he's a private detective."

"And what's he to you?"

"He's been working for me."

"Doing what?"

"If you must know, I've been having some business problems lately. Somebody in my organization has been leaking confidential information. I hired Baxendale to find out who."

"And has he?"

"Not yet—as far as I know. Last Friday he told me he was on to something and might have it wrapped up over the weekend. But I haven't heard anything yet. No doubt later today . . ."

"So, what was he doing here last night?"

McCallum looked startled. "Baxendale was here?"

"You didn't know?"

"No, of course not. Why didn't he report to me? Who did he see?"

"Baxendale was caught by Preston Giles and Grady Fletcher searching Fletcher's room during the party. Seems he got in through a window."

McCallum was looking staggered. "I can hardly believe it! I heard there'd been an intruder, but I'd no idea it was Baxendale." He frowned suddenly. "But, look, why are you bringing this up now? I thought you were interested in this body in the pool . . ." He broke off. "Good Lord, you don't mean . . ."

"Mrs. Fletcher seems to think so."

"Mrs. Fletcher? What on earth's it got to do with her?"

"Smart lady, Mrs. Fletcher," Gunderson said ruminatively. "She spotted the corpse's shoes were a lot like Baxendale's—and not like yours. Anyway, my men are checking the body's fingerprints now, comparing them with the intruder's, lifted from Grady Fletcher's room. We should have a positive ID soon. And while we're waiting, I want answers to a few more questions."

"Such as?"

"What the dead man was doing in your costume, for one."

"I've told you I know nothing about that."

"What happened to the costume? When did you take it off?"

"I don't know exactly. I'd decided to go out for some fresh air."

Gunderson looked at him skeptically. "Oh, yeah?"

McCallum's jaw was working angrily. "All right, if you must know, I left with a young woman—a guest at the party."

"Left for where?"

"We, er, spent the night at a local inn. I knew nothing about anything that had happened until I arrived back here and ran into your deputy."

"That still doesn't explain the Sherlock Holmes costume."

"I took it off and dumped it in the front closet before I left here. I wasn't going to prance into the lobby of that inn looking like a refugee from a costume ball."

"I see." Gunderson nodded slowly. "Well, that makes sense. About the only thing that has so far. What was the name of this girl?"

"Look, Gunderson, do we have to drag her into it?"

"Don't see we have much choice, considering she's your only alibi."

"But you can't suspect me of killing this man. Even if he *is* Baxendale."

"You told me yourself Baxendale had been investigating your company. Suppose he happened to find out something he wasn't meant to, and decided to try a spot of blackmail."

"That's nonsense!"

"Or maybe dug out something about your private life. That's not exactly pure as the driven snow. Oh, that reminds me—the girl's name."

Unwillingly, McCallum muttered, "Tracy something. I don't know her other name. At the party she was dressed as Little Red Riding Hood."

Gunderson made a note. "Thanks. I'll get her full name from Giles."

At that moment there was a tap on the door.

"Yeah?" Gunderson yelled.

The door opened and the young deputy put his head in.

"Yes, Jim?"

"Positive, Chief."

"Thanks, Jim. Quick work."

The deputy went out. McCallum looked at the police chief. "I suppose that means . . ."

Gunderson nodded. "Yup. The guy in the pool *was* Dexter Baxendale."

# Chapter Seven

BY one p.m. that day the police had interviewed and taken statements from all the people in the house, and Gunderson gave permission for everybody who so wanted to leave. Most wasted no time.

Jessica decided to start back to Manhattan immediately after lunch. Preston was upset and anxious, waiting for the imminent descent of the media, and there could be no enjoyment left in the weekend. She felt a little guilty about leaving him in the lurch, but, in fact, he encouraged her to go.

"I'd like you away, out of it all," he said. "Come back again soon, when it's all over, and spend a truly restful weekend."

He was apologetic that he couldn't return with her; but as he explained, he felt he had to stay on hand for the time being. In spite of her assurance that she could perfectly well return to the city by train, he insisted on arranging for a limousine and chauffeur.

"You arrived in style; you'll go back the same way," he said firmly.

He came outside and kissed her gently on the cheek.

"Safe trip," he said. He waved her off as the car bowled down the drive.

In the back Jessica settled down to chew over the possibilities of her embryonic plot. However, just as the car reached the end of the driveway and was about to turn onto the road, a figure with his hand raised stepped out from behind a tree. The driver hesitated.

"It's all right," Jessica said, "do stop. I know the gentleman."

It was Roy Gunderson. He opened the rear door. "Would you mind dropping me at police headquarters, ma'am?"

"Delighted, Mr. Gunderson."

He climbed in and the car moved off.

"How strange you haven't an official car available," Jessica said dryly.

He grunted. "Can we talk?"

"By all means."

Gunderson closed the partition behind the driver, then sank back into the deep seat. "I want to know about your problem," he said.

"Problem? I don't know . . ."

"You've had a look on your face, Mrs. Fletcher. Somethin's worrying you—somethin' about this case. I want to know what it is."

Jessica shook her head firmly. "No, Mr. Gunderson, this is really none of my business."

"I'd like to make it your business. You see, I figure this is a screwy sort of crime, like in a book. Not the usual sort of thing we have to handle. Now, seems to me you have the sort of brain . . ."

"The *screwy* sort of brain, do you mean?"

"The, let's say, ingenious sort of brain that could see to the bottom of this mystery."

"It's kind of you to say so, but I'm sure that's not true. You think I know something that I haven't told you. I assure you I don't."

"I'd like to tell you some of the things I learned this morning," Gunderson continued, "particularly what McCallum had to say."

"Should you do that?"

"Why not? Cops talk to each other about what they're told. And sometimes to outside experts they think can help. Let's call you one of those. Want to hear?"

Jessica gave a little chuckle. "Mr. Gunderson, you know quite well I do."

"So, there it is," Gunderson finished. "What d'you think?"

"Dear me, it's all extremely interesting, isn't it?"

"Any . . . observations?"

"Not just at the moment. I'd like to mull it over for a while first."

"You goin' to tell me now what's on your mind?"

"It's nothing specific, just vague ideas. There's only one definite point that occurs to me."

"What's that?"

"Well, someone killed Sherlock Holmes."

"That New York gumshoe was no Sherlock Holmes."

"Ah, but he was, Chief. At least, he was at the moment he was killed. The question is: did the killer know he was?"

Gunderson narrowed his eyes. "What?"

Jessica took a deep breath. "At first you thought you were investigating the murder of Captain McCallum. You said you wanted to find a motive. Then the Captain turned up and you discovered the true identity of the victim. Now, quite obviously, you're going to be looking for somebody with a motive for killing Baxendale."

"Of course."

"Such a person might have followed him to New Holvang and have no connection with anybody at the party. Indeed, I hope that *is* the case."

"So?"

"Well, we mustn't forget that it was the *Captain* who went to the party as Sherlock Holmes. Suppose the murderer didn't know Caleb had taken the outfit off?"

"You mean . . . thought he was shooting at McCallum? But the shooting was done from the front."

"Yes, but it was night. There was probably only enough light for the killer to see that very distinctive cape and deerstalker."

Gunderson frowned. "What you're telling me is that we have *two* possible intended victims—*two* sets of suspects—depending on who the killer thought he was killing."

"I'm afraid so. And you can't afford to neglect either line of inquiry, can you?"

Gunderson sighed and stared disconsolately out of the window. "Mrs. Fletcher, between church and football and the fact that the town council never calls me, this is my favorite day of the week. Now you've just made it the worst Sunday I've spent in ten years."

On arriving in New York, Jessica went straight to her hotel. She spent a quiet evening and went to bed early.

The next morning she awoke having come to a firm decision. She had just finished dressing, when there was a knock on the door. It was Grady. He was carrying a bundle of newspapers.

"Seen these?" he asked, after they'd greeted each other.

"No, are they very bad?"

He handed her a copy of the *Daily News*. The front page carried a blazing headline: BIZARRE MURDER STALKS POSH PARTY. Below, in slightly smaller type were the words: Society Detective Slain.

There was a photo of Preston's home, and one of Dexter Baxendale.

"I don't think I want to read all this," Jessica said.

"Just listen to this bit."

He took the paper back from her and ran his eye down the column. "Ah, here we are: 'McCallum had registered at the inn shortly after ten-thirty. The internationally known fast-food king was accompanied by a young woman whose identity has not yet been divulged by authorities.' "

"Oh, poor Louise," said Jessica.

"I suppose it had to come out eventually. By the way, you're mentioned, Aunt Jess."

"Oh no! Am I?"

"Relax. It only says, let me see, er . . . , 'Also present at the party were best-selling mystery novelist Jessica Fletcher and ex-Broadway composer Peter Brill.' " Grady chuckled. "Peter will just love that 'ex.' Oh, and something else rather funny: one of the other papers refers to you as *Mr.* J. B. Fletcher."

"That's fine. Fame is not for me. The fewer people who know about me, the better I'll be pleased. Which is why I'm going home today. In fact, now."

She crossed the room, picked up a suitcase, put it on the bed, and began packing.

"Yeah, I thought you might decide that," Grady said. "I think it's a pity, though. I bet you could solve this case. You were the first to realize the body wasn't Caleb's."

"I'm not a detective, Grady. I'm a substitute English teacher."

"You mean a writer."

"I don't know what I mean, but I do know that Ethel Jenks is leaving Wednesday to visit her daughter in Montpelier and I promised I'd take her class."

"They can get somebody else."

"The truth is, I want to go back. Maybe I'm old-fashioned, but I don't have much use for city life, and frankly, except for you and Kitt, I don't much care for the people either."

"Including Preston Giles?" he asked quietly.

Jessica looked at him for a moment, then carried on with her packing.

"At least you could have called and told him you were leaving."

"I'll call him from Cabot Cove." She smiled. "You know, it's a bit unseemly for you to be fixing up your old auntie with a suitor, no matter how pleasant or distinguished he might be."

"Hey, I wasn't. Honest."

"Oh, but you were. Honest."

He shrugged. "Well, I'm sorry you guys didn't hit it off."

"But, my dear, that's the trouble." Jessica's voice was almost sad. "We were starting to hit it off much *too* well."

She snapped shut her suitcase, then reached into her purse and took out a five-dollar bill. She was just putting it under the ashtray next to her bed when the phone rang.

"Answer that, will you, Grady?"

Grady did so, listened for a few seconds, then covered the mouthpiece. "Somebody called Chris Landon—*New York Times.*"

"Oh, tell them I've been forced to go home today. I'm starting for Cabot Cove within the hour. If they want to send somebody there to interview me, fine; but I can't possibly see them today."

Grady relayed the message and hung up. He looked at his watch.

"Sorry I can't come to the station and see you off, Aunt Jess, but I must get to the office."

"Of course you must."

Jessica moved to him and gave him a big hug. "Take care of yourself, dear. My love to Kitt, and my thanks to her for making last week almost tolerable. Bring her up to Cabot Cove soon. Promise?"

"I promise, Aunt Jess," Grady said.

Half an hour later Jessica was walking along the platform of the railway station, about to board the train, when she suddenly heard a voice calling frantically from behind her.

"Mrs. Fletcher! Aunt Jess!"

She turned her head in surprise. Dashing toward her was Kitt.

Jessica stopped and stared as the girl came running up. She caught at Jessica's arm and stood panting, trying to get her breath.

"My dear, what on earth's the matter?" Jessica exclaimed.

Kitt gulped down a big mouthful of air. "Oh, Aunt Jess—it's Grady."

A cold hand clutched at Jessica's heart. She felt herself go white.

"What about him?" she whispered.

"He's been arrested!"

*"What?"*

"On suspicion of murder."

They gazed speechlessly at each other.

# Chapter Eight

"CHIEF Gunderson," Jessica said forcefully, "my nephew did *not* kill that private detective."

Gunderson fumbled for matches and relit his cigar. "I sure hope you're right, Mrs. Fletcher. He seems like a nice young man—for a thief."

"Thief?" Jessica was indignant. "What *are* you talking about?"

"Fact is, Mrs. Fletcher, he's been stealing confidential information from his company."

"I don't believe it!"

Gunderson shrugged. "I wouldn't expect you to, ma'am, but right now he's being questioned by county detectives who aren't so sure."

Jessica threw up her hands in exasperation.

They were in a New York City precinct station. She had rushed straight there as soon as Kitt had explained where Grady was being held. But she hadn't yet been able to see him. Kitt herself had gone to phone Preston.

"County detectives?" Jessica said. "Why aren't *you* questioning him, Mr. Gunderson?"

"Matter of jurisdiction. When it comes to murder, the county cops have a way of taking over. Guess they figure a small-town chief like me is in over his head."

"If you believe Grady is guilty, they may be right."

The muscles around Gunderson's mouth tightened for a moment. Then, as he looked at Jessica, and perhaps sensed the anguish she was feeling, he softened his manner.

He crossed the sparsely furnished room, pulled out a chair, and sat down opposite her.

"Look, Mrs. Fletcher, I know how you feel. I realize he's kin. But listen to the facts."

He took his cigar from his mouth. "At daybreak this morning we found Baxendale's car parked a half mile from the Giles place. In the glove compartment there was a confidential real estate report belonging to Caleb McCallum. We've checked with him, and he tells us it must have been taken from his office sometime Friday morning."

"But why do you assume the thief was Grady?"

"He had access, ma'am."

"So, I'm sure, did many other employees."

"Not too many. Half a dozen, according to McCallum."

"Miss Vickers among them, I assume."

"Yes. And she's being questioned this very minute. Remember, however, Baxendale was discovered in your nephew's room."

"But assuming for a moment that Grady did take it, he would never have been so crazy as to carry it around with him—right out to New Holvang—and then leave it unguarded in his room."

"He might have. Could be he was about to hand it over to somebody, somebody who was going to contact him, though he didn't know just where or when. But he had to have the report handy. He'd figure it was safe enough. If the report wasn't missed and no hue and cry started, he could reasonably assume the theft wouldn't be discovered until this morning—by which time he would have gotten rid of the report. As he would have done if things had gone according to plan. And it wouldn't even matter if anybody—'cept McCallum himself—happened to see the report in his room. To a servant, for example, it'd just be business papers, which they'd assume your nephew had a perfect right to have."

Jessica considered this. Things were not looking good for Grady. "Chief Gunderson, I don't want to cast undue suspicion, but all you've said applies equally to Ashley Vickers."

"Except for one thing: there's no evidence that Baxendale was ever in Miss Vickers' room; it would be much more dangerous for her to keep the report there—because she might well expect McCallum himself to visit her."

"I don't agree," Jessica said. "I heard her say that for several months her relationship with the Captain had been a purely business one."

"Well, she would say that, wouldn't she—once she discovered McCallum had found another playmate in Little Red Riding Hood? But I don't figure she found *that* out until late Saturday night. Don't forget, either, that *Mrs.* McCallum certainly thought there was something going on between her husband and Vickers."

Jessica didn't say anything. Gunderson seemed to be warming to his task. He took a puff on his cigar, then went on:

"However, say Vickers was telling the truth. Fact remains, McCallum brought her with him for some reason. Say it was just business. Or again, McCallum knew one of his employees was leaking information. Suppose he suspected Vickers and wanted to keep an eye on her. She wouldn't realize his motive. But whatever his reason for having her along, she must have thought there was a good chance McCallum would be in and out of her room. It would have been a risk to have the report there. Oh, I know none of this is conclusive. But the truth is that the evidence against her is not so strong as against your nephew."

Jessica sighed. "Grady himself raised the alarm when he saw someone in his room . . ."

" 'Course he did. And if he had that report hidden there, it'd explain why he got so steamed up when he saw the beam of that flashlight bobbing about."

"That's nonsense. If he'd had anything incriminating in his room, he wouldn't have drawn attention to the intruder. He would have made an excuse to Miss Donovan, then hurried quietly up the back stairs. He'd never have come charging through the living room the way he did, letting Kitt tell us all what was going on."

"He panicked."

"He's not the panicking sort. And his manner was not that of a guilty person. At the party he was very relaxed and rather pleased with himself."

"So you say, Mrs. Fletcher. But I'm afraid your nephew's manner is not evidence."

"All right," Jessica asked suddenly, "answer me this: how did the papers get to Baxendale's car?"

"What do you mean?"

"Well, according to your theory, when Grady took Baxendale downstairs to see him off the premises, he knew there was a chance Baxendale had found the report and had it on him. Are you telling me that, with a possible jail sentence staring him in the face, Grady just let him walk off without searching him?"

"Could be he tried."

"What do you mean?"

"Your nephew got the better of Baxendale once. But he might not have a second time. Baxendale was a pro. He'd be on his guard. Say your nephew demanded that Baxendale turn out his pockets, Baxendale refused, they fought—and this time Baxendale won. He got away, took the report back to his car, locked it in safely. Then it occurred to him: why turn in your nephew to McCallum? Why not seek a partnership? Your nephew knew where the report could be sold, so Baxendale would need him. He goes back to the house again, sees your nephew a second time, and starts to apply the pressure—let him in for fifty percent, or he turns your nephew over to McCallum. Your nephew sees red, and bang . . .''

Jessica tried another tack. "If this leaking of information has been going on for some time, whoever's responsible will have made a good sum of money already. I know the state of Grady's bank account: anemic.''

"Naturally he wouldn't put the dough in his regular account. And incidentally, neither would Ashley Vickers. But we're looking into it, all the same.''

Jessica looked up. "Fingerprints," she said abruptly. "If Grady had been handling that report, his prints would be all over it.''

"We checked. Prints are all smudged.''

Jessica got to her feet. "Nothing I can say will shake you, will it?''

"I got an open mind, Mrs. Fletcher. But I gotta go by the facts. Bring me some facts, something solid in Grady's favor—or something solid against another person—and I'll be pleased to shake hands with your nephew and tell him I'm sorry. But until then . . .''

When Jessica went outside she found an anxiety-stricken Kitt awaiting her.

"Well?" the girl asked eagerly.

Jessica shook her head. "He's got an answer for everything, my dear. He's built up quite a formidable case, even if it is purely circumstantial.''

Kitt took her by the arm. "Well, I have some good news. I got through to Mr. Giles. He was terribly shocked. He said he'd call his lawyer friend, Karl Teretsky, to get Grady released on bail today.''

"Oh, thank heavens. Karl Teretsky? I've heard of him. He's very expensive, isn't he?''

"One of the most expensive in New York, but one of the best. And Mr. Giles is coming straight here himself.''

"Oh, good." Jessica gave a wry smile. "Not, I suppose that there's a lot he can do. But just having him here will help.''

By early afternoon Grady had been released and Preston had arrived hotfoot from New Holvang. He, Grady, and Teretsky had a hurried conference; then Teretsky went off to put some inquiries in motion.

Preston, Grady, Jessica, and Kitt went for a late lunch at a small Italian restaurant across from the police station.

At the close of the meal Preston slipped away to phone Teretsky. He came back looking a little grim.

"Well, things aren't really any better, I'm afraid," he said. "It seems

Baxendale *did* have a reputation as a blackmailer—which supports the police theory about his attempt to pressure Grady."

Grady gave a groan. "I'm sick of saying it! I never saw that report. And I didn't set eyes on Baxendale again. I took him downstairs and saw him off the premises. That was that."

Jessica tapped his hand. *"We* know that, dear, but we must look at it from the police viewpoint."

"I know," he sighed.

"There's one thing," Jessica said slowly, "that I should have raised with the chief: the Sherlock Holmes costume. Why was Baxendale wearing it?"

"I mentioned that to Karl," Preston said. "The cops just figure he slipped back to the party and took it out of the front closet as a sort of disguise so he could mingle with the guests. At least it would cover his hair and that very expensive suit."

"Oh, that's fiddle-faddle, Preston," Jessica said impatiently. "Baxendale wasn't a mind reader. How could he possibly have known the costume was in the closet? Anyway, why should he want to mingle? If he had been meaning to blackmail Grady, all he had to do was phone the house, ask to speak to him, and demand that Grady come outside to meet him. To wander around the house looking for him, knowing he might run into you or me or Kitt, would have been crazy."

"Even so," Grady said, "there must be a reason he was dressed that way."

Kitt spoke up suddenly. "Perhaps Captain Caleb gave him the costume, or told him where it was, and asked him to put it on."

"What reason would he give?"

"As the police think: so he could mingle easier. But not to look for you."

"I don't get it."

"Afraid I don't, either," Preston put in.

"Look: Caleb was going off with Little Red Riding Hood. Baxendale was working for him, but still hadn't found the report. He needed to go on searching. Or perhaps keep somebody under surveillance. He needed a disguise to do so. Say he phoned McCallum, told him he'd been rumbled and evicted, and wanted to get back indoors. So McCallum *didn't,* as he says, put the costume in the closet, but took it out and left it somewhere on the grounds for Baxendale to find."

Grady said thoughtfully: "Well, it's logical up to a point. Trouble is, that costume just wasn't a very effective disguise—not in bright lighting, indoors. From behind, for a few seconds, okay—but people would only have to get a glimpse of his face . . ."

"With most of the guests that wouldn't matter," Jessica said.

"It wouldn't if Caleb hadn't been wearing the costume all evening. I mean, can't you imagine people going up to Baxendale, momentarily thinking he was McCallum? 'Oh, have you and Caleb changed costumes?' Or: 'I didn't know there were two Sherlock Holmes here.' No, that costume would have been useless as a disguise; it would only have drawn attention to him. Don't you agree, Aunt Jess?"

But Jessica had stopped listening. She had just seen a familiar figure enter the restaurant and hurry across to a wall phone.

"Look who's here," she murmured.

"Ashley Vickers," Grady said slowly. "So she's been released too." He grinned wryly. "I honestly don't know whether to be glad or sorry."

"Excuse me a moment," Jessica said.

She rose and moved slowly across the restaurant toward the phone. Ashley got a number and Jessica waited while she talked urgently for a few seconds, then hung up. Jessica moved to her as she turned.

Ashley raised her eyebrows. "Mrs. Fletcher. What are you doing here?"

Jessica nodded her head, indicating the group seated across the room.

"I think it's called a war council. Would you like to join us?"

"Thanks, but no," Ashley said. "I've just spent several hours being hounded by two homicide detectives, and all I want now is a hot bath and a cold drink."

She started to move. Jessica put a hand on her arm.

"Ashley, often there is strength in numbers. You know the police are convinced that either you or my nephew murdered that private detective."

"But that's not true," Ashley said sharply.

Jessica frowned. "What do you mean?"

"Didn't you know? They've pinpointed the time of death. Preston's neighbors heard a loud noise at eleven-fifteen. They thought it was a sonic boom, so they didn't investigate. The police checked. There were no jets overhead Saturday night. That sonic boom was the sound of the shotgun."

Jessica cast her mind back. "Eleven-fifteen . . ."

"Yes," said Ashley, "a time for which I could gratefully provide them with an ironclad alibi."

"Oh, was that when . . . ?"

"Right. At eleven-fifteen I was sitting half-naked in an upstairs bedroom while *you* were washing my dress out. So I'm afraid that leaves Grady as the one and only suspect. Excuse me."

She walked away.

Thoughtfully Jessica went back to her table. She relayed Ashley's news. Grady and Preston looked grim, but Kitt said excitedly:

"Eleven-fifteen! But that's wonderful! Grady and I were together at that time."

Preston said gently: "My dear Kitt, I'm afraid that's like Bonnie Parker alibiing Clyde Barrow."

Her face fell. "Oh yes, I suppose so."

Suddenly Grady sprang to his feet. "I'm going back to the office."

They stared at him. "Today?" Jessica said.

"Why not? I have to do something or I'll go crazy. I can usually manage to lose myself in figures."

"But won't you mind showing yourself?" asked Kitt. "Everybody there will be sure to know . . ."

"So what? I've done nothing to be ashamed of. I want McCallum to know that. And I have to face the others sometime."

"You won't find Caleb at the office this afternoon," Preston said. "He told me he'd be spending the day on his yacht at Bayside."

Grady shrugged. "Just as long as he knows sometime."

They left the restaurant. Grady and Kitt went off together. Preston hailed a taxi. He and Jessica got in, and he gave the driver the address of Coventry House.

There was a companionable silence for a moment or two. Then Preston said quietly: "Worried?"

"I can't help it."

"I know. But cheer up. Karl Teretsky is the best trial lawyer in the state."

"Will it come to that, Preston? A trial?"

He shook his head. "I don't suppose so for a moment."

Then he took her hand and spoke gravely. "Jess, you have my word: Grady will be exonerated."

"Thank you, Preston. I know you're trying."

He looked at her a little sadly for a moment. "Kitt tells me she caught up with you at Grand Central."

Jessica looked awkward. "I was going to call you, Preston, I give you my word."

"From Maine." He looked out of the window. "I feel somewhat foolish. This weekend—before the trouble—was the happiest time I'd spent in years." He looked at her. "Did I misread you so badly?"

Jessica hesitated. "Of course not. But back home we have a saying: flowers that bloom too quickly are fair game for a late frost."

Preston looked amused. "Do you really say that?"

"Actually, no." Jessica smiled.

They both laughed. "That's better," he said, and squeezed her hand.

"You will be going home then?"

She shook her head decidedly. "Oh, not now. Not until I know that Grady is all right."

A minute or so later the taxi drew up outside Preston's office. He got out, then turned around. "Dinner tonight?" he asked.

"Well," Jessica replied, "there's a lot to do . . ."

"But you do have to eat. Why not with me?"

Jessica smiled. "All right, I'd love to. Thank you."

"Great. I'll call you later."

He took a twenty-dollar bill from his pocket and handed it to the driver. "Take the lady to her hotel." He gave a wave and was gone.

Jessica stared after him absently for a moment, then started to rummage vigorously in her purse. She was recalled to reality by the cabdriver. "Lady, which hotel?" he asked in a tone of superhuman patience.

"Oh, I'm sorry," Jessica said, "I was thinking of something else. No, I've changed my mind. Driver, do you know a place called—now dear me, where is it? Bayview? Baytown?"

"We got a Bay Ridge, lady. That's in Brooklyn. In Jersey you got your Bayonne. Out on the Island, you got your Bay Shore, your Bayville, your Bayside . . ."

Jessica snapped her fingers. "That's it! Bayside! The Bayside Yacht Club. Would you please drive me there?"

The driver held up Preston's twenty-dollar bill. "Won't get there on this, lady."

"Oh, I'm prepared to pay the difference, naturally."

The driver turned right around in his seat. "Listen, lady, to tell you the truth, I wanna get home. My feet are killing me. Yeah—I know—a guy in my job should have problems somewhere else, but with me it's my feet. Some joke, huh?"

"Oh, it's no joke. My friend Lena Miller had an awful time for years. She had these little calluses—like corns, only they're not corns . . ."

The driver's face lit up as though he had met an old friend.

"Say, that's what *I* got!"

"Really? Then we're going to have to get you some ointment."

"Naw, I've tried all that stuff."

"Not *all* that stuff, you haven't. Back home, we make some ourselves. Very secret."

"You're kidding. You know, my old man's got the same problem. I think it's heretical."

"I think you're very probably right," Jessica said gravely.

"This ointment stuff—it does the trick?"

"It cured Lena Miller."

"That so? Gee, this I gotta try. How can I get hold of some?"

"Well, if you like I can tell you how to make it. Or write it out for you."

"Aw, would you do that?"

"Certainly, but it's quite complicated. It'll take some time. So, if you'd like to drive on . . ."

"You win, lady. For something that'd fix my feet, I'd drive to California."

He faced front again, and the cab pulled away from the curb.

Jessica took out her notebook. "I'll explain what I'm writing," she said. "Now, this is how we make it . . ."

# Chapter Nine

WHEN the taxi drew up at the Bayside Yacht Club, the meter read thirty-three dollars and eighty cents.

Jessica looked up from her purse in dismay. "Oh dear," she said, "how awful."

"You can't make it?"

"I'm sorry, Bernie, I was sure I'd brought more cash with me. I don't suppose you'd take a credit card, would you? No, I didn't think so."

He gazed at her indulgently. "Look, Mrs. Fletcher, you gonna be here long?"

"Well, I can't be sure. But not if I can help it."

"Okay, then, I'll wait for you and drive you back to the city off the meter."

"Oh, Bernie, I couldn't ask you to do that."

"What you gonna do—take the subway? Forget it. Go do what you're gonna do."

Jessica stared at him. "Do you know something, Bernie?"

"I don't know nothing."

"All the same, you've taught me a valuable lesson."

"That so? What?"

"That there are some very kind people in New York."

" 'Course there are."

"In fact, probably just as many as there are anywhere else. They just take a bit of digging for." She got out. "I'll be as quick as I can."

"No rush. It's peaceful here. I got my paper and the radio. And your secret recipe." He held up some pages torn from her notebook.

It didn't take Jessica long to locate McCallum's boat, the *Chowder King*. It was one of the largest yachts berthed at the Bayside Yacht Club.

As she walked along the wharf, she spotted the familiar figure of Mc-Callum, hosing down the deck.

"Hullo?" she called out. *"Chowder King* ahoy! Captain Caleb."

He spun around. His expression was momentarily grim. Then he recognized her and made an effort to smile.

"Mrs. Fletcher. What a surprise. A delightful one, of course."

"I hope you don't mind my coming," Jessica said.

"Not at all. Come aboard."

He stopped the hose and dropped it on the deck. She climbed the short gangplank and he assisted her off it.

"Thank you, Captain."

"What can I do for you, Mrs. Fletcher? I assume this isn't just a social call."

"Unfortunately not. Captain, you know, of course, that Grady was arrested this morning."

He gave a shrug. "The evidence is conclusive, I'm afraid."

"The evidence is far from conclusive, Mr. McCallum. It's wholly circumstantial."

"Circumstantial evidence can be as strong as any other kind."

"I suppose you've been talking to Chief Gunderson," Jessica said.

"Thankfully, no. Gunderson is an incompetent fool. He's a political hack, putting in time till his pension comes. However, in this case he does have his facts straight."

He turned away, took a mop out of a bucket that was standing nearby, and started to swab the deck with it.

Oh no, Jessica thought, you're not going to get rid of me as easily as that.

She looked around and spotted a canvas and aluminum chair near the rail. She walked across to it, carried it to the center of the deck, and sat firmly down in it.

"What facts are those, Mr. McCallum?" she asked.

He stopped swabbing and stared at her for a few seconds. Then he straightened up. "All right, I'll tell you. Can't do any harm."

He walked across and stood in front of her, resting his hands on the handle of the mop.

"Someone in my organization has been stealing information on proposed sites for my Chowder Houses. Those leaks have cost me a great deal of money."

"Yes, I'm aware of that."

"I hired Dexter Baxendale to ferret out the guilty party. He eventually narrowed the list down to six possible culprits."

"Among whom no doubt was Grady?"

"Right."

"And Miss Vickers?"

McCallum's eyes narrowed. "She was a theoretical possibility. I don't know if you'd care for the names of the other four?"

"Not at this stage, thank you," Jessica said seriously. "They wouldn't mean anything to me. Please go on."

"At Baxendale's suggestion I made those six people—and only those six—aware of a confidential real estate report I had just received. The contents of it could be worth big, big money to someone if I acted on it. Of course, if the information did leak out, I didn't have to. I let it be thought, though, that I *was* going to act on the information. Today."

"I see. Your object in this being to force your traitor to act quickly."

"Yeah. He or she'd have to steal the report on Friday and dispose of it over the weekend."

"And it *was* stolen on Friday?"

"That's right. But I still didn't know who by."

Resisting the impulse to correct him with an admonitory *by whom,* Jessica asked, "Wasn't that rather careless? Wouldn't it have been preferable to leave the report somewhere in your office, apparently unguarded, but with Mr. Baxendale watching covertly to see who took it?"

McCallum looked embarrassed. "Well, that was the original idea. But there was a foul-up, Baxendale, the fool, left his post for five minutes, and in that time the report vanished."

"Dear me," Jessica said, "now that seems to me rather suspicious. Didn't it occur to you that Baxendale might have been in, er, cahoots with the traitor and have deliberately left his post for five minutes?"

McCallum scowled. "It crossed my mind," he admitted. "But he convinced me it was a genuine mistake. Besides, at that stage I had no choice but to trust him. There wasn't time to call in another detective agency. So I didn't let it be known I'd discovered the theft, and Baxendale arranged, at no extra charge, for all five suspects to be closely watched over the weekend by himself and his operatives . . ."

Jessica interrupted. "Five suspects? I thought you said six . . ." She broke off. "Oh, I see. You yourself were going to keep an eye on Miss Vickers, I presume."

"Nothing of the sort," he snapped.

"No? Then may I ask why in fact you invited her to Preston's house with you?"

"That's my business, I reckon, Mrs. Fletcher."

"I think not, Mr. McCallum. Not when my nephew is facing a murder trial. However, I won't press the point. You were saying the five other suspects were put under surveillance . . . ?"

"That's right. From the moment they left the office."

"Really? That means somebody must have followed Grady to Grand Central when he caught up with me there?"

"I guess so."

"How interesting," Jessica said thoughtfully. "I've never been kept under surveillance by a detective before. At least, not as far as I know." She gave a sudden decisive nod. "Yes, of course! It would have been that big burly man with the brown hair."

McCallum looked startled. "You spotted him?"

"Well," Jessica said, "naturally, I couldn't be absolutely *sure* . . ."

A point to me, she thought, with satisfaction. Definitely cheating, of course. But among Baxendale's operatives there was almost certain to have been one who was big, burly, and brown-haired; and no one could ever *prove* she hadn't spotted him.

Without giving McCallum a chance to work this out, she went on quickly. "So you knew Grady was being watched at the party on Saturday night?"

"I sure hoped he was."

"You suspected from the start he was the culprit?"

"No. He's one of my brightest boys. But I wanted to be sure it wasn't him. Naturally, when Louise and I accepted Press' invitation, we had no idea your nephew was going to show up there."

Jessica furrowed her brow. "But I'm puzzled. You believed Grady was being watched. Yet when you were told by Chief Gunderson that Baxendale had been in the house that night, you were apparently surprised."

"That Gunderson's sure got a big mouth," McCallum said disgustedly. "But it's true. I *was* surprised. I didn't know Baxendale was tailing your nephew *personally*. I figured that one of the guests in fancy dress was a Baxendale operative. I still do. My bet is that Baxendale came along late, knew your nephew was safely under surveillance downstairs, and decided to search his room. Where he found the report. 'Course, he didn't know your nephew was outside the house and would see his flashlight. So he was caught."

"And why didn't he produce the report then and expose Grady?"

McCallum shrugged. "Probably because he had no proof where he'd found it. But we know he found it somewhere—it was discovered later in his car—and we know he had been in your nephew's room. The inference is obvious."

"Do you really think so? Then explain to me why the document was found in Baxendale's car. Why walk half a mile, lock the report in his car, and come back to the house? Why didn't he bring the report to you?

He did know you were there, I suppose. You did tell him where he could contact you over the weekend?"

"Naturally I did. Look, Mrs. Fletcher, I'm not denying Baxendale was a crook—had decided to double-cross me and perhaps sell the report himself. It's possible—probable, even. But it doesn't alter the situation regarding your nephew. And if it is true—well, Baxendale sure paid the penalty."

Jessica nodded. "Yes, he did, didn't he?"

Something in her tone angered McCallum. "What d'you mean by that?" he asked hotly.

"Just that I don't think you'd take kindly to being double-crossed, Mr. McCallum. You'd get very angry with anyone who tried."

He flushed. "You saying I killed Baxendale?"

"Merely that you had means and motive—just as strong a motive as Grady, in fact—even admitting he was the thief, which, of course, I don't."

"I also have an alibi, Mrs. Fletcher."

"Ah yes, the young, er, lady in the Red Riding Hood costume. So does Grady. Quite as good a one, if not better. I mean, granted that Grady and Kitt are very fond of each other, so she could perhaps be expected to lie for him—well, so are you and Little Red Riding Hood fond of each other. After all, you couldn't resist the temptation to go off with her when Louise's departure gave you the opportunity. That left Miss Vickers unwatched and with a wonderful chance to get rid of that report."

"I never seriously suspected Ashley. Besides, the cops have cleared her. They called to tell me. You yourself give her an alibi for the time of the murder."

"Yes," said Jessica, "for the time of the *murder.*"

"Well, there you are. Now, Mrs. Fletcher, you must excuse me. I have lots to do."

"Oh, certainly, I'll go."

Jessica stood up and moved toward the rail. "You know, Mr. McCallum," she said pleasantly, "there's one thing we may be forgetting: how can we be sure *anyone* intended to kill Baxendale? With him wearing that Sherlock Holmes costume, the killer may have been after you."

He shook his head. "Not a chance. The police say the shot was fired from no more than fifteen feet away."

"I just can't help thinking: it was such a dark, cloudy night. And you know, if a mistake *was* made . . ." She broke off. "Oh well, you're probably right." But she sounded far from convinced.

"Mrs. Fletcher, you're a pretty shrewd cookie," McCallum said, "but you're scratching up the wrong tree. You see, nobody has a motive to kill me. My employees know full well that I *am* Cap'n Caleb's Chowder Houses. Without me, it all falls apart. As for my wife, Louise—we have a prenuptial agreement. While I'm alive, she lives like a queen. If I die, she gets almost nothing." He smiled. "So much for your theory of mistaken identity."

Jessica put her foot on the gangplank. "But on the basis of that, can you really say *nobody* has a motive to kill you? I don't think *I* could be so confident. There is such a thing as pure hatred, you know."

She started down the gangplank, then paused and turned. "All the same, I'm glad you said none of your employees has a motive to kill you."

"Why?"

"Because if mistaken identity should be proven, I have your word for it that Grady didn't have a motive."

"If he's still technically an employee of mine, he won't be for long."

"Technically? But he's at his desk at McCallum Enterprises this afternoon."

The Captain's face darkened. "You mean he had the colossal nerve to go to work today?"

"Why not? He's done nothing wrong. And that's something I know. I appreciate your hospitality, Captain Caleb. And no thank you, I *won't* have a drink."

Jessica stepped off the gangplank, turned, gave him a cheerful little wave, and tripped away along the wharf.

It was late afternoon when Jessica got back to her hotel. She went up to her room and immediately telephoned Grady. He answered almost at once.

"Grady?"

"Oh, hullo, Aunt Jess."

"How did it go at the office?"

"Not too bad. I got a few fishy looks, and one or two people kept their distance. I felt like the guy who uses the wrong toothpaste."

"Well, I think you were very brave to go. Grady, what time does the office close?"

"What's it matter?"

"What time, Grady?"

"Six-thirty, seven. Why?"

"That real estate report . . ."

"Oh, Lord, am I tired of that report!"

"Listen, Grady, this is important. Baxendale found it at Preston's house. The only two employees who could have brought it there were you and Ashley. That automatically eliminates the other four suspects. We know it wasn't you . . ."

"Thanks," he said dryly. "Sometimes I'm beginning to have doubts even about that."

"Be serious, Grady. Ashley had to be the culprit. You agree on that?"

"Yes, I suppose so," he said somewhat reluctantly.

"Then we have to prove it."

"But how on earth . . ."

"I want to look around her office," Jessica interrupted.

He drew his breath in sharply. "Aunt Jess, that's police business."

"At the moment, my dear, the police seem to be making it their business to convict you of murder."

"But if you were caught . . ."

"I don't think I'd face a very severe sentence, not as a first offender. But anyway, I shall take great care not to be. Of course, I'll need your help."

"I don't like it."

"Grady, you must trust me. I'm going to get you out of this. You would never have been at that party if it hadn't been for me."

"Well, *you'd* never have been there if it hadn't been for *me*. I submitted your book to Coventry House, remember."

"If it comes to that, I introduced your father and mother to each other, so you wouldn't *be* if it weren't for me. However, this is pointless. Now, will you cooperate?"

Grady gave a sigh. "I suppose, as there's obviously no way I'm going to talk you out of this, I'll have to. When were you thinking of mounting this expedition?"

"Tonight. Can you pick me up here at the hotel in"—she looked at her watch—"about an hour?"

"All right, if you're set on it. They can tack breaking and entering onto my murder-one sentence."

"Think positive, my boy. See you in an hour."

Jessica put down the receiver. That had been quickly settled. Fortunately. One of the reasons she had been so firm was that if she'd let him argue for long, he'd have talked her out of the project.

Almost as soon as she hung up, her phone rang. It was Preston.

"Where have you been?" he asked. "I've tried several times to get you, but the clerk said you hadn't been back since lunch. I was getting worried."

"I'm sorry, Preston. I went to see someone. I forgot you said you'd call."

"Oh, that's okay. Look, about tonight: I know a little restaurant . . ."

"Preston, do you mind if we keep options open for tonight? I may not be able to make it—or only rather late."

There was silence, and when he spoke she could hear the disappointment in his voice.

"No, of course, that's all right. If there's a chance of your having another dinner engagement . . ."

"It's nothing like that, I assure you. It's just I have a job to do. If you don't mind possibly wasting an evening, call me here later, about nine o'clock."


"Listen, Aunt Jess," Grady was saying, "Ashley may have taken those papers, but you know yourself she couldn't have killed Baxendale."

"Agreed. But her accomplice could have."

The two were in Grady's car, en route to McCallum Enterprises. Grady glanced briefly at her. "What accomplice?"

"I don't know. But she not only stole that report, but actually took it with her to New Holvang. Why?"

"Obviously to pass on to someone . . ." He broke off. "Oh, you mean to someone at the party?"

Jessica shrugged. "Well, that certainly seems most likely. It's clear she had to dispose of the report on Saturday or Sunday. Knowing that, she took the report with her to Preston's house—in spite of the risk involved. She must have had an arrangement with someone to hand it over. And remember: that someone was just as vulnerable as she was—and just as likely to commit murder."

Grady nodded thoughtfully. "Yes, it makes sense. But, Aunt Jess, it doesn't figure from any of this that Ashley would keep anything incriminating in her office."

"I realize that. But we'll never know unless we look. And there has to be something incriminating somewhere. It may be in her apartment."

Jessica paused and a very determined expression came over her face. "Tonight may be the first of several expeditions we have to make."

Ten minutes later Grady and Jessica entered the lobby of the McCallum Enterprises building. It was deserted, save for a uniformed security guard sitting at his desk. He looked at them with some surprise as they approached.

Trying to mask his nervousness, Grady said cheerily, "Evening, Tom."

"Evening, Mr. Fletcher. Working late tonight?"

"No. I just want to show my aunt where I work. She's visiting from Maine."

The guard nodded. "How do, ma'am. Hope you're enjoying your stay."

"Oh, it's been a rare experience, believe me," Jessica said.

"Anybody else around?" Grady asked casually.

"No, sir, you'll have it to yourself."

Grady nodded, took Jessica's arm, and escorted her toward the elevators, pointing like a tour guide to various extremely uninteresting objects as he did so.

They entered an elevator, Grady pressed a button, and the doors closed. They both breathed a sigh of relief as the elevator started to ascend.

"First obstacle cleared," he muttered.

"Now, when we get there," Jessica said, "I'm going to search Ashley's office. I want you to check the sales records."

He stared at her. "What?"

"We need to know the names of the people from whom the company bought the properties. Can you get them?"

He ran his fingers through his hair. "I guess so. They'll be in the computer."

"Good. Whoever bought and then resold those overpriced properties has to have some connection to Ashley—or to her contact."

The elevator stopped and the doors opened with a chime. Grady and Jessica stepped cautiously out, glancing both ways along a carpeted, dimly lit corridor.

Grady pointed and put his mouth close to Jessica's ear. "Ashley's office is at the end of the corridor. Her name's on the door."

"Why are you whispering?" Jessica asked brightly.

"*Quiet!*" he hissed.

"Grady, for heaven's sake, there's no one to hear you. Now, off to your computer. Scoot!"

"All right, but it may take a while."

They went their separate ways.

The door of Ashley's office was open. Jessica slipped in. The lights of the city outside a huge glass panoramic window provided just enough illumination. She looked around for a few seconds, then moved quickly to Ashley's desk. She flipped on a desk light and sat down. Then she started to go through the drawers of the desk.

Five minutes later she sat back in disappointment. Nothing. Nothing but completely innocuous business papers.

However, one drawer was locked.

Jessica eyed it speculatively. In that drawer might be pay dirt. On the other hand, quite possibly it contained papers that were just normally confidential.

It was while these thoughts were flashing through Jessica's mind that she heard a faint sound. She jerked her head up. What was it? The next second she knew.

It was the whir of the elevator ascending.

Jessica froze. Then, like lightning, she switched off the desk lamp and flitted silently to the door. She peered cautiously along the corridor toward the elevators at the far end.

She told herself there was no need for alarm. Hundreds of people were employed in this building. Obviously, some of them worked late. There was no reason to assume that anybody would come near this office.

Jessica heard a chime. The doors slid back. There was an agonizing moment of suspense during which nothing happened. And then out of the elevator stepped Ashley Vickers.

# Chapter Ten

JESSICA gave a muted gasp of horror, and her head shot back into the office like a tortoise withdrawing into its shell. Her mind whirled.

She was virtually certain Ashley had not seen her, because as the girl had stepped from the elevator, she was in the act of studying her face in a compact mirror.

But she would certainly be here within sixty seconds.

Jessica gazed around the room frantically.

There was no hiding place in the office. But there was one other door leading out of the room—set in the far wall. It was her only chance not to be caught in a highly embarrassing situation.

Almost willing the door not to be locked, Jessica darted across the room. She turned the knob and experienced a throb of relief as the door opened. She shot through it.

She found herself in a small private bathroom. She turned and pulled the door almost closed behind her, leaving it about an inch ajar—just enough to see through. There was a risk that Ashley would notice this and remember she had left the door closed. But if it enabled Jessica to see exactly what the girl was up to, it was a risk worth taking.

Jessica remained frozen, practically holding her breath, one eye glued to the crack. She was unable to see the whole office, but had a clear view of the desk and a couple of filing cabinets.

What seemed like an age passed. Yet it could not have been more than half a minute before Jessica heard someone enter the room. The door to the corridor closed, and a second or two later Ashley came into her view.

The girl was carrying a purse, which she put down on the desk and opened. She fumbled inside it for a moment and took out a bunch of keys. She selected one, bent over the desk, and unlocked the one drawer Jessica had been unable to search.

Ashley reached in and took out a file folder. She then carefully removed a sheaf of papers from it. She folded these and put them in her purse. Next she closed the file and replaced it in the drawer, which she locked.

For several seconds Ashley stood quite still by the desk, staring at the floor as though in thought. At last she seemed to come to a decision. She raised her head and looked directly at the bathroom door.

She hesitated for a moment—and then started to walk straight toward it.

Jessica's heart missed a beat and she shrank back against the washbasin—desperately, but hopelessly, trying to think up some feasible explanation for her presence.

She heard Ashley's footsteps approaching. The door started to move. It was at that moment that the telephone rang.

Jessica nearly jumped out of her skin. She heard Ashley give a little gasp.

There was an agonizing wait while the girl obviously stood, indecisive, her hand on the knob. Jessica held her breath, her fingernails pressed hard into the palms of her hands.

At last, Ashley retreated across the room. The next moment the telephone bell cut off sharply as she lifted the receiver. Her voice came—low, cautious.

"Yes?"

Then she audibly relaxed. "Oh, it's you. You scared me." Suddenly she sounded markedly annoyed. "Why are you calling me here?"

Ashley listened for a few seconds. "Well, I don't want you calling me *anywhere*. And yes, I *do* have it."

After a further short pause, she said angrily: "Talk? About what? I told you—after this, it's over. I won't have any part in murder."

Jessica smothered an involuntary gasp. She could hardly have hoped for anything as good as that. She strained her ears, trying to hear something—anything—of the voice on the other end. But she was too far away from the phone, even though Ashley's silence meant her caller must now be talking at length.

Eventually Ashley plainly cut in. "What, now? Tonight? No." After another wait she said: "All right, stop being hysterical. If it's that important, I suppose I can. Where are you?"

Ashley waited again, and Jessica imagined her jotting down an address. Sure enough, a moment later the girl said, "Got it," and Jessica heard the tearing of paper.

"I'll be there as soon as possible. But listen—they may be following me."

This time Ashley was silent for the longest period yet. "Well, all right,"

she finally said. Her voice sounded doubtful. "I'll do the best I can."
Then came the sound of her replacing the receiver.

Once more Jessica waited, tense. Nonetheless, her apprehension of
being discovered had now vanished. She would almost have welcomed a
confrontation. That one word—*murder*—had changed the situation entirely.

However, a confrontation wasn't to be. Jessica again heard Ashley
moving—this time away from the bathroom. The door to the corridor
opened and closed. Then all was still.

Hastily Jessica emerged into the office. She badly wanted to sit down,
get her breath, and collect her thoughts. But there was no time. She had
to know who Ashley was going to meet.

She hurried to the corridor, opened the door, and peered out. Ashley
was walking briskly toward the elevators.

Jessica waited until she had entered a car and descended before starting to run down the corridor herself. She got to the elevators, jabbed
impatiently at a button, and looked around her. She had no idea where
Grady had gone. She tried a sort of muted shout, like a stage whisper.

"Grady!"

But there was no response. She had no choice but to go without him.

Jessica waited, gnawing at her lip, watching the indicator showing
Ashley's car approaching the ground floor. Then the doors of another
elevator slid back. Jessica shot in and pressed the ground-floor button.

When the elevator reached the lobby and Jessica emerged, there was
no sign of Ashley. But the security guard, Tom, was still at his desk,
writing in a big book.

Jessica hurried across to him. As she did so, she opened her purse and
took out the first object her fingers met, which happened to be a fountain
pen.

The guard looked up as she reached him.

"Has a young lady just left?" she asked breathlessly.

"Yes, ma'am—Miss Vickers. I was just signing her out. She seemed in
a hurry."

"You didn't see which way she went, did you?"

He shook his head.

Jessica held up her fountain pen. "She dropped this," she said menda-
ciously. "I wanted to give it back to her."

He stuck out his hand. "That's all right, ma'am. Leave it with me. I'll
see she gets it in the morning."

"Oh, no," Jessica said hastily. "She may need it tonight. I'll just see if I
can catch her."

She turned and almost ran to the doors.

The guard stared after her. "But, ma'am . . . it can't matter tonight. It's only a pen. Ma'am . . ."

But Jessica ignored him. The guard shook his head in disbelief and returned to his book.

Jessica emerged from the brightness of the lobby into the night and stood helpless and lost for a moment, peering up and down the street. There was still no sign of Ashley.

Then, miraculously, she spotted her quarry. At least . . . yes, it had to be. The girl in question was some distance away, and there was only street lighting to go by, but it was impossible to mistake that magnificent outline. Ashley had halted and was waiting by a corner bus stop seventy or eighty yards away.

Jessica considered. The problem now was going to be to get close to the girl—and actually follow her onto the bus—without being spotted. If only there were a few other waiting passengers she could hide among, but at present Ashley was the only one.

The next moment Jessica's problem was, in one sense, solved: as she stood wavering, a bus swept past her from behind. It drew up at the stop, Ashley hopped nimbly aboard, and the bus moved off.

Jessica could have wept from sheer frustration. To have come so close, and then . . .

But no! She wouldn't be beaten!

Traffic ahead of the bus was heavy. Already it was slowing down. It *must* be possible to catch it.

A taxi!

Jessica ran to the curb, searching the traffic stream for a cab. Almost immediately she spotted one. She threw up a hand and called.

It passed by, unheeding. Occupied.

Jessica cast a despairing glance toward the back of the bus. It didn't seem to have progressed much farther. But obviously this couldn't last. At any moment the traffic ahead was bound to clear.

Another occupied cab passed. Then at last one responded to Jessica's frenzied waves. She gave a sigh of relief, stepped off the curb, and spoke urgently through the window to the driver.

"Follow that bus." She pointed down the street.

She had her hand on the passenger door. But then she noticed that the driver was staring at her in disbelief.

"Are you kidding, lady?" he said. "D'you know where that thing's going?" And before she could get the door open, he pulled away into the traffic stream.

"No, I do *not!*" Jessica yelled. *"That* is the problem!"

She stood in the road, staring furiously after the taxi. Amazingly, she could still just see Ashley's bus. But obviously now the situation was hopeless.

The next second Jessica nearly leaped in the air, as from behind her came a raucous horn blast. She spun around and saw a bus bearing down on her. About to leap for the sidewalk, Jessica suddenly realized that this was her final chance.

There was no time to reflect. She took a deep breath, raised her arm in an authoritative halt signal, and stood her ground. The bus, its horn still blaring, continued to hurtle toward her. She closed her eyes and prayed.

There was a harsh squeal of brakes. Jessica stood stiff, waiting for the terrifying noise to stop. Eventually it did so and she opened her eyes. The front of the bus had come to rest about three feet from her. The driver was glaring and gesticulating at her through the windshield.

"Thank heavens," Jessica murmured devoutly.

She trotted hastily to the side of the vehicle and made to step on board. Her left foot was actually off the ground when suddenly the bus jerked forward, leaving her still standing in the road.

She stared after it speechlessly. Then, once again, she started to run.

The bus came to a halt by the stop at which Ashley had boarded, and a couple of passengers alighted. Panting, Jessica arrived in the nick of time and mounted the step just as the driver was about to close the doors. She clung to the pole, trying to get her breath, and he looked coldly at her.

"You!" he grunted. "Tired of life, lady?"

"Far from it," she answered with dignity.

She heard someone in the doorway behind her and moved to one side. Rummaging in her purse, she allowed a burly young black man to push past her. He dropped some coins in the farebox and took a seat about halfway down the aisle.

The bus moved forward. Having found a dollar bill, Jessica looked up and peered through the windshield. The other bus was now about a block and a half away.

She addressed the driver. "Excuse me, but does this bus go to the same place as that bus up ahead?"

He sighed as though the burdens of the world were on his shoulders.

"That's the way it works, lady. Up the street, down the street. Seventy-five cents."

"Oh, good."

She held her dollar bill out to him. He ignored it.

"Exact change, lady." He pointed to a notice on the coin receptacle.

"But I don't have the exact change," Jessica said wearily.

"Then off you get at the next stop."

She bridled. "I will do no such thing."

"Yes, you will."

"You mean you'll hurl me off bodily?"

"Nope. I'll just sit here till a cop comes along and does it for me. Unless the other passengers get a bit fed up and decide to do it themselves."

In desperation, Jessica glanced once again through the windshield. Ashley's bus was still in sight—just. She looked the opposite way and let her eyes run over the other passengers. Most stared stonily ahead, apparently completely uninterested, and seemingly most unlikely to attempt a mass assault upon her person.

Only the young black man was watching her—with, she fancied, a rather odd expression. As he saw her looking at him, he glanced hastily away, out of the window.

Then her gaze fell on a very large old lady in the front seat. She was bestowing a wide, twinkly smile upon Jessica. Delighted at the sight of a friendly face, Jessica was about to smile back when she noticed something that seemed completely inexplicable. Around the old lady's considerable girth was hanging a change dispenser.

Jessica stared for a moment, then leaned toward her, holding out her bill. "Excuse me," she said politely, "but would you have four quarters for a dollar?"

Without ceasing to smile, the old lady shook her head. "No."

Jessica blinked. "I beg your pardon?"

"Said I ain't. What I do have is *three* quarters for a dollar."

Light dawned on Jessica. "I see."

Resignedly, she handed over the bill and received three quarters in return.

"Do many people get on board without the right change?" she asked.

"You'd be surprised, dearie."

"Nothing would surprise me," Jessica said. "You must do quite well out of it."

"Beats welfare, any day."

Jessica dropped the quarters in the receptacle and then looked once more through the windshield at the bus ahead. She fancied they might have gained on it slightly in the last minute. She continued standing, not taking her eyes off the vehicle in front. She had no idea where the stops were situated on this route, and at any moment the bus might halt and Ashley alight.

Suddenly the driver spoke again.

"Lady, for seventy-five cents, you're entitled to a seat."

"Oh, I'm fine like this, thank you," she said.

*"Will you sit down!"*

Jessica looked at him sadly and clicked her tongue. "You know"—she bent and looked at his badge—"you know, George, rudeness does not become you."

Steam was by now practically coming out of the driver's ears. He opened his mouth, fully primed to emit some choice expletives. But Jessica, who still had her eyes fixed on the bus ahead, laid a soothing hand on his arm.

"Wait a moment," she said sharply.

He swung around and glared at her, his eyes bulging. "Whaddya mean, wait a moment? I'm driving a bus."

"That one is stopping."

"What?" He looked front again. Then he gave a snort that nearly choked him. "Of course it's stopping, you silly old bag! That's a stop! What are you trying to . . ."

But Jessica wasn't listening. Ashley had stepped off the other bus and was walking back along the sidewalk.

"Stop here, please," Jessica said suddenly.

The driver gave a groan of despair.

'George, I'd like to get off. Quickly, please. It's very important."

Abruptly, George slammed on the brakes and the bus lurched to a stop. Jessica, gripping the pole, just managed to maintain her balance.

George was staring at her with grim satisfaction.

"I'm only supposed to open the doors at official stops," he said quietly. "Except in cases of emergency. Lady, you *are* an emergency. A walking emergency. Please"—he touched a control, opening both the front and rear doors of the bus—"get off. Back or front, but just get off. Now!"

She stepped down onto the street. Then she turned. "George," she called, "it's been delightful. We must do this again."

The bus roared off. Jessica did not notice that another passenger had emerged from the rear doors at the last moment and had moved silently into the shadow of a nearby doorway, where he silently watched her. It was the young black man.

But Jessica's attention was given entirely to Ashley Vickers, whom she could still see a hundred yards away. Now Ashley was coming toward her.

How best to keep Ashley under observation was the problem. Jessica knew that if she waited at this point, there was the danger the girl would turn off down some side street and would disappear again before she herself could reach it. On the other hand, if Jessica walked toward her, and Ashley did *not* turn off, they might end up meeting face-to-face. Although such an encounter would not be the disaster here it would have been in Ashley's office, it would put an end to discovering whom the girl was going to meet. Jessica could hope to rely on finding some alleyway or niche to dart into at the last minute. But it would be a risk.

She was just telling herself that she had only moments to reach a decision when, for the second time that evening, a decision was made for her. For Ashley paused, gave a somewhat furtive glance around her, and then quickly disappeared through the door of some building that Jessica could not at this distance identify.

Jessica hurried forward, being careful not to take her eyes for one instant from the spot at which Ashley had disappeared.

As she drew closer she could see that the building in question was brightly lit. Some kind of store? A bar? No. She was now close enough to see that the place was a small café.

Jessica drew level with it. A garish little place, its stonework crumbling, its windows plastered with posters.

Keeping her head turned away, Jessica hurried past and stopped in the doorway of a TV store abutting the café. She considered. This was a most unlikely place for the elegant Ashley to have a rendezvous. No doubt there was a good reason, if only that she would be extremely unlikely to encounter any of her other friends here.

Jessica longed to know whether the person Ashley had arranged to meet was already in the café. If so, it might only be necessary to walk boldly through the door to face the murderer of Dexter Baxendale.

On the other hand, if Ashley was so far merely waiting, to go in now could ruin everything. Or it might be that Ashley and her unknown friend had retired to some back room, and that by going in Jessica would learn absolutely nothing.

It really seemed that she had no choice but to wait and see.

She looked around her and for the first time became fully conscious of her immediate surroundings.

Oh dear. This really was a pretty grim neighborhood. Litter everywhere, graffiti, loungers wandering aimlessly back and forth, ragged alcoholics lurching about, prostitutes chatting in little groups or strutting up and down. So incredibly different from Cabot Cove that it might be another world. Or at least a movie set.

But if this *were* a movie, seen on TV from the comfort and safety of her living room, with the press of a button she could switch it all off. *These* people couldn't be switched off. They were very much there, and it was clear some of them were becoming as conscious of her as she was of them.

Jessica realized that in this neighborhood she must stick out like a sore thumb: the personification of conservative, middle-class respectability—and of comparative affluence.

Jessica came to a sudden decision. She had to know whether Ashley had yet met with her phone friend, or whether she was still waiting. She couldn't wait here any longer, a cynosure for all eyes, and not do anything.

She took a deep breath and stepped out firmly from her doorway.

Perhaps it wouldn't be necessary to go inside the café; a quick peek through the window might be sufficient. And it was fairly bright inside; it might not be possible from there to see much that occurred outside.

Speed was the important thing: not to give the girl, if she was watching the street, too long to be sure of just whom she had seen.

Jessica fairly shot up to the café window, put her face against the glass, and blinked into the interior. For a few seconds she could make out nothing. Then . . . yes! There was Ashley. And she was alone. What was more, she had her back to the door. Jessica relaxed slightly and studied her for a moment.

The girl was sitting at a small table against the wall. She was smoking with quick, nervous movements of her hands. In front of her was an apparently untouched cup of muddy-looking coffee. Several of the other patrons were casting interested glances in her direction. She seemed oblivious to them, no doubt being used to this reaction wherever she went.

As Jessica watched, Ashley looked up at a big clock on the wall. It showed exactly nine p.m. She glanced at her watch, as if to confirm this, then got to her feet and opened her purse.

Jessica scurried quickly away. She gazed around in a mild panic, spotted a deserted and darkened store with a deep entryway a few yards down the street, hurried along, and stood well back in it.

She watched the café door, and a moment later Ashley emerged and walked off briskly in the opposite direction.

Jessica thanked her lucky stars she had decided to look through the window. Had she remained in the TV store doorway, she would now almost certainly have assumed that Ashley had completed her meeting—and would have waited to see who emerged from the café after Ashley got clear. By the time she had discovered her error she would have lost the girl for good.

Jessica let Ashley get a lead, then started off after her.

This was all decidedly odd. Ashley presumably had had no rendezvous in that café after all. It surely couldn't be that she had just suddenly got tired of waiting: she couldn't have been in there more than ten or twelve minutes.

No. The way the girl had checked the time indicated a prior decision to leave there exactly on the hour. She had just been filling in time until her "talk" could take place somewhere else. Yet what an odd spot to choose to wait in.

However, speculation at this stage was useless. The important thing was not to lose her again.

Ashley was now striding briskly along. And even though many heads were turning to look at her, she seemed impervious to her surroundings and quite unaware of possible danger. She was either a remarkably brave or a remarkably foolish girl. And it seemed clear that she did not know she was being followed.

Ashley was not slackening her pace at all, and Jessica felt thankful that she kept so fit: Ashley was much younger than she was. It had been a long and tiring day, and her legs were beginning to ache. But there was no question of having to abandon the expedition. She'd collapse in the street first.

# Chapter Eleven

TO Jessica's relief, Ashley's pace finally slowed. Jessica let herself draw slightly closer. The girl still did not look behind, but she had started glancing around. It seemed she might be getting a little edgy. Could the end of her journey be near?

Then, without warning, she turned abruptly at right angles and disappeared from Jessica's sight.

Jessica broke into a run and quickly reached the spot at which the girl had vanished.

She discovered that Ashley had simply turned down a narrow alley between two large, dark buildings. Jessica gazed along the alley.

It looked most forbidding. It was long and narrow and illuminated by only two dim lamps. Ashley was just passing under the first of these. At the far end could be seen the lights and traffic of the street running parallel to the one Jessica was on.

She hesitated, then squared her shoulders. Anywhere Ashley Vickers could go, Jessica Fletcher could go too.

She stepped resolutely into the alley.

She had gone about twenty-five yards when she heard the footsteps behind her.

She felt a sudden prickling up her spine. The impulse to glance back was enormous. But she resisted it and simply increased her pace. Immediately the footsteps behind her also quickened.

Jessica broke into a run. She came to the small pool of light cast by the first lamp and passed out of it into the virtual blackness beyond. The footsteps were now running too.

She told herself that if she could only reach the street at the far end, she might yet be safe.

She tried to run faster. But the ground underfoot was potholed and rutted. In the darkness she kept stumbling.

Gasping with exhaustion and fear, she was approaching the second of the lamps. Suddenly a big figure loomed up from the side of the alley in front of her.

Jessica ran straight into his arms. She could see almost nothing of him, but could tell he was big and obviously young.

She heard him chuckle. "Not so fast, mama."

She opened her mouth to scream, but he must have sensed rather than seen her intention, for he suddenly clasped a hand over her mouth.

She jerked her head back and bit his hand hard.

He gave a yell and momentarily his grip loosened. Jessica pushed him as hard as she could and again started to run.

As she did so, she caught a brief glimpse of Ashley at the far end of the alley, staring back. Then the girl moved quickly out of sight.

Jessica heard an urgent voice shout behind her.

"What happened?"

"She bit me!"

"You zombie! After her, quick!"

She carried on running as fast as she could, but it was hopeless. They caught up with her under the second lamp, grabbed her by the arms, and forced her back against the wall.

She got her first good look at them. They appeared oddly alike—in their late teens or early twenties, long-haired, lean and pale, and with something strange about their eyes. Junkies, she said to herself.

She continued to struggle and had the satisfaction of kicking one of them sharply on the shin.

He swore and gripped her more tightly. Then he put his face up close against hers. He hissed: "All we wanted was the purse, mama. But just for that—and the bite—we're gonna give you a free blood test."

There was an ominous click, and she saw the glint of a knife blade appear in front of her eyes.

For the second time a hand was clapped over her mouth, and this time she could not dislodge it. She watched with horrified eyes as the point of the knife was brought slowly closer and closer to her face.

Then there was an intervention.

Inexplicably, from somewhere in the darkness a hand shot out and twisted sharply at the wrist of the knifeman.

He gave a howl of pain and the blade clattered to the ground.

The next moment the space around her was a maelstrom of action. She heard punches land. Gasps. Thuds. Yelps of pain. Somebody fell heavily. A fist whizzed past, an inch from her nose. She leaned up against the wall, gasping for breath, nearly fainting.

Suddenly she heard a voice call hoarsely: "Split!"

Then she became aware of someone clambering to his feet, and of two sets of footsteps retreating down the alley.

After that, all was silence.

Jessica shook her head dazedly, looked up, and managed to get her eyes focused. Staring down at her, a concerned expression on his face, was the young black man from the bus.

"You all right, ma'am?" he asked gently.

Jessica nodded dumbly.

"They didn't hurt you?"

She was getting her breath back. She gulped. "No, I'm all right. Thank you very much."

"You're welcome."

Jessica was fast recovering her wits—also, remembering why she was here. And a realization suddenly hit her. Everything in the alley had happened fantastically quickly. It was certainly still less than a minute since she had last seen Ashley.

She grabbed the young man by the lapels.

"Please—do something else for me?"

"Sure."

"Run to the end of the alley, quick as you can. Turn right. Look for a girl. Beautiful. Black hair. Wearing a blood-red suit and white blouse. Follow her. Find out where she goes. I'll make it worth your while, I promise."

"What about you?"

"I'll be okay. I'll wait for you at the end of the alley. Only please hurry. It's desperately urgent."

He gave a quick nod, turned, and ran off at an easy lope. At the end of the alley she saw him outlined for a second against the lights of the street. Then he was gone.

Jessica slowly and painfully made her way in the same direction. Suddenly she felt very old.

She emerged from the alley into the bright lights of the street. She blinked around, saw a low window ledge, walked across, and gratefully sank down on it.

Then she closed her eyes and tried to collect herself. After a few minutes she felt better and opened her eyes again.

What absolutely appalling luck that mugging had been. Just when, she felt sure, she had been within minutes of seeing the end of Ashley's journey.

On the other hand, it wasn't bad luck but her own foolishness in venturing into such a place alone that had gotten her into trouble.

Jessica's train of thought came to a sudden halt.

That was very odd. Those youths must have planned the mugging, because one of them had been lurking in the alley in advance, while the other had come up from behind. Yet there was no way they could have known *she* was going into the alley. They surely wouldn't have expected *anyone* to venture into it alone, at night; therefore, it couldn't have been just a question of hoping a possible victim might happen along.

So they must have been waiting for Ashley. But no. That couldn't be. The one who had already been in the alley had let Ashley pass.

It didn't make sense. Unless he had spotted her, Jessica, following Ashley, and decided to let the girl go and concentrate the attack on this second person instead.

That was possible. However, if the mugging had been planned, that meant that someone—presumably the man who had called Ashley's office—had tipped them off as to her movements.

And that made it a whole new ball game.

Then again, where did the black youth come into the picture?

He must have followed her all the way from the bus. Why?

She gave a deep sigh. It was all too much. She'd been a fool to get involved like this. What had made her think, just because she had a knack for creating and solving fictional mysteries, that she was qualified to solve a real-life one? Much better to have left it to the professionals.

"Ma'am?"

Jessica looked up with a start. The young black was standing over her.

She got quickly to her feet, her heart sinking. "No luck?" she asked quietly.

He hesitated. "Well, I think maybe . . ."

Jessica caught her breath. "What do you mean?"

"I saw a girl who looked like the one you described. I followed her."

Jessica's fatigue suddenly lifted. "And what happened?" she asked eagerly.

"She went into this building. I figured she might be in there hours, so I came back for you."

"Yes, you did quite right. What building was it?"

"I'll take you there. It's not far."

"Yes, please."

They set off, Jessica practically trotting to keep up with his loping, long-legged stride.

He said: "Maybe she left after I came back for you."

"I don't think so," Jessica said decidedly.

They rounded a corner and suddenly the young man stopped. He pointed.

"That's where the lady went."

Jessica stood still and stared at the building he indicated. She looked behind her at the street sign and her expression changed. Then she walked slowly forward and read a notice on the door of the building.

A great feeling of triumph welled up within her. She'd done it!

The young man came up to her shoulder. "Want me to come in with you?"

She turned to him with a smile of pure contentment. "No, thank you. I'm not going in—now. I've found out all I need to know." She couldn't resist sharing her triumph. "Do you know what I've just done, er . . . ?" She paused interrogatively.

"Oh, Joe."

"Do you know what I've . . ." She corrected herself. ". . . what *we've* just done, Joe? We have just solved a murder."

His eyebrows went up. "We have? That's great. And what are you . . . we . . . goin' to do now?"

Jessica took a deep breath. "The first thing I'm going to do is have a drink. Will you join me, Joe?"


Joe found a fairly respectable bar, and ten minutes later they were sitting in a corner booth, sipping their drinks. Jessica had made a strong effort to repair the ravages the night had made on her appearance. With her immediate mission accomplished, her weight off her feet, and refreshment in front of her, she was feeling quite her old self.

Joe was regarding her thoughtfully.

"Sure like to know what this is all about," he said.

"Oh, you will, Joe, I promise. But not yet. I have a lot of thinking to do first. Now." She opened her purse. "I promised I'd make this worth your while."

"There's no need for that, ma'am."

"Well, let's argue about that later. First, I want to know what this is all about."

He shifted in his seat. "What do you mean?"

"I want to know why you tailed me tonight."

"I didn't tail . . ."

"Oh, but you did. You followed me onto the bus and you must have gotten off when I did. Then obviously you were right behind me all the way, or you could never have rescued me so quickly in that alley. Now, why?"

He shrugged. "I did follow you onto the bus. I was hoping to talk to you. But you hopped off so quick I didn't get a chance. I figured you were in some sort of trouble. Now, I know this neighborhood. Some awful bad people hang around here. Lady on her own's likely to find herself in need of a friend. So I decided to tag along and make sure you were okay."

Jessica eyed him thoughtfully. "Well, that's wonderful, Joe. I'm more grateful than I can say. But you still haven't explained why you wanted to speak to me."

"Well, Mrs. Fletcher, you're a celebrity, you know."

She stared. "You know who I am."

"Sure. Seen you on TV. Besides, I had this, with your picture on the back."

And to Jessica's astonishment, he reached into his jacket pocket and brought out a copy of *The Corpse Danced at Midnight.*

"I been reading this," he went on. "I think it's really great."

She said weakly: "And that's all you wanted to say to me?"

"Well, not completely." He pushed the book across the table toward her. "I wanted to ask you to autograph my copy."

In the lobby of Jessica's hotel, three people were waiting. All were plainly anxious. Preston Giles fidgeted and glanced constantly at his watch. On a sofa opposite him sat Grady. He was trying to occupy himself by studying several sheets of computer printout, but he glanced up toward the doors every time somebody came in. Next to Grady sat Kitt, nervously smoking a cigarette.

"Well, Grady, I have to say it," Preston said suddenly. "I think it was rather irresponsible of you to go along with her in this scheme."

Grady sighed. "Mr. Giles, you don't know my aunt as well as I do. She was dead set on it. And when Aunt Jess is dead set on anything . . . well, *I* can't stop her."

"But chasing around New York City at night . . . alone . . . maybe following a killer."

"I explained I hadn't a clue she was doing that," Grady said. "When she wasn't in Ashley's office and I went looking for her, I was staggered when Tom told me Ashley had been there and Aunt Jess had gone racing after her. And all to return a pen, according to him."

"Well," Kitt said, "we realize that was a blind, of course."

Preston gave a groan. "But what happens if Ashley discovers she's being followed?"

"Well, naturally, I'm anxious too," Kitt said, "but not so much as you two. I think Aunt Jess . . . Mrs. Fletcher . . . can take care of herself." She stubbed out her cigarette, looked up, and then jumped to her feet. "And I'm right!"

Preston and Grady followed her gaze and hastily rose as they saw Jessica entering the hotel. She started to make for the desk, then saw them and changed direction.

Preston gave an exclamation. "Jessica! Thank heavens!"

"Aunt Jess, where on earth have you been?" Grady said urgently. "We've been worried stiff."

"Well, you needn't worry anymore. As you can see, I'm perfectly all right."

She sat down and smiled around at them.

"What have you been doing?" Kitt asked.

"Solving the murder."

They stared at her. "You mean you know who killed Baxendale?" Grady said incredulously.

"I know who was behind the murder, if not who pulled the trigger."

"But who?" They all spoke together.

Jessica considered. Then she shook her head. "I'm not saying yet."

"Really, Jessica!" For the first time since she'd known him, Preston sounded quite irritated with her.

"Now, Preston, you must allow me my sense of drama and suspense. I *am* a mystery writer, after all."

Her eyes fell on the computer printouts in Grady's hands. "Oh, are those the real estate sales figures I asked you for, dear?"

He looked awkward. "Actually, no. I must have hit the wrong button. These seem to be last year's wholesale fish prices." He paused, then added defensively: "Well, I was nervous."

"I'm sure they make riveting reading," Jessica said. "Thankfully, we shan't need those other figures, after all."

"We won't?"

"No."

"But why?"

"Wouldn't you like to know."

Grady became exasperated. "Aunt Jess, you told me once that you hate those mystery stories in which people keep vital information to themselves for absolutely no reason. And now you're doing that very same thing."

"And you know what invariably happens?" Preston put in grimly. "Those people always get knocked off before they can tell what they know."

"Now, don't get fiction confused with real life, you two. Besides, I have no intention of keeping vital information to myself for long. First, however, I want something to eat. You did promise me dinner tonight, you know, Preston. I realize I'm a *little* late, but how about us all going out for something? Then I promise I'll tell all."

Jessica drank the last few drops of coffee in her cup and wiped her mouth with a napkin.

"That was a delightful meal, Preston. Thank you."

The four of them were in a small, quiet, and very expensive restaurant near Coventry House. It was a place Preston frequently patronized when he had business to discuss, because there was ample space between the tables and it was possible to speak perfectly freely without being over-heard.

"Glad you liked it," he said. "Now, Jessica, please . . ."

"Very well." She paused to collect her thoughts. "You know Ashley Vickers came to her office while I was searching it. I had a minute's warning and hid in the bathroom. She took some papers from a locked drawer. Then the phone rang. She had a very interesting conversation, the strong implication of which was that she *is* the one who's been leaking information. But more important, she actually said, 'I told you that after this is over I won't have any part in murder.' "

"Good Lord!" Preston said.

Grady gave a whistle. "But that's fantastic!"

"Not all that fantastic. You see, there were no other witnesses, so there's no corroboration."

"But who was she talking to?" Kitt asked.

"That's what I didn't know. But then the person on the other end obviously asked her to come and see him—right away. She agreed, which is why, clearly, I had to follow her. Even though it meant walking out on you, Grady."

He nodded. "I can see that. Though I wish you hadn't taken the risk. It was terrifically brave of you."

"Oh, fiddle-faddle. Anyway, I followed her quite a long way, first on a bus and then on foot. I had one or two little adventures en route, and nearly lost her . . ."

"What sort of adventures?" Preston asked sharply.

"I'll tell you all about it some other time. The important thing is that I did discover where Ashley went." She paused.

"And saw who she met?" Kitt asked eagerly.

"Not exactly *saw.*"

Grady's face fell. "Then I can't understand . . ."

"Patience, Grady. You see, it was the building she entered that gave it away."

"Well, what building was it?" Preston asked.

"A theatre. The Serendipity Theatre, to be exact."

They all looked blank. Preston said: "I've never heard of it."

"I'm not surprised. It's very small and shabby, one of those hole-in-the-wall storefront theatres tucked away in a commercial area. Its precise location is just off Seventeenth Street."

Still they all stared at her without reaction.

Jessica said: "Perhaps none of you were there when it was mentioned, but as soon as I saw Seventeenth Street on the sign, I remembered."

"Remembered what, for Pete's sake?" Grady demanded.

"Something that was said at the party. I hardly had to go up and look at the poster on the door."

"Poster?" Preston queried.

"Yes. It said that they were holding tryouts for a new musical by Peter Brill."

Preston's face was a study. "Peter? *He's* the killer? I can't believe it. He just doesn't seem the type."

"I don't know," Kitt said. "He's pretty bitter. Seems to dislike everything and everybody."

"So did Jonathan Swift," Preston exclaimed. "So did Ambrose Bierce. They didn't kill people. Besides, with Peter I'm sure the bitterness is just a reaction against the bad luck he's been having. He simply seems too fastidious to blow a man's face away with a shotgun." Kitt winced. Grady coughed.

Jessica broke the silence. "Peter Brill may not have done the shooting himself. Perhaps he paid somebody else to pull the trigger."

Preston shook his head. "I can't even see him doing that."

"I admire your loyalty to a friend, Preston, but it's amazing what people will do when they're desperate for money."

"You think he's desperate?" Grady said.

"I believe so, yes. His lack of success recently is hurting him deeply. Preston, you yourself said that he's been scared his talent is gone for good. This musical could be his last chance. I remember hearing him say it takes a quarter of a million just to get started—money which apparently he's found, or believes he can get. Now, Mr. McCallum told me today that that report could have been worth big, big money to somebody if it fell into the wrong hands. It would have been a godsend to Brill, even after Ashley had taken her cut. Remember, too, there have been other costly leaks from McCallum Enterprises before, which is why Dexter Baxendale was called in."

"Then what exactly do you figure happened Saturday night, Aunt Jess?" Grady asked.

"Well, Ashley took the report down to hand over to Brill at the party. It was a risk, but they were playing for very high stakes. Brill no doubt had the contacts enabling him to dispose of the report in the most profitable quarter. Now, she arrived at your place with the Captain before Brill, didn't she?" She raised her eyebrows at Preston.

He nodded. Jessica went on: "So she couldn't dispose of it immediately. Even after Brill arrived, however, she must have realized that there was a possibility she was under surveillance and had to be very cautious about handing it over. And while she was waiting, Baxendale found the report. We don't know what he was doing in your room, Grady, but I think it quite possible Ashley hid the report there and that's where Baxendale found it."

Grady stared. "You mean she was intending to frame me?"

"Not strictly. Obviously, she hoped it wouldn't be found at all. But if it *was,* she'd clearly rather it be found in your room. The vital point is that Baxendale got hold of the report. Ashley discovered this—no doubt guessed the worst as soon as she heard about the intruder—and immediately reported to Brill."

Jessica broke off, took a sip of water, then continued. "Brill must have been frantic at the thought of losing all that money, so he went after Baxendale. As a result, Baxendale was shot, either by Brill or by a thug working for him. But from Brill's viewpoint it was too late. Baxendale had already taken the report to his car, locked it in, and had come back —hoping, I believe, for a cut in the profit or to apply a spot of blackmail. So although his death did save Brill from exposure, it didn't get him the report back."

There was silence for a few moments while they all digested what had been said.

Grady was the first to speak. "It all fits in. No snags that I can see."

"I wouldn't go quite as far as that, dear," Jessica said. "There are a few snags, but none that can't be surmounted."

She frowned and looked suddenly thoughtful.

"What's the matter?" he said.

"I'm just wondering if one can surmount a snag." She gave a firm nod. "Yes, one can—quite correct usage."

He gave a groan. "English teachers! Authors!"

"What do you think those papers were that Ashley took from her desk?" Kitt asked suddenly.

"Probably a duplicate of the report. Brill must have asked her for it today, so she went along to the office tonight to get the photocopy while no one was around. Meanwhile, Brill found he could dispose of it—and get paid for it—tonight. So he took the chance of calling Ashley's office and caught her while she was there. He told her to bring the papers straight to him at the Serendipity Theatre, and she did so."

"Good Lord!" Grady suddenly looked alarmed. "That means the report's probably already in the wrong hands. I ought to warn McCallum quick."

Jessica raised her eyebrows. "In spite of the way he's treated you?"

He looked awkward. "Well, I owe the firm some sort of loyalty."

She patted his hand. "Good boy. But actually you needn't worry. The Captain told me today that that report would only be valuable to outsiders if he acted on its recommendation. He only let it be *thought* he was going to."

Grady relaxed. "Oh, I see."

Kitt gave a frown. "Wouldn't Ashley know that?"

"I don't think so," Jessica said. "There's certainly no intimacy between her and the captain now. And I don't suppose she was at work today, was she, Grady?"

He shook his head. "I don't believe so."

"She wasn't," Preston said. "I called in to see Caleb late this afternoon. He'd just arrived there from his yacht. He happened to mention she hadn't been in."

"There you are. As far as she's concerned, the position regarding the report is the same as it was before the weekend."

Grady grinned. "Poor old Brill's really going to be in hot water if he sells the report for a fat profit, and then the buyers find out it's worthless."

"Well," Kitt said, "what's the next move, Aunt Jess? I mean, Mrs. Fletcher . . ." She stopped. "Sorry."

"Please do call me Aunt Jess, Kitt. I think it's a very good sign."

"Thank you," Kitt said. "I was going to say, hadn't you better tell the police what you've found out?"

"No, I don't think so."

"Oh, but surely . . ."

"What do you think, Preston?" Jessica asked.

Somewhat reluctantly, he shook his head. "No, I agree with you, Jessica."

He looked at Kitt. "Jessica realizes that we have absolutely nothing the police could act on. It's pure suspicion—logically based, I agree, but completely without substantiation."

"But Ashley's going to see Peter tonight . . ."

"That's no crime," Jessica said. "Why shouldn't she go and watch a friend holding auditions for a new show?"

Grady grew insistent. "But, Aunt Jess, Chief Gunderson respects your opinion. You told me he more or less asked you to put your mind to the problem. If you told him your deductions, it would at least make him think."

"Perhaps," she said. "But since he spoke to me in the car, he's become very suspicious of you. I fear he'd think my theory was cunningly contrived to get you off the hook. Besides, it seems the county detectives have taken over the case from him. Matter of jurisdiction, he said. And I don't think *they'd* take too kindly to my butting in."

Kitt banged the table in frustration. "But there must be something we can do!"

Jessica nodded thoughtfully. "I think that probably our best bet is a frontal attack on Peter Brill himself."

"How do you mean?" Grady asked.

"Well, on the phone Ashley told him not to get hysterical. With a murder and robbery hanging over him, and at the same time trying to put on a new show, he must be living very much on his nerves. If he was suddenly confronted with the information that I know of his involvement, he might well panic. And he might be pushed into making a serious blunder."

"Yes—such as trying to kill you," Grady said grimly.

"Well, that would be excellent," Jessica said. "The best thing that could possibly happen, especially if there were witnesses."

"Now, Jessica, don't be foolhardy," Preston cautioned. "You've taken quite enough risks today already."

She looked at him quizzically. "Where is the risk, Preston, if, as you say, Peter Brill is not the type to commit murder?"

He spread his hands. "You've got me there. I still feel that about him. But if there's the slightest chance of danger, I don't want you risking it."

"I don't really believe for a moment he'll try to harm me. And I promise I won't take any risks, Preston."

"Then I suppose I must give my blessing—partly to preserve my self-respect, because it won't make a blind bit of difference if I don't." He smiled at the truth of his statement.

"When will you talk to Brill?" Kitt asked.

"Tomorrow, I think. At the theatre. Judging by the poster, he should be there most of the day. You can drive me, if you will, Grady."

"Yes, sure."

She pushed her chair back and got to her feet. "And now it's me for my hotel—and bed. This has really been quite a day."

# Chapter Twelve

AT ten o'clock the next morning Grady's sports car pulled up at the curb outside the Serendipity Theatre. Grady got out, went around to the sidewalk, and opened the passenger door. Jessica, with his assistance and some difficulty, extracted herself.

Grady opened the theatre door. From within they immediately heard the distant tinkle of a piano.

"Sounds of life," Grady remarked. "Look, Aunt Jess, I'm still not happy about letting you go in there and confront him alone."

"Grady, he wouldn't dare try to harm me here. Not when I make it clear that other people know I've come to see him. You stay just where you are. Keep an eye on that lovely car—and an ear open for me. If he attacks me, I'll scream. I assure you, Fay Wray has nothing on me when I'm in full voice. Then will be the time for the fighting CPA to go into action."

She gave him a wink and disappeared into the theatre.

Jessica crossed a small foyer, pushed open another door, and emerged into an auditorium. It was in darkness, but the light from a bare, uncurtained stage revealed this as a small, cramped theatre with a general air of tattiness. It smelled both stuffy and musty.

On the stage were three people. At center was a young lady of obvious physical endowments, but considerably less musical talent, struggling to perform a song with little tune and an unrhyming lyric. Nearby a flashily dressed man was seated backward astride an old kitchen chair, gazing at the singer with an expression of intense delight. Seated at an upright piano downstage and providing accompaniment was Peter Brill. On his face was a look of anguish that nicely counterbalanced the other man's expression, reminding Jessica of the before and after sections of an indigestion-tablet advertisement.

She made her way quietly about halfway to the front, lowered herself onto an extremely uncomfortable aisle seat, and settled down to listen.

For one raised on the musicals of Kern, Rodgers, Gershwin, and Berlin it was a painful experience. If this was a typical number, could Brill's new show ever make the grade? She knew tastes had changed, but had they really changed this much?

After a few more minutes the routine blessedly came to an end. The flashy-looking man applauded enthusiastically and got to his feet, beaming. "Well, Petey boy, ain't she great?"

Brill rubbed his eyes. "Marvin," he said wearily, "your client's talent is exceeded only by her monumental capacity for flagellation of the treble clef."

"You got it," the agent said happily.

The singer put her hands on her hips and stared at Brill. "We through?" she asked peevishly. "I gotta be on the switchboard by eleven."

"I've heard all I need to, Miss Devine," Brill told her.

She sniffed. "That means I stink, right? Well, listen, buddy, you don't play so hot, either."

"But I've only had two hours' sleep," Brill said, "whereas with you, sweet thing, the oblivion of Morpheus seems to be a perpetual state of mind."

"Oh, yeah?" She clearly regarded this as a brilliant riposte.

Marvin took her by the arm. "Come on, honey, let's get out of here. Petey, I'll be in touch."

They started toward the wings, but the agent turned back and cast a quizzical eye at Brill.

"Listen, you got the dough for this thing, right?"

Brill gave him a smug smile. "Yes, Marvin, I got the dough."

Marvin shrugged and he and the girl left the stage.

Brill remained at the piano. The smug smile disappeared. Suddenly he seemed like a frightened, harried man. He played a couple of chords, then abruptly slammed the piano lid in apparent frustration.

Jessica got to her feet. She spoke loudly. "And just where did you get the dough, Mr. Brill?"

Brill gave a start and stared into the darkness. He shaded his eyes. "Who's out there? If you're here to audition, honey, come on up."

Jessica walked down the remainder of the aisle, till she was at the edge of the stage and inside the bright pool cast by the stage lighting.

Brill stared down at her in amazement. "Mrs. Fletcher! Good grief! Surely you've not come to audition?"

"Actually, I was hoping we might have a little chat."

His eyebrows went up. "Chat? About what?"

"The murder of Dexter Baxendale."

"Really? Nothing would delight me more than to hear your no doubt highly ingenious theories, Mrs. Fletcher, but another time, perhaps? As you can see, I'm conducting auditions this morning and I'm expecting another performer at any moment."

"Ah, but there's nobody here yet, so you do have a few minutes to spare, at least. My friends know I'm here, but they're not expecting me back for a while."

"I don't really see that there's anything I can say about the murder, Mrs. Fletcher, so the exercise seems pointless."

"Very well, then. Let's discuss your show instead."

"That's something I'm always pleased to do. But even that will have to be brief."

"Well, it wouldn't take long to answer the question I asked just now."

"What was that?"

"Where you raised the dough to finance it."

He frowned. "I think that is my business, don't you?"

"Not solely. I take it, then, that you decline to discuss it?"

Brill got suddenly to his feet. "Mrs. Fletcher, I've explained to you that I have a very busy day ahead."

"So you'd like me to leave, is that it?"

"Yes, that is it."

"I see. You won't even discuss the theft of secret documents from Caleb McCallum?"

Did she spot a momentary gleam of concern on his face? If so, it was gone quickly. "Quite correct, Mrs. Fletcher. The matter is one of complete indifference to me."

"I see." She shrugged. "So you wouldn't be interested in the startling information I heard yesterday from the captain himself?"

She began to turn away.

"Startling?" There was a new note in Brill's voice now.

"Yes, but I won't bore you with it."

With what seemed to be a great effort, Brill smiled. "Well, now, don't let my manner upset you, Mrs. Fletcher. I do have a lot on my mind, but as an inveterate gossip, I like to be up-to-date. What is this startling information?"

"May I come onstage?"

"Please do."

Jessica mounted the few steps to the stage. Brill gave her his hand to assist her up.

"Now, where was I?" she said. "Ah, yes. Well, you know that stolen confidential report there was all that fuss about. It was found in Baxendale's car."

"I heard something about it."

"It was supposedly very valuable. But the Captain himself told me that it's quite worthless."

Brill stood perfectly still. His face did not change. If not a picture of guilt, his reaction was neither that of a man to whom the matter was one of complete indifference.

"Worthless?" he said. His voice suddenly went higher in pitch. "What do you mean?"

"Just what I say. The value of that document depended on the Captain's acting on its recommendations. He doesn't intend to do so."

Brill continued to stand quite motionless. Was it her imagination, the effects of the stage lighting, or had he gone decidedly pale?

"Surely you must be wrong?"

"Definitely not, Mr. Brill. It's quite a blow to you, isn't it? Have you actually sold the photocopy and been paid for it yet? Was that what you were up all night arranging—why you had only two hours' sleep?"

At first, it was as if he didn't take in what she was saying, but suddenly he swung around on her.

"What do you mean?" he shouted.

"You know what I mean, Mr. Brill. Ashley Vickers stole that report from the office and passed it on to you—as she has done with other information in the past."

"What utter garbage!"

"But the private detective found it," Jessica went on imperturbably, "so last night she fetched a spare photocopy from her office and brought it to you here."

"She did no such thing!"

"I followed her, Mr. Brill."

He drew his breath in sharply. *"You?* It was . . ." He broke off.

"Yes, and I have an independent witness who saw her come into this theatre."

Brill had been making a great effort to control his emotions. Now he gave a casual shrug.

"So what? Sure Ashley was here. She's taking an interest in this show and wanted to watch some of the auditions."

"And what about the papers she had locked in her office drawer and which, at your request, she brought along with her last night?"

*"How did you know about that?"*

The female voice rang out sharply from the wings. Jessica turned toward it.

Ashley emerged from the darkness and glared at Jessica. "I want to know how you knew about those papers."

"Oh, it's quite simple, Miss Vickers. I was in your private bathroom when you entered the office. I saw you take them."

Ashley gave a gasp. "Why, you nosy, meddling old . . ."

Jessica nodded calmly. "Yes, I am nosy, and I'm meddling. Because my nephew Grady's whole future is at stake. Which is why I'm not at all ashamed at spying on you. I consider it fully justified."

Ashley shook her head incredulously. "I don't believe this! Well, Mrs. Clever-Detective Fletcher, I'm glad your conscience is clear, because so is mine. Those papers in my desk were simply confidential reports on people in the company in line for promotion. Caleb asked me to look them over and make recommendations. I merely wanted to leave them home to study at my leisure."

"I see," Jessica said slowly, regarding her judicially. "That's not too bad a story. But I think you should fabricate something sturdier before the case comes to trial."

"What are you talking about?" Ashley said harshly. "No one can prove I stole that report."

"I think they can," Jessica said. "Now that I and my friends know of the connection between you two, I'm sure we can convince the police to dig into it. Somewhere you have quite a lot of money hidden away, Miss Vickers, which will be traced to you eventually. If you continue to deny all involvement, you will almost certainly find yourself charged as an accessory to the murder of Dexter Baxendale."

Ashley went white. But before she could speak, Brill cut in. "Accessory? Are you suggesting she was *my* accessory, Mrs. Fletcher? If so, I must inform you that at the time of that detective's unfortunate demise, I was seated at the piano, delighting my fellow guests with a few dozen melodic gems from my incomparable repertoire."

"Yes, I thought perhaps you might have a convenient alibi," Jessica said.

"Well, then?"

"To be guilty of murder, one doesn't actually have to do the deed oneself. The person who pays a hired thug to commit a killing is just as guilty as the thug himself. It would have been extremely simple for you to have smuggled someone into Preston's fancy dress party and given him detailed instructions for the disposal of Baxter."

"I am not in the habit of employing hired thugs, Mrs. Fletcher."

Jessica stared hard at him. "Aren't you, Mr. Brill?" She looked at Ashley. "Nor you, Miss Vickers?"

Seeing Ashley's discomfiture, Jessica continued her line of attack. "Last night when Mr. Brill phoned your office, he asked you to come here. You said you'd be here as soon as possible. But why did you stop off at a very cheap and nasty little café, order coffee, which you didn't drink, and stay there about ten minutes? You made a point of leaving there at exactly nine p.m. I'm certain the proprietor will remember you. You attracted quite a lot of attention."

For the second time Ashley seemed at a loss for words. She cast a despairing glance at Brill. But he avoided her eyes. Jessica thought she detected beads of perspiration on his brow.

"Would you like me to give you *my* explanation for your actions?" Jessica said.

With an attempt at casualness, Ashley shrugged. "Go ahead. I'm sure it will prove very entertaining."

"I hope it will. Well, on the phone, after agreeing to come here, you used these words: 'They may be following me.' Then you listened for quite a time while Mr. Brill plainly gave you some instructions. Eventually, you agreed to comply. Now, I don't know exactly who you thought might be following you. Perhaps the police. Perhaps operatives of Dexter Baxendale, whom Captain McCallum had retained to shadow all the suspects. Or perhaps representatives of some rival third party after the real estate report. However, their precise identity is not relevant. Suffice it to say you were frightened of *someone's* following you here."

She paused. Ashley, however, still did not speak. She just licked her lips.

Jessica went on. "Mr. Brill's instructions were for you to come part of the way here and then wait in the café until exactly nine o'clock. After that you were to continue on foot, being sure to pass through a certain dark alley."

Jessica transferred her gaze to Brill. "The delay gave you time to contact a couple of young louts, whom no doubt you've had dealings with before. You gave them strict orders. Miss Vickers was to go unharmed through that alley. But the person tailing her was to be stopped, allowing Miss Vickers to proceed unmolested and unseen to this theatre. And that, Mr. Brill, is why I take with a very large pinch of salt your claim that you are not in the habit of employing hired thugs."

Again Jessica paused. She looked from one of them to the other. For a moment Ashley seemed about to speak. But then she caught Brill's eye and obviously changed her mind.

Eventually Jessica resumed. "What you didn't know, Mr. Brill, was that there was yet another person involved, an independent witness who saw the whole thing. He followed me to the café, watched me following Miss Vickers, *and* spotted somebody shadowing me."

Jessica gave a smile. "It really was quite a little procession. Anyway, I'm sure you know what happened. My young guardian angel took care of your thugs. It must have been quite a surprise when those young men later reported back to you that the person following Miss Vickers had been what they no doubt described as an old dame. I'm sure you spent some time puzzling out who it could have been. Which, by the way, explains your exclamation, *'You!'* when I first mentioned having followed Miss Vickers here. You nearly said, 'It was *you* they stopped.' "

At last Brill found his voice. "That's a highly ingenious scenario. Of course, you have not one iota of proof."

"There I must disagree. First there's my independent witness. He's perfectly willing to testify to everything he saw. Given that the police believe our combined account, which they're bound to, the theory I have advanced is the only logical explanation of Miss Vickers' passing through that alley unmolested. Or, in fact, for her ever walking that route. After all, if her visit here was quite innocent, her obvious course would have been to take a cab the whole way."

"It may be logical," Brill said, "but courts want hard evidence."

"They shall have that as well," Jessica said quietly. "The evidence of those two young men."

Brill went white. "What do you mean? You don't know who they were."

"Not yet. But I had a very close look at them. They're certain to have criminal records. I'll go to the police and look through the mug shots. I'll pick out those boys. They'll be arrested. And they'll talk—when I promise not to press charges if they tell who hired them."

Brill's hands were clenched at his sides. There was now no doubt about the sweat on his face. Ashley didn't look any better, and Jessica suddenly realized how fear could obliterate beauty from a face.

"All right," the girl said suddenly, "you win, Mrs. Fletcher."

Jessica and Brill both swung to face her.

Jessica caught her breath. "You mean . . . ?"

"I stole that report. I gave a photocopy of it to Peter last night."

Brill yelled at her. "Quiet, you little fool!"

At that, Ashley lost her temper. "You call *me* a fool?" she stormed. "You're too stupid to see that it's all over. She knows. Everything. It's all going to come out. All thanks to you. Doing everything on the cheap.

Hiring those pathetic little creeps to do your dirty work for you. But I suppose they go along with this crummy dive and fifth-rate singers and all the rest of your shoddy little life. Why did I ever get mixed up with you? Well, this is the end. Mrs. Fletcher: I repeat, I know nothing about the murder. I'm a thief. But only a thief. I'm not taking the rap for anything else this idiot's got himself involved with. I . . ."

"Will you shut up?" Brill shouted. Then he turned on Jessica. "She's mad! Do you understand? She's flipped her lid. You repeat one word of what she said . . ."

Jessica interrupted. "I shan't repeat it. I shan't need to."

She pulled open the coat of the suit she was wearing to reveal the small tape recorder fastened to the lining. "This will do all the talking that's necessary," she said.

Brill's face went purple. "Why, you slimy old . . ."

He made a lunge toward her.

Jessica screamed.

The sheer volume of the sound in the little building took Brill aback and checked him momentarily. Jessica hastily glanced around, picked up the chair recently vacated by the agent, and held it out in front of her like a lion tamer.

"Keep back," she warned sharply.

But Brill was already advancing again. "You old bat, if you think I'm letting you walk out of here with that tape . . ."

Jessica screamed once more. The door at the back of the auditorium burst open and Grady's voice rang out.

"Hang on, Aunt Jess! I'm coming." He charged down the aisle.

Brill froze, and then seemed to deflate. He took a step back, stared at Jessica in silence for a few moments. Then, his shoulders drooping, he walked slowly away, sank down onto the piano stool, and buried his head in his hands.

Jessica lowered the chair as Grady came running up onstage and crossed to her.

"Aunt Jess, you all right?"

She gave him a rather shaky smile. "Yes, dear. I'm fine."

"What's happened?"

"Quite a lot has happened. But only one really important thing. And that, my boy, is that you have been finally and completely cleared."

# Chapter Thirteen

"THANK you, Sergeant. That's wonderful news. Tell Chief Gunderson we appreciate his having you let us know."

Preston Giles put down the phone and turned around.

"Ashley and Brill have signed statements admitting their involvement in the theft of the documents. Gunderson's gone to the yacht club to report to Caleb. It's official: Grady's off the hook."

Jessica gave a deep sigh. "What a relief!"

"The cops could hardly do anything else after they heard that tape, Aunt Jess." Grady gave her a kiss on the cheek. "I don't know how to thank you."

She handed him her glass. "Just fill this up again, dear."

They were in Jessica's hotel room. After taking her precious tape to the police, she and Grady had returned there for a celebration drink. Shortly after, Preston arrived to be regaled with a detailed account of the incident in the theatre.

Grady poured another drink and handed Jessica her glass.

"I suppose Brill hasn't admitted any involvement in the murder yet, Mr. Giles?"

Preston shook his head. "Vehement denials from both of them on that score. Nor is Ashley admitting anything about framing you. The sergeant said they accept she wasn't involved in the killing. But they're confident they'll make a case against Brill."

Jessica raised her eyebrows in surprise. "Well, that's more than I am."

Preston looked at her quizzically. "You think he'll have covered his tracks that well, eh?"

"Not that," she said. "I just don't think Peter Brill had anything to do with the murder of Dexter Baxendale."

Preston and Grady stared at Jessica speechlessly.

Preston was the first to find his voice. "You're not serious?"

"Oh, perfectly."

"But, Aunt Jess, you went to the theatre to try and prove he was involved."

"Not at all."

She put down her glass. "My principal concern in this case was not who killed Baxendale. As I've repeatedly said, I am not a detective and solving the murder wasn't my job. Naturally, like everybody else, I was curious. But I got involved for one reason only: to obtain proof that Ashley Vickers was responsible for the theft of that report. Because that would automatically clear you of suspicion, Grady; if you didn't steal it, you had no motive for murdering Baxendale."

"But I heard that tape," Grady said. "You virtually accused Brill of arranging the murder."

Jessica smiled. "I was a bit sneaky, I'm afraid. I was willing to say anything that might draw from either of them an admission about the stolen report. I thought at one time Brill might be the killer. But it was always in the cards he would have an alibi. So in order to get him—and Ashley—rattled, I had to make up a plausible case for his having employed a hired killer. The fact that he *had* hired those two punks to stop me gave the theory feasibility. I tested it on you last night, and you seemed to think it made sense. So I then tried it out on Brill. Well, the ruse worked. Actually, of course, it was Ashley who got scared. But it didn't matter who. Once she cracked, my job was over."

"But why don't you think Brill hired a killer?" Preston asked. "It would, as you said, have been easy to hide somebody among all those guests in fancy dress."

"But there's a fatal flaw in that theory. Brill didn't think of it at the time. But if he hasn't yet, his attorney soon will."

"Well, what is it?" Grady asked.

"It's very obvious. For Brill to have smuggled a killer into the party, he would have had to know beforehand that Baxendale was going to be there, was going to find the report, and was going to be a threat to his security. There was no way he could have known that. Nor, incidentally, is there the slightest evidence that Baxendale ever knew Brill was involved in the theft. It seems that, at the time Baxendale was shot, Brill had never even handled the document."

Grady was thoughtful for a moment. "But suppose the target was really McCallum, as you once suggested?"

"Well, the Captain himself rather put to bed that idea when I saw him on his yacht. But the same argument would apply. Brill would never have been so foolish as to plan to have *anybody* killed under those circumstances. If he'd thought there was any danger of being exposed as a thief that night, I'm certain he would simply have arranged with Ashley to postpone the hand-over until a safer time. She wouldn't have liked it, but there would have been nothing she could have done."

"Well, then, who do you think *did* kill Baxendale?"

"I haven't the foggiest idea. And I don't really care."

"Oh, Aunt Jess!"

"No, Grady. Murder's a very pleasant thing to pass a few hours with —if it's in a book or on a TV screen. But real-life murder isn't at all nice. And neither, I'm afraid, are any of those people. Don't think I've enjoyed being mixed up in it."

"What about all those deductions you were making that first morning?"

Jessica had the grace to look a little awkward. "I admit that for a short time I did get involved in the intellectual puzzle side of it. But my interest has worn very thin now. Besides, it would be virtually impossible to solve the case by deductive reasoning. We've now discovered the murder had nothing to do with the stolen documents. There were dozens of people we know of at the party, in addition to possible gate-crashers. Any one of them might have had a motive for killing Baxendale. And to check out every one of those is the sort of job only the police can tackle."

"And you're not going to take any more interest in the case?"

"I didn't say that. I shall follow it in the papers."

"The New York papers?" Preston asked quietly.

Jessica looked at him enigmatically.

"If that's a way of asking if I'm staying in New York any longer, the answer is no. As you know, I've been wanting to go home for some time, but things have kept stopping me. Now, however, there's nothing to keep me here any longer."

"I'm sorry you should think that," Preston said quietly.

She smiled. "Cabot Cove, Maine, isn't the other end of the world, Preston. I owe you a return weekend. I'd be thrilled for a chance to show off my rich and sophisticated New York publisher to all my friends."

He grinned. "I may take you up on that sooner than you imagine."

"Any time. Just don't expect a fancy dress party."

He raised his hands in mock horror. "Please! Don't ever let me hear that phrase again."

He got to his feet. "I must get back to the office. I'm sure my in-tray is piled three feet high with stuff. When are you leaving?"

"Tomorrow morning, I think."

"Dinner tonight?"

"That would be lovely."

"Great."

"I'd better get along to McCallum's," Grady said. "I look forward to seeing the red faces when I show up again—reputation white as the driven snow."

"Do you think the Captain's face will be red?" Jessica asked.

"Not his. Doubt if he'll even apologize. But I'm sure going to see he asks me to stay on after all."

"And what will you say then?"

"I shall take great pleasure in telling him to . . ." He broke off with a grin. "All right, Aunt Jess. I won't say it—here. Let's say I shall inform him forcefully that from now on he's going to have to manage without my invaluable services."

"I think you're very wise, dear."

At the door Preston turned back to the young man. "Come and see me in a day or two, Grady. Publishers are always looking for good accountants, and I have lots of contacts."

Grady's face lit up. "Gee, thanks, Mr. Giles. Books would sure make a nice change from clam chowder."

# Chapter Fourteen

CHIEF Roy Gunderson walked heavily along the wharf at the Bayside Yacht Club and stopped alongside the gleaming hull of the *Chowder King*.

The boat appeared deserted. He called out. "Mr. McCallum!"

He waited a few moments but nobody appeared on deck. He swore under his breath. They'd told him at McCallum's office that the Captain was spending the day on his yacht. But it looked to Gunderson as if he might have had a wasted journey. It would, of course, have been easy to phone McCallum, or send a subordinate. But Gunderson, on whom the Captain's insult of Sunday morning still grated, had been looking forward to seeing McCallum's face when he was told that Ashley had been the traitor all along. It seemed, though, that this was a pleasure he was going to have to forgo.

Gunderson started to turn away. Then he hesitated. McCallum might be sleeping. Besides, he might not be alone.

Gunderson grinned to himself. If so, there could be a laugh in walking in on him. It was worth a try.

He mounted the gangplank, stood for a moment looking around for signs of life, then made his way below deck. He paused outside the door of the main cabin and raised his hand to tap on the panel. Then he changed his mind, took hold of the knob, turned it, and walked straight in.

To his disappointment, the cabin was deserted. He was about to go out again when his eye caught a dark stain on the luxurious cream carpet.

He crossed to it, stood staring at it for a couple of seconds, then knelt down and touched the stain with one finger.

Blood. Definitely blood.

Gunderson remained on his knees for half a minute, looking thoughtful. Along one wall of the cabin was a large closet, and there seemed to be another smaller stain on the floor in front of it.

He straightened up, walked across, and opened the closet door. It was full of clothes.

It was at that moment that he heard the unmistakable click of a revolver being cocked.

A voice spoke, hard and unemotional.

"Hold it, mister. Right there."

Gunderson froze. He felt, rather than heard, footsteps approaching. The voice spoke again. "Keep your hands where I can see them. Turn around—slowly."

Gunderson did so, then let his breath out. The man standing a few feet away, a .38 revolver leveled at him, was a uniformed policeman. In the doorway behind him, his revolver also drawn, was his partner.

Gunderson started to move. "Boys, for a moment you had me scared there . . ."

"*I said hold it,*" the policeman barked out. "Stand facing the wall. Hands over your head."

Gunderson complied. "I know the drill, son. My name is Roy Gunderson. I'm the chief of police up at New Holvang. My identification's in my right jacket pocket."

The two policemen exchanged glances. Then, while the one in the doorway kept his revolver trained on the chief, the first reached gingerly into Gunderson's pocket and extracted his wallet. He opened it, scanned it, then visibly relaxed.

"Sorry, Chief," he said. "Can't be too careful."

He handed Gunderson his wallet back and both policemen holstered their guns.

Gunderson returned his wallet to his pocket and eyed them curiously. "What you boys doing here?"

"We got an anonymous tip. Said there'd been a murder on this boat."

"Did you now? Well, that may interest you, then." He pointed to the stain on the carpet.

"Blood?"

"Yeah."

"What d'you think it means, Chief?"

"Could mean he cut his hand opening a can of chowder. But in view of your tip-off, we'll take a look around. Let's go topside."

On deck again they separated and started poking around.

Then the second policeman called out. "Over here, Chief."

Gunderson joined him. The officer pointed down at the deck. What appeared to be a trail of small blood spots led toward the mainmast.

Gunderson walked slowly over to it. The mainsail was rolled and lashed. He surveyed it for a few seconds.

"You boys know anything about sailing?" he asked.

"A little, Chief," the first one said.

Gunderson began to untie the lashes on the mainsail.

"Get on those ropes and hoist up the mainsail," he ordered.

The two policemen moved to the mast and did as instructed. Gunderson loosened the last lash. Then he stepped back. The sail started to rise, unfolding as it went up.

The first policeman grunted. "Something's holding . . ."

He stopped short. Out of the folds of the sail had flopped the lifeless arm of a man.

For a moment the three of them stood without moving. Then, apparently of its own accord, like a slow-motion film, the rest of the body appeared, gradually rolling clear of the sail and, gaining momentum, falling with a thud onto the deck.

His face expressionless, Gunderson looked down at the corpse.

The second policeman, who could not have been long out of his teens, had gone pale. "Is that . . . ?"

The chief nodded. "Sure is. Captain Caleb McCallum has sold his last bowl of clam chowder."

McCallum's body was dressed in just an open-neck shirt and white linen trousers. The shirtfront was perforated with five or six small, blood-encrusted bullet holes.

"Looks like someone really hated him," said the older policeman.

"Lot of people did, son."

Gunderson continued to stare down at the body, rubbing his chin. Almost under his breath he muttered, "So Baxendale's murder *was* a mistake after all."

"What's that, Chief?"

"Oh, nothing. Okay, boys, let's get moving. You know the routine."


"So," Preston said, "it's goodbye for the present."

"I'm afraid so," said Jessica.

They had just returned to Jessica's hotel room.

"Sorry I can't come to see you off tomorrow," he said. "Kitt will be there, of course, but there's no way I can skip an appointment with one of Hollywood's most important producers."

"Of course not. I wouldn't let you, anyway."

"Sorry, too, if I was a bit subdued over dinner, Jess. But as you know,

Caleb was an old friend. I knew him when he was a very different man from what he'd become."

"I quite understand. And it was a very pleasant and peaceful evening, all the same."

He gave a wry grin. "Do you realize that after the first minute we didn't discuss the murder at all?"

"No, and we're not going to now. After all, what is there to say? Besides, I'm absolutely *sick* of talking about crime. In fact, in reaction, my next book is likely to be a very mushy love story without the teeniest bit of violence."

"I promise to publish it sight unseen. I'm sure J. B. Fletcher could write a beautiful love story."

"Why, thank you, Preston."

He took her hand. "Jess, despite the insanity that's surrounded our brief acquaintance, these days have been very special to me. You know, for the past several years I've acquired every luxury a man could ask for, but I've been operating on automatic pilot. Automatic banking, automatic security systems, automatic lights—I'm a pampered rich man who does nothing for himself, and I'm miserable. Or at least I have been."

She drew away. "Preston, wait. I do like you a great deal . . ."

"I know. And that's all there is to it, right?"

"So far, yes. As you say, our acquaintanceship has been absurdly brief —and all the circumstances have been so abnormal. Everything's moved much too fast for a widow lady from Maine."

"I can respect that."

"Can you?"

"Absolutely. Look, Jess, you and I are going to be joined professionally for a long time. And if something else is destined to come out of this relationship, then so be it. If not, then at least I'll have made a very good friend."

He kissed her. And at that moment there came a tap on the door.

Preston gave a groan. Jessica called, "Come in."

The door opened and Roy Gunderson stood in the threshold.

"Sorry to call so late, ma'am," he said.

"Not at all, Mr. Gunderson. Won't you come in?"

"Thanks."

He closed the door behind him, giving a nod to Preston.

"To what do I owe this pleasure, Chief?" she asked.

"Well, first off, I came to say goodbye. New York City homicide has taken over the McCallum case, so I'm heading back home. Only want to tell you it's been a real pleasure meeting you. Any time you want to horn in on one of my cases, you're welcome."

"Thank you, Mr. Gunderson; from a professional I take that as a real compliment. And any time you get to Maine, you let me cook you up some lobster stew."

"I'll do that, Mrs. Fletcher. Thanks."

"Any developments in the McCallum case, Chief?" Preston asked.

"Not since the arrest, Mr. Giles."

They stared blankly at him.

"Arrest?" Jessica said.

"Who's been arrested?" Preston asked.

It was Gunderson's turn to stare. "I thought you'd heard. It was on all the evening news."

"We haven't seen or heard any news," Preston said. "Tell us who's been arrested?"

"Louise McCallum."

"Louise? Now I wonder . . ." Jessica said slowly.

"You had your doubts about her on Sunday morning, if I remember correctly, ma'am," Gunderson said. "Well, you were right then. We had the wrong victim. But there's no doubt about it this time: Caleb McCallum is positively dead. And there's a very strong case against his wife. Late last night, around midnight, they had a flaming row. It woke the servants, some of whom heard Louise . . . er, Mrs. McCallum . . . threaten to kill Captain McCallum."

Preston interrupted this recital of events. "Mrs. Fletcher doesn't want to get involved, Chief," he said firmly. "She doesn't even want to talk about the case."

Gunderson rubbed his face with a big, beefy hand. "That's a shame."

"Why?" Jessica asked. "You say you have a strong case against Louise. Why should you want me involved?"

"It's not me, ma'am. It's Mrs. McCallum. She wants you to go and see her. She's sure you can clear her. That's the second reason I'm here. To pass on her message: please will you help her?"

"Oh dear." Jessica wearily rubbed her eyes with forefinger and thumb. "What on earth can *I* do?"

Gunderson shrugged. "Frankly, Mrs. Fletcher, I don't know. But as I wanted to tell you so long anyway, I volunteered to give you the message. You see, I felt kinda sorry for her."

"She wants me to go and see her tonight?"

"No, tomorrow will be fine."

Jessica looked at Preston. "I can't refuse, can I?"

"You could, my dear," he said gently. "Many people would."

Jessica gave a sigh. "Very well, Mr. Gunderson, I'll do what I can."

He beamed. "That's swell."

She eyed him shrewdly. "Just why is it swell, Chief?"

He looked a bit embarrassed. "Well, it's—it's just that deep down she seems a real nice lady."

"Why, Mr. Gunderson." Jessica was suddenly mock-coy. "I do believe that beneath that rough exterior beats a heart of gold. And a chivalrous one, to boot."

From his expression, she almost expected him to start scuffing up the rug with his toe, go red, and say, "Aw, shucks."

In fact, all he did was clear his throat. "Don't know about that, ma'am?"

"But you're far from convinced of her guilt, aren't you? Well, I don't think I can actually *do* much. What I will do is listen to the evidence, talk to Louise—and think. If I see any weaknesses in the case against her, any points in her favor, then I'll get in touch with her lawyer. And, of course, I'll tell you as well."

"Reckon I can't ask more than that, Mrs. Fletcher. So you'll be going to see Louise tomorrow?"

"That's a promise. Shall I give her your love?"

Gunderson hesitated. "Better make it my best wishes."

"As you like. And now, Chief, you'd better tell me everything you can about the case. When I see her I must be fully briefed."

# Chapter Fifteen

"JESSICA, I swear to you I'm innocent. I did not shoot Caleb. I give you my word."

Louise McCallum spoke with a desperate, pleading urgency.

"My dear Louise," Jessica said quietly, "it's not me you have to convince, you know."

"But I want you to believe me. You do, don't you?"

Jessica didn't answer immediately. But she knew this was a time for complete honesty. "I don't know."

Louise gazed at her in blank dismay. Then, with a gesture of despair, she got to her feet. She went over to the barred window and stared sightlessly out.

Jessica rose. She crossed the bare room, with its drab gray walls and door, its single unshaded light, its plain wooden table and four hard chairs, and joined the other woman.

"My dear," she said, "I'm not saying I *dis*believe you."

"That's all? And I thought we were friends."

"No, we're not."

Louise looked at her coldly. "My mistake, Mrs. Fletcher."

"Now, don't misunderstand me. I only mean that we hardly know each other. We certainly got on well last weekend. We could have become friends. We may yet. But so far, I don't know you nearly well enough to say whether you were capable of shooting your husband. Or to know when you're lying to me. If it's any consolation, my instinct is to believe you."

Louise looked at her for a moment, then managed a sort of smile. "Sorry. My nerves are all on edge."

"Of course they are."

She took Louise by the arm. "Now, come and sit down again and tell me everything."

They went back to the table and seated themselves on opposite sides of it. Jessica felt rather like a lawyer interviewing a client. "Oh, incidentally," she said, "Roy Gunderson sends you his best wishes."

Louise raised her eyebrows. "I wonder why."

"He likes you. He thinks you're a real lady. It's clear he doesn't believe you're guilty."

It was a slight exaggeration of what Gunderson had actually said, but Jessica felt, under the circumstances, it was justified.

Louise looked amazed. "You're joking!"

"Not at all. You have one friend, you see."

"I can sure use all I can get."

"Tell me about your fight with Caleb."

Louise shrugged. "What is there to tell? It was the usual sort of thing. We shouted a lot. It ended with him storming out of the house, yelling that if anybody wanted him he'd be on the yacht."

"The usual sort of thing you say? Yet you threatened to kill him. Was that usual? You've threatened to kill him before?"

"Frequently. But, just between ourselves, I never did. Not once."

"So, it was merely an expression—didn't mean anything?"

"Exactly."

"Could you find witnesses who'd heard you threatening him like that in the past?"

"Well, we didn't usually go at it hammer and tongs in public. But there might be one or two who'd remember. Probably the servants would admit that last night wasn't the first time they'd heard me say it. I don't suppose the police bothered to ask them."

"Well, I should get your attorney to ask them. And anybody else you can think of. The longer ago the better. It's one good point in your favor."

"You talk as if there weren't any others. What about the fact that I actually stood to lose by Caleb's death? Do you know about that?"

"Your prenuptial agreement? Yes. Though I'm afraid it won't carry much weight. The prosecution's case will be that this was a *crime passionnel*—that you weren't thinking rationally."

"That's nonsense!"

"Yet you did chase after him—immediately on top of the fight?"

"Yes. I followed him—maybe ten minutes later—in my own car."

"Why?"

"I wanted to catch him with his floozie. I'd never actually found him with one of them . . . well, let's put it delicately . . . in his arms. I thought this was a good opportunity."

"And you didn't take a gun?"

"No, just a camera. I thought I might get a picture of them."

"You took a camera with you?"

"Yes."

"Where is it now?"

"In the glove compartment of my car, I guess. I don't honestly know. All I remember is having drunk so much I could barely drive. After just a few miles, I pulled off the road to sleep it off." She smiled ironically. "I seem to make a habit of that. Anyway, I never reached the yacht."

"But I should certainly see your attorney has an independent witness check that it's in the glove compartment. It could be another little point in your favor, suggesting the real reason you followed Caleb. And enough little points, all put together . . ."

"Make one big one?"

"Something like that. Tell me, though, what made you think your husband would have a girl with him that night?"

"It was obvious."

"Why?"

"Because earlier he'd told me he was going out to play some poker with the boys. That was absurd. He plays poker Thursday nights— played, I should say—with the same guys every week, and never on the yacht. And they never start as late as that. So of course I knew he had a date. He probably didn't even expect me to believe him."

"Let me get this straight," Jessica said slowly. "He'd already said he was going out *before* you had the fight?"

"That's right."

"Interesting."

Louise looked excited. "It is? Why?"

"Because the impression that's around is that Caleb suddenly decided to go out *as a result* of his fight with you. In other words, no one but you knew he'd be on board the yacht. Now you tell me he had a date there. So at least one other person did know."

"The girl," Louise breathed. "You think *she* could have killed him?"

"Well, it's certainly possible."

"Of course. I should have thought of it before. But my mind's been in such a state . . ."

"Do you know her name?"

Louise shook her head.

"Is it the one who was at the party—Little Red Riding Hood?"

"It could have been, Jessica. I honestly don't know. He changed them like he changed his socks."

"Well, no doubt she can be traced." Jessica looked thoughtful. "The only thing is, it's difficult to see what motive she could have had. Whether she was just a gold digger, or genuinely in love with him, it was obviously in her interest to keep him alive. However, even if she is innocent, she might well have told somebody else about her date. Girls of that type are quite likely to boast about having a millionaire for a sugar daddy —especially to their girl friends."

Jessica stood up. "Louise, I've learned all I need to from you. You've given me a lot to think about. And I feel much surer of your innocence now than when I came in."

Louise gave a smile such as Jessica had not seen from her before. "That's wonderful, Jessica. Thank you."

"I'll report our whole conversation to Roy Gunderson. Now I'm going home. But I promise I'll give this matter a lot of thought. The whole trouble with this case is that it's all been so rushed. There's been no time for reflection. It's had a New York tempo. Well, I'm going to play it over in a Cabot Cove tempo. It might come out much clearer."

Jessica walked along the station platform, in the shadow of the great train. She was possessed by a strange sense of what might be called double *déjà vu.* Twice before she had tried to leave New York City, and twice she had been stopped on the platform.

Surely it couldn't happen again. Well, one thing was sure: Kitt was not going to come running up with disastrous news of Grady this time. For both Kitt and Grady were with her—Grady laden with her suitcase.

At last they reached her sleeper car and Grady deposited the case on the platform.

Kitt took a notebook from her purse and consulted it.

"Just a few last points, Aunt Jess. First, there's been talk of a movie deal. But I'd better warn you not to get your hopes up. These things usually fall through."

"I certainly hope so," Jessica said. "After New York, I know I'm not ready for Hollywood."

"Second, the tape with Barbara Walters will probably be on the air next Friday."

"Thank you, dear. I shall make a point of not being near a TV set. I was terrible."

"I was there. You were fine. Third, the *New York Times* book reporter assigned to cover you—Chris Landon—will be calling by phone for the interview."

"Very well. Now, is that it?"

"That's it."

"I'm free?"

Kitt laughed. "You're free."

"Thank heavens. At last."

"Sorry to have been such a pest."

"You, Kitt, have been a dear."

Jessica embraced her. "I'd never have gotten through it all without you. Now, see that this nephew of mine keeps out of trouble."

"I'll do my best. If he can just curb this unfortunate tendency to get himself arrested."

Jessica turned to Grady and gave him a hug. "And you look after her."

"I will. If she can just curb this unfortunate tendency to find bodies in pools. Sure you have to go, Aunt Jess?"

"Positive."

"And I was certain you'd solve the mystery."

"Well, I couldn't and I didn't and that's that. But I have promised to keep on reflecting."

"Ah," Grady sighed, "like Monsieur Poirot, you sit back and employ ze leetle gray cells."

"I don't know about sitting back. I usually think best when I'm doing something physical but routine, like washing up."

At that moment the conductor swung down from the train. He gave a yell: "All aboard!"

Jessica turned to him. "Why, hullo, Daniel. You again."

"Hi, Mrs. Fletcher. Nice to see you. Leaving at last?"

"Definitely."

Jessica's case was lifted on the train, and she followed it. Kitt handed her a thick wad of newspapers and magazines, Daniel slammed the door, and Grady and Kitt waved and called goodbye.

As the train started to move, Jessica leaned out of the window. "And one other thing, young man," she called. "No surprise telegrams mentioning the word *elopement*. I expect the deed to be done in my parlor."

The train gathered speed. Jessica continued waving until Grady and Kitt were a couple of specks in the distance, then withdrew her head.

Daniel escorted her to her seat and placed her bag on the rack. "Well, ma'am," he said, "I guess you must have had a fine visit staying all that extra time."

"I could hardly drag myself away. Tell me, Daniel, did your boy hear from the university?"

He beamed. "Yes, ma'am. He starts next September."

"You and your wife must be so proud."

"That we are, ma'am. Well, if there's anything you need, just let me know."

"Thank you. But I don't think I shall. I shall be quite happy to sit here and relax."

He went away. Jessica stared out of the window. She was *not* going to think about the case until she reached home. She just had to have a rest from it.

Distraction. She needed a distraction. She went through the pile of papers and magazines on the seat beside her and selected the *New York Times.*

For ten or fifteen minutes she tried to concentrate on the big national and international news stories—the economy, elections, the Middle East. But her mind kept wandering.

Perhaps something a little less serious . . . Jessica turned to the book section. Now, what was new?

Her eye caught the name Chris Landon. Ah, that was the man who was to interview her. How did he write? she wondered. The column was headed "Book Beat." Jessica soon discovered that he had a nice, informal style. He liked the personal touch—brought in references to the tastes and comments of his family, his friends, his . . .

Jessica stopped short. She blinked. How very odd. It couldn't be!

But yes. There was no mistake.

Slowly Jessica lowered the paper. Thoughts whirled crazily through her mind. All sorts of odd phrases, things seen and not seen, half-absorbed facts . . .

Fancy dress . . . favorite characters . . . Sherlock Holmes . . . Ebenezer Scrooge . . . Edmond Dantes . . . Little Red Riding Hood . . . automatic appliances . . . sonic booms . . . newspapers . . . Chris Landon . . . J. B. Fletcher . . . Justice . . .

Like a kaleidoscope, the pieces came together in Jessica's brain. For the first time they made a pattern, a pattern in which all the elements blended.

If only she could be wrong. But she wasn't. It had to be so . . .

Poor Grady . . .

# Chapter Sixteen

FOR a full ten minutes Jessica sat motionless in her seat. She so much wanted to go home. She was tired in body and in mind. It would be so easy just to continue with her journey and forget all about the murders of Dexter Baxendale and Caleb McCallum. Louise would never be convicted. Nor, she was sure, would anyone else. The police investigations would drag on for a few more weeks and then the case would join the great list of unsolved mysteries.

And would that matter? Murders went unsolved all the time—murders worse than these. Both these victims had probably gotten what was coming to them. A lot of people would be better off for their absence from the world. All that she, Jessica Fletcher, had to do was just remain sitting here. It would be so simple. And such a relief.

After all, bringing killers to justice was not her responsibility. It was the job of the police. Nobody could ever blame her or claim she could have done more.

But it was no good. In her heart she knew that to do nothing was impossible. Because Baxendale and McCallum had been human beings. No one had the right to take their lives from them. Besides, a murderer was always dangerous. And one who'd killed twice was especially so. Such a person, if threatened, would probably kill a third time. Perhaps a fourth. Then where might it end?

Therefore, no matter how much she wanted to let this killer go free, she couldn't do it. For however much she tried to rationalize such lack of action, her own conscience would never cease to tell her she was wrong.

Nevertheless, it was with a heavy heart that Jessica got to her feet and went in search of Daniel, to find out which was the train's first stop, and when, from there, she'd be able to get a train back to New York.

On arrival in New York Jessica first phoned Coventry House. There were questions about the night of the party, and about the house, that Preston could answer best. Unfortunately, the office had closed, and the automatic answering machine gave no indication as to where he might be. Nor did the one at his rooms in town. She decided to call the New Holvang house, but found the number was unlisted. To her chagrin, she suddenly realized that in spite of having stayed at the house, she didn't know its number. Kitt would no doubt have it, but Grady, she knew, was meeting Kitt straight from work and they were going out for a long evening.

Jessica could think of nobody else she could ask. Roy Gunderson would probably obtain it for her, but she did not want him to know, at this stage, that she was back in town and on the case.

There seemed no alternative but to go to New Holvang herself. There was one important thing she might be able to discover even without Preston's presence.

First, however, she had time to do a bit of writing.

It was about ten minutes to eight when Jessica's cab pulled to a halt outside the front door of the Giles mansion. She got out and gazed up at the building. It was in total darkness.

The driver stared out of his window. "Hey, lady, you sure you got the right night?"

"No, not at all sure. Look, I don't think there's much point in ringing the front door bell. I'll go and see if I can find any sign of life in back of the house. Will you please wait?"

"Sure, but remember the meter's running."

"Of course."

She looked around hesitantly, then started toward the side of the house.

Around the corner, without even the glow of the cab's lights, it was completely dark. Jessica groped inside her purse, took out a small flashlight, and switched it on.

By its light she made her way somewhat gingerly to the pool. At the edge of it she stopped for a few seconds, shining her flashlight around and getting her bearings. Then she walked slowly around to the spot at which on Sunday morning she had seen Dexter Baxendale's bloodstains. She bent down. They were fainter but still visible. She straightened and shone her flashlight upward at the ring of unlit lights that surrounded the pool area. She stood quite still for a few minutes. Then she continued on along the side of the pool to the far end. Here was situated an equipment shed, which housed the pool's filtration and heating systems. Jessica went up to the door. It was padlocked.

At that moment out of the darkness she heard a voice.

"Who's there?"

She spun around—and was blinded by the brilliant beam of a powerful flashlight.

"Good grief! Jessica!"

She raised her hand to shield her eyes. "Preston?"

"Yes. My dear, what on earth are you doing here?"

She continued to hold her hand up. "Preston, do you mind?"

"Oh, sorry."

The flashlight was lowered as he came toward her. "Jess, you're supposed to be on your way to Maine."

"I know. I changed my mind."

"But that's wonderful!"

He came right up to her. "I can't say how pleased I am! You can tell me why inside. Come on." He took her arm.

"In a moment. How did you know I was here?"

"I was in my study. The taxi set off a silent alarm as it came up the driveway. I went out to see who it was and spoke to the cabbie. He told me he'd just dropped a lady, who'd disappeared around the side. I couldn't for the life of me think who it might be. Jess, I assume, knowing you, that you have a good reason for prowling around my pool at night. A sort of reconstruction perhaps?"

"Something like that."

He chuckled. "So J. B. Fletcher's still on the case. I might have guessed. Finished now?"

"Not quite. Come with me, Preston."

She led him along the side of the pool and again located the bloodstains with her flashlight. "This is where Baxendale was standing when he was shot, right?"

"Yes, so it seems."

"Stand just here yourself, will you, Preston? Right."

She started to walk away, counting as she did so. She stopped. "And, according to Chief Gunderson, the experts think the shot was fired from about *here*. Correct?"

"Near enough."

"I'm going to switch off my flashlight. Switch yours off too, Preston."

He did so, and heard her voice: "I don't know about you, Preston, but I can't see you at all."

"No, I can't see you either. But what are you driving at?"

"The police believe—and I thought it possible once—that the killer saw an outline of somebody wearing a cape and deerstalker and assumed it was Captain Caleb. But nobody could possibly have seen even *that* much in this sort of light. It would have been just a question of firing blindly into the darkness."

She switched her flashlight on again and walked back to him.

"Well, it obviously wasn't as dark that night," he said. "The moon's waning, remember, and it's overcast now."

"Yes," she said thoughtfully. "But I can't think it would make that much difference."

"Look, let's not stand around here any longer. Come indoors."

"Very well."

He took her arm again and they turned away.

And just then, without any warning, the whole area was suddenly engulfed in brilliant light.

They blinked around, for a moment disoriented. Then Jessica spoke triumphantly: "I thought it might be that! Automatic timing. Am I right?"

Preston was looking dazed. "Yes. Good Lord!"

"What time do they cut off?"

"Er, midnight, I believe. Yes, that's right."

"And the murder took place at eleven-fifteen. So when Baxendale was shot it was as bright as day here."

"That certainly explains a lot."

"Did you let the police know about the lights?"

"No. To tell you the truth, Jess, I'd completely forgotten about that automatic timer. What put you onto it?"

"Something you yourself said about automatic appliances. *I* don't have a pool, of course, but I know some people who do who have just the same arrangement. I tried to call you at the office and ask you about it, but you'd left. I didn't know your number here, or anyone to ask, so I just had to come down and check it out. When I saw the house in darkness, I assumed you weren't here either and decided to have a look myself anyway."

"I'm very glad you did. All the same, I've had enough of this pool now. Let's go inside."

"Aren't you going to turn the lights out now?"

He laughed. "The master switch is in the shed and I don't have a key on me. After all these months, another four hours isn't going to make much difference to my electric bill."

He led her to a side door of the house. "Oh, my taxi!" she exclaimed. "I'd better warn the driver I'm going to be some time."

"I'll pay him off and send him away."

"Oh, Preston, no . . ."

"Why not? When you leave, I can run you to the station. Now, come to my study. That's the coziest place at the moment."

He led her to the pleasant, book-lined room where he had talked to Gunderson on the morning of the murder, and told her to sit down in a big leather arm chair. "Back in a moment."

Jessica sat down, but she didn't relax. She was tense and full of apprehension. What she had to tell him about her deductions was, she knew, going to be an appalling shock; and she just didn't know how he would react.

He came back after about two minutes. "He's gone."

"It's very dark and quiet here, Preston. Where are the servants?"

"I gave them all a few days off. I didn't expect to be here myself. But I decided I had to get away from town for a bit. I can manage quite well on my own." He sat down opposite her. "Now, I'm aching to know what this is all about. I can't believe that it was only a sudden thought about my pool lighting that got you off the train and all the way back to New York."

"No, it wasn't." She took a deep breath. "Preston, I know the identity of the murderer."

His eyes widened. "You mean that? Literally? You really *know?*"

"Yes."

"You have proof?"

"Nothing tangible—but logical proof, yes."

"You'd better tell me who it is," he said quietly.

"I hate to say it, Preston. It's going to be an even bigger shock to you than it was to me. But I'm afraid it's Kitt."

For a second or two Preston sat staring at her without speaking. "You can't be serious."

"I'm sorry. But . . ." She trailed off.

He stood up suddenly and took several aimless steps about the room. "I . . . I just don't believe it."

"I didn't expect you to—at first. But it all fits in. Just listen."

With obvious reluctance, he sat down again.

Jessica began her recital of events. "Ashley Vickers said that for several months her relationship with the Captain had been on a strictly business basis. I believe that. Now, he only met his latest girl friend, Tracy Ellison, the night of the party. He must have, because he told Chief Gunderson he didn't even know her second name. But he hasn't been without a girl during that intervening period. Ask Louise. She says he changed his girls like he changed his socks."

Preston broke in, his voice incredulous: "You're saying *Kitt* was that girl?"

Jessica bowed her head. "Until Little Red Riding Hood—Tracy—pushed her out. Kitt saw it happening the night of the party. She's a proud girl. She wouldn't stand for it. I believe she confronted McCallum that night and he told her they were through. She went out to the pool area, probably just to be alone, and—as she believed—saw him there. The gun had been left lying around; she picked it up and shot him. Though, actually, of course, she shot Baxendale. My, but she did a good acting job the next morning, feigning such shock at finding the body. Or perhaps it wasn't all acting. Perhaps something about the corpse made her realize that it wasn't McCallum—that she'd shot the wrong man. If so, her shock was no doubt genuine."

Jessica paused and moistened her lips before continuing.

"I think McCallum guessed the truth. But he had no proof, and probably wouldn't have given her away to the police anyway. However, he either told her of his belief, or somehow she realized he knew. He then presented a tremendous threat to her. She couldn't relax, knowing that at any time he could give her away. She had to kill him.

"I know from Louise that Caleb had a date on the yacht the night of his death. I believe Kitt called him, pretending to be Tracy, and arranged to meet him there. She got there ahead of him and lay in wait. Then, when he arrived . . ." Jessica stopped.

Preston lowered his head and held it between his hands. She watched him silently. At last he looked up. It was plainly an effort, but he spoke calmly and quietly. "You say you have logical proof of all this. What, exactly?"

"It consists of things Kitt said, things she knew which she couldn't have known unless she were guilty; how they tie up with things Louise said, Grady said. It's all very complicated. Difficult to explain clearly in words."

She reached into her purse and took out an unsealed envelope. "I've written it all out, in the form of a long letter to Chief Gunderson. As soon as I leave here I'm going to mail it."

Preston looked at the envelope, then lifted his eyes to hers. He said heavily: "Jess, don't send that letter."

"I must, Preston. Do you think I'm not tempted—desperately—to let things be? But I can't let the girl get away with two murders. I can't let her marry Grady. Double murderers don't stop at two. I *must* send it."

"I wouldn't try to stop you if I thought she was guilty. But she isn't."

"You can't know that."

"I do know it."

"Your belief in her character isn't knowledge, Preston."

"It's not that. I know it because . . ."

He stopped. He'd gone very pale. "I know it, Jessica, because . . . *I* murdered Baxendale and McCallum."

The only sound was the tick of an antique silver clock on the mantelpiece. There was no movement. For what seemed a long time they sat as though figures in a tableau.

Then Jessica let her breath out very slowly. "I see," she said softly.

"You don't seem surprised."

"I'm not."

He stared at her in amazement. "You're telling me you *knew?*"

"Yes."

"But . . . but"—he was stammering—"all that about Kitt . . ."

"A lot of fiddle-faddle. I didn't believe a word of it."

"But that letter . . ."

"Read it." She held the envelope out to him.

He took it with a hand that shook only slightly and removed several sheets of paper covered with small, neat handwriting. He unfolded them.

*Dear Chief Gunderson,* he read. *It is with deep regret I have to inform you that without question the murderer of Dexter Baxendale and Caleb McCallum is Preston Giles. My grounds for this statement are as follows . . .*

Preston read no more. He looked at Jessica, his face a study of bafflement. "But why?" he said blankly.

"Why did I accuse Kitt? Because I couldn't bear to accuse *you* to your face, Preston. Perhaps because I'm a coward. I wanted to give you a chance to confess."

He got to his feet again. He went slowly to the window, pulled open the drapes, and stared out into the darkness. With his back to her he said lifelessly: "How did you know?"

"You made one mistake—and only one. It was that phone call on the night of the party."

"Phone call?"

"When Ashley and I came into the kitchen to get some things to clean her dress, you were on the phone. You mentioned my name. After you hung up, you told me the caller had been a *New York Times* reporter called Chris Landon. You said he wanted to interview me, but that you'd agreed to see him. I thought nothing of it. But today on the train I was reading Chris Landon's column. And halfway through it Chris Landon refers to . . . her *husband*. Yes, Chris Landon is a woman. And you didn't know that. At first I just couldn't understand it. Then I remembered how one paper had referred to me as *Mr.* J. B. Fletcher. Because it's nearly always *men* who designate themselves only by their initials, the paper had assumed *I* was a man.

"My guess is that Chris Landon had in fact called earlier, but you hadn't spoken to her, only been given a written message. You just assumed Chris Landon was a man. When I overheard you mention my name on the phone and you were forced to say whom you'd been speaking to, you said the first name that came into your head. But I realized on the train that you must have been lying—you'd obviously never spoken to Chris Landon at all. I couldn't think *why* you'd have lied.

"I'd been idly puzzling for a long time over something else—something Baxendale said to you about your being dressed as the Count of Monte Cristo. He said it after very obviously catching sight of that figure of Blind Justice in your bedroom. It seemed quite irrelevant, yet oddly meaningful. It was as if something had suddenly clicked into place with him.

"And then, while on the train, I linked the two facts—Baxendale's words and your lie. I realized his words had been a sort of secret message to you, though I don't think you grasped the fact at the time. It had been he on the phone. He asked you, didn't he, to meet him outside that night? You went."

She paused. Preston didn't react. "Go on," he said without turning around.

"It was the first time I'd suspected you and I was horrified. But I had to follow it up. Could you have shot Baxendale deliberately in that sort of light? And then I thought of my friends' automatic pool lights. Surely any such automatic gadget that was available, *you* would have. And when those lights came on, any lingering doubts I might have had vanished. For frankly, Preston, I don't for one moment believe you forgot about that automatic timing. You're just not the sort of person to forget a thing like that. You knew it had been bright as day by the pool when Baxendale was killed. He was shot from the front, from close range. That was the big flaw in my argument which you didn't spot, when I was accusing Kitt just now: the fact that nobody for one second could have mistaken Baxendale's face for McCallum's. Baxendale was the target all along. Yet you let the police—and me—assume the light was poor by the pool, and that perhaps Baxendale had been shot in error. You even went so far as to dress the body in the Holmes costume, which you knew the Captain had discarded, in order to foster the belief that Caleb was the intended victim. You feared if the police investigated Baxendale's affairs too closely they would eventually trace some connection with you. Tell me, Preston, am I right?"

He turned around, came back to his chair, and sat down. "Many years ago," he began, "I was betrayed by three partners in a business venture. An apartment house we'd built collapsed. Several people were killed. Although I had nothing to do with the construction end, I was made the scapegoat. They got off free and I was sentenced to fifteen years in prison. After two years I managed to escape. Don't ask the details—but the police assumed I'd died in the attempt."

"Like the Count of Monte Cristo," Jessica said.

"As you well know, my favorite fictional character. Well, not everyone was convinced I was dead. A hotshot detective, third grade, had a hunch I was still alive. He was even more positive when, over the next couple of years—like the Count of Monte Cristo—I financially destroyed my three ex-partners from a safe distance. He looked for a while longer, but eventually gave up. Saturday was the first time I'd seen him in twenty-two years. He'd changed his name, as I had, and I didn't recognize him, though he did, as I soon discovered, recognize me. He must have thought his ship had come home with a vengeance: two possible sources of big money hit on within a few minutes—Caleb's real estate report and dirt on me. Naturally, he wasn't going to risk losing the report—which I'm sure he had no intention of returning to Caleb, incidentally—so he took that back to his car and locked it in. Then, deciding to strike while the iron was hot, he went to a pay phone and called me. That was the first time I realized who he was. He insisted I meet him by the pool at eleven o'clock. Blackmail was his game. He said he had a thick dossier on me in his office. Baxendale threatened to tell everybody who I was if I didn't meet him. He was especially insistent he would tell *you,* as though he'd somehow sensed during that few minutes he was with us in my room how I felt for you. That was how I happened to mention your name—just as you came into the room.

"I couldn't let him do it to me, Jess. I went to the rendezvous. But I took the skeet gun with me. The rest you know."

"You took a tremendous risk," she said.

"Not so great as the risk of losing everything. And there was always the chance the sound of the gun would be taken for a sonic boom. It was just bad luck there were no flights that night. So those neighbors of mine were able to pinpoint the exact time it happened. If they hadn't, *nobody* would have had an alibi and there'd have been many more suspects for the police to check out.

"Not that it's really mattered, as things have turned out."

He sounded very, very tired.

He looked at her steadily. "He was a slimy blackmailer, Jess. He threatened to destroy my life. Morally, it was a case of self-defense."

"Even if I could bring myself to believe that, Preston, there's no way you can justify the murder of Caleb McCallum."

"Caleb wasn't much of a human being either. In killing him I did a good turn to Louise, and to the next young woman he would have taken up and then dumped."

"But he didn't deserve *killing,*" she said fiercely. "And you didn't do it for Louise, or anybody else. You did it to divert suspicion from yourself, by switching the investigation away from Baxendale—proving his death was just a mistake."

"Oh, that was part of it, but not all, by any means. You see, Caleb had known for years I had some sort of guilty secret. We were great buddies at one time, and once or twice I probably spoke a bit too freely. For a long time it didn't matter, for whatever his faults he was a loyal friend. But then, after Baxendale's death, he became suspicious of me."

"He did?"

"Yes. Remember, he knew Baxendale, and probably guessed he wouldn't be above a little blackmail. He also knew Baxendale had seen me, had left the house and gone to his car, and then come back. He realized that once Baxendale had gotten away from the house with that real estate report, it would take something special to make him return. Finally, Caleb was aware *I* knew he'd taken off the Holmes costume and put it in the closet. Knowing that I was vulnerable to blackmail, it didn't take him long to start suspecting me. After you saw him on his yacht that day, he called me and asked me to come to his office late that afternoon."

"And you went. You mentioned it."

"Most of the staff had left by the time I got there. Caleb was very odd. Didn't in so many words accuse me of the murder, but made it pretty clear he wasn't in much doubt. He didn't actually say he was going to the police, but I couldn't possibly take the risk of letting him.

"While I was there that girl Tracy phoned. Quite openly he made a date to see her on the yacht that night. Then he let me go—still giving no clue what he meant to do. That evening I phoned Tracy's apartment, spoke to her roommate, said I was Caleb, and canceled the date. Later after you and I'd had supper with Kitt and Grady, I drove out to Bayside, boarded the *Chowder King,* and waited for him. And—well, you know what happened."

"I know you let Louise be arrested—for your crime."

"Jess, that was a nightmare! How on earth could I have known that that night, of all nights, she and Caleb were going to have a fight, that people would overhear her threaten to kill him, and that she'd drive off after him and disappear for the rest of the night? However, as I knew she was innocent, I couldn't believe she'd be found guilty. I was tremendously relieved when Gunderson doubted her guilt and you agreed to take a hand. All the same, if the worst had happened, I swear to you I wouldn't have let her be convicted."

"I believe you, Preston. I'm sure, you see, in spite of all this, that in your own way you're a man of honor."

Suddenly, for the first time, Jessica broke down. She turned her head away. "Oh, Preston," she said in a distraught voice, "I'm so angry I don't know whether to scream or cry. All the way to the train station today I kept thinking about you. Twice I nearly turned around and came back. And then, when I saw that newspaper, when I realized . . ."

He stood up, moved across to her chair, and put his hand on her shoulder. "I'm sorry, Jess. I truly am."

She straightened, dived into her purse, took out a handkerchief, dabbed vigorously at her eyes, and blew her nose.

"Well, Preston, what are you going to do now?"

"The question is, my dear, what are you going to do? Go to the police, I suppose?"

"I hope I shan't have to."

"You mean you expect me to give myself up? Well, as no doubt you've already told someone else of your deductions, I have little choice."

"But I haven't."

"Then you've left a letter with an attorney or somebody."

"I haven't done that, either."

He looked flabbergasted. "You mean . . ."

"I mean that nobody but you and I knows of your guilt, Preston. Only the taxi driver, who I'm sure didn't recognize me, is aware I've been here. I've seen not a soul who knows me since I got off the train this afternoon."

He straightened up and stared down at her. "You do realize what you're saying? That I could kill you here and now; and very probably get away with it—as well as the other two murders."

"Yes."

"And you talk of my taking a risk! A few minutes ago you said double murderers don't stop at two, remember?"

"I remember. And I'm staking my life on my firm belief that you, Preston, will not harm *me.*"

Jessica's heart was beating very fast. She didn't know whether she looked frightened, but she certainly felt it.

He continued to gaze down at her. Every muscle of his body was tense, and she knew beyond doubt that the temptation to kill her was very real. She had never been in greater danger than now.

Then the moment passed. As if by a conscious effort he relaxed, and it was as though a pressure gauge had suddenly been turned down. He went across the room to a small cocktail cabinet, poured himself a glass of whiskey, and downed it in one go.

"Do you want a drink?" he asked.

"No, thank you."

He put down the glass and returned to his chair. "You're right, of course. I could never hurt you, Jess. You can walk out of here unhindered whenever you like."

"And you? Will you go to the police and tell the truth?"

"What will you do if I say no? Go yourself?"

"I don't think I could bring myself actually to go into a police station and inform on you. I shall mail my letter to Chief Gunderson."

He was silent. Then: "You won't need to do that."

"You will give yourself up?"

"I promise I'll let Gunderson have a full confession. And for good measure, I'll see he gets your letter as well. I'm sure it lays out the facts much more succinctly than I shall be able to."

Jessica hesitated for only a moment. Then she bowed her head. "Very well. Your word is good enough for me, Preston."

He stood up, walked to the phone, dialed, and asked for Chief Gunderson. He listened for a moment, then hung up. "He'll be here in ten minutes."

He got to his feet and went over to her. "Another time, Jess, a different place, we might have had something."

She took his hand. "We might indeed."

He drew her to him, took her in his arms, and held her close for a moment. Then he pulled away, put his hands on her shoulders, and looked into her eyes.

"Forgive me, Jess?"

"What is there for *me* to forgive?" She turned aside. Her voice broke. "I . . . I think . . . if you don't mind, I'll walk down the driveway and wait for the Chief there."

"As you wish, my dear."

"Don't see me out."

"Very well."

Without looking at him again, she walked quickly to the door and opened it.

"Goodbye, Preston."

The door closed behind her.

"Goodbye, Jessica," he said softly.

But she didn't hear.

# Chapter Seventeen

"AUNT Jess, how did you hatch that story you told Preston Giles about Kitt?"

"The whole thing was just a product of my overfertile imagination."

She took Kitt by the hand. "I'm so sorry, my dear, for maligning your character in that way to Preston. It was just the only way I could think of to make him tell me the truth."

They were in Kitt's apartment. Grady and Jessica had stopped off on their way to the station for Jessica to say a final goodbye.

"Oh, I don't mind in the least," Kitt said airily. "In fact"—she tossed her head at Grady—"I'm quite flattered that anybody would believe all that of me."

Grady shook his head sorrowfully. "Hopeless. Just a natural-born delinquent, this girl."

Kitt turned to Jessica. "And speaking of natural-born delinquents, why did you phone asking me for Tracy Ellison's number earlier?"

"I wanted to clear up all the loose ends. That anonymous phone call to the police about the murder on the yacht. I had my own idea. And I was right. Tracy, suspecting she'd been ditched for another girl, made her way to the yacht club that night to try to find out. She waited on the quay about fifty yards away. Preston must have been there by then, but she saw the Captain arrive and go aboard. A few minutes later she saw and heard . . . well, not enough to know exactly what had happened, or identify the murderer, but enough to know Caleb had been shot. She panicked and ran away. But later she phoned the police. She spoke in a whisper so they wouldn't identify her voice as a woman's."

"Must have been a terrifying experience for her," Grady said. "Poor kid."

"I shouldn't waste too much sympathy on her," Jessica assured him. "I don't think she's exactly overwhelmed with grief. In fact, she's already collaborating with a ghostwriter for some scandal sheet on an article to be called 'My Love for Cap'n Caleb.' As she said to me, 'A girl's got to take care of herself.' "

"Things seem to be working out quite well all around," he said. "Ashley's making a deal with the D.A. that will keep her out of jail. Brill will probably get a comparatively short sentence. Louise is out of prison and on the wagon. *And* is so very grateful to Roy Gunderson, who is now a frequent caller at her house. Finally, J. B. Fletcher vindicates her nephew, solves the mystery, gives her book a tremendous boost of publicity—and builds herself an overnight reputation as a crackerjack amateur detective. Highly satisfactory."

"For everybody but you, my dear," she said sympathetically. "Do you know, almost the first thought that occurred to me when I realized Preston might be guilty was, 'poor Grady.' Just when he'd promised to help find you a job in publishing."

"Oh, don't worry about me, Aunt Jess. There are always openings for guys like me: brilliant, dynamic, charming . . ."

". . . modest, unassuming," Kitt murmured.

He put his arm around her waist. "Besides, we're thinking of pooling our talent and experience and going into partnership."

"Oh, doing what?"

"Producing a book. How does this grab you as an eye-catching title? *History and Practice of Accounting in the Clam Chowder Industry.* Think it'll make the charts?"

"Very possibly," Jessica said. "But I shouldn't bank on selling the movie rights."

She looked at her watch. "Well, if you're taking me to the station, we'd better get moving."

"Do you think it's really worth the bother this time?"

"Grady, this time I *am* going home. And I am not coming back to this city. Not next month, not next year. Never."

"Point taken," he said.

She turned to Kitt. "Goodbye, Kitt, dear. And again, thanks for everything."

"Thank *you,* Aunt Jess."

They embraced and a minute later Jessica and Grady left.


At the station Jessica said: "I seem to have spent half my life on this platform lately."

"Well, let's hope this is the last time. Tell me, Aunt Jess, how do you feel now?"

"Still rather shattered."

"You really like Preston, don't you?"

"Yes, I really like him. Oh, Grady, if I hadn't been such a terrible busybody, if only I'd let it be . . ." She took a grip on herself. "Anyway, now I've had enough. Enough murders, enough suspects, enough puzzles. I'm not even sure I'm going to write another book."

"Sure you are. And I'll be the first one to read it."

She smiled. "Well, we'll see."

She kissed him and boarded the train. Then she turned and looked out of the window. She was about to say goodbye, when suddenly she heard a voice calling.

"Aunt Jess—wait!"

Flying down the platform toward them was Kitt.

Grady gave an exclamation as the girl came running up to them. "Kitt, what on earth's the matter?"

She was panting for air. "Aunt Jess, the police have just phoned my apartment. They've been trying to find you all morning. They won't say it, but I think they need help."

"Help from *me?*"

She nodded. "The bodies of two dead wrestlers were found this morning at Madison Square Garden—lying side by side in the middle of the ring. One had been stabbed. The other drowned."

"No!" Jessica said. "Absolutely not!"

At that moment the train started to move.

Kitt called breathlessly, "They said they're sure there's a logical explanation, but . . ."

Jessica cut her off. "Grady, *tell* her. Goodbye, children. Be sure to write—and remember, I expect to see you soon."

She gave a wave and withdrew into the train.

She made her way to her seat, sank gratefully down on it, and closed her eyes. She'd made it! Soon she'd be back in Cabot Cove, and . . .

Jessica's eyes opened. She sat up and stared blankly ahead of her. One had been stabbed. And the other . . .

*"Drowned?"* she said out loud.

# HOORAY
# FOR HOMICIDE

# Chapter One

"YES. I shall kill him with a bayonet. Clean, quick and very certain."

Jessica Fletcher gave a firm nod. It was so difficult to think of original weapons with which to dispose of one's victims, but she couldn't recall anybody who'd used a bayonet. It would throw suspicion on the ex-GI, and while people would soon realize this was a red herring, probably not many would suspect a woman of having done it.

Now—wait: could a woman kill a man with a bayonet?

Well, Maude was a fit, athletic girl. All the same . . .

How could she find out if it was feasible?

Well, Major Harris could no doubt lend her a bayonet from his collection of World War II souvenirs. Bert Stradling, the local butcher, would probably let her borrow a side of meat for an hour or so. And if somebody like—like—Jean Pollard, who coached the high school girls in tennis, and was a keen fencer—if she were willing to come along and try her hand at stabbing the meat . . .

Or was it worth going to such trouble? Who could prove, after all, that it wasn't possible for a girl to kill a man with a bayonet?

Jessica sighed. The trials of a mystery writer's life . . .

It was at that moment that the light in the cozy kitchen, where she did most of her writing, flickered and went out. Jessica groaned. That was all she needed. She had to admit, though, that in this weather it was hardly surprising.

Jessica sat still in the darkness and listened to the storm howling outside. For the first time she became really aware of what a fierce one this was. Rain and wind were beating furiously against her house. It honestly sounded quite frightening. Jessica gave a shiver. In all the years she'd lived here she didn't think she could remember a storm of such intensity.

Jessica Fletcher was an attractive, kindhearted widow in her mid-fifties. For over twenty-five years she had lived in the small coastal town of Cabot Cove, Maine. Most of those years had been spent in the large Victorian house that was now creaking and groaning under the onslaught of the storm. Until a few years ago she had shared this home with her husband, Frank. Then had come the shattering blow of his death. Jessica had gone through a bad time, which her work as a substitute English teacher in the local high school had only partly eased.

Her life had been transformed when, in an attempt to keep her mind occupied, she had embarked on the writing of a mystery novel, entitled *The Corpse Danced at Midnight.* Against all her expectations the novel had been published and had even become a best-seller. To publicize the book, a hectic and traumatic visit to New York had followed. In the midst of the publicity junket, Jessica had been instrumental in solving two murders, and she returned home to Cabot Cove feeling she never again wanted to hear the word *murder.*

However, she found she had been well and truly bitten by the writing bug and had recently started on her second whodunit.

Already, however, she was beginning to regret the decision.

Sitting in the darkness, Jessica let her mind flit from one subject to another. At last, though, she pulled her thoughts together and got to her feet. Better go and find some candles. However, at that moment, to her great relief, the lights came on again. She tilted her head back, looked at the ceiling, said "Thank you" devoutly, and bent again over her typewriter.

But as she did so, above the noise of the storm came the sound of someone hammering on the rear door of the house.

Jessica murmured: "Now who on earth would be out on a night like this?"

She stood up and crossed to the door.

"Who is it?" she called.

"Ethan."

"Oh, good Lord!"

She unlocked the door and opened it. A large figure in oilskins and a sou'wester was practically blown into the room by a strong gust of wind, and the din of the storm momentarily filled the kitchen.

Hastily, Jessica forced the door closed again as her visitor drew off his sou'wester and gave a gasp. Ethan Cragg was a tough, weather-beaten man of about Jessica's age, who made his living operating charter fishing boats. Taciturn, blunt and often irascible, he had nevertheless been a good friend to Jessica since Frank's death.

He took out a handkerchief and mopped his face dry. "Whew, what a night!"

"What is it, Ethan? Something wrong?"

"Nope. Just thought I'd come and see if you were okay. Don't often get a hurricane as bad as this so far north. A real deadly lady, this one. Wanted to make sure your place was still in one piece; the phones are off, so I couldn't call."

"Oh, Ethan, you shouldn't have bothered! I do appreciate it, but everything's fine. As a matter of fact, I got so engrossed in my new book I hardly noticed how bad the storm was until the lights went out for a few minutes."

"Everyone's not so lucky," he said. "The Coast Guard's picked up distress signals from some fools out there on a yacht." He jerked a thumb in the direction of the sea.

"Oh, how awful! Surely they'll never make it?"

He shrugged. "Might. No way of telling. Can't get to 'em till it clears. Anyway, guess I'd better be getting along."

"Not till you've had a cup of coffee, you're not," she said firmly. "Now take off that oilskin and go into the living room."

Three minutes later, Jessica entered the living room carrying a tray of coffee and sandwiches, to find Ethan seated by the fire, reading the typescript of her novel, which he'd brought in from the kitchen.

"Now, Ethan," she said sharply. "I've told you before: nobody reads my books until they're finished."

"Sorry." He put down the sheaf of papers. "How's it coming?"

"The book? Slowly. I've heard that one's second novel is always the hardest. Now I believe it."

She poured a cup of coffee and handed it to him, saying, "Oh, by the way, I had some exciting news today."

"Oh, that so?"

"Marilyn Dean, my editor, phoned from New York. A Hollywood producer has just bought an option on my first book."

"What's an option?"

"Well, it means he's interested in making a movie out of it but isn't ready to commit himself. So he sort of pays a fee to reserve it for a year then the publisher can't sell the film rights to anyone else until the option expires."

"I see." He sipped his coffee appreciatively. "Mean a lot of money for you?"

"Not a great deal. Of course, if he decides to go ahead with the picture, then I'll do very well. But let's face it, he probably won't. Marilyn warned me that most options aren't picked up. But it's exciting to know somebody's considering it."

"Well, I sure hope it works out for you."

"Thank you." She poured herself some coffee and sat down.

"Ever since I heard I've been casting the picture in my mind. Trouble is, nearly all the actors and actresses I'd really like in it are dead or retired."

She paused and at that moment a particularly strong gust of wind rocked the house. Her face clouded. "Oh dear, I can't help thinking of those poor people out in that storm."

"Now, Jess, it's no use worrying about things you can't do anything about. If worrying'd help 'em, I'd say go ahead and worry. But it won't."

"I know. I'll try not to think of it." She drank some coffee.

"Oh, by the way, keep it under your hat about the film business for the time being, won't you? Otherwise, sure as eggs, it'll get around town a movie's going to be made from the book. Then if nothing happens, it'll be a letdown."

"You can rely on me," he said.

During the night the storm blew itself out, and when Jessica left her house early the next morning it was a fine bright day. Signs of the hurricane's path, however, were everywhere: uprooted trees, smashed road signs, shingles torn from roofs, broken shutters. On the whole, though, no serious damage seemed to have been done.

Jessica made her way down to the harbor to see if she could pick up any news of the yacht that had been in trouble. But there was no sign of Ethan, or of his boat. She walked over to a shop that bore the sign ANDERSEN'S BAIT AND TACKLE SHOP. The owner, Nils Andersen, a slim, rawboned man in his early forties, was outside selling a teenage boy bait from an ice chest.

"Good morning, Nils."

"Morning, Jessica." He took the boy's money and turned to her.

"Nice morning for the fish," she said.

"They'll be biting, sure enough. Always do after a storm."

"I don't see *The Pilgrim.*"

"No. Ethan went out about an hour ago—helping some folk who got stuck last night out on the water."

"Yes, I heard about them. Are they all right?"

"I couldn't say. They lost radio contact."

"I see. Well, have him call me when he gets in, would you, Nils?"

"Sure thing."

She turned away, but at that moment from within the shop there came the crackle of static, followed by somewhat distorted voices.

"Hang on, Jessica," Nils said. "That's my ship-to-shore radio. I left it tuned in. That could be Ethan, reporting to the Coast Guard now." He turned into the shop. Jessica followed him just in time to hear Ethan's voice from the radio.

"I just hooked up with that yacht," he was saying. "We're about eight miles off Spruce Head. Towing her in now."

"Do you need assistance?" asked the voice of a Guardsman.

"No." There was a pause, then Ethan added: "But there's something strange going on here. You'd better get Sheriff Tupper down to the dock to meet us coming in."

"Okay, Ethan, will do."

"Be there in about an hour. Over and out."

The radio fell silent. Jessica looked at Andersen.

"Now, I wonder what that's about," she mused. "*Strange* is a strong word for Ethan. He takes everything in his stride."

Nils shrugged. "Well, we'll soon know."

Jessica nodded and looked at her watch. "Yes, he said about an hour, didn't he?"

"Right."

"Then you can forget that message, Nils. I'll be back."

Jessica retraced her steps toward home. Within a few minutes she was regretting her last words to Nils. After all, whatever the "something strange" was, it was no business of hers, and she really should put in a hard morning's work on her book. But now, unless she did return to the harbor, it might be ages before she discovered what was going on.

"You really must curb this insatiable curiosity of yours, my girl," she told herself firmly. On the other hand, she reflected, as a mystery writer she should always be on the lookout for good material.

Then as she opened her front gate, the matter was put suddenly out of her mind. There was a man in her flower garden. He was bending over a bed of nasturtiums, but straightened up as he heard the sound of the gate. He was, she judged, in his late sixties, with gray hair, and sporting a three days' growth of beard. He was wearing a worn red-and-black lumberman's shirt, faded jeans, shabby shoes and an old fisherman's cap.

Jessica approached him a little warily. "Excuse me, but this *is* private property."

He touched the cap respectfully. "You the lady of the house, ma'am?"

"Well, yes, I suppose you could say that."

"It's a shame letting these weeds get a toehold like this," he said, poking at the earth with his foot. "This is too good a garden to go to ruin."

"You can hardly say those nasturtiums are going to ruin." She spoke a little frostily.

"Still, you have to admit these beds could use a good weeding."

"Are you offering your services, Mr.—er?" She broke off.

"Oh, just call me Ralph, ma'am. Yes, I am, after a fashion. I'm mighty hungry, but I don't believe in taking handouts. If you could spare me a good breakfast, I'm willing to work for it. There's quite a few jobs I could tackle: shutters need paint—whole house does, for that matter—water pump out back wants a new washer. No offense intended, but I believe in being direct."

"Well, I certainly wouldn't expect you to do all that in return for one breakfast."

She eyed him appraisingly and came to a decision.

"All right, Ralph. Suppose you make a start on these flower beds, while I get some bacon and eggs on? We can talk about the other jobs later."

"That'll be fine, ma'am."

He touched his cap again, turned away and knelt down by the flower bed. Jessica went indoors.

Fifteen minutes later Jessica opened her front door again and called out: "Breakfast's ready."

Ralph straightened up and walked somewhat stiffly across the grass to the door.

"Come on through to the kitchen," she said.

He wiped his feet carefully on the mat and followed her.

"You can wash your hands at the sink if you don't mind slumming it," she told him.

"Oh, right."

He turned on the faucet and started scrubbing his hands vigorously.

Jessica went back to the stove, lifted off the frying pan and deftly flipped a second fried egg onto a plate. "Been doing this long?" she asked over her shoulder.

"Hobo-in'? Yes, ma'am. As long as I can remember. But I'm no bum, you understand: I work for what I get."

He dried his hands and came across to the table as Jessica placed the plate of sizzling bacon and eggs down on it.

"My, that looks good." He sat down. "You not eating, ma'am?"

"Not right now. I'll just have some coffee." She sat down at the table opposite him. "How do you like yours?"

"Just black, please."

He cut himself a thick slice of bread from the crusty loaf on the table, and started to dig into the food. Jessica watched him surreptitiously as she poured two cups of coffee and pushed one across the table to him.

"Tell me," she asked suddenly, "do you figure that story makes people more likely to give you work than the truth would?"

He stopped with his fork halfway to his mouth and gazed at her blankly.

"Sorry, ma'am, I don't rightly follow."

"That fiddle-faddle about living like this all your life. You're no more a tramp than I am."

He didn't move for a few seconds, then he gave a sigh.

"How d'you know?"

"In the first place, the term is *bo-in'*, not *hobo-in'*. Secondly, your clothes may be old and faded, but they're of fine quality and very expensive. Thirdly, your table manners are too good. Finally, on your wrist is the imprint of where a watch used to be. Where did you stash it, Ralph?"

He hesitated, then reached into his pocket and rather sheepishly brought out an expensive-looking gold watch.

"I didn't steal it."

"I didn't say you did."

He buckled it on to his wrist. "Well, truth is, ma'am, I *am* bumming around, but, like you guessed, I haven't been at it long. My company just retired me, after forty-two years. Gave me a small pension and the proverbial gold watch. It suddenly hit me I had no idea what I was going to do with my life. I mooched around at home for a while, then realized there was a lot of the world I hadn't seen. How to see it was the problem. I figured I had two choices: hop on a tour bus with the rest of the old fogies, or see America from the ground up. Sorry I spun that yarn. Mad with me?"

"Why should I be? Though it's my belief you'd get on better if you told the truth. As you said, there's a lot needs doing around this old place—if you're still interested."

"You bet, ma'am."

"Very well. I'll make up a list of jobs."

He finished his breakfast and returned to the garden. Jessica washed up, did a few chores around the house and then looked at her watch. It was no good: she just *had* to go down to the harbor and see what strange thing Ethan had discovered and why he wanted the sheriff to be there.

Then she hesitated. She'd just remembered her publisher might be calling this morning—something about the German translation of *The Corpse Danced at Midnight,* which would require a prompt decision on her part. She considered that Ralph, of course, could take a message—

but she didn't want to leave a virtual stranger with the complete run of the house.

Then a solution occurred to her. Five minutes later she put on a coat, picked up her purse and went out, locking the door behind her.

Ralph was still busily weeding as she walked across the yard to him. "Ralph, I have to go out for a while, but I'd like you to do something for me."

He straightened. "What's that?"

"I may be getting a phone call this morning. A firm called Coventry House. Now I've moved the phone to the ledge just inside that little window there." She pointed. "The window is open. Will you listen for the phone and if it rings, reach in through the window, answer it and tell them I'll return the call the minute I return."

He nodded casually. "No trouble."

"Thank you." She cast a quick glance over the flower beds.

"You're making a very good job of that."

She hurried off.

# Chapter Two

WHEN Jessica reached the harbor she saw at once that *The Pilgrim* had returned and was docked alongside the pier. Just behind, and making *The Pilgrim* look a very humble craft indeed, was a big, gleaming white, oceangoing yacht. A small knot of people were standing on the dock near the two crafts.

Jessica drew closer, seeing as she did so that the group consisted of Ethan Cragg; Amos Tupper, the sheriff; and, standing a few yards from them, four young women who were strangers to her. Nils Andersen, two or three fishermen and a few children were grouped around as interested spectators to the proceedings.

Somewhat diffidently, Jessica approached the group. After all, it was nothing to do with her. Nothing at all.

Ethan and the sheriff were arguing. Well, there wasn't anything unusual about *that*. Suddenly Tupper glanced up and spotted Jessica. To her slight surprise, he looked definitely pleased to see her, then raised a hand and beckoned her. Feeling a little self-conscious, she walked right up to the group.

"Good morning, Sheriff. Hello, Ethan." She gave a half nod toward the four other women.

Tupper returned her greeting. "Mrs. Fletcher, I'm glad you showed. I hate to bother you, but something mighty peculiar's happened, and frankly I could use some advice. I figure it's more in your line than mine."

The sheriff was a man in his early fifties, an amicable career officer, honest, conscientious and perfectly adequate at his job. However, while by no means a fool, he had never been noted for his intellectual powers and at the moment looked a bit out of his depth.

Ethan said crossly, "Amos, you old fool, there's no need to involve Jessica in this."

"Will you zip it up, Ethan, for the love of Mike! I'm conducting an official investigation here."

"And I'm telling you there wasn't any murder! These nice little girls wouldn't have murdered anybody, especially their own daddy."

Jessica pricked up her ears. "Murder?"

"No!" Ethan said fiercely.

Tupper sighed. "Maybe. It's got to be looked into."

"Perhaps," said Jessica, "somebody could kindly tell me just what has been going on?"

"A man off that boat was drowned last night," Tupper told her.

Jessica lowered her voice. "The father of these four girls?"

Tupper looked relieved at her perspicacity. "Precisely."

"Well, that's very tragic. But hardly surprising, is it? I'm amazed *anyone* survived being out in that hurricane."

Ethan gave a satisfied nod. "My sentiments exactly."

Jessica eyed him quizzically. "On the other hand, Ethan, I did hear you on Nils Andersen's radio distinctly tell the Coast Guard that something strange had been going on and to have the sheriff meet you when you got in."

He looked a little embarrassed. "Yeah, well, that was just a few minutes after I met up with the yacht. Things did look a bit strange. I didn't know the girls then. Since then I've heard the whole story. Two of 'em rode back with me on *The Pilgrim*. They're nice kids."

"And mighty attractive ones," Tupper growled. "You always were a sucker for a pretty face, Ethan."

Ethan went red. "It was an accident, I tell you—pure and simple. Amos, you're—"

Jessica interrupted hastily. "Just what is it you want me to do, Sheriff?"

He took her arm, drew her a few feet away from the young women and lowered his voice. "Talk to 'em, Mrs. Fletcher, listen to their story, see if you think it ties together. I mean being a woman, educated, like them, you can handle it better than I can. Size 'em up properly. If you decide there's nothing suspicious in their old man's death, that's what I'll put in my report."

Jessica raised her eyebrows. "My, that's quite a responsibility. All right, Sheriff, I won't pretend I'm not interested—and flattered. You'd better introduce me to them."

"Thanks, Mrs. Fletcher. Appreciate it." He led her across to the four young women.

"Ladies, I'd like to have you meet Mrs. Fletcher—Mrs. Jessica Fletcher. She's a good friend and from time to time I like to rely on her advice. Mrs. Fletcher, these are, er, Miss Earl, Miss, er, let's see now . . ." He started leafing through his notebook.

The eldest of the young women stepped forward. "Perhaps I'd better do the introductions." She held her hand out.

"I'm Maggie Earl."

Jessica smiled. Maggie, she judged, was about thirty-five or -six. She was attractive in a quiet way, her hair simply styled; she wore no makeup. As Jessica took her hand she received the clear impression that it was quite an effort for Maggie to push herself forward in this way.

Maggie went on. "These are my sisters. Grace . . ."

Grace didn't offer her hand, but instead gave a rather curt nod. She was about thirty. She had good features, which, however, she seemed intent on hiding under a pair of large, severe spectacles. Her hair was drawn back into a bun. She wore a wedding ring.

"How do you do, Mrs.—?" Jessica deliberately broke off with a query in her voice.

"Lamont." Grace spoke unwillingly.

Maggie continued. "Lisa."

The third girl stepped forward with a dazzling smile and held out her hand. "Lisa Shelby, Mrs. Fletcher. It's a pleasure to meet such a distinguished author."

Jessica bowed her head. "Thank you, my dear. It's a pleasure to meet such a beautiful young lady."

This was not flattery. "Beautiful" was an overworked word and one frequently misused with women, but in Lisa's case it was strictly true. Everything about her—features, complexion, hair, figure—was flawless. Unlike her elder sisters, she was wearing makeup, but it was so subtly applied that it took a very close observer to be aware of the fact. She accepted Jessica's compliment easily, being obviously quite used to such remarks and considering them no more than her due. Justly so, of course, but Jessica could have wished Lisa a little less aware of the fact.

Maggie continued the introductions. "And this is Nan—the baby."

The fourth girl smiled and said, "Hello."

She was about twenty-four and, while she did not have Lisa's breathtaking beauty, was delightfully pretty with a natural and infectious smile. On this occasion, however, the smile faded quickly after she spoke to Jessica.

"Well, that's everybody," Tupper said. "Now, ladies, suppose you tell Mrs. Fletcher just what happened out there last night?"

"Just a minute, Sheriff," Jessica said. "Wouldn't we all be more comfortable indoors somewhere?"

"Oh, I guess so. Well, we can go along to the station house, if you like."

"Oh, I hardly think that's necessary." She looked around and spotted Andersen, still watching interestedly. "Nils, could we use the back room of your shop for a while?"

The eyes of everyone present turned on Andersen. He looked momentarily embarrassed, then pleased to find himself the center of attention. "Yeah—sure," he said.

"Thank you." Jessica looked around. "Let's go, shall we?"

The little procession, led by Nils, made its way across to the Bait and Tackle Shop, watched curiously by the uninvolved bystanders. Jessica felt they looked as if they should be headed by a drum majorette. She repressed the thought. They were, after all, dealing with a man's death— even if there had so far been little evidence of grief from any of his daughters.

She heard footsteps coming up behind and turned to see Grace Lamont alongside her.

"Excuse me if this sounds rude, Mrs. Fletcher," said Grace, "but what exactly is your involvement in this?"

Jessica smiled sweetly. "I'm the official town snoop, my dear; and you *do* have the right to remain silent."

Somewhat self-importantly, Nils led them through the shop to the back room. It was small, rather dusty and crammed with stock. The four girls perched themselves on various barrels and cartons; Ethan crossed to the window and remained standing, his elbow on the ledge. Tupper leaned up against the wall just inside the door and folded his arms; it must have been the position he'd assumed many times when as a young policeman he'd been the guard while his superiors were interrogating suspects.

Nils went out, to return a few seconds later with a somewhat rickety upright chair for Jessica. She sat down on it, feeling rather like the chairman at a board meeting, and almost expected someone to pass her a gavel.

She hoped Nils wouldn't decide to stay. After all, while she had been asked to conduct the questioning, and Ethan was no doubt some sort of witness, the girls might well object to having a complete outsider present. However, it would be awkward to ask him to vacate his own room. For a moment, indeed, he looked as if he intended to stay, then the voice of a customer was heard, calling from the front of the shop. Somewhat regretfully, he went out. The sheriff pushed the door shut after him.

Jessica cleared her throat. It was the first time she had been officially involved with interrogating suspects in what Amos plainly thought might be a murder case, and already she was beginning to regret agreeing to take part.

"I'm afraid I'm quite in the dark about what exactly has happened," she said. "I don't even know the name of the—the missing man."

Tupper said: "Oh, sorry, Mrs. Fletcher. Well, these young ladies' father was Stephen Earl, the makeup tycoon. You may have heard of him."

Jessica's eyebrows went up. "Yes, indeed, Mark of the Earl cosmetics. I've used them; they're very good. Though expensive." She frowned. "Didn't he start out as an actor, many years ago?"

It was Maggie Earl who answered. "That's right. He went to Hollywood, couldn't get work, and a friend got him a job in the makeup department of one of the studios. It was supposed to be temporary, but . . ." She trailed off.

"I believe he wrote his autobiography some time back?"

Maggie nodded. "Yes, *Greasepaint Millionaire.* That must be twenty years ago, though. Have you read the book, Mrs. Fletcher?"

"No, I'm afraid not. But I've noticed it at our local library. So twenty years ago, Mr. Earl was already a millionaire. And his company certainly seems to have been flourishing—if the displays on the cosmetic counters in the stores are anything to judge by. So I imagine he'd be a very rich man?"

"You can say that again." Lisa spoke dryly. "And yes, Mrs. Fletcher, my sisters and I are the legatees under his will. We'll share an estate that can be conservatively estimated at one hundred million dollars. So we all had a very good motive for killing him. Satisfied?"

"Lisa!" Maggie spoke sharply. "That's no way to talk."

"Sorry, darling, but there's no point in not facing facts. I'm sure Mrs. Fletcher's abristle with suspicion already, anyway, just like the sheriff."

"Not at all," Jessica said calmly. "Offhand I can think of no instance of a millionaire being murdered for his money by one of his children. After all, the children know that under normal circumstances, they'll get the money eventually anyway. And if they find themselves in financial difficulties, their father will usually come to their rescue. So I see no *prima facie* reason for suspecting any of you young ladies of murder. Of course, I still don't know the circumstances of Mr. Earl's death, or what other motives there might be. Suppose you begin by telling me about this cruise you were on."

The girls glanced at each other, and again the job of principal spokeswoman seemed to devolve on Maggie.

"Well, we left Bridgeport four days ago. We had a pleasant, uneventful trip."

"Just the five of you?" Jessica interrupted.

Maggie nodded. "Yes—well as I say—"

Again Jessica cut her off. "Excuse me, but wasn't that rather unusual? Two of you are married, I know, and I'm sure the others have boyfriends in the offing."

"Well, in my case, no," Maggie said rather coldly.

Grace said: "And I'm separated from my husband."

Nan gave a bright little laugh, that didn't sound very natural. "While I'm still treading water after the end of a beautiful romance. Oh dear, that wasn't a very good figure of speech, was it?"

Jessica looked at Lisa, whose beautiful face flushed.

"Yes, I did leave my husband behind—as the others would have left their men behind, if Dad had insisted. If they had any to leave, that is."

There was silence. Grace opened her mouth and drew a deep breath to respond to this, but Jessica spoke before the younger woman was able to do so. "Was there any particular reason he wanted to get the four of you alone?"

Lisa said: "Well, he wasn't going to test us to see who was best suited to run his business empire, if that's what you mean."

"Fortunately for you, dear," Grace said.

Maggie said hastily: "It was just that years ago we all used to sail together every summer. That was the only time we got to spend with Dad, really. But for several years now we've never all been together, and he thought it would be nice to revive the custom just once, for old time's sake. I think he thought it might be the last chance." She looked round for support.

Nan said quietly: "Yes, that's all there was to it."

"Like we were a bunch of teenagers," Lisa muttered.

"No one forced you to come along, Lisa," Grace snapped.

"That's right, Lisa. You seemed quite willing." Maggie was speaking now. She went on. "And you did say Brian was too busy for a vacation right now; you didn't mind leaving him."

"Oh, no," Grace said. "Lisa wasn't going to be the odd girl out. After all, what dastardly plotting might have gone on behind her back?"

"You'd have liked me to stay away, wouldn't you, Grace?" Lisa said in a low voice. "What a great chance that would have been for you to spread more venom about Brian."

"Girls, stop it." Maggie spoke briskly, but without undue irritation or embarrassment. "We're here to explain what happened, not air family differences."

She turned to Jessica. "There was no question of Dad insisting we come, Mrs. Fletcher. He urged us to come—and that was all."

Jessica, who had been sitting quietly, her eyes darting from one to the other, spoke placidly. "Well, that all seems very natural. Quite a charming idea, in fact. I understand the background now, and perhaps we could turn to the events of last night."

"We've already told it all to the sheriff once," Lisa said.

Tupper spoke quietly from near the door. "And you may have to tell it a few times more, ma'am. Better get used to it."

Lisa gave a disgruntled shrug.

Grace said, "I suppose *I'd* better tell it, since I may be the only one who can deal with what's happened without falling apart." She drew a breath. "We'd been at sea for three nights. We knew the storm was approaching, but we felt sure it would head out to sea long before it came this far north."

"They usually do," Jessica said.

Maggie cut in. "By the time we realized our mistake it was too late. We made for shore, but the storm caught us. Last night, shortly before midnight, we were three miles due east of Monhegan Island. The boat was yawing badly. The four of us were huddled below decks, when we suddenly realized that Father was topside. Lisa was the first one up on deck. She saw—"

"I can tell my own part quite well, thank you," Lisa interrupted. "When I got on deck I could barely see. The wind was raging and the rain was pouring down in sheets. I could just see Father at the boom. One of the sails was starting to unfurl and he was trying to lash it. I started toward him. Just then—"

Grace interrupted in turn. "Just then I came on deck. Lisa was moving toward Father. Suddenly a huge wave smashed into the boat. In an instant he was swept overboard. I struggled to the rail but it was too late. He was gone. By then Maggie and Nan had come topside. We knew it was hopeless. It was all we could do to get ourselves safely below decks. We managed to ride out the rest of the storm—and that's about it. This morning Captain Cragg spotted us, got a line on board and towed us in."

There was silence for a few seconds, then Ethan said: "Seems pretty straightforward, doesn't it, Jess?"

"Apparently your sheriff doesn't think so," Grace said. "What about you, Mrs. Fletcher?"

All eyes were on Jessica. She was silent for a moment before saying slowly, "Well, of course, I know very little about sailing, but I do know that was a really exceptional storm last night. If Mr. Cragg here thinks it could have happened just like that, I certainly wouldn't be able to say he was wrong. Nor would I dream of accusing anybody of murder on the basis of what I've heard so far."

If there was a certain ambiguity in this sentence, nobody seemed aware of it.

Lisa, in fact, got to her feet at once. "Well, thank the Lord that's over." She looked at Tupper. "I suppose we can leave now?"

"Sure you can leave . . . this store. You'll stay in town, though, till after the coroner's inquest."

"And when is that likely to be?" Grace asked.

"Depends."

"Depends on what?"

"On when your father's body shows up. With so much money at stake, my feeling is there are special circumstances here, and before we go holding any inquests I want to see that body."

Lisa shuddered. "Do you mean we have to hang around this God-forsaken dump perhaps for weeks. Until . . ."

"Won't be anything like that," Tupper said. "The way the tides are, it'll wash up tonight or tomorrow for sure."

Maggie, too, stood up. "Then of course we'll stay. The sheriff is obviously quite right. Tell me, Sheriff, is there a hotel in this town?"

He nodded. "Hill House. Daresay they'll be able to fit you all in."

"I can just imagine what it'll be like," Lisa said.

"Well, it's no Cabot Cove Hilton," Tupper said. "And I don't suppose they've had four multimillionairesses at the same time before, but I reckon they'll make you comfortable enough."

"Then let's go," Lisa said. She started for the door.

Just then Jessica stood. "Oh, ladies, forgive me. I'm forgetting my Yankee hospitality. I have this big house and there's only me. I'd be delighted to have you all as my guests."

Lisa gave a short laugh. "And spend the next twenty-four hours being grilled about Father's death by the sheriff's unofficial deputy? Thanks, I prefer to take my chances at the hotel." She opened the door and marched out.

The other girls looked embarrassed.

Maggie said a little stiffly, "Thank you, Mrs. Fletcher, but I think perhaps we'd better all stick together. Er, how do we get to this hotel?"

Ethan said: "I'll show you."

Maggie went out, with Ethan on her heels.

"It's a very kind offer, Mrs. Fletcher," Nan said. "Thank you. I'd like to say yes, but as Maggie says, we'd better stick together."

She, too, left the room. Only Grace remained. She looked at Jessica. "I apologize for my sister, Mrs. Fletcher. Tact is not one of Lisa's virtues."

"Naturally, you're all upset," Jessica said.

Grace eyed her curiously for a while. "Yes," she said. "Naturally." And went out.

Sheriff Tupper closed the door, moved across the room and lowered himself onto a barrel recently vacated by Maggie. He reached into his pocket, took out a pack of cigarettes, lit one and regarded Jessica. "Well, Mrs. Fletcher?"

"Well what, Mr. Tupper?"

"What do you make of it all?"

"It's very interesting, isn't it?"

"You could put it that way."

"Tell me, what aroused your suspicions in the first place?"

He lifted a hand and raised the thumb. "First: motive." He straightened his index finger. "Second: lack of any grief—in any of 'em." He held up another finger. "Third: fact that Earl was a very experienced sailor, who would have known what a tremendous risk he was taking messing about on deck without a line attached and—as they told me before—without a life jacket."

He was about to continue, but Jessica stopped him. "Let's take those points first. Yes, they did have a motive. But as I pointed out, no greater motive, so far as we know, than the children of any rich man. It's rare for rich people to be murdered by their children for their money. No, I agree they showed no grief. And I think it highly likely they don't feel any. But that is far from proof that one or more of them pushed their father overboard. And, you know, if they had done so, I would have expected that person or persons to *simulate* grief. I should think that in such circumstances a show of grief would be almost irresistible. It could be argued, I suppose, that there was an element of double-bluff involved, but that, I feel, is rather too subtle."

She was thoughtful for a moment, then said, "As to your third point, I agree Mr. Earl was taking a risk. But it might have been necessary. If he suddenly became aware that the yacht was in danger of foundering and only prompt action would save it, he might have taken that action in spite of the danger. Because his daughters didn't love him, it doesn't follow he didn't love them."

Tupper drew on his cigarette. "So you're saying the death is all aboveboard?"

Jessica shook her head firmly. "Oh no, I'm not saying that at all."

Tupper sat up. "You're not? But you said—"

"All I said was that those particular points you mentioned don't weigh all that heavily with me. That does not mean I think those girls are telling the truth. In fact, I'm sure they're not."

"What specially makes you think that?"

"There was one thing . . ." She broke off. "But you hadn't finished listing the things that made you suspicious. I cut you off after the third one."

He scratched his chin. "It was simply something Grace said, when she was talking about the storm. She said they were huddled below decks." He stopped as he saw a smile come over Jessica's face. "What is it?"

"I'm delighted to see our minds were working in exactly the same way. Grace said: 'We suddenly realized Father was topside.' That seems to me very odd. Why *suddenly?* They obviously weren't asleep. They knew their father wasn't with them. Where did they think he was? Below decks in another part of the yacht? But if so, how did they suddenly realize he was topside? They didn't hear him calling. They would have said if they had. Anyway, I doubt you *could* hear anybody calling in that storm. Yet suddenly they realize he's topside and all rush up on deck. Is that what you were going to say, Sheriff?"

"Well, I wouldn't have said it as well as that, Mrs. Fletcher. But, yes, it did strike me as kinda suspicious."

"Mind you," Jessica told him, "I'm not saying we definitely have a murder here. It *may* have been an accident, though not such a simple one as they described. Perhaps one of the girls was to blame in some way, and they're all covering up for her. It might even have been suicide, and they just don't want it to get out. All I am sure about is that they are covering something up."

Tupper dropped his cigarette butt onto the floor and ground it to dust with his heavy shoe. He gave a sigh. "Well, I sure don't have grounds for charging any of them with a crime, so I don't see much chance of getting at the truth. Seems I'll have to let it ride."

"Well," Jessica said, "certainly the only way the facts will come out is if one of the girls decides to tell the truth. If you could get each one alone, in turn, and just chat with them till they're relaxed—draw them out, simply let them talk . . ."

He shook his head. "They wouldn't talk to me—not in that way. They'd be on their guard the whole time. Whereas, you, Mrs. Fletcher . . ."

"Oh dear," Jessica said. "I really can't afford the time, Sheriff. I have a book to write."

"You're interested, though, aren't you? You said as much. And you could do it. They would talk to you."

"I believe so, yes. At least, two of them would."

"Which two?"

"The oldest and the youngest: Maggie and Nan. Maggie, I think, has a lot bottled up inside and is probably aching to let it out to a sympathetic stranger. Nan—well, Nan interests me. Did you notice how little she spoke? Hardly said a word—just sat and listened. Of course, she is the youngest by quite a few years. But I wouldn't think she's normally the shy type. I got the impression she was definitely uneasy about what was going on."

"So will you do it, Mrs. Fletcher? Talk to them?"

Jessica stood up. "Well, I'll do the best I can, but don't be too disappointed if the result's inconclusive. And will you do something for me?"

"What's that?"

"Can you have some discreet inquiries made about the girls? I'd like to know a little about their backgrounds before I start on them."

"Oh, sure, that'll be no trouble."

"How long do we have, Sheriff?"

He pursed his lips. "Well, after the body comes ashore there'll have to be an autopsy, then an inquest. Don't rely on more than three days. Couldn't keep 'em here after that—not without concrete evidence of foul play."

"Hm, not very long, is it? Still, we might get somewhere."

"Let's hope so. Oh, and Mrs. Fletcher—officially it's an accident, for the time being. Okay?"

"Of course."

# Chapter Three

JESSICA walked home, deep in thought. The sheriff had set her quite a challenge. Now, how would she approach it? That was the problem. If the girls weren't to suspect what she was up to, she would have to be very subtle. Even then, if they stuck firmly to their guns, there would be virtually nothing she could do about it. Oh dear, how very much less satisfactory than fiction real life was. If this had been a story, one of these girls would have made some small but vital slip, which nobody noticed but the detective, but which gave the whole thing away.

Now, hang on.

Her hand on her front gate, Jessica stopped. There *had* been something. Some small point in the girls' story—apart from the bit about suddenly realizing their father was topside—*had* struck her as odd, not ringing true. The trouble was she had not grasped it at the time and now it was gone. She concentrated hard. Oh, what was it? No—it wasn't any good: the thing wouldn't come.

She went up the path and let herself into the house. She was just taking off her coat when the phone rang. She turned toward where it normally stood, stopped short and remembered she'd moved it to the window ledge. She went across and lifted the receiver.

"Hello?"

"Jessica? This is Letitia."

"Oh, hello, Letitia," Jessica said to Cabot Cove's telephone operator. "What can I do for you?"

"I have the cost of that call."

Jessica frowned. "Which call was that?"

"The long distance from your number a little while back. A man placed it. To Paris."

Jessica's eyebrows shot upward. "Paris!"

"Yes; say, it was all right, wasn't it?"

Jessica gulped. "Oh yes, quite all right, Letitia. At least—well you'd better tell me how much it was."

She listened, then said: "Oh well, that's not too bad, I suppose. Thank you, Letitia."

She hung up, stood quite still for a moment, then walked quickly to her kitchen, opened the rear door and went outside. There was a gleam in her eye.

She looked around. But there was no sign of Ralph. Then she heard a familiar slow and lazy creaking sound. She moved purposefully toward it.

At the far end of the garden, a hammock was slung between two trees. A bulge in the underside indicated that it was now occupied. Jessica walked grimly across and looked down at Ralph. There was a handkerchief over his face and he was breathing gently and easily.

Jessica drew a deep breath, casting around in her mind for some gem of sarcasm, when, without removing the handkerchief, he spoke quietly.

"How's the latest murder?"

Jessica was a little taken aback.

"What did you say?"

"Murder. The guy on the boat."

"What do you know about that?"

"Couple of kids went past, gassing about it. Seems they were down at the harbor. I asked them what was going on. They told me you were there."

"Oh, I see. Well, it wasn't a murder at all. The man was swept overboard by the storm. An unfortunate accident."

He removed the handkerchief and gazed up at her. "An accident? Really? Someone local?"

"No, a stranger. Now, suppose you stifle that morbid curiosity. I thought we had work on the agenda."

He sat up and swung his legs to the ground. "I finished the weeding. Not much else I could do without supplies: paint, lumber . . ."

"You didn't by any chance call France for an estimate?"

He stared. "What?"

"The local operator just phoned with charges on your Paris call. Nine dollars and eighty-seven cents."

To her surprise, he gave an amused chuckle. "That was Paris, *Kentucky.* I've got a friend down there who's a horse breeder. Don't worry, I'll make good on those charges."

"Is that before or after the horse comes in?" Jessica asked dryly.

"Believe me, it's nothing like that. Now, about this work, can we go indoors for a moment?"

"Of course."

She led him into the house and through to the living room. Ralph

crossed to the window casement. "I was having a look at this before you
went out." He pointed. "See there: wood's starting to rot. You need new
putty and paint, or come winter you'll be having bad drafts."

"I've already got them. Can you fix it?"

He nodded. "I'll just need about ten or fifteen dollars for supplies."

"Seems a bargain," Jessica said.

She went to her purse and started fishing in it for the money. While she
was doing so, Ralph drifted across to the nearby table, on which was a
rack of pipes and a tobacco humidor. He took a pipe from the rack and
examined it. Jessica came toward him, with a twenty-dollar bill in her
hand.

"Fine-looking meerschaum," he said. "Your husband's?"

"Yes."

"He had good taste."

"Do you smoke a pipe?"

"Have for over forty years."

"Then take that one, please."

He looked suddenly embarrassed. "Oh no, I couldn't."

"Yes, I'd like you to. Better you smoke it than let it sit there, gathering
dust."

She blinked two or three times rapidly, then said, "Here," handed him
the twenty-dollar bill, turned and rather hurriedly left the room.

Ralph looked after her sympathetically. Then he slipped the pipe into
his pocket, went back to the window and started examining the frame
more closely.

For the next several hours Jessica worked on her book in the kitchen.
She found it somewhat difficult to concentrate, but managed to make
some progress.

It was about four P.M. (and she'd just got to the stage where the
inspector had discovered the bloodstained bayonet in the ex-GI's garage,
where Maude had planted it) when there was a knock on the door.
Jessica went to answer it. It was Tupper.

"Oh, hello, Sheriff. Come in."

She showed him into the living room, which smelt noticeably of lin-
seed. Ralph had completed the puttying stage of his job and was now
outside fitting the new washer on the pump.

"Sit down, Sheriff. Any developments?"

He lowered himself gratefully into a big easy chair.

"Not a lot. Brian Shelby's arrived—in very grand style: private heli-
copter, no less."

"Brian Shelby? Oh, that would be Lisa's husband. What's he like?"

"Very much the smart young executive. Self-assured. Rather pushy. Better manners than his wife, I might add."

"He needs them," Jessica murmured.

"He's executive vice-president with the old man's company. And has his eyes firmly fixed on the top job, if you ask me."

"As somebody once wrote, 'The Son-in-Law Also Rises.' "

Tupper grinned. "Mr. Shelby's *very* anxious for an immediate inquest. 'So that the reins of leadership can pass quickly to his successors,' as he put it."

"An original phrase. What did you tell him?"

"No inquest without a body. He's not at all happy. Seems to think the company could be thrown into financial chaos if there's any delay in certifying the old man dead. I told him it must be in a pretty parlous state if a few days' delay can do that to it. He didn't like that, either."

"Sheriff, what happens if the body doesn't turn up in a day or two?"

"Meet that problem when we come to it. Reckon it will, though. They always do."

Tupper reached into his pocket and took out a notebook. "Anyway, why I really called was to give you what I've dug up about those girls."

"My, that's quick."

"Unofficial channels. I phoned a pal of mine on the L.A.P.D. He put me in touch with a gossip writer on one of the local papers. The Earls are a pretty well-known family there, and in return for a few harmless scraps of inside information I was able to give him about the old man's death, this journalist handed me quite a bit of data about the daughters."

"I'm all ears," Jessica said.

"Well, Stephen Earl's wife died nearly twenty years ago. Maggie was seventeen then, and Nan, the youngest, only about four. Stephen never remarried, so Maggie became more of a mother than a sister to the others —as well as housekeeper and hostess for her father. She's lived at home always."

Jessica nodded thoughtfully. "And as a result she missed out on marriage *and* a career. Does she resent that, I wonder?"

He shrugged. "No evidence of that. Or that her father forced her into it. She's very much the peacemaker. Relations between the other girls, particularly Grace and Lisa, have been kinda prickly. But they all look up to Maggie. Course there's an age gap of about six years between her and the next eldest, Grace."

"What do you have on Grace?"

"Well, she's the brains of the outfit. Got a Ph.D."

"Yes, and I should imagine she has always been used to hearing people say how brainy she is—so she feels she has to live up to the image. She could certainly make herself much more attractive, if she put her mind to it. But she prefers the intellectual look. What about her husband?"

"Walked out on her four years ago. She didn't seem to mind too much. Threw herself into the business."

"She works for the company?"

He nodded. "And is Brian Shelby's chief rival for the number-one job now."

"I see. I imagine she'd be a very efficient businesswoman. Though a bit intimidating, perhaps, to be really popular. That explains the prickliness of her relations with Lisa, no doubt."

"I guess so."

"Lisa doesn't work for the company, I assume?"

"No; Lisa doesn't like work. She did try—unsuccessfully—to make it as an actress. Had the looks, but not the talent. Anyway, she enjoys going to parties and sitting around pools too much. However, though she doesn't want to be boss of Mark of the Earl, she does want to be the boss's wife. She picked out Brian Shelby when he held a very junior position in the firm, married him—against her father's wishes at first, though he came around at last—and has pushed him nearly all the way to the top. Having met him, I figure he'd have made it himself eventually. He's a tough cookie."

Jessica smiled at him. "You know, Sheriff, I'm seeing quite a new side to you. You should have been a writer yourself. You're making it all so vivid."

"Well, most of this is secondhand of course." He consulted his note-book.

"That just leaves Nan."

"Ah, yes. I'm very interested in Nan."

"Apple of her father's eye."

"I'm not surprised."

"Nicest of the four, according to my informant. Was engaged a couple of years back to some guy called Jones. It was broken off. She left the West Coast then, went to New York. Been working as a fashion designer. Has great promise apparently, but hasn't made her name yet. Could have used her father's name and money to help her on her way, but chose not to."

"Good for Nan."

Tupper flipped his notebook closed and leaned back. "That's about it."

"And much more than I expected, Sheriff."

"Given you any ideas?"

"Oh, lots. Presented with a scenario like that, all sorts of possibilities spring to my mind."

"Such as?"

She shook her head. "Not yet. My ideas are just guesses, really—and they contradict each other. I'd only mislead you if I told you them at this stage."

"Er, when do you think . . . ?" He trailed off.

"I hope you're not expecting miracles, Sheriff. I'm no Sherlock Holmes. All I promised to do was talk to the girls. I may get nothing out of them at all. You must face the fact that the truth might never come out. And your best chance of reaching it may well be the autopsy results —once the body is found."

"Yeah, I suppose you're right. But you will talk to 'em?"

"Oh, certainly. In fact, I'm looking forward to it. Just don't build on it getting you anyplace, that's all."


At a little after seven that evening Ralph pushed his empty plate away from him and gave a sigh of satisfaction.

"That sure was a fine meal, ma'am. I'll bet one thing: your husband didn't die of malnutrition." He stopped, then added hastily: "Oh, I mean no disrespect."

"I'm sure you didn't," Jessica said.

"I lost my wife many years ago. It hit me hard. For a long time I couldn't talk about her. Couldn't even say her name. Then it came to me: by recognizing what she had been, what she had meant to me—well, that was a way of keeping her alive in my heart."

"That's a sweet thought, Ralph. I'll remember it."

"Do you have children?"

"No, Frank and I were never blessed that way."

"Blessed? Well, I'm not sure kids are always a blessing."

Abruptly, he got to his feet, pushing back his chair. "Well, with your permission, I'll excuse myself."

"You're not leaving?"

"Yes. Got a few things that need doing. I might be back later this evening. It all depends."

"Well, I'm going out myself shortly, to see some ladies. I won't be late, but I'd better give you my spare key."

"No, don't bother. I'm liable to be late. Lock up normally, and if I do return, I'll sleep out in the hammock."

"Oh, don't be silly," Jessica told him. "I have a perfectly good guest bedroom."

"No, ma'am, thanks all the same. Folks have a way of talking in a little town like this."

He moved to the door. "Well, thanks again for the supper. Good night."

"Good night, Ralph."

He went out, closing the door behind him.

Jessica stared after him thoughtfully for a second or two, then looked at the clock, got to her feet and started clearing the table. She carried the dishes to the kitchen and washed them. Five minutes later, the job completed, she pulled out the sink plug and stood drying her hands, thinking deeply. As her thoughts went around, her eyes were fixed unseeingly on the water in the sink as it disappeared down the drain. As the water level descended, it suddenly gave a loud gurgle, which jerked Jessica's thoughts back to the present. For a second or two, however, she remained staring at the little whirlpool of water eddying around the outlet pipe.

Suddenly her eyes widened. She stood quite still, doing some rapid mental calculations, and trying to dredge from the back of her mind various scraps of information—knowledge gleaned from many years living on this part of the coast; from the overheard talk of fishermen and yachtsmen; from half-forgotten old schoolbooks; and from the weather reports she had heard early that same morning on the radio, and, later still, something said by one of the daughters of Stephen Earl.

She felt a fluttering of excitement within her. Maybe she was entirely wrong. But this wasn't something she could just let go by unchecked.

And the first thing she needed was some professional advice.

It was eight o'clock when Ethan Cragg, who'd been doing some routine maintenance on the engine of *The Pilgrim* and was taking a breather in the cabin, heard his name being called urgently. He got to his feet, went to the cabin door and peered out to see Jessica walking up the gangplank. She looked pleased when she saw him.

"Oh good. You're here."

He went out on deck. "Jess! This is an unusual time for you to be calling."

"This isn't a social call, Ethan. I need your help and advice."

His eyebrows went up. "Suppose there has to be a first time for everything. Come on below."

He led the way back to the brightly lit, spotless little cabin.

"What can I do for you, Jess?"

"Get out your charts and weather logs or whatever you call them, and your compasses and rulers, and if necessary call up the Coast Guard and the weather station. And then tell me the course of that hurricane—and its precise location at midnight last night."

Twenty minutes later Ethan and Jessica looked up and gazed at each other across the top of the paper-strewn table.

"I'm right, aren't I?" Jessica said slowly.

"Got to hand it to you, Jess, you are. Don't see any alternative. Can't understand why I didn't spot it myself."

"I think you did, Ethan. First thing this morning when you met up with the Earl yacht. Something subconsciously struck you as wrong. Strange, you said. Perhaps you didn't actually put your finger on what it was. But I bet at the back of your mind that was it."

"Then I let myself be sweet-talked out of it."

"Don't blame yourself. That story they told was very plausible."

"And what do we do now?"

"Go to see Amos Tupper and tell him just what we've worked out."

# Chapter Four

THE sheriff's car drew up outside the Hill House Hotel. Amos Tupper got out and opened the rear door for Jessica and Ethan. They all went inside the hotel. The lobby was empty. Tupper crossed to the desk and rang the bell and a moment later the clerk emerged from his office.

He gave an amiable nod to all three. "Evening, Sheriff. Mrs. Fletcher, Ethan."

Tupper said, "Evening, Harry. I want to see the Earl ladies. They in?"

"I think some of them are in the lounge. They were ten minutes ago."

"Thanks."

He beckoned to Jessica and Ethan and made his way across the lobby to a door opposite. He opened it and went into the lounge, Jessica and Ethan following.

The four people in the room abruptly turned their heads toward the door, and two of them—Maggie Earl and a tall, slim, good-looking young man, who Jessica realized must be Brian Shelby—got to their feet.

Maggie said anxiously: "What is it, Sheriff? Do you have news?"

"Not exactly news, ma'am."

He looked around the room. There was nobody else present.

"Where's Miss Nan?" he asked.

"We've no idea," Maggie said.

"Oh, is that so?"

There was an awkward silence for a few seconds, then Lisa spoke, her voice sharp and high-pitched. "Sheriff, I'm sure you haven't come to make small talk. For heaven's sake, tell us why you're here. Presumably our father's body hasn't turned up yet."

"No, Mrs. Shelby, and I'm not sure it's going to in a hurry."

Brian Shelby frowned. "Just what do you mean by that, Sheriff? If this is a ruse to postpone the inquest still further—"

"I'm pulling no ruses, Mr. Shelby."

Grace said: "You told us that our father's body would wash ashore in a day or two."

Tupper nodded. "I did. Because I believed your father had gone overboard about three miles out, during a heavy storm. My experience has been that people lost in those conditions do get washed ashore somewhere along this stretch of coast within twenty-four hours or so. But—"

Ethan interrupted. "What he's saying is that your story about the storm's a crock of chowder. And we can prove it."

Tupper turned to him in exasperation. "Zip it up, Ethan. I'm running this investigation."

"Then get on with it, man. It's almost next week."

"A crock of chowder," Maggie said dazedly. "What does he mean?"

"It's a colloquial metaphor, quite common in this part of the world," Jessica said. "Meaning—frankly—that it's nonsense."

Shelby stared at Tupper. "Look, what's going on? Who are these people?"

Before the sheriff could reply Lisa broke in. "I told you about them, darling: Captain Cragg—he towed us in—and Mrs. Fletcher."

"The self-styled town snoop," Grace drawled.

Jessica smiled sweetly at Shelby. "How do you do, Mr. Shelby?"

"Oh, yes, you're the mystery writer. How do you do?" He spoke coldly. He looked at Tupper again. "I understand you've called in Mrs. Fletcher to help you, Sheriff. Seems rather irregular to me, but no doubt you can consult with whom you like. However, I don't see why my wife and her sisters should be cross-examined by people with absolutely no official status."

Tupper said: "Mrs. Fletcher's not here to cross-examine anybody. I'll do any questioning that's necessary. She and Captain Cragg have come up with evidence that, to say the least, casts doubt on the story these young ladies told. I want Mrs. Fletcher to put it to them herself." He gave a nod to Jessica.

She stepped forward and addressed Maggie. "Miss Earl, you said it was shortly after midnight when your father was swept overboard."

"That's right."

"And at that time you were three miles due east of Monhegan Island."

"Yes."

"Not so, I'm afraid," Jessica said calmly. She looked around the group. "At that time and at that place your yacht would have been in the eye of the hurricane—the very center. And in the eye of a hurricane there is no wind or rain. The sea would have been dead calm."

There was a hush. Grace bit her lip, then glanced quickly at Maggie, who suddenly went pale. Lisa opened her mouth to speak, then obviously thought better of it.

It was left to her husband to break the silence. "This is absurd!" he said angrily. "Obviously they had their position wrong."

"They were very exact about it—this morning and now," Ethan said.

"But we're amateur sailors," Lisa said. "We don't know much about navigation or plotting a position. We tried to work it out, but obviously we got it wrong."

"A hurricane moves," Grace exclaimed. "The eye doesn't stay in one place. I just know what I saw and heard. My father was swept overboard in the teeth of a gale, and—"

"No!"

The voice barked out and Grace stopped dead. It was Maggie who'd spoken. Her face was still pale. She walked forward to confront Jessica.

"I congratulate you, Mrs. Fletcher," she said quietly. "That was a smart piece of work. I might have known the story wouldn't wash. You mustn't blame my sisters for lying. They're only doing it to protect me."

"Maggie! No!" Lisa's voice came in a kind of wail.

Grace said, hoarsely: "Don't be a fool!"

But Maggie ignored them. She turned to Tupper. "Mrs. Fletcher is right, Sheriff. My father's death was no accident. I killed him."

Grace looked away and slumped back in her chair. Brian turned to Lisa, who took his hand. Tupper looked at Maggie, but for a few seconds didn't speak.

"Aren't you going to read me my rights, Sheriff?" she asked.

He reached into his pocket, took out a card and began to do so.

Ethan spoke quietly in Jessica's ear. "Tell me, Jess, why do I feel like a dirty rat?"

"I don't know, Ethan," she said softly. "Same reason I do, I expect."

Tupper put away his card. "Do you want to tell us just what happened, Miss Earl?"

"Be careful, Maggie," Brian Shelby said sharply.

"It's all right, Brian. I know what I'm doing. Mind if I sit down, Sheriff?"

"Go right ahead."

Maggie resumed her seat. "Anyone got a cigarette?"

Tupper took a pack from his pocket and held it out to her. She extracted a cigarette and he lit it. She inhaled deeply, then spoke slowly.

"Dad didn't die last night. It happened the night before. He and I were on deck alone. He was drunk. As usual, we started fighting. I forget what it was about this time—money, my sisters—it doesn't matter. He could pick a fight over anything. He got madder and madder. Suddenly he started toward me, waving his arms, threatening me. I was really scared.

I keep a gun in my purse for protection. I took it out and pointed it at him. He just laughed and came on. I vaguely remember firing—once, twice. He staggered back, then went over the side. That's it."

Lisa spoke quietly. "We heard the shots from below. By the time we came on deck, Father was gone. His pipe was lying there. Still warm. Maggie was holding the gun, staring straight ahead of her, as if in a trance. I don't think she knew what had happened."

Grace stood up. "Sheriff, you can't *blame* her!" she spoke vehemently. "After everything she'd put up with all these years—taking orders, sacrificing whatever life she could have made for herself . . . And for what?"

Lisa said: "It was self-defense. I'm sure of it."

"Maybe so, ma'am," Tupper said. "That's not for me to say." He looked at Maggie. "I'm sorry, Miss Earl, I'm going to have to take you in."

Maggie nodded and stood up. She seemed quite composed. "Of course. May I fetch my coat and purse from my bedroom?"

"Sure, I'll have to come with you, though."

"I'll come, too," Grace said.

"Now, don't worry, Maggie," Shelby said consolingly. "You'll have the best legal representation available."

Grace threw him a vicious look. "She doesn't need *you* to tell her that, Brian."

Shelby shrugged and turned back to his wife. Maggie and Grace left the room, followed closely by Tupper.

Jessica and Ethan stood somewhat awkwardly for a few seconds before he touched her shoulder. "Let's go, Jess."

They walked through the lobby and out into the night. Ethan gave a sigh as they strolled away from the hotel.

"Who'd have thought it? Nice quiet young woman like that. Real lady. Finding herself in that sort of situation—having to shoot her own daddy."

"Oh, Ethan," Jessica said. "Surely you don't think what we've just heard is what really happened, do you?"

# Chapter Five

ETHAN Cragg stopped dead in his tracks.

"What in tarnation do you mean, Jess?"

"Simply that we still haven't heard the truth."

He stared at her in bewilderment. "But—what do you reckon did happen, then?"

"I've no idea. Yet. But don't tell me that a levelheaded girl like Maggie suddenly lost her head and started blasting away at her father with a pistol because he got drunk and shouted at her. And all over something they've apparently argued about dozens of times before—so routine that she can't even remember what it was."

"You mean she's covering for one of the others?"

"I don't know. I'll only say that that is the sort of thing one might well expect Maggie to do. Actually, though, my mind is working in a somewhat different direction. I feel that the mystery here is a much deeper one than simply an eldest daughter taking the blame for a younger. I am virtually certain, though, that Maggie Earl did *not* kill her father—whatever she might claim."

Ethan regarded her thoughtfully for a few seconds before speaking. "Jess, you sure you're not—well, letting your professional interest in the subject get the better of you? I mean, making a straightforward family tragedy into a bigger mystery than it actually is?"

"Making it more like a detective story, you mean?"

"Well, yeah."

"An astute observation, Ethan, but I don't think so. You see, I don't like being mixed up in real murders. You don't know how hard I tried to avoid involvement in that case in New York. I only did so to clear my nephew of a murder charge. This morning I was curious to know what was going on because I thought it might give me some ideas for a book. But I only got involved in the investigation because Amos Tupper asked me to. And believe me, I'd be very happy if I could go home now, forget the whole thing and get on with plotting my make-believe crime."

"Well, why can't you?"

"A good question. Maggie Earl is presumably satisfied with the situation. So are her sisters. So's the sheriff. I suppose with me it's a matter of having too much respect for the truth to let a falsehood be accepted as fact. That and a dislike of injustice—even if it's people who have deliberately brought that injustice on themselves."

"But, my dear, can you be *quite* sure injustice *is* being done?"

"I believe so, Ethan, yes."

"Just because of your reading of that young woman's character?"

Jessica shook her head. "No; you see, I know certain things that nobody else knows."

"What sort of things?"

"I'll tell you later. But if I didn't know them I might reluctantly have accepted Maggie's account of her father's death. Which is why, incidentally, I ought not to criticize you or blame Tupper for believing it. I had additional data."

He gave a sigh. "Well, what are you going to do now?"

"I'm going to see Mary Parsons."

"What for?"

"I want to look up something in the library."

"Library'll be closed now."

"I know. That's why I'm going to Mary's house. I want her to lend me the keys for half an hour."

"She's not supposed to let unauthorized people wander around the library on their own at night."

"I'm not exactly unauthorized. I have helped Mary out there once or twice when an assistant's been sick. Besides, I *am,* in the words of our local paper, 'the famed Cabot Cove author.' As a matter of fact Mary has loaned me the keys before when I've urgently needed to look up things for my writing. I think she will again. You can come with me, if you like. I'll be happy to have your company."

He looked at his watch. "Oh, might as well, I suppose. I've nothing else to do."

"We'll make a detective of you yet," she said.

"Me? Not on your life. Huntin' down bass is good enough for me."


Twenty minutes later Jessica unlocked the door of the Cabot Cove Public Library and pushed it open. She groped for the switches and the building flooded with light. Ethan, who, in spite of having official approval, couldn't help feeling like a trespasser, followed her in.

Jessica crossed to the card catalogue and started searching through it.

Ethan stood waiting for her, looking around as if he expected to see the ghosts of long-dead authors peering at him from the corners. Indeed, at night the library was an eerie place, the long silent shelves packed with volumes seeming somehow to be reproachful that they weren't being read.

Jessica sighed. "Ah."

"Found the book you want?"

"Found its number, know it's still here and where to find it. This way."

She marched off down the center aisle, her eyes reading the categories and code numbers written on the ends of the shelves. Resisting an irrational impulse to walk on tiptoe, Ethan tramped after her.

She stopped. "Here we are."

Ethan followed her pointing finger, and read the words: BIOGRAPHY & AUTOBIOGRAPHY. Jessica darted up to the shelves and started running her fingers along the rows of books, muttering to herself as she did so: "Boswell's *Life of Johnson* . . . farther back . . . Gibbon's *Decline and Fall of the Roman Empire!* What's *that* doing in this section? Careless, Mary . . . Fox's *Book of Martyrs* . . . Evans . . . Edwards . . . Eureka!"

For a moment Ethan wondered what Eureka had written. He saw Jessica snatch a book from the shelf in triumph.

"What is that?" he asked.

She held it out for him to see. He read aloud: *"Greasepaint Millionaire.* Oh, Stephen Earl's story."

"Exactly. Now, keep your fingers crossed, Ethan."

She opened the book and glanced at the dust jacket. Then she gave a sigh of relief.

"Found what you wanted?"

"Yes, I have."

"Great. Can we go now? This place gives me the jitters."

"Oh, don't be silly, Ethan." She was peering at the book. "There's not enough light here. Come to the desk."

She hurried back to the librarian's desk, near the door. She switched on the reading lamp, placed *Greasepaint Millionaire* on the desk, burrowed in her purse and took out a small magnifying glass.

"Oh, we're really getting down to the Sherlock Holmes stuff now," Ethan said.

"Shh!"

Jessica sat down, opened the book under the lamp and peered at it through the glass. Ethan saw that what she was studying was the portrait-type photograph on the jacket flap.

"That Earl?" he asked.

For a moment Jessica didn't reply. She closed the book, sat back and looked at him.

"That is indeed Stephen Earl," she said, "as he was twenty years ago."

"So, what does it prove?"

"That Maggie Earl did not shoot her father two nights ago. I know it now."

"Just from looking at that photo?"

"Yes; because, you see, this man"—she tapped the book in front of her —"Stephen Earl, had supper at my house less than two hours ago."

Jessica opened the front door of her house and went in. She turned on the lights, calling as she did so, "Ralph!"

There was no reply. She went hastily through the ground-floor rooms, then hurried upstairs. When she came back down half a minute later, Ethan had ensconced himself in his usual chair in the living room.

"Excuse me not waiting to be invited," he said.

Jessica said absently: "Oh, don't be silly, Ethan."

"You going to tell me what this is all about?"

She didn't answer, and he had to repeat the question. Then she came to herself and smiled. "Sorry, Ethan. yes, I am."

She sat down opposite him. "Actually," she said, "I don't know that I *can* explain. But I'll tell you what happened. This morning I found a man in my garden. He said he was a hobo, and was looking for odd jobs . . ."

Five minutes later Jessica had concluded her account.

"And that's all I know." She sat back and looked at Ethan, awaiting reactions.

Ethan rubbed his chin. "You're quite certain this guy Ralph is the man in the photo in Earl's book?"

"Yes, I am . . . Oh, he's changed in twenty years, of course, but not that much. No—Ralph *is* Stephen Earl."

"What first put you on to the idea that he might be?"

"I think it was when Lisa mentioned her father's pipe lying on the deck. It suddenly occurred to me what a strange coincidence we had here. An elderly, wealthy man; a pipe smoker; a widower for many years; and a father of troublesome children disappears off a yacht. Within a few hours an elderly man, wearing expensive clothes; a pipe smoker; a widower for many years; and a man who thinks children aren't always a blessing appears from nowhere in the nearest coastal town and tells a lot of lies about himself. It just seemed too coincidental to be true. I could then have asked the sheriff, or one of the girls, to let me see an up-to-date photo of Earl. But just going down to the library and looking at that picture in the book was quicker. And meant I didn't have to show my hand."

"Well, it was sure smart thinking, Jess. Going to call Amos now?"

She shook her head. "Not yet."

"Why not?"

"For one thing I don't have any proof."

"Easy enough for the cops to get proof. Let 'em dust this house and Earl's boat for fingerprints. If they find the same prints in both places, that's proof enough."

"That's true, of course. All right, say that was an excuse on my part. Say I just don't want to go to the sheriff until I have a bit more to give him. For instance, until I know *why* Earl went through all of that elaborate charade."

Ethan shrugged. "That's obvious: he wanted to disappear. Maybe his company's on the rocks and he knew he'd soon be facing fraud charges or something. Perhaps he was being blackmailed. So he decided to fake his own death. His girls agreed to help him—by saying he'd gone overboard in the storm."

"Yes," Jessica said, "but why hang around in Cabot Cove afterward? He must have known there was a chance somebody would recognize him. You expect him not to come ashore at all, but just to have another boat standing by out there, and have it take him straight to South America, or somewhere."

Ethan considered. "Well, that might have been the original scheme, but then the hurricane put the kibosh on his plans. He couldn't rendezvous with the other boat, and so he had to hang around till whoever was helping him could make other plans. Probably when he went out this evening he was going to call them and see what had been arranged."

Jessica nodded judicially. "Yes, that does make very good sense, Ethan, I agree."

"But?"

"Well, for one thing, Ralph's manner wasn't that of a man who was disappearing for good and who was scared he might be recognized. He was much too relaxed."

"An act. Remember he started out as an actor."

"Yes, but can you imagine a man virtually on the run—in the sense that he must get away and nobody must know he's still alive, a man discarding his old life, everything he holds dear . . . Can you imagine his spending the day pottering about here, weeding my nasturtium beds, fixing a washer on my water pump and puttying my window frames—all as happy as a sandboy?"

Ethan looked doubtful. "Well, must admit it doesn't seem likely."

"There's something else, too," she said. "When I came back from the harbor, he asked me about the drowning. He'd heard some kids talking about it and he referred to it as the *murder.*"

"Well, probably that's what the kids called it."

"Yes, but when I told him—as the sheriff asked me to—that it was only an accident, he seemed definitely surprised."

"You mean he was expecting the death to be put down as homicide?"

"Yes. Yet surely it couldn't have been part of the plan that Maggie would be charged with his murder? That a man should fake his own drowning, that his daughter, or daughters, should help him—that I can understand. However, you and I expose that story as phony—and in order to save the situation, Maggie impulsively changes the story, says she killed her father. In that way, she thinks, he'll still be officially certified as dead. All that, too, I can believe—even though, unless Maggie is prepared to serve a long jail term for something she didn't do, she must realize she'll have to tell the truth eventually. But surely Earl can't let her go through with it? I mean, however bad their relationship, he couldn't be *that* heartless. Then again, what about her sisters? Will *they* let it happen?"

"You mean, to save her from a jail term Earl's going to have to come back from the dead?"

"Exactly. At least get in touch with the authorities, prove he's still alive—even if he doesn't actually show up."

"Perhaps that was the idea all along."

"How do you mean, Ethan?"

He frowned, struggling to find words to express his meaning. "Well, maybe the plan was for the girls to cover for him just long enough for him to get away. They'd try and put across the story he'd died accidentally. As a result of the storm. If that didn't work Maggie'd confess to killing him—just so as no one'd start hunting for him. Then in a few days, or weeks, he'd emerge somewhere in South America, produce proof of his identity to the authorities down there, they'd contact the U.S. cops —and Maggie'd be off the hook."

Jessica was silent for a moment. She shook her head slowly. "If Earl only wanted a chance of getting away to South America, why not just *go?* The only point in staging a phony death would be so that he could come back later under a different name and start a new life. If it's known he's still alive, he can't do that."

"What exactly are you saying, Jess?"

"There's more to this than meets the eye. As it stands now, there's no sense to any of it."

"Well, what are you going to do?"

Jessica sighed. "I don't know, Ethan. I don't know what I can do. I don't know why I should do anything. It's . . ."

"I know. It's nothing to do with you. All the same, you are going to do something, aren't you?"

Jessica got to her feet. "I suppose so. But not tonight. I want to sleep on it. Now I'm going to make some coffee and we're going to sit here and drink it and talk about anything but murder. Even fishing."

Jessica was a long time getting to sleep that night. As a result, unusually for her, she slept late the next morning. However, by the time she'd finished breakfast, she had come to at least one decision: She had, after all, to tell the sheriff that Stephen Earl was alive. It wasn't fair to withhold the information.

She stood up and went toward the telephone. Before she reached it, though, it rang. Jessica lifted the receiver.

"Hello?"

She heard the sheriff's voice. "Mrs. Fletcher? Amos Tupper. Thought you'd like to know: Stephen Earl's body was found on the beach a mile along the coast early this morning. He'd been shot."

Jessica didn't speak. Her face was blank. "Mrs. Fletcher? Did you hear me?"

At last she spoke. Her voice was flat and unemotional. "Thank you for letting me know, Sheriff. Now I must think. I'll be in touch. Goodbye."

She hung up.

# Chapter Six

IT was nearly noon that morning when Jessica was shown into Sheriff Tupper's office by a deputy. Tupper seated her in the most comfortable chair, offered her coffee, which she refused, then sat down himself behind his big paper-strewn desk and lit a cigarette. He smiled.

"Well, Mrs. Fletcher—done your thinking?"

"Till my head's buzzing."

"I don't really see what's worrying you about the case now. It all seems straightforward."

"The body has been officially identified as Stephen Earl's?"

He nodded. "Yep. By Lisa and Nan—in Elias Cobb's mortuary just half an hour ago."

"And tell me: was Stephen Earl a man in his late sixties, gray-haired? And was he wearing an old red-and-black lumberjack's shirt and faded jeans?"

He stared. "You been talking to the girls?"

"No."

"Cobb, then? Or one of my deputies?"

She shook her head. "I know nothing except what you've told me."

"Then how on earth did you know what he was wearing?"

"I'll tell you," said Jessica.

And she did.

By the time Jessica had finished her story, Tupper was sitting back staring at her with an expression of utter incredulity on his face.

At last he spoke. "Mrs. Fletcher, you telling me that Stephen Earl was alive and well at seven o'clock last night?"

"I am."

"But how could he have been? Maggie shot him the previous night. The girls all testified to that."

"The girls are lying."

"But *why*, for heaven's sake?"

"That's what I've been trying to work out all night. And so far I don't have an answer."

Tupper got to his feet and walked aimlessly about the room. "I'm sorry, Mrs. Fletcher, I just can't buy it. It must be a coincidence. This guy Ralph must've just happened to be wearing the same sort of gear as Earl. After all, there're plenty of lumberjack's shirts and jeans around."

"Well, there's an easy way to settle it: let me look at Earl's body."

"You wouldn't mind?"

"I've seen bodies before."

"Okay, if you're sure. Let's go." He opened the door.

They went to Tupper's car and started the short drive to the mortuary. As they were going along the main street, however, Jessica said suddenly: "Oh, stop, Sheriff, please."

He drew the car to a halt and Jessica pointed. He followed her finger. Across the street was a bar. Standing rather aimlessly on the sidewalk outside, obviously just having emerged from it, were Lisa and Nan.

"Could you wait for me a moment?" Jessica asked. "I must have a word with them."

Without waiting for an answer, she jumped from the car and hurried across the street.

The two girls glanced up as Jessica approached them. Nan managed to dredge up a smile. Lisa was less welcoming. "Oh, Mrs. Fletcher," she said coldly.

"My dears," Jessica said. "The sheriff's told me everything. I'm so very sorry."

"Well, it's a relief in a way," Nan said. "The shock came the other night. I was dreading what we had to do this morning. I'm just glad it's over."

"Oh, what a shame you had to do it," Jessica said sympathetically. "Surely, somebody else—"

Nan interrupted her. "No! I wanted to. I mean, I *was* dreading it. But I did want to see him once more. It was pretty horrible all the same. And only having heard about Maggie's arrest early this morning made it a sort of double shock."

"Of course, it must have been terrible." Jessica looked at the other girl. "For both of you," she added.

For the first time since Jessica had met her, Lisa's face softened.

"Yes, it was," she said. "In fact, we both felt we needed a bracer, afterward. We're not in the habit of frequenting bars at this time of day."

"I think you were very wise."

Jessica was about to say more when a sudden screech of brakes made them all turn toward the road. A stylish if somewhat flashy red convertible had just drawn up alongside them, and the driver was grinning with delight.

He gave a yell. "Nan!"

Nan gasped. "Terry!" There was no mistaking the joy in her voice.

"Oh no!" Lisa exclaimed.

The driver threw open the door and leapt from the car. He was a tall, handsome man in his late twenties.

Nan ran toward him and hurled herself into his arms. They embraced passionately, to the considerable interest of the passersby and the obvious disgust of Lisa, who turned away, muttering some uncomplimentary remark under her breath.

"An old friend, presumably," Jessica murmured.

"Terry Jones. A year ago he and Nan were engaged. Then he just walked out of her life. He sure picked the right time to show up again."

Terry was now holding Nan at arm's length, his hands on her shoulders. "Darling," he was saying, "I heard the news in Kentucky this morning and I flew right in. Nan, I'm so sorry."

"I know, Terry. I know."

Suddenly she broke down and started to sob. He drew her to him again and they stood together, not moving. Jessica gave a nod to Lisa and walked thoughtfully back to the sheriff's car.

"Who's the feller?" Tupper asked as she got in.

She explained as he started the engine and got the car moving again. He gave a grunt.

"Didn't waste much time, did he? Love—or the fact she's now worth about twenty-five million?"

Jessica shrugged. "I couldn't say. One is naturally suspicious of a young man in such circumstances. On the other hand, it's not at all unlikely that somebody should fall in love with Nan."

A few moments later the car drew up in front of Elias Cobb's mortuary, an old building on a side street. Tupper and Jessica got out. He said: "A word of warning—don't say anything, one way or the other, in front of Cobb or his assistants. Wait till we get out here again."

She gave a nod and he escorted her inside.

Only five minutes passed before Jessica and the sheriff emerged once more into the sunlight. They stopped on the sidewalk. "Well?" Amos asked anxiously.

Jessica nodded. "Yes, Sheriff, that's the man who spent most of yesterday at my house."

"No possibility of a mistake?"

"Only if he had an identical twin . . ."

"He didn't."

"What a shame. It would be so interesting to be involved in an identical-twin case. You know, it's a motif that runs right through literature, back to Shakespeare's *The Comedy of Errors* and probably further back still . . ." She broke off. "I'm sorry."

"I'll have to check it out, you understand, Mrs. Fletcher. It's not that I don't believe you, but . . ."

"Of course. Ethan suggested you could send fingerprint men along to my house."

"Yeah, we'll probably do that. Trouble is, I just don't know what else to do. It was all panning out so nicely." He swore under his breath.

"May I make a suggestion?"

"I wish you would."

"Has Maggie Earl been told yet that her father's body has been found?"

"No. Didn't want to tell her until we had a positive identification."

"Then tell her now. And if I might be present?"

"Sure. But why? I mean, she already knows he's dead . . ." He broke off. "Or doesn't she?" He scratched his head. "Oh, Lord, I don't get this."

Jessica smiled. "Well, that really is the point, Sheriff. Was Maggie consciously lying or not when she confessed? Did she truly believe, for some reason or another, that she had killed her father, or didn't she? Whichever way, her reaction when she's informed that her father's body has been found should tell us quite a lot."

After Jessica had left the two sisters and Terry Jones outside the bar, Nan and Terry got into his car and roared off. Lisa watched until the car was out of sight, then made her way back to her room at the hotel. She went in, and Brian, who was lying on the bed in his shirt-sleeves looked up at her.

"Well?" he said.

She dropped her purse on the nearest chair, slipped off her coat and let it fall to the floor, then walked across to the window and stared out.

"Well, what?" she asked.

"Well, was it your old man?"

"Of course it was."

"Oh. I'm sorry."

She turned to him. "Are you, Brian? Are you really sorry."

He lifted himself from the bed and went across to her. "Hey, Lisa, you're really upset, aren't you?"

"Naturally I'm upset."

"Oh, come on, don't tell me you loved the old barracuda?"

"No, I didn't *love* him. But he was my father. And seeing him lying there . . ."

"You were overwhelmed with pangs of filial remorse?"

"No! I was not. I had nothing to be remorseful about. All the same, it wasn't a nice experience. And I could have done with my husband there for moral support."

He shrugged. "Sorry, honey, I told you I had some business calls to make. I didn't realize it would particularly worry you. You had Nan. If I'd known how you felt, naturally I'd have come along. But you always seem so . . ."

"So hard-boiled?"

"I was going to say strong."

She gave a sardonic smile. "Thanks for the compliment."

"Strong—but also stupid."

She flushed. "What do you mean?"

"You know what I mean. All that business about a storm accident—lying for Maggie like that."

"She's my sister, Brian."

"Yes, your sister and Stephen's daughter; and as such entitled to one quarter of his estate. Unless, of course, she's convicted of murdering him, in which case she'd be out of the will and your share would increase by the little matter of eight or nine million dollars. Did you think about that, dear wife?"

"No. Because I might just be able to get by on twenty-five million. Plus the odd million or so."

He stared at her for a moment, then gave a harsh laugh and turned away. "Your trouble, my sweet, is that you lack ambition."

"That's the first time anyone has accused me of that."

"Have a drink," he said.

"No, I had one with Nan."

"Then I will."

He went over to the dresser, picked up a bottle of Scotch, practically filled a glass and downed it without batting an eye. Then he poured another and turned back to face her.

"Anyway," he said, "what's the difference? It's all worked out. Maggie's eliminated, and Nan won't be a problem. She'll be pursuing her designing career in New York. Or perhaps I should say in New York she'll be pursuing her career as a designer. Or was I right the first time?"

"I shouldn't rely on that," she retorted quickly.

"What do you mean?"

"Terry's turned up again."

Brian gave a whistle. "Has he, indeed? Crafty dog."

"And he's ambitious—even by your standards. He'd like nothing better than to work his way into the company. If Nan decides to put her weight behind him . . ."

"Don't you worry about Mr. Terry Jones. I can handle him. No, the problem is little Gracie."

"Oh, Brian, I'm so sick of this feuding between you two! Can't you somehow manage to work together?"

"Never in a million years, my dear. So I'm afraid there's only one answer: Grace will have to be disposed of."

Lisa drew her breath in sharply. "Brian, what are you saying?"

For a moment he looked puzzled at her reaction, then he suddenly started to laugh. "Good heavens, darling, you don't think I meant . . ." He broke off. "Oh, Lisa, what a morbid imagination is housed in that fevered little mind of yours. I'm talking business, not murder."

Lisa went up to him and put her arms around him. "Sometimes, Brian," she murmured, "you frighten me."

He held her close and stroked her hair. "I never want to frighten you, darling. Never."

They kissed. Then he said: "You know the thing that amazes me?"

"What's that?"

"Where Maggie finally found the guts to do the old man in."

Lisa drew away and then abruptly raised her arm and tried to slap his face. He caught her wrist, gave a laugh and kissed her again.

Lisa tried to fight him off for a moment, then submitted.

# Chapter Seven

BACK at the police station, Tupper gave orders for Maggie Earl to be brought to his office. A few moments later she was led in by a middle-aged policewoman. Jessica eyed the girl closely. Maggie was pale and looked tired. But she seemed perfectly composed and neither frightened nor resentful.

Tupper said: "Come in and sit down, Miss Earl." He dismissed the policewoman with a nod and she went out.

Maggie sat down. "Is there any news, Sheriff?" she asked.

"Well, yes. Oh, by the way, I hope you don't mind Mrs. Fletcher being here?"

Maggie gave an impatient shake of the head. "Of course not. Sheriff, what's happened?"

Tupper hesitated. "Your father's body has been found, Miss Earl—on a beach about a mile away early this morning."

There was dead silence. Maggie didn't move. For seconds she didn't speak. Then very quietly she said: "I—I don't . . ." She stopped.

Gently, Tupper repeated the words. And as he did so the spell seemed to be broken. Maggie jumped to her feet.

"No!" Her voice was hoarse. "My father . . . *dead?* He can't be!"

"There's no doubt, I'm afraid," Tupper said. "Two of your sisters have just identified the body."

Maggie's face was a picture of horror and incredulity. She seemed to freeze. Then slowly she sank back on to her chair. She looked at Tupper. "He was drowned," she said. It wasn't a question, so much as a statement of the obvious.

Tupper shook his head. "No, Miss Earl, not drowned—shot. Twice in the chest."

"What?" The word came in a whisper. If Maggie had been pale before, now she was ashen.

"Just as you described," Tupper said deliberately.

Maggie didn't reply to this. She shook her head dazedly. Then at last she spoke. "Could I have some water, please?"

Tupper stood up, crossed the room, filled a paper cup with water, came back and handed it to her. Maggie sipped. To Jessica she looked as if she could have used something stronger.

Tupper resumed his seat. "I don't quite see why you're so surprised, Miss Earl," he said. "You knew your father was dead. You knew we were waiting for his body to be washed up. Your sisters were upset, sure, but they weren't shocked or surprised. Whereas you, who actually shot him, act like you can't believe it could have happened."

Maggie put down the water cup. She kept her eyes fixed on it. "I didn't shoot him, Mr. Tupper."

"I've got your confession, Miss Earl." He tapped some typewritten sheets on the desk in front of him.

She looked up. "I know. But that wasn't true." She spoke with a kind of desperate vehemence.

"Then why say it? Because one of your sisters shot him? You've been covering up for Grace or Lisa or Nan. Is that it?"

"No! Nobody shot him!"

"I assure you somebody did, Miss Earl. The medical examiner's preliminary—"

"Nobody shot him on the yacht, I tell you! When he left, he was perfectly all right."

She buried her head in her hands. "Oh Lord, this is awful. It's like a nightmare." She raised her head. "It just doesn't make sense!"

Jessica spoke. Her voice was crisp. "Exactly what I have been saying for some time now. Maggie, I think it would be highly advisable if you were to tell us the truth now without equivocation."

Maggie was silent for a moment. After reflection she said quietly, "Very well." She picked up the water cup, took another sip and cleared her throat.

"My father left the yacht voluntarily the night before last. I helped him. He had an inflatable raft on board, which he'd hidden away before we started the cruise. I made sure my sisters were below when he pushed off and I arranged with him that I'd put around the story that he'd fallen overboard. It's as simple as that."

Tupper gave an exclamation of disbelief. "You call this business simple? Okay, suppose—just suppose—I buy your story: what was the point of this screwy rigmarole?"

Maggie flushed slightly. "It was Father's idea. It's a rather long story."

"Oh, please go ahead, Miss Earl," Tupper said, with elaborate politeness. "We have all day."

Maggie drew a deep breath. "It has to do with Nan. She is—was—Dad's favorite. He desperately wanted her to be happy—particularly to make a happy marriage, like he and Mom had had. He'd seen Grace's marriage break up, and Lisa marry a man he was sure was just on the make. Personally, I'm not quite certain of that with Brian. I think there really is something between Lisa and him, and—"

Tupper sighed. "Get on with it, please, Miss Earl."

"Sorry. Well, as I say, he'd seen two daughters make unsatisfactory marriages—and a third miss out altogether. He was determined Nan's life should be different. More than determined. Almost desperate. Nan had lots of boyfriends, but never anything serious, until about two years ago.

"That was when she met Terry Jones. Nan fell for him in a big way. Dad, though, was convinced Terry was no good—just a fortune hunter. And I must say I agreed with him. Eventually Dad hired private detectives to check Terry out, and they turned up some rather suggestive facts. Nothing conclusive—not enough to turn Nan against him. So Dad waited for his opportunity. Once, when Nan was out of town on her own, Dad went to see Terry. And he . . . well, he bought him off. I was there. Terry was happy to accept a very substantial sum—paid in installments —in return for getting out of Nan's life permanently. At first Dad thought this would cure Nan of Terry for good. But I argued that knowing Dad had meddled in her affairs would be just as likely to alienate her from him as from Terry. So Dad made it a condition of the payment that Nan was not to know about it. Terry agreed to this—and he just split. It hit her pretty badly, of course, and I felt quite a monster for my part in it. However, after a time she seemed to get over it. Eventually she decided to go to New York and try to carve out a career for herself as a fashion designer. She has real talent, you know . . ."

"Miss Earl," Tupper interrupted quietly, "just what has all this to do with your father going ashore in an inflatable raft?"

"I'm coming to that. I told you it was a long story. For some months Dad stopped worrying about Nan. Then she came home for a short vacation—and it became obvious that she was as much in love with Terry as ever. Dad got very depressed. He kept saying, 'If I die, that guy'll come straight back into her life—take her for every cent she has.' I got irritated and one day I said something like, 'Well, *if* you die at least you won't be around to see it.' That gave him the idea, and a week or two later he came to me with it: he would fake his own death—disappear in such a way that it would seem certain he was dead. Terry, he was sure, would show up again. Then Dad would resurrect himself and unmask Terry for what he was. The sailing trip was planned for only that purpose. It was a pretty way-out scheme—and unfair to Grace and Lisa, too —but Dad was set on it. And when Dad is set on something, it's useless to argue. So I . . . well, I went along."

Maggie sat back in her chair and took another sip of water.

There was silence for several seconds. Then Jessica spoke. "You say the plan was for you to tell people your father had been swept overboard?"

"Right."

"Why then did you say you'd shot him?"

"Because of that eye-of-the-hurricane business. Once you'd got on to that, I could see there was no way of making anyone believe that Dad had been swept over."

"You fired the shots?"

"Yes. Into the air, well after Dad had pushed off. You see, we hadn't expected the hurricane, but the forecast had said it would be rough. Rough enough for my sisters to believe Dad could have been lost that way. We hadn't figured on it being so absolutely calm. So at the last minute, we cooked up the idea of my telling the girls I'd shot him."

"Whose idea was that?" Jessica asked.

"Dad's."

"And you went along with it, quite willingly?"

"I always went along with my father's ideas, Mrs. Fletcher."

"All the same, you did tell the sheriff in the first instance that Mr. Earl had been drowned."

"Well, there was no harm in trying. I didn't especially want to be arrested, even for a few days. I think I would have been believed, too, if it hadn't been for you, Mrs. Fletcher—working out the position of the eye of the hurricane. May I ask what gave us away?"

Jessica smiled. "Watching the dishwater running out of my sink. I thought of whirlpools and whirlwinds and all I knew about the behavior of storms generally. However, at the back of my mind I was already aware of something not quite right, though I couldn't put my finger on it. Then it came to me: you had been able to state the yacht's position so precisely. It seemed hardly likely in the teeth of a storm. If, though, it were actually calm and if your father were planning to go ashore, he would need to know his position before pushing off. If you were helping him, you would no doubt know it, too."

Maggie nodded thoughtfully. "He must have just made it ashore before the hurricane caught up with him."

She was silent for a moment, a faraway look in her eyes. Then she raised her head and stared at Tupper. "And no sooner than he makes it, somebody shoots him! It's ghastly! And it's senseless. It couldn't have been just casual robbery. He only had a few dollars on him. And yet no one knew what he was going to do, where he'd be."

"Except you, Miss Earl," Tupper said quietly.

She stared at him. "I'm in a mess, aren't I? It's absolutely no use my swearing Dad left the yacht alive and well. You won't believe me. I can see that."

Tupper gazed at her calmly for a moment before speaking. "Well, as a matter of fact, Miss Earl, I do."

For several seconds it was clear that Maggie just couldn't take this in. Her expression was blank. At last she said jerkily: "You . . . believe me? I don't understand. Why?"

"You can thank Mrs. Fletcher." He looked at Jessica. "Tell her, ma'am."

"There's really no call for thanks," Jessica said. "It was purely fortuitous. You see, my dear, the fact of the matter is that your father spent a good part of yesterday at my house."

For what seemed a long time Maggie didn't move; then she slowly let out her breath and slumped back her chair.

"Oh, my word, what a relief."

Jessica watched her sympathetically. Maggie's color was starting to come back. "That means my father did make it safely to shore that night?"

Jessica nodded.

Maggie said simply: "Tell me about it—the day he spent with you."

Quietly and without embellishment Jessica recounted the details of what Stephen Earl had said and done the previous day.

"He was happy, I think," she ended up.

Maggie nodded. "Yes, he would have been. He was *being* Ralph the hobo, do you see? He'd put his troubles behind him." She gave a wary smile. "He always was a frustrated actor." She lowered her head for a moment, then raised it again and looked straight at Jessica. "Thank you for making his last day a happy one." There were tears in her eyes.

Tupper cleared his throat. "You understand, Miss Earl, that I can't let you go just yet. Mrs. Fletcher's story has to be checked out first. Naturally, I believe her, but I have to have proof of it before I can act officially. However, I think I can promise you you'll be free in a couple of hours."

"Oh, that's wonderful," Maggie said. She turned to Jessica. "Mrs. Fletcher, I hated you when you started, as I thought, interfering, and showed Dad couldn't have been washed overboard. But now I don't know how to thank you."

"I assure you there's no need for thanks," Jessica told her. "I'm only after the truth. And I'm afraid we're no nearer to that—so far as identifying your father's murderer is concerned."

Maggie's face clouded. "That's true. Do you have any ideas at all?"

"Oh, yes, I have lots of ideas. But so far not an iota of proof to back any of them up."

Maggie looked at Tupper. "What about you, Sheriff?"

"Until a short while ago, I thought we had our culprit, Miss Earl. Now it's back to square one. Might learn something from the medical examiner's full report that will help."

"When do you expect that?" Jessica asked.

"This afternoon, with luck. Miss Earl, you ought to be able to give me some leads. Did your father have any enemies?"

She shook her head. "No. I mean that's such a melodramatic word, isn't it? Obviously he had business rivals, there were people who didn't like him. There must have been many of them who would have been glad to see him down. But not *kill* him."

"What about people who would have gained by his death?"

"Apart from my sisters and me, you mean? There's nobody to speak of. I imagine he's remembered a few old friends in his will; but not enough to make it worth anyone's while to murder him. I suppose if the company were to get into difficulties as a result of what's happened, our competitors would all gain to a certain extent. But I imagine the benefit would be shared out pretty equally between eight or ten firms. Besides, I don't believe Mark of the Earl is going to get in trouble."

"You sound very confident, my dear," Jessica said.

"Well, yes; of course, I know little about it really. But I know it's well organized. We have efficient managers, a good work force and a first-rate product. We can thank Dad for all that. But the idea that it could collapse because he's not there to run it is absurd."

"Somebody has to run it, though."

"Of course."

"Who will that be, do you suppose?"

"Brian, I imagine."

"You're happy about that?"

"Oh, yes. Brian's smart and tough. And a trifle ruthless. He'll do a good job."

"Would your father have been happy to know Mr. Shelby was running his company?"

"Yes, I'm sure he would."

"But you said your father thought he was just on the make."

"That's right. He didn't like Brian personally, and he didn't want him as a son-in-law. But he did respect him as a businessman. He wouldn't have let Brian get to such a position of influence in the company if he hadn't. After all, somebody on the make is just the sort of person you want to run a big commercial venture, isn't it?"

"Do you think your sister Grace will agree with you?"

"Probably not. There's no doubt Grace wants to be number one."

"But you won't support her?"

Maggie frowned. "I love Grace," she said thoughtfully. "And I admire her talents. She'd certainly change the nature of the business. She's a scientist and a bit of a visionary. She'd want to experiment—for instance, go in more for natural beauty products. It would all be very interesting with Grace in charge. But perhaps risky."

"You wouldn't be in favor of that?"

"You have to think of the stockholders, don't you? A business exists to make money. And I'm not sure Grace understands finance all that well. I suppose since she's not only a woman but my sister, I ought to support her. But you have to be pragmatic about these things."

"You've thought about the matter a lot, haven't you?" Jessica said.

Maggie looked just a little disconcerted. "I suppose I have. I'm sort of the observer of the family, you see. Dad ran the company. Grace worked for it. Lisa was involved through Brian. Nan simply wasn't interested. I just looked and listened. Then again, Dad had a minor heart attack a while back and afterward, as I explained, kept talking of dropping out. So I couldn't help speculating about what would happen if he did."

"And your speculations have led you to believe Brian Shelby will be the new head?"

"I'll be surprised if he isn't."

Tupper broke a long silence. "Think Shelby's come to the same conclusion himself?"

"Of course. He has no doubts."

"That'd seem to give him a pretty good motive for wanting your father out of the way."

Maggie stared at him. "Brian? You're suggesting *he* killed Dad?"

"Nope. Just saying it's possible."

"Never!"

"Why are you so sure? You said he was tough. And ruthless."

"And also smart. He'd never take the risk. He'd know he only had to wait for a few years, anyway. Dad would have been bound to retire before long. Besides, from a purely practical standpoint, there was no way Brian could have known Dad was going to be here last night, walking around, a ready-made target."

"Suppose your father told him his plan?"

"He would never have told Brian: it would have meant telling him why he was doing it—all about Terry Jones. It would have got back to Lisa, and then to Nan. Lisa can never keep her mouth shut. The whole scheme would have been ruined. The essence of it was secrecy."

"Yet somebody found out about it, Miss Earl."

"Well, *I* didn't tell anybody, I assure you."

"I believe you," Jessica said firmly.

Tupper looked at the young woman, hesitated, then gave a shrug of resignation. "Then your father must have told somebody himself. The only alternative is this was just a random killing by some psycho, which I don't buy for a moment. Any ideas who he might have told?"

Maggie shook her head in perplexity. Tupper turned to Jessica again. "He spent most of his last day with you, Mrs. Fletcher. Was there anything at all he said or did that might give a lead?"

Jessica was silent for a moment. She was thinking of a certain phone call—and of a casual remark by Terry Jones. Should she mention it? She came to a rapid decision. That young man had too much stacked against him already. She didn't want to make things worse for him by repeating something that, though on the face of it suspicious, might bear an innocent explanation, or even be merely a coincidence. Which didn't mean she wasn't going to look into it . . .

"There's nothing I can tell you at the moment, Sheriff," she said at last.

If Tupper perceived equivocation in this he gave no indication of it. He just sighed. "Looks like this is going to be a long job," he said.

# Chapter Eight

TUPPER had Jessica driven back home in a police car. She was accompanied by a fingerprint expert. She took him in and pointed out several things that "Ralph" had handled, including the window to which he'd applied the new putty. The man got several prints with which he seemed highly pleased, then left.

As soon as he'd gone, Jessica went to the telephone. She lifted the receiver and after a few seconds heard the familiar voice of the operator.

"Letitia? Jessica Fletcher. I'm fine. And you? . . .Yes, isn't it shocking? . . . No, I know nothing. Letitia, I am *not* in the sheriff's pocket . . . All right, I promise, you'll be the first to know. What? No, I don't want a number. I want some information. A friend was over at the house yesterday and made a call to Paris, Kentucky. You remember? . . . That's right, you did. Nine dollars and eighty-seven cents. Letitia, is there some way I could find out whose number it was? Yes, I'll hold on."

After almost a minute, she heard Letitia's voice again. She listened, and gave a nod of satisfaction. "Thank you, Letitia, that's a great help . . . What? No, I didn't get the money for the call. And somehow now I don't think I'm going to. Bye."

She hung up.

Jessica made herself a light lunch, ate it, cleared up and spent an hour answering some correspondence which just wouldn't wait one more day.

Then she got her bike and cycled to Hill House Hotel. She propped her bike up against the front porch and went in. Today a woman was on duty at the desk. As Jessica approached, she looked up with a smile. "Afternoon, Jessica."

"Hello, Marge."

"Let me guess: you want one of the Earl sisters?"

"Actually, no. Well, I may have to see one of them, but I was really looking for a Mr. Terry Jones. Is he staying here?"

"Miss Nan's boyfriend? Yes, checked in this morning. I put him in

Room 212, but he and Miss Nan went straight out again and haven't been back since."

"I see. Well, when they come in, will you tell Mr. Jones—in confidence —that I'd like to see him before I speak to Sheriff Tupper again? Nan can explain my involvement to him. It's urgent."

Marge looked interested. But she had been in the hotel business long enough not to ask questions. "I'll tell him, Jessica."

"Thank you, Marge. I must rush. Bye."

She was just about to remount her bike when she noticed a car coming up the drive. She waited and saw that Brian Shelby was behind the wheel. His wife was next to him and in the back was Maggie. The car drew up and they got out. Maggie saw Jessica and came straight across, hands outstretched.

Jessica smiled. "Maggie, I'm so glad you're out."

"Thank you again, Mrs. Fletcher. It's a tremendous relief."

"I take it the fingerprint man confirmed my story of your father being at my house yesterday?"

She nodded. "Yes; and besides, the sheriff's had the medical examiner's report. The shots that killed Dad came from a .32 caliber—not my gun."

Brian and Lisa came up.

"I see," said Jessica. "And could he say when it happened?"

It was Brian who answered. "He thinks between six and ten o'clock last night."

"Really? Well, I can narrow it down a bit further. He was at my house until shortly after seven."

Lisa tugged at Brian's arm. "Come on inside. Let's find Grace and Nan."

"You won't find Nan in," said Jessica. "She's out with Mr. Jones."

Lisa gave an exasperated exclamation. "Not back yet! We haven't set eyes on her since that creep turned up. Nan is a little fool!"

Jessica said: "I understand then that neither she nor the young man know of the latest developments—including the fact that Mr. Earl was still alive early yesterday evening?"

Lisa shrugged. "I don't see how they can. *We* didn't know until fifteen minutes ago."

"Well, if I see them I'll give them the news. I'd like to speak to them both."

She positioned her bike for a quick start, but before she could do so Brian took hold of the handlebars. Jessica stared at him. He was smiling, but when he spoke there was no mistaking the threat in his words.

"Mrs. Fletcher, I have no wish to be rude, and we do appreciate the information you've been able to provide, but I would remind you that this is purely a family affair. We don't need outsiders poking their noses in where they don't belong."

Jessica eyed him coolly. "You're wrong, Mr. Shelby. This is not purely a family affair: it's very much a Cabot Cove affair. And in Cabot Cove *you* are the outsider. And as for my nose, it is right where it belongs. Good afternoon."

Jessica twisted the handlebars out of his hands, mounted her bike and rode briskly away. As he gazed after her, Brian Shelby's face was full of undisguised anger.

"Nan, I've always loved you. You know that."

Terry Jones spoke with utmost sincerity. He took Nan's hand and squeezed it reassuringly.

Nan gave a sigh. "I wish I did know it, Terry, but I don't."

They were sitting in his car, which was parked on a high promontory looking down over the sea a short distance outside Cabot Cove.

"What more can I say or do?" he asked.

"I don't know. Nothing, I guess. I'm afraid it's what you've already done."

"You mean going away."

"I mean walking out on me, Terry. Or to use a simple, old-fashioned word, jilting me."

"Don't say that!"

"Why not? It's true, isn't it?"

"No! I tell you, your father threatened to ruin me if I didn't leave you alone—completely."

She drew her hand away gently. "I find that very hard to believe."

"You're saying I'm lying?"

"No! Oh, I know he didn't like you. He'd never have found anybody he thought good enough for me. I'm sure he tried to split us up. But threatening to ruin you? You must have misunderstood him."

Terry gave a hopeless shrug. "Okay, have it your way. I misunderstood him. But I tell you this: he scared me half to death."

"He's scared a lot of people in his time. I was hoping you'd be one who wouldn't scare so easily."

"Nan," he said, "why have you started talking like this? When I first arrived you were . . . well, you were pleased to see me. I thought that other business was in the past. Why suddenly drag it up again?"

"Because it was always there—at the back of my mind. I *was* glad to see you. Over the moon. Because everything had been so ghastly, and to have you suddenly turn up again was like a breath of fresh air. You swept me off my feet. You could always do that. But I guess I'm too much my father's daughter to let my heart rule my head for more than a few hours. The memory of what you did was nagging away all the time."

Terry was silent for a few seconds. He took out a pack of cigarettes and lit one before speaking. "I can only say I'm sorry, again. I know I should have stood up to him. I just didn't have what it takes—then. And I guess it's too late now to prove things would be different. I just know one thing: I love you, I want to marry you and spend my life with you."

She looked at him. "You're sure of that?"

"Positive."

"I envy you, Terry. Because right now I'm not positive about anything, least of all myself. And I warn you, I'll probably be irrational for some time."

"Nan . . ."

She raised a hand to cut him off.

"No, Terry, not now. We've talked enough. Drive me back to the hotel. I've been out too long. I must see the girls, find out what's been happening."

For a moment he was about to argue. Then he obviously thought better of it, threw his cigarette out of the window and started the engine.

They drove back to the hotel in silence. He dropped her right outside the entrance, parked the car, then went inside himself. As he was crossing the lobby, Marge at the desk called him over.

"There's been a lady asking for you, Mr. Jones."

"Who would that be?"

"Mrs. Fletcher, Jessica Fletcher."

He raised his eyebrows. "The famous Jessica Fletcher. I've been hearing about her. What does she want?"

Marge relayed Jessica's message.

Terry frowned, then glanced at his watch.

"I just have time to go and see her now. Can you give me her address?"

# Chapter Nine

"I'M glad you came, Mr. Jones," Jessica said, leading him into her living room. "Won't you sit down?"

"Thanks." He lowered himself into an armchair and crossed his legs. His manner was easy and casual.

"I'm intrigued as to why you want to see me, Mrs. Fletcher. And what's all this about the sheriff?"

Jessica sat down on a high-backed chair facing him. She said: "I wanted to talk about who killed Stephen Earl."

His eyes narrowed. "What do you mean? We know who killed him: Maggie."

"No."

He stared in disbelief. "But Nan says she confessed."

"She did, but it was a false confession."

"But why on earth . . . ?"

"It's a long story, and I'm sure you'll hear it soon. But there isn't time to go into it now. However, you can take my word that Maggie was released from jail early this afternoon and the sheriff is still seeking the killer."

Terry whistled. "This sure is a turnaround. But I still don't understand why you wanted to see me."

"Mr. Jones, when you drew up in the street this morning, jumped out of your car and ran across to Nan, I was standing nearby with Lisa. You may have noticed me."

He grinned. "Well, only vaguely, I'm afraid. Sorry, but I had eyes only for Nan."

"I couldn't help overhearing what you said to her. Quote: 'I heard the news in Kentucky this morning and I flew right in.' "

"So?"

"That wasn't true, was it?"

"Sure it was true. I heard it on the early morning news."

"I think not. In reality you heard about Stephen Earl's death yesterday."

"You're crazy."

"The phone company says I'm not. A man placed a call here in Cabot Cove to your number in Paris, Kentucky, at around noon yesterday. The charge was nine dollars and eighty-seven cents."

Terry was silent for a moment. Then he shrugged. "Okay. There's no reason I should hide it, really. I did get a call yesterday from a reporter. He told me about Earl's death being announced here. He seemed to know about my previous relationship with Nan and wanted a comment. I gave him one. You're a lady, so I won't repeat it."

Jessica gazed at him. He seemed only slightly embarrassed and not at all guilty. And his story was perfectly reasonable: Stephen Earl, having baited his trap and wanting to be quite sure Terry walked into it, wasted no time in guaranteeing the young man knew about his "death" as soon as possible by phoning him, disguising his voice and pretending to be a reporter. Yes, it made sense so far.

"And then you flew immediately up here to Maine?"

"Not immediately."

"But yesterday. Not today?"

For a moment he seemed to be trying to make up his mind about something. "Oh, what the heck! There's no way of keeping it secret, I suppose. I traveled under my own name. Yes, I got a plane yesterday afternoon."

"To Portland?"

"Of course."

"Arriving there at what time?"

"About eight P.M. And I spent the night in a motel near the airport. Look, what is this?"

She studied his face. "Why did you conceal this and pretend only to have arrived in Maine today?"

"I . . . I'd rather not say. And Mrs. Fletcher, what gives you the right to question me like this?"

"Well, for one thing, the sheriff asked me to take an interest in the case."

"The case? You mean the murder? But I know nothing about that. I was in Kentucky when it happened. I have dozens of witnesses."

Again Jessica gazed at him. It really seemed he did not know Stephen Earl had died only last night—possibly *after* Terry had himself arrived in the state. And, plainly, if he *was* innocent, there was no way he could have known it, having been out with Nan since before Jessica's own testimony had put Stephen Earl alive and well at seven last night in this very house.

On the other hand, Terry Jones might be just a highly accomplished actor. Indeed, Jessica thought, he almost certainly was. But that didn't necessarily make him a killer.

"Mr. Jones," she asked suddenly, "is the reason you don't want to answer my question because you spent a large part of last night with Nan Earl?"

Terry swore. "How did you find out?"

"Believe it or not, Mr. Jones, simple deduction. When the sheriff and I went to the Hill House yesterday evening, Nan was the only sister not present. Now there's not a lot for a young unaccompanied girl to do in Cabot Cove of an evening. I couldn't imagine that she would go to Portland or anywhere else on her own for a night out so soon after her father's death. On the other hand, if someone had phoned and invited her to meet him . . . When I learned you were in Portland last night, and remembered Nan indicating this morning that she hadn't got back till the early hours, the solution was obvious."

"Yes, you're quite right," Terry shrugged. "I was a bit dubious about coming. Wasn't sure what my reception would be. But I followed the advice to the letter—even phoned Nan first, told her I was on my way. I rented a car as soon as I arrived in Portland, drove out, picked Nan up, and we went to a motel. Spent most of the time talking. Then I took her back to her hotel in the early hours and returned to Portland."

"Why did you lie to me just now about spending the night in a motel near the airport?"

"I thought Nan might not want people to know she'd been with me. That's why I shouted out in the street this morning about just arriving from Kentucky. I could see Lisa standing there, her ears like great question marks."

Jessica said dryly: "Nan did a good acting job, too. Anyone would have thought she hadn't set eyes on you for years and was amazed to see you."

"Oh, that wasn't acting. She thought I'd gone back to Kentucky. You see, things didn't go too well last night. As a matter of fact, we had a fight. I wasn't very complimentary about her old man. When I dropped her off at her hotel, relations were rather cool. Then, later this morning, I decided to come back here and patch things up. So Nan *was* surprised to see me."

Jessica nodded thoughtfully. "And how are relations now, if I may ask?"

"Frankly, I don't know. Nan's being rather strange. One minute it's as if nothing had ever been wrong between us—you saw her this morning. Then suddenly she seems all suspicious and uncertain again."

"You must remember she's been through a very traumatic time."

"I realize that. But it makes things difficult."

At that moment there came an urgent ringing of the doorbell.

Jessica excused herself and went to answer it. She opened the door to reveal Nan standing on the step.

"Is Terry here?" the girl demanded abruptly.

"He is. Come on in."

Nan hurried into the living room, Jessica following. Terry got to his feet in surprise. "Hello, darling."

Without preamble she asked urgently, "Have you heard the news?"

"About Maggie? Yes. Nan, I'm very pleased . . ."

"No, not that. Dad didn't die the night before last. He was killed yesterday."

"What?"

"Last night between six and ten."

Terry sat down again suddenly, his face white. "That . . . that doesn't make sense! How do they know?"

"From Mrs. Fletcher."

He turned a bewildered gaze on Jessica. "From you? I don't understand."

"It's quite simple," Jessica said briskly. "Mr. Earl came ashore near Cabot Cove early yesterday morning. He spent most of the day right here in this house. The police have checked the fingerprints he left about. He went out just after seven last night, and then somebody shot him."

"But why would he stay here all yesterday when everybody thought he was dead, and—?"

Nan interrupted impatiently. "Never mind about that now. The thing that matters is that he was probably killed after you'd arrived in Maine. Your precious alibi's absolutely worthless."

Terry sat quite still. He licked his lips. Then he spoke quietly. "I didn't do it." He looked from one of them to the other, and repeated more urgently: "I didn't. Mrs. Fletcher, you do believe me?"

"Frankly, Mr. Jones, I don't know. You certainly had a stronger motive than anyone else: you knew that as long as Stephen Earl was alive you had no chance of marrying Nan."

"But how could I possibly know he was going to be in Cabot Cove last night? I thought he was dead by then!"

"So you say, Mr. Jones, so you say."

"But that reporter told me. We must find him. He'll confirm it."

Jessica was silent for a moment. Did Terry Jones really believe it was a reporter who had phoned him? Or was this a clever bluff? Had he in fact recognized the voice of Stephen Earl, realized something fishy was going on and flown north immediately to investigate it?

Before she could speak Nan said: "He may confirm he called you. That doesn't mean you believed him."

Terry gave a groan. "Nan, you just have to believe me!"

Her expression softened slightly. "I'd like to, Terry. I wish I could."

He stood up again suddenly. "I must go. I have to trace that reporter. Damnit, I don't even remember the guy's name or his paper. And I was devilish rude to him, too."

Jessica looked at him thoughtfully. Was this the time to test his reaction to being told the real identity of the "reporter?" No. Apart from the fact that it was not her place to tell him about Stephen Earl's trap, one of the first rules of criminal investigation was never to give away information unnecessarily. Besides, she was still far from sure that Terry wasn't pulling a clever bluff. She didn't trust this young man, even though she couldn't help liking him.

"Mr. Jones, before you leave, one more thing. There was something you said earlier that puzzled me."

"What was that?"

"It was before Nan arrived. You said you'd been dubious about coming to see her, but that you'd followed the advice to the letter. What advice?"

He looked a little embarrassed and glanced at Nan, who was gazing at him interestedly, awaiting his reply. This was obviously news to her, too.

Terry gave the girl a somewhat nervous grin. "Well, I didn't tell you about this, honey, because she suggested I shouldn't. But yesterday, about an hour after I had that phone call from the reporter, I got another one. From your sister. She said she thought you'd be glad to see me and suggested I fly up to Maine on the double—but to call you first, just to be on the safe side. I'm sorry I didn't mention it, Nan, but I didn't want you to think I had to be put up to coming. I would have come anyway, honest."

But Nan had stopped listening. She was frowning.

"My sister?" she said. "Which one?"

"Oh, sorry. It was Grace."

"What can I do for you, Mrs. Fletcher?"

Grace Lamont drew on her cigarette and surveyed Jessica coolly through the smoke.

Jessica let her eyes wander around the girl's hotel room. Already Grace had succeeded in turning it into an office. Two extra tables had been brought in. One was strewn with business papers. On the other was a portable typewriter and a tape recorder. Grace, who wore no makeup, was dressed in a plain shirt and trousers. She glanced hastily now at a large and chunky digital wristwatch on a steel strap.

"I'm sorry to interrupt your work," Jessica said.

"That's okay. I can spare a few minutes. Only I'm expecting a call from London at any time. Sit down."

Jessica perched herself on a rather uncomfortable upright chair. Grace crossed to the bedside table, on which stood a bottle of whiskey and a tumbler.

She picked up the bottle and turned around, raising it high. "Drink? I think there's another glass around somewhere."

"Thank you, no."

Grace poured some whiskey into the glass, saying as she did so, "Sorry I don't have anything lighter."

"Oh, I quite like an occasional slug of Scotch. But not—"

"I know, not when you're on duty. All detectives say that, don't they?"

"I'm not a detective, Mrs. Lamont."

"You could have fooled me."

"I'm taking an interest in the case at the request of Sheriff Tupper."

Grace sat down on the bed and drank some whiskey. Then she asked, "Are you really interested in finding out who killed my father?"

"Yes."

"Want the culprit to get his just desserts?"

"No, I leave that to the law. I just want to learn the truth. And please don't say, 'What is truth?' I'm sure that as a scientist you know quite well what I mean."

Grace gave a short laugh. "Scientist? That's a good one. I was one once. Now I'm an accountant, p.r. person, personnel officer and general manipulator."

"Then why don't you go back to science?"

"Somebody has to keep the business going. We have over five thousand employees. We owe them a debt. Not to mention our stockholders."

"You feel a personal responsibility—now your father's gone?"

"Well, at least there's a chance to get the firm back on its feet again now. It's been going slowly but steadily downhill for the last several years."

Jessica raised her eyebrows. "You blame your father for that?"

"Of course."

Jessica paused, then said brutally and deliberately, "So you must be glad he's dead."

"No. Just glad he's out of the business."

"But on a personal level?"

"Oh, on a personal level I stopped letting him affect me one way or the other several years ago—after he broke up my marriage."

"You blame him for the breakup of your marriage?"

"No, I blame my husband. What Dad did was probably good for me in the long term. Though I still resent it. Illogical, isn't it? Not very scientific. But no, Mrs. Fletcher, I haven't been harboring a burning desire to get even all these years, and I didn't shoot him."

Jessica said dryly: "There was obviously no love lost between you, though."

"You're shocked I should speak as I do? I don't believe in being hypocritical. There was no love lost between Stephen Earl and any of his daughters, if you ask me, though the others are probably too well behaved to say so outright. But he turned Maggie into a dull *Hausfrau* and Lisa into the spoiled brat she is today."

"And Nan?"

Grace took another drink of whiskey and refilled her glass. "He interfered in Nan's love life, too. Broke up the great romance of her life."

"What did you think of Terry Jones?"

"I don't know him well, of course. Nan didn't bring him home a lot, as you can imagine. I met him briefly about three times. He's very attractive, plenty of charm. But definitely crooked, I'd say."

"So you think your father was wise to try and break them up?"

"No! Far from it. He shouldn't have meddled. Nan was over twenty-one. She could have had some fun with Terry and found out what he really was in her own time and way. She couldn't have come to any real harm. And Dad could have found some legal way of keeping Terry's hands off her money. But no! He had to employ private detectives, dig into Terry's background, threaten him. So eventually Terry turned tail. Dad humiliated Nan, don't you see?"

"Yes, I think so. And is that why you phoned Terry in Kentucky yesterday and suggested he come see Nan?"

Grace stopped with her glass halfway to her mouth. "Did what?"

Jessica repeated the words.

"You're joking."

"Not at all."

"Where on earth did you get such an idea?"

"From Terry himself."

"Terry said that? The dirty little liar. Why on earth would he make up a thing like that?"

"I've no idea. You *did* call him, though?"

"Certainly not."

"You've had no contact with him of any kind?"

"Not a word. For over a year."

Jessica frowned. "How very odd. I mean, it was a lie so easily exposed. And one can't see what he could possibly gain by it."

"I hope you're not suggesting *I'm* lying, Mrs. Fletcher."

At that moment the phone rang. "That'll be my London call," Grace said. "If you'll excuse me?"

Jessica got to her feet. "Of course."

"Sorry I haven't been able to help you." Grace lifted the receiver.

Jessica crossed to the door. She spoke over her shoulder. "Oh, I wouldn't say you haven't helped me, Mrs. Lamont. I wouldn't say that at all. Goodbye."

She went out.

# Chapter Ten

JESSICA left the hotel and made her way to the police station. She felt the time had come to consult again with the sheriff. He was out when she arrived, but a deputy told her that Tupper had just radioed that he was on his way back. It seemed now that Jessica was regarded almost as a member of the force, for the deputy let her wait in Tupper's office. Ten minutes later the sheriff came in. He looked tired, yet excited.

He grinned when he saw her. "Well, Mrs. Fletcher, what you got for me?"

"Nothing very concrete, I'm afraid. But I've discovered a few things that are, shall we say, suggestive?"

He dropped down into his chair and lit a cigarette. "Shoot."

Jessica told him of her conversations with Terry, Nan and Grace. He listened in silence until she'd finished. "So," he said slowly, "Terry Jones was in Maine last night. Nan was with him part of the time. And he lied about being advised to come here by Grace Lamont."

"Perhaps he lied."

"You saying Grace was lying?"

"Not necessarily."

"One of them has to have been."

"I repeat: not necessarily."

He gazed at her silently for a few moments. Then he said: "I won't ask just what you mean by that, Mrs. Fletcher. I think I may know, and I don't want to be told I'm way off beam. Anyway, *I* got something for *you.*"

With an air of triumph, he reached into his pocket and took out a small object wrapped in paper. He unwrapped it and laid it on the desk. It was a pink high heel from a woman's shoe.

"Kinda fancy, isn't it?" he said.

Jessica bent over it. "May I touch it?"

"Oh, sure."

She picked it up and examined it closely. "Yes, quite fancy. Good quality, I should think. Although it would be easier to tell if one had the whole shoe. Where did you find it?"

"On the beach, near where Earl's body was discovered. Footprints indicate he walked—wasn't taken there and dumped after he was killed. So I've had a gang of volunteers searching the beach and rocks behind it. Hoping we might find the murder gun."

"But you didn't?"

"No. This is the only interesting thing we turned up. We found several impressions that this heel and it's partner had made in the sand very near where the body was lying. I reckon that when I find who this belongs to, I'll have found the killer."

"I think I can tell you who it belongs to, Sheriff," Jessica said quietly.

He stared. "Who?"

"I'll bet my bottom dollar this heel came off a pair of shoes belonging to Nan Earl."

Tupper whistled. "What makes you so sure? You seen her wearing them?"

"No, it's just that everything points to it."

Tupper tapped his fingers on the desk. "You saying she shot her father almost immediately after she left the hotel last night, and then went on to meet with Jones afterward? Or were she and Jones in it together? Did they rendezvous last night, come back and waylay the old man on the beach? Or did Jones do the actual shooting and was Nan just the accomplice?"

Jessica shook her head. "I'm not prepared to speculate on anything like that at the moment, Sheriff."

"I agree. The details aren't important right now. But you realize this means that all along they knew—or at least *she* knew—that the whole business about Earl going overboard off the yacht was phony and that the old man was alive all—"

Jessica coughed. "Sheriff, I don't want to interrupt, but I would feel a lot happier if, before you do any more surmising, you'd confirm my theory about those shoes. I know I said I'd bet my bottom dollar on it, but that doesn't mean I want you staking your reputation—and perhaps your job—on it, too. I am, after all, only an amateur."

Tupper grinned. "Some amateur, Mrs. Fletcher, some amateur." He got to his feet, stubbing out his cigarette. "I'll get over to the Hill House now and have a word with Miss Nan Earl. Want to come along?"

Jessica stood up. "I wouldn't miss it for the world, Mr. Tupper."

* * *

Nan said: "Off my shoe?"

She took the heel from Tupper's hand and examined it. "Well, it certainly looks like it. But it can't be. I haven't unpacked those shoes since we started the holiday. Naturally, on the yacht I wore casual shoes, with low heels."

"Do you mind checking, miss?" Tupper asked her.

"Of course not." She gave the heel back to him, then crossed to a closet, opened it and took out a small case. "These are custom-made shoes I designed myself. I've hardly worn them. I only brought them on the trip in case we went ashore to any special functions."

She took a brown paper package from the case, tore a hole in it and drew out a stylish pink leather shoe. "Here we—" She broke off with a gasp of dismay.

The shoe had no heel.

Nan stared at Tupper blankly. "I . . . I don't understand it."

Tupper held out his hand. "May I?" She handed the shoe to him. He turned it upside down and placed the heel against the underside. "Fits perfectly," he said. He turned the shoe over in his hands. "You say these shoes are practically unworn, Miss Earl? Then how come they're so scratched and marked?"

He pointed out a number of scores and scuff marks on the leather. Nan shook her head in bewilderment.

He turned the shoe upside down again and, holding it in one hand, shook it over the palm of his other hand. Then he peered into his palm. "Ever worn these on a beach, Miss Earl?"

"I don't—" She stopped short. "I can't remember. Why do you ask?"

He held out his hand for her and Jessica to see. "Sand in the shoe."

Nan's face changed. Suddenly she seemed to grasp the drift of what he was saying. "Was that heel found on the beach?" she whispered. "Near my father's . . . ?" She left the sentence unfinished.

Tupper nodded slowly, his eyes on her face. She had gone pale.

"I didn't kill my father." Her voice was hoarse.

"I didn't say you had, Miss Earl."

"No, but the implication is clear. You're saying I went to the beach, wearing these shoes, shot my father and lost the heel of my shoe while I was there. So I came back here and hid the shoes away. But I tell you, I wrapped them up before I left New York and I've never had the paper off them since." She was still holding the package containing the other shoe.

Jessica stepped over to her. "Could I have that, please?"

She took it from Nan's hand and drew out the second shoe. They all stared at it. From this one also the heel was missing.

Nan sighed. "I suppose you're going to say that both heels came off at the same time?"

Tupper shook his head. "No, but it would be mighty difficult to walk with one heel on and one off. If you couldn't find the missing one, the obvious thing would be to wrench the heel off the other shoe, so at least they'd match and you wouldn't be limping."

Nan made a gesture of despair.

"D'you mind putting these shoes on, miss?" Tupper asked. "I want to see if it's possible to wear them without heels."

"I don't see why I should help you convict me for murder."

"I should do as the sheriff asks, my dear," Jessica said to her gently. "It won't make things any worse for you. He only has to get someone else to try them out, if you refuse, and it's always best to cooperate with the police."

"Oh, very well." With rather bad grace, Nan took both the shoes, sat down on the bed, kicked off the shoes she was wearing and slipped the pink ones on. She stood up.

"Walk across the room, will you?" Tupper said.

She did so.

"How do they feel?" Jessica asked.

"Extremely uncomfortable."

"Well, they look okay," Tupper said. "I figure you could wear those for a bit and nobody'd notice there was anything wrong, unless they were specially looking for it."

As if with a sudden distaste for them, Nan shook both shoes from her feet, left them where they fell and put her original footwear back on. Jessica picked up the pink shoes and stood gazing at them closely.

Nan addressed Tupper. "Look, if what you are saying is true, why would I hang on to those shoes? Wouldn't I realize you might discover the heel and start looking for them?"

For a moment Tupper seemed at a loss. It was Jessica who replied.

"Oh, that's easily answered."

Tupper cast her a quick glance. "Mrs. Fletcher!" Nan said. "Are you trying to convict me, too?"

"Just answering a hypothetical question. Suppose you shot your father, lost the heel off one shoe and tore the other off deliberately, as the sheriff said. Now, you were going straight to meet Terry. You couldn't come back to the hotel, and you had to have something on your feet. So for the rest of the night you kept these shoes on. You really had no choice. In the early hours Terry brought you back here. You took these shoes off immediately. But what could you do with them? You couldn't just throw them in the wastebasket or hurl them blindly out of the window. Now tell me, what happened immediately after you got back here? I'd advise you to tell the truth."

"If you're so clever, you tell me."

"Well, I would guess that either Lisa or Grace, or both of them, had been waiting up for you, heard you moving about and came in to tell you about Maggie's arrest. Am I right?"

Nan nodded reluctantly. "About that, yes. But the rest's a load of—"

Jessica interrupted. "You asked why you wouldn't have disposed of the shoes. I'm giving a reason. To continue: you and your sisters talked about the situation for some time before they went back to their rooms. You could then have gone out again and disposed of the shoes in the only practical way, by burying them. But you realized you might be seen leaving the hotel—by the night clerk, say—and be asked the reason for it later. So you decided it was a lesser risk to keep them until morning. But daylight came and you wondered how you could be sure you wouldn't be seen burying them. To be completely safe you'd need to go right out into the country to do it. But you didn't get a chance: first you had to go to the mortuary to identify your father's body. While you were out you met Terry and went off with him. After a few hours he brought you back. Then you might have had a chance to dispose of the shoes. But again you were prevented: you found out Maggie'd been released. You had to speak with her. Next, you learned that Terry had gone over to see me, and you needed to know what we were talking about. So you rushed over and joined us. Eventually Terry went off to trace the reporter who phoned him. That was your first real opportunity. But it was still light. You wondered if now it would be safer to wait until dark. And while you were hesitating the sheriff and I turned up."

Jessica paused for breath. Tupper looked at her admiringly. Then he switched his gaze back to Nan.

"Well, Miss Earl?"

Nan sat down slowly on the bed again. "What can I say? You've built up a case against me and I can't disprove it. I don't think I'd better say anything else until I've spoken to an attorney."

"That's your privilege."

"Are you going to arrest me?"

"I have good grounds."

Suddenly she stormed at him. "That's not an answer! Stop playing with me and tell me what you're going to do!"

Tupper opened his mouth, but before he could speak Jessica cut in: "Nan, what do you *expect* the sheriff to do? You've admitted there's a good case against you. Obviously he has no choice but to arrest you."

Jessica looked at Tupper. "Have you, Sheriff?" she said deliberately.

Tupper gazed at her silently for a moment. Then he shook his head. " 'Fraid not, ma'am. Miss Earl, I'm going to have to take you in."

Nan got to her feet. She looked quite composed. "Very well," she said. "I'll get a coat."

She went to the closet, took out a coat and put it on.

"Shall I go and tell your sisters?" Jessica asked.

"They're not here. Brian took them out to celebrate Maggie's release. Funny, isn't it. One sister comes out, another goes in. They should be back soon, though."

Jessica said: "Leave it to me. I'll wait in the lobby and catch them as they come in."

"And Terry, too, please. Tell him I'd like to see him."

"I will."

"Thank you." Nan turned to Tupper and held out her hands. "Going to put the cuffs on me, Sheriff?"

"That won't be necessary, Miss Earl," he said gruffly. "Let's go."

# Chapter Eleven

ABOUT an hour later Maggie, Grace and Lisa, together with Brian Shelby, came rather boisterously into the lobby of the Hill House. All except Grace seemed to have been celebrating, and they were talking and laughing. Jessica rose from her chair in the corner, came forward as they crossed the lobby in a group and confronted them.

"Well, well, well, our lady sleuth." Brian's voice was loud and the words slightly slurred. "Have they signed you up as house dick, Mrs. Fletcher, or is this your usual Saturday night hangout?"

Lisa, clinging to his arm, giggled. Maggie stepped forward with a smile. "Don't mind Brian, Mrs. Fletcher. He's had one or two too many. In fact, I'm afraid we all have. We've been celebrating my exoneration."

"Speak for yourself, dear," Grace said.

"Grace! Do you mean you *haven't* had one or two too many, or that you haven't been celebrating sister Maggie's exoneration?" Brian pointed a finger at her. "Answer yes or no, madam," he thundered. Lisa giggled again.

"Don't be a fool, Brian," Grace said coldly. "You know I rejoiced at Maggie's being cleared."

"It's just that your rejoicing is like other people's mourning, isn't it, Grace?" said Lisa.

"Oh, for heaven's sake!" Grace snapped. "Our father died twenty-four hours ago."

"I know; and you're consumed with grief, aren't you, darling?"

"No, I'm not, Lisa. But we should show a little respect and not make public exhibitions of ourselves."

Jessica said firmly: "I want to speak to you all, privately."

"My, my," Brian said, "that sounds serious."

"It *is* serious."

Maggie caught her breath. "Is anything wrong? Nan? An accident? Oh, I *knew* we should have insisted she come with us."

"No, Maggie," Jessica said. "Nan hasn't had an accident. She's perfectly fit. Look, come into the writing room. I know it's empty."

She ushered the somewhat bewildered and mildly protesting group toward a room off the lobby. They went in. As Jessica was about to follow them she glanced over her shoulder and saw Terry Jones coming into the hotel.

"Mr. Jones!" she called. "Could you come here, please?"

"Oh, really," Lisa muttered. "Do we have to have that creep in here?"

"He has a right to hear what I have to tell you," Jessica said.

Terry joined her in the doorway.

"What's up?"

"Please go in," Jessica told him.

Terry entered the room, nodding awkwardly to the others. Jessica followed him in, closed the door and stood with her back to it. Five pairs of eyes were fixed on her. She began: "I have to tell you that Nan was arrested an hour ago for the murder of her father."

For several seconds there was complete silence. Then there was a sudden outbreak of exclamations and questions. Jessica waited for this to die down before continuing. "I'm sorry I had to tell you like this."

Maggie said blankly: "But . . . but why? I mean what possible reason . . . ?"

"The sheriff found the heel of a woman's shoe near where your father's body was found. It was off one of Nan's shoes. She's admitted it's hers."

"But that's not conclusive!" Grace exclaimed.

"No, not conclusive," Brian said slowly. "But it looks bad."

"Brian!" Lisa stared at him. "You're not saying you think she's guilty?"

"No! But I'm not prepared to say she's not guilty, either. Sometimes I've thought your Nan just a little too perfect."

Maggie said hurriedly: "We must get down to the police station right away."

Brian looked at his watch. "And I must get hold of a lawyer."

"Please, just a moment," Jessica said. "There's one question I want to ask before you go."

Everybody paused, staring at her.

"One of the points against Nan is that the shoes in question are badly scratched. Nan says she's never worn them anyplace where they could get so marked. Now, I know how sisters are: very often they trade clothes. I'm wondering if it's possible that any of you three could have worn Nan's shoes?"

Simultaneously the three sisters shook their heads.

"We never trade shoes," Lisa said. "I take a size smaller than Nan."

"And I'm half a size larger," Grace added.

"I take the same size, but I never wear pink," said Maggie.

Jessica gave a nod. "That's what I expected. I simply wanted confirmation."

"You're making it look as if we're putting Nan even deeper in trouble," Grace said defensively. "But what would be the point of lying about it?"

"None at all," Jessica said. "And what you've told me doesn't put Nan deeper in trouble. From her point of view it's good testimony."

"I don't understand," Lisa said.

"Well, you've confirmed what Nan said: that those shoes haven't been worn much. Now, I've examined them. For shoes that haven't been worn much they are very badly scratched indeed. Too badly, even if they had been worn on a beach or for walking along a rocky path for a few minutes. It looks, in fact, as if they've been deliberately scratched, by being rubbed against a rough surface."

It was Lisa who spoke first. "You're saying Nan was framed?"

"I'm saying it's possible."

Grace said slowly: "Any of us girls could have got Nan's shoes on. Even though they'd be too small for me and too large for Lisa, we could have worn them—uncomfortably—for half an hour or so. Now, if I'd been trying to frame Nan by means of her shoes, that's what I'd have done: worn them so the scratches would look natural. If they were just rubbed against a rough surface, doesn't that suggest it was done by someone who couldn't get the shoes on at all?"

"That's very clever of you, my dear," Jessica said quietly. "Congratulations."

There was an uncertain silence for a few seconds, before Brian broke in. "Look, do you girls want to hang about here theorizing or do you want to see Nan and try and get this business cleared up? Come on."

He shepherded the three girls to the door. "Thanks for passing on the information, Mrs. Fletcher."

They went out. Terry Jones waited until they'd disappeared, then started toward the door himself. But Jessica called him back.

"Mr. Jones."

"Yes?" He turned.

"Nan said she especially wanted to see you. I promised I'd tell you."

"Oh, yes, of course. I don't want to be with her family, though. I'll go later."

"Well, not too much later. I understand Sheriff Tupper is keen to talk to you, too. It wouldn't look good for you if he had to have you picked up."

Terry gave a slight start. "Me? Why does he want to talk with me?"

"Well, you were with Nan during most of the evening when, if she's guilty, she must have done it."

His voice slightly higher pitched than usual, he said: "But I know nothing about it. Nothing at all."

"Don't tell *me,* Mr. Jones. Tell the sheriff."

"You said *if* she's guilty. Do you think she might not be?"

"Why ask me? You should know better than I."

He drew in his breath. "Why do you say that? I've told you I know—"

"All I meant was that you know Nan so much better than I. Do *you* think she's capable of murder?"

He shrugged. "Isn't everyone supposed to be, given the right circumstances?"

"It has been said."

"I think it's true. Nan's not a natural killer, of course. But I'd be crazy to say that she, or anyone else, is incapable of murder."

"What a remarkably dispassionate judgment, Mr. Jones."

He remained staring at her for a few more seconds, then turned abruptly on his heel and went out.


Jessica stood silently for a few moments after Terry had left. Her face was very grave. Then she gave herself a little shake, went out of the room and walked to the pay phone in the lobby. She called the police station. Tupper himself answered.

"Sheriff? Jessica Fletcher. Look, the sisters are on their way down to see Nan. Should be there any moment. And Terry Jones will be along later. If he doesn't show, you should have him brought in."

Tupper didn't reply directly. Sounding a little exasperated, he said: "Mrs. Fletcher, what was the idea of making me arrest Nan?"

*"Making* you, Sheriff? You know I couldn't make you do anything of the sort."

"You know what I mean. You wanted me to. You made that quite clear."

"Agreed."

"Why?"

"You had a strong case against her. She had motive, opportunity."

"I know, but it was too soon. I went along with you, but I haven't been happy."

"You needn't worry, Sheriff. You did the right thing. You must hold her."

"You really think she's guilty?"

"No. I know she's not."

He gave a gasp. "What? You encouraged me to take her in, knowing she—"

"I didn't know *then*. There was just a possibility she was guilty."

"Then why do you want her held?"

"For her own good."

For a moment the line went silent. Then he asked: "You mean, for her protection? You think she's in danger?"

"Perhaps not in the sense you mean. I don't think her life is in danger —at least, not at this stage. But in one sense, yes."

He sighed. "I give up. Mrs. Fletcher, are you sure you know what you're doing?"

Jessica chuckled. "No. But I do know who the killer is."

An explosive exclamation caused her to shift the receiver hurriedly from her ear.

"You serious?" Tupper said incredulously.

"Perfectly."

*"Who?"*

"Not yet, Sheriff."

He gave a groan. "Mrs. Fletcher, please. This is not a mystery story where the killer can't be revealed until the last chapter."

"Sheriff, if I told you, and you believed me, you'd be duty-bound to act on my information. Because if you didn't and the killer struck again, you'd be in deep trouble. But if you did act now, it would spoil everything, because I doubt you'd ever get a conviction."

He gave a sigh even deeper than the first. "Mrs. Fletcher, I have the greatest respect for you, and especially for your brain. But I think you're plumb crazy."

"Good. I suggest you tell everybody that."

"What?"

"Tell everybody I claim to know the identity of the killer, but that I won't reveal it yet. Say you think I'm a stupid old biddy, that I'm just showing off, anything you like. Tell them I've promised to give you my deductions tomorrow, but you're sure it'll be a lot of baloney. All right?"

"Well, if that's what you want." He sounded doubtful. "Anything else?"

"Well, I do have one or two more suggestions, if you're sure you don't mind."

"Go ahead, Mrs. Fletcher," he said wearily. "I've played along with you so far. I'm not going to back out now."

"Thank you, Mr. Tupper. I appreciate your confidence. Now this is what I'd like you to do . . ."

# Chapter Twelve

THERE was an air of bravado about Terry Jones as he walked past the deputy into Tupper's office. When he spoke his voice was loud and blustering.

"Sheriff, what's this about? I called to see Nan Earl and was told I had to see you first. Now I really . . ."

He trailed off as Tupper looked slowly up from his desk and fixed him with a beady eye.

"Sit down," he said.

"Now, look, I don't have—"

"*I said sit down!*" Tupper positively snarled the words and Terry dropped into a chair. Tupper continued to glare at him for a couple of seconds, then bent his head over his desk and continued writing.

The seconds passed. Terry cleared his throat. At the end of a minute Tupper got to his feet, crossed to a filing cabinet, opened it, removed a folder, came back to his desk, sat down, opened the folder, read the top sheet, then looked at Terry again.

"Your full name is Terence Arthur Jones?"

Terry licked his lips. "Yes, but Sheriff . . ."

"Just answer the questions. Born October 15th, 1959?"

"Yes."

"Presently a resident of Paris, Kentucky?"

"That's right."

Tupper leaned back. "Right, Jones, I want a full account of your movements yesterday evening from 7:30 on."

"Well, that might be kinda difficult."

"Why?"

"To remember everything I did."

"We're only talking about twenty-four hours ago."

"I know, but . . ."

"Listen, Jones, Nan Earl claims to have been with you most of that time. Is it true?"

"Well, yes, I guess so."

"Right. Now she's given us a very detailed account of how you spent your time. I want you to do the same. And I warn you, Jones, the accounts better tie up."

Terry was very pale. "But what happens if . . . if . . ."

"Nan Earl's facing a charge of first-degree murder. If you can't account for all your time, and produce witnesses, from the moment you met her, you may well find yourself charged as an accomplice. And in this state being an accessory's about the same as being the killer. Clear?"

Terry nodded. He made a great effort to get himself under control. "I know Nan didn't kill anyone from the time she met me, and I guess I may be able to give you an account of how we spent the evening. But I'll need a spell to think . . . remember . . . work out the timings. But answer me one question, will you?"

"What's that?"

"Between what times was Earl killed? What are the outside limits?"

Tupper considered before he spoke. "Between about 7:30 and 10:00 P.M."

"Well, look, I didn't get off the plane until 8:00 P.M. I didn't meet with Nan until after 8:30. So couldn't she have done it before she met me?"

Tupper scratched his chin. "It's possible."

"Then there you are!" Terry sounded triumphant.

"You're saying you believe she's guilty?"

Terry checked. "No! *You* say she's guilty. I say if she did it, it was before she met me."

"What was her manner like?"

"A bit, well, strange."

"I see." Tupper was thoughtful for a moment. "Okay, Mr. Jones, you can see her now."

Terry hesitated. "Perhaps that's not a very good idea after all."

Tupper shrugged. "That's up to you. Any message for her?"

"You can give her my . . ." He stopped. "Tell her I'm sorry I couldn't see her. I hope it all works out, and I'll be in touch."

"I'll see she's told. Okay, that's all."

"You don't want me anymore?"

"I'll probably still want that report, but I can see you need time to recall the details. You can go for now."

Terry got to his feet with haste.

"Thanks, Sheriff. I appreciate it."

Tupper gave a grunt and bent once more over his desk. Terry hurried out. Tupper waited until the door had closed behind him, then he said loudly:

"You hear all that, Miss Earl?"

A door behind him, which had been open about an inch was pushed wide. Nan came through. She was unguarded. Her face was very white and her hands were trembling. Tupper stood up and faced her.

"Yes, I heard," she said quietly. She took a deep breath. "That was cruel, Sheriff."

"Sorry. Sometimes you've got to be cruel."

"To be kind?" she finished. "So I've heard. Was that your idea, Mr. Tupper?"

He hesitated, and before he could reply she added: "Or Mrs. Fletcher's? All right, don't say anything. I know the answer."

It was night. The house lay bathed in pale moonlight. All was quiet. A distant clock struck one, and as it did so a shadowy figure approached the house; a figure dressed in a black sweater, jeans and black cap.

The figure flitted silently up to the house and cautiously tried a window. It was locked. The figure crept around to the rear of the house. Here it went up to the door and gingerly pulled at it. But this, too, was firmly fastened. The figure hesitated indecisively for a few seconds, then raised an arm and brought an elbow into sharp contact with the glass pane of the door.

As the tinkle of falling glass fragments broke the silence, the figure froze, merging into the shadow of the wall.

A minute passed, then another, before the shadow stirred again. Slowly a hand reached through the window frame, groping for the key inside and turning it. A moment later the door was open. The figure slipped inside. The narrow beam of a small flashlight momentarily cut through the darkness of the kitchen and was then extinguished.

The intruder crossed the room, crept in dead silence down the short corridor leading to the living room and stopped again. Once more the flashlight's beam darted around. But the next second it was suddenly neutralized as without warning the lights came on.

The intruder's hands were instinctively thrown up to hide the face as Jessica Fletcher, standing by the light switch, said calmly: "That wasn't very thoughtful. Now I'll have to have that glass pane repaired."

For seconds both she and the intruder stood motionless. Then the latter's hands were slowly lowered and Maggie Earl said unemotionally: "You were expecting me."

* * *

The words were a statement more than a question and Jessica did not reply. But then Maggie said: "I slipped up, didn't I?"

"Yes. I never said those shoes were pink."

"I realized my mistake the second the words were out of my mouth."

Jessica nodded. "I thought you had. You went very quiet after that."

"I wasn't absolutely sure you'd spotted it," Maggie said. "But when Sheriff Tupper told us you were going to give him your deductions tomorrow, I couldn't afford to chance it."

"If it makes you feel any better, I was virtually certain you were the guilty one before that."

"How did you know?"

"Nan had obviously been framed. The shoes had deliberately been scratched. Besides, she'd never have worn those shoes for such an expedition. No; you removed them from her closet, took them with you when you went to kill your father, made footmarks with them in the sand afterward, deliberately scratched them and got sand in them. Then you wrenched off both heels, left one near the body, threw the other away, and later wrapped the shoes up again and replaced them in Nan's closet."

"But what made you think it was me? I thought when you congratulated Grace on her theory that you accepted it."

"I congratulated her on its ingenuity. But it was too subtle. She obviously hoped Brian was the murderer; hence her implied suggestion that the killer had to be a man. But she ignored the time element: *anyone* who was in a hurry would scratch the shoes the way you did, by rubbing them on a rough surface. That fact didn't mean the shoes were necessarily too small for the killer. As to why I believed you were the culprit, there were three reasons. First, your father obviously went out that evening to meet somebody. Who was it likely to be but the only person in on his scheme to fake his own death and trap Terry? You. Second, there was the phone call to Terry, suggesting he come to Maine and see Nan. If you were going to frame her, you had to be sure she left the hotel that night. Only for *Terry* would she be certain to do that. He told me Grace had phoned him. She denied it. I felt they were both telling the truth as they believed it. In fact, you phoned him and said you were Grace. Your voices are not unalike; Terry had never had a lot of connection with either of you and hadn't been in touch for over a year. It wasn't likely he'd spot the deception. So, given Grace's denial was genuine, the impersonator could only have been Lisa—unlikely—or you."

"And the third reason?" Maggie asked harshly.

"Your father's death was plainly what I might call a family murder. I couldn't believe the motive was financial. I thought that it was much more likely to be a matter of pure hatred and jealousy. I asked myself which of the other three girls was most likely to hate her father and be jealous of her youngest sister. Answer: the one who'd been closest to him and lived at home with him. I'm afraid all roads led to you, Maggie."

"You're very clever, Mrs. Fletcher," the girl said.

"Merely logical. You're the clever one, Maggie. Taking advantage of your father's plan—actually confessing to shooting him—because you knew investigation would exonerate you."

Maggie smiled, the pleased, self-contented smile of the egoist. "Yes, it was clever. And yet you know it had never occurred to me to kill him until he came up with this idea of pretending to die. And then I thought: wouldn't it be nice if he really died? It was actually my idea to confess to killing him. Of course, he didn't suggest it."

"No, I didn't think any father would suggest his daughter put herself through all that. Not unless he was an absolute monster, and he didn't strike me as a monster."

Maggie's eyes flashed. "You didn't know him! You don't know what he did to me. I hated him for it. My whole life was spent catering to that man, keeping the peace, running his house, raising his daughters. All my youth was just frittered away on my family. It wasn't too bad with Grace and Lisa: Grace was always too busy studying to be any trouble. And Lisa never needed anybody to look after *her*. But Nan was the last straw. It was because of her I had to stay on years after the others had left home. 'Just stay a bit longer,' Dad said, 'just till Nan's grown up.' She was his baby, she was vulnerable, she needed a mother around. So I stayed until it was too late for me. And they were so close, always laughing and joking together. I got no love or appreciation. I was the outsider. They had each other; Lisa had Brian; Grace had her career, even after her marriage broke up. I had nobody and nothing. I hated them. I knew Terry was no good, and I wanted Nan to leave him—just because he was a rat. I wanted her to suffer—and I wanted Dad to suffer, seeing her suffer. And then Dad roped me into this crazy scheme to save Nan from her own stupidity. And I thought, I'll make them both sorry."

She was panting. Jessica looked at her with deep pity in her eyes. "Well, you succeeded," she said softly. "Your father is dead. And Nan has nobody."

Maggie looked pleased. "Yes, I have, haven't I?"

"And what now? What about me?"

"I can't let you spoil it all for me. I'm sorry. I like you, I really do, but I have to protect myself."

"Oh, dear me," Jessica said. "That's not a threat, is it?"

"It'll all look very natural," Maggie said quietly. "You were home alone. A defenseless widow. A burglar entered. You surprised him and there was a struggle."

Jessica shook her head gently. "Maggie, really, for a clever woman you have devised a terrible scenario. First of all, we have no burglars here in Cabot Cove. Second, and I suppose more to the point, as soon as I heard the window shatter I called Sheriff Tupper. He was standing by and he's been listening to this entire conversation."

She pointed to a nearby table. Maggie looked—and gave a gasp of horror. The receiver was off the hook.

Jessica walked to the table and picked up the receiver. She took a few steps toward Maggie, saying into the receiver as she did so: "Did you hear all that, Sheriff?"

She held it out for Maggie to hear the reply: "Sure did, Mrs. Fletcher. And it's all on tape."

Jessica spoke into the receiver again. "Then I think you'd better come over to my house right away. I have a young woman here who wants to surrender herself into your custody."

# Chapter Thirteen

"IT'S very strange," Jessica said. "When the three of us went to the hotel that night and confronted the girls with what we'd found out about the eye of the hurricane, Maggie immediately confessed to having shot her father. In that respect she was telling the truth. The clever thing was that she confessed to killing him on the yacht the previous night. That was a lie—and she knew it would be proved so. In actuality she must have only gotten back to the hotel a short while before, having just done it."

Ethan Cragg nodded. "She shot her old man about the time you and I were working out the course of the hurricane?"

"I'm afraid so."

"And, of course," Tupper said, "when it turned out that first confession was phony, I was checking everybody else's movements at the real time of the murder; but it never occurred to me to check Maggie's. I thought she was in the clear."

"That's what she was counting on," Jessica said.

It was the following afternoon. The three of them were in Jessica's living room, where she had been serving Ethan a cup of tea when Tupper had arrived to announce the final developments of the case.

Now he said: "By the way, lucky Maggie signed a full confession and that you told me in advance what to say over the phone last night. Because I couldn't hear half of what you and she were saying."

Jessica chuckled. "I realized you might not. Fortunately, in moments of stress people don't think of things like that."

"One thing I don't get," Ethan said. "You told me Maggie gave herself away by talking about pink shoes. Why didn't you jump on her then?"

"Two reasons. First, Maggie could have said that Nan had mentioned she'd bought pink shoes and she'd guessed those were the ones I was talking about. I didn't know if Nan could or would deny having told her; but even if she did, it would only be a question of one girl's word against another's. I had to lure Maggie into doing something that would be conclusive proof. The second reason was that I didn't want the case tied up too quickly—not until the sheriff had had a chance to grill Terry, with Nan listening in."

"You told me you wanted me to hold her for her own good," Tupper said. "I thought you meant her protection, but you didn't, did you?"

"In one sense. I wanted her protected from marriage to Terry Jones. I wasn't sure about that young man for a long time. Then I thought that a good test of his love would be Nan's arrest for murder. It was only when I saw how he reacted to that news that I knew he was no good. But how to convince Nan? She was in love with him. It occurred to me that if you could grill him, so he really thought he was in danger of arrest, and Nan could be made to listen in, then her eyes would be opened. Fortunately, his cowardice turned out to be greater than his greed. He preferred to lose a stake in her fortune rather than risk facing a murder-one charge."

At that moment there came a ring of the doorbell. Jessica went to answer it.

Nan was standing on the step. She smiled shyly. "I'm just leaving." She indicated the taxi parked outside. "I thought I'd come and say good-bye."

"Oh, my dear, I'm so glad. Do come in."

She took the girl through to the living room. Ethan and the sheriff got to their feet.

"I hope this means you've forgiven me?" Jessica said.

Nan nodded. "Yes, of course. It did hurt hearing Terry turn against me like that. But I can see it was a good thing I did hear it. It's certainly what Dad would have wanted you to do."

"That was in my mind," Jessica said.

Nan said slowly, "I can't get over that I'm really the one responsible for his death. If it hadn't been for my infatuation with Terry, Dad would never have hatched that scheme."

"You mustn't think like that," Jessica told her firmly. "It was your father's own idea. All you did was fall in love with a very good-looking, charming and clever young man. And let me say this: I'm sure your father would have been quite content to die to insure your happiness."

"Yes, I think you're right." She paused for a moment, then said, "He was really a decent man, you know—whatever may have been said about him. And he did care very deeply for the others, and worry about them. I know. We'd talk about them sometimes. It was they who distanced themselves from him—not the other way around. I'm sure that's the reason I became his favorite, if it's true I was."

"I'm certain you were. I think if you give love, that's what you get

back. And you, my dear, have a great capacity for giving it. So make sure
your father didn't die in vain. Be happy."

Nan smiled. "I'll try."

"So, Miss Earl," Tupper said, "back to New York now, is it?"

"Yes, to try and pick up the threads of my career once all the publicity's died down."

"What do you think's going to happen to your father's company?"
Ethan asked. "Who do you figure's going to gain control?"

"Grace, I think. She'll get my vote, anyway. I want to keep in touch
with Grace. Basically she's okay—and as straight as an arrow. Just a bit
too ambitious for her own good."

"Well, that may not be a bad thing right now," Jessica said. "If she's to
win this battle. When she achieves her ambition, she'll probably soften.
People usually do."

"I hope she does achieve it. I should hate the firm to fall into the hands
of Brian and Lisa."

"Folks like that deserve each other, I reckon," Ethan grunted. "Oh, no
offense."

Nan grinned. "None taken, Captain." She looked at her watch. "I
must go."

Jessica walked with her down to the front gate. When they reached it,
Nan suddenly turned and gave Jessica a hug. Then she drew back and
said:

"Thank you. From me—and Dad."

"Be sure and write now," Jessica told her.

"I will. Promise. Bye."

Jessica stood waving until the taxi was out of sight. A sweet girl. If
ever she'd had a daughter . . .

She turned and made her way back up the path to the house. As she
approached the front door, Ethan appeared in the hallway beyond.

"Hey, Jess," he called urgently. "Come in quick—there's a guy on
television talking about your book."

# Chapter Fourteen

JESSICA hurried into the house. "Ethan, are you sure?"

"Sure I'm sure. I turned the set on to get the weather forecast and heard this fellow mention *The Corpse Danced at Midnight.*"

He followed Jessica into the living room, where Sheriff Tupper was staring at the television screen. Tupper looked up. "This is weird, Mrs. Fletcher. The guy's talking about it being made into a horror movie."

*"What?"* Jessica sat down on the edge of a chair, her eyes glued to the set.

The program on the screen seemed to be coming direct from a film-studio sound stage. In the background a troupe of dancers was rehearsing. In the foreground two men were seated on canvas chairs. Jessica recognized one of the men as a well-known talk-show host. The other was a tanned, handsome man in his late forties, with flashing white teeth, that seemed to be exposed in a perpetual smile.

As Jessica sat down, the host was saying: "Jerry, just why do they call you Hollywood's most controversial producer?"

Jerry would obviously have liked to grin, if he hadn't been doing so already. Instead he contented himself with a graceful shrug.

"Well, Ted, I guess because the critics hate my pictures. Everybody hates them except the public."

"There's a bit more to it than that, though, isn't there? I mean, haven't you been accused of pandering to the lowest tastes of the moviegoing public?"

Jerry threw back his head and laughed. "There's a lot of jealousy in this business, Ted. I'm successful. I know what the public wants and I give it to them. I don't pass judgment. If people don't like my movies, they don't have to see them. Fortunately for me, millions do like them."

"Okay, Jerry, now let's revert to the picture you started shooting to-day: *The Corpse Danced at Midnight,* starring Eve Crystal."

Jessica gave a gasp. "They've actually started shooting it!"

The interviewer was continuing. "I described it just now as a horror picture. Is that accurate?"

Jerry made an elegant gesture with his hands. "Not really, Ted."

"Well, thank heavens for *that!*" Jessica exclaimed.

"I mean, it's so much more than just a horror movie," Jerry went on. "It really has everything the young, modern moviegoing audience wants: music, dancing, plenty of sex, violence."

"Too much violence, perhaps?"

"Just what is too much? We live in a violent world."

"Well, I was thinking, for instance, of the scene where the psychotic killer uses a flamethrower on a group of breakdancers."

Jessica shot out of her chair with a shriek of dismay. "I didn't write anything like that!"

Jerry chuckled. "Just good clean fun."

"For you, perhaps. But won't it scare the kiddies?"

"They'll love it."

Ted obviously decided to let this point go. "Now the screenplay, by Allan Gebhart, is based on the novel by J. B. Fletcher."

"It's not!" Jessica shouted.

Jerry nodded. "Correct."

"That book, of course, was a best-seller," Ted continued, "but it was also praised for its literary qualities."

Jerry interrupted. "That so?"

"Haven't you read it?"

"Never got around to it, Ted. Saw a synopsis, of course."

"Let's move on to your next project, Jerry: a new up-to-date version of *Little Women,* with some alterations made in the girls' characters. For instance—"

Abruptly Jessica switched off the set. Her face was white.

Ethan said: "Seems Mr. Lydecker's tossing some of his own ideas into the picture."

"Is that his name? Lydecker?"

"So the other guy said."

"Can he do that, Mrs. Fletcher?" Tupper asked. "Change everything?"

Jessica's expression was set firm. "Not if I have any say in the matter, Sheriff. I assure you, I'm going to fight tooth and nail to stop that man from mutilating my book."

She looked at her watch. "First thing in the morning my editor is going to get a call that will probably melt the phone wires between here and New York. I shall instruct Coventry House to buy back that option from Mr. Jerry Lydecker. I don't care what it costs."

*  *  *

When Ethan Cragg called at Jessica's house the following morning, he expected to find her busily working on her book, as usual. Instead, to his surprise, she was in the throes of packing a suitcase.

"Where you off to?" he asked.

"Hollywood."

*What? Hollywood?* Now?"

"In just an hour. So I don't have much time, Ethan. I'm sorry."

"But what for? Say, have they invited you? You going to rewrite the script for 'em or something?"

"No, I have not been invited."

Jessica deftly folded a silk blouse and put it in her suitcase.

Ethan scratched his head. "Well, what on earth's happened, Jess? Did you call your publisher?"

"Yes, I did." Her voice was grim.

"And?"

"And nothing. Marilyn—that's my editor—is off on a three-week vacation in Europe. I got no satisfaction at all. As you know, Coventry House was taken over by some big conglomerate. Practically everybody I knew there when my novel was first published has left. Even Kitt Donovan has gone to work for Avon Books. So it's all become extremely impersonal. Anyway, it seems that they're not handling the matter there. All business pertaining to the movie rights of their books is handled by a firm of attorneys in Los Angeles."

"And you're going out there to see them?"

"That's right."

"For heaven's sake, Jess, can't you phone?"

"I could, but I have a strong suspicion that I'd get nowhere. If I'm going to stop this appalling thing happening to my book I'm going to have to *be* there—and make a perfect nuisance of myself. I may have to hire lawyers of my own—try and get on TV shows myself to object publicly, talk to the press, take advertising space to denounce the project."

"Jess, this could cost you a small fortune."

"No, Ethan. It could cost me a big fortune."

She closed the suitcase and snapped shut the catches.

He said helplessly: "Look, Jess, why not just let it ride? Let it be known the picture's nothing to do with you, that you dissociate yourself from it, and just sit back and enjoy the dough. Or if you feel that's unethical, give it to charity. Don't bang your head against a brick wall."

Jessica looked at him. "No doubt what you say makes sense, Ethan. But—"

"I know, I know: it's a matter of principle, something you just gotta do."

"Precisely."

He sighed. "Then it's a waste o' time me trying to talk you out of it. But you can't go alone. Better let me come along with you. I can manage to take a day or two off."

Jessica looked at him affectionately. "Ethan, that's sweet of you. But no."

"Why not?"

"I can manage on my own. Besides, you know that you can't afford the time."

"Place like Hollywood's no spot for an unescorted lady. Dangerous."

She smiled. "Why, Ethan, you don't think someone's going to offer me a screen test and I'll find myself drugged and in a crate on my way to South America?"

"No, course not, but . . ."

"My dear, it's lovely of you to offer, but I assure you I'll be quite all right. Besides, to be absolutely frank, you'd probably cramp my style."

He frowned. "How d'you mean?"

"You're too straightforward, Ethan, too honest. It may be necessary for me to play dirty and be very devious. And I'd hate you to have any illusions you might still have about me shattered."

# Chapter Fifteen

MARTIN Strindberg, of Carr, Strindberg & Roth, Attorneys at Law, was a man in his forties, with beautifully styled wavy hair and charming manners. Smooth was the one adjective that came irresistibly to Jessica's mind as she sat across the big shiny desk from him: smooth white hands; smooth unlined face; smooth mohair suit; smooth silk shirt and tie; smooth, soothing voice. A voice he was now using in the most persuasive way he could manage.

"My dear Mrs. Fletcher, I'm extremely sorry you should feel like this, and I assure you I do understand. I must, however, point out that it is always a shock for a novelist to see his or her work translated to the screen. I don't suppose any author has ever been completely happy with the movie version of his book. You see, the Novel and the Motion Picture"—he clearly bestowed mental capital letters on the words—"are two entirely different art forms. Changes have to be made in—"

"I am well aware of that, Mr. Strindberg," Jessica interrupted. "I never imagined, if a movie was made from my book, that the story would be unchanged. I was prepared for drastic alterations. What I was not prepared for was the whole thing to be made completely unrecognizable. My book is a mystery story—"

"And a brilliant one, if I may say so."

"Thank you. It's chiefly an intellectual puzzle, a character study, and I suppose to an extent a morality tale—with a bit of humor thrown in. It's quite clear this picture is going to be nothing like that."

"Have you read the screenplay?"

"No, I haven't. But I heard Mr. Lydecker talking about it on television. He's introducing music and dancing—farcical but harmless, and I wouldn't object to that—and plenty of sex and violence. Mr. Strindberg, my book includes one very chaste romance between two of the murder suspects: all they do is kiss—once—at the end. The murders all take place offstage, and in the end the murderess gives herself up without a struggle. She's a ballerina, not in the least psychotic, and she wouldn't know one end of a flamethrower from the other!"

Strindberg nodded understandingly and judicially. "Believe me, I do appreciate your feelings, Mrs. Fletcher. But do let's look at the bright side. If this picture is a box-office success—as I feel sure it will be—your name will be made. Every producer in Hollywood, many of them more high-minded than Jerry Lydecker, will be after the rights to your next book. Out of the whole thing, Mrs. Fletcher, you could make a fortune. Well, already, you are guaranteed . . . er, let me see, exactly how many thousand dollars is it . . . ?" He looked down at some papers on his desk.

"That is immaterial," Jessica said.

Mr. Strindberg looked up quickly. He blinked.

"I beg your pardon?"

"I said that's immaterial. I have quite enough money for my needs."

Mr. Strindberg was shocked. It was as if Jessica had questioned a sacred article of his faith. He was also baffled.

"You mean you don't want a piece of the action?"

Jessica sighed. "Naturally, all those thousands of dollars would be very acceptable. There's a lot of good I could do with the money."

He brightened. "Well, then . . ."

"How could I justify my book, if while on the one hand the proceeds of it are doing good, at the same time the movie version is having a corrupting influence on young people?"

"Oh, Mrs. Fletcher, I'm sure you're exaggerating. There are many pictures made which are far wo—" He broke off. "Er, far more extreme than—"

Jessica interrupted. "Were you going to say far *worse* than Mr. Lydecker's? I don't doubt it. But my name isn't associated with those pictures. I can't do anything about them."

Strindberg was silent for a moment. Then he said: "What exactly are you asking be done about yours?"

"That the movie rights be purchased back from Mr. Lydecker."

Strindberg shook his head firmly. "Quite impossible, I'm afraid. There's no clause in our contract with him which gives us that right."

"But don't I have any say in the matter at all?" Jessica asked angrily. "Surely you shouldn't have sold away the rights to my book without consulting me?"

"I'm sorry, but we were perfectly justified, legally. I have a copy of your original contract with Coventry House here." He picked up a sheaf of papers from his desk. "When you signed this you granted to them—

quote—'sole and exclusive rights to reproduce and to authorize the re-production of the work in cinematographic form in any language in all parts of the world.' The publishers authorized us to act on their behalf."

"I cannot understand how I came to sign that," Jessica said exasperat-edly. "I must have been crazy!"

"Not at all. It's perfectly standard practice. I do agree that as a matter of courtesy you should have been contacted when Lydecker made his initial approach several months back. If you'd made your views plain then, and the publishers wished to retain your goodwill they might—*might*—have respected your objections and instructed us to refuse his offer. Now it's too late."

"The first I heard of it was four or five days ago," Jessica told him bitterly.

"There was obviously a regrettable breakdown in communication. We thought New York would inform you. They left it to us. I'm extremely sorry. And let me emphasize that my job is not to make critical or moral judgments, but simply to obtain the best possible financial deal for our clients."

"Oh, I realize that," Jessica said.

Strindberg stood up. "So, it looks as if you'll just have to make the best of it, Mrs. Fletcher. You've made your protest, and you can rest assured I will see that Jerry Lydecker is informed of your views. But I'm afraid that will be the end of the matter."

Jessica also got to her feet. "Oh, no, it won't, Mr. Strindberg."

He stared. "What's that?"

"I haven't flown two thousand five hundred miles to let the matter rest like that. The fight's only just started."

"But what can you possibly do?"

"In the first place, see Mr. Lydecker myself."

"And say what to him, for heaven's sake?"

"I don't know precisely. Yet. But I shall probably start by appealing to his better nature—if I can find it, that is. Thank you for your time, Mr. Strindberg. Good day."

And Jessica walked briskly to the door and went out.

As Jessica was making her way thoughtfully along the corridor toward the elevator she heard footsteps coming up behind her and a voice saying somewhat nervously: "Oh, ma'am. Excuse me, ma'am."

She stopped and turned to see a young man approaching her. He was thin, bespectacled, with an earnest and anxious expression. For a moment he looked strangely familiar; then she realized that in hairstyle and dress he'd obviously modeled himself on Martin Strindberg. However, as he'd had to do it on a much lower income, he'd failed to achieve the same impressive effect.

The young man stopped a few feet from Jessica. "Yes?" she said encouragingly.

"Oh, Mrs. F-Fletcher?" He stammered slightly.

"That's right."

"I—I just wanted to say before you left how m-much I enjoyed your book. It was terrific."

Jessica smiled. "That's extremely kind of you, Mr. . . . er . . . ?"

"Lester, Norman Lester. I'm a junior member of the f-firm."

"I see. So you know all about this movie deal?"

"Well, not *all* about it. But I understand Mr. Strindberg . . . er, Martin . . . made a very satisfactory arrangement."

"It depends how you define satisfactory. Do you know what sort of film Lydecker is making from my book?"

"Well, I saw him being interviewed on television. And I know his reputation, of course."

"And what do you think of his plans?"

He hesitated, then took a deep breath. "Frankly, Mrs. Fletcher, not much. In fact—well, I think it's a crying shame." Then he went red. "I say, I'm sorry. Please don't think I'm criticizing you. I know you can't afford to turn down that sort of money."

"Oh, but I can, Norman. And if I *could* I would. Like a flash."

He looked amazed. "Really?"

"Really. That's what I've been telling Mr. Strindberg. But it seems I have no power to turn the offer down."

"No, of course, you wouldn't have. But if I may say so, Mrs. Fletcher, I think it's great you should want to." He was rapidly gaining in confidence.

Jessica regarded him reflectively. "Well, it's nice I should have one ally in Los Angeles. Tell me: would you be willing to help me?"

He stared at her owlishly through his spectacles. "In what way?"

"I'm not quite sure at the moment. But I'm not giving up the fight. I might require legal advice—or just information. To know that I could call on you, if necessary, would be reassuring. I promise I won't be too much of a nuisance."

"I couldn't act in any way contrary to the interests of the firm. Or break any confidences."

"Of course not. I wouldn't ask you to."

"Then in that case, Mrs. Fletcher, I'll be delighted to do anything I can."

"Thank you, Norman. That's very good to know. I'll probably be in touch. Goodbye."

She gave him a warm smile and walked away.

Jessica took a cab back to her hotel and went straight to the phone. She dialed the number of Lydecker's studios and asked for his office. A girl answered.

"Can I speak with Mr. Lydecker, please. My name is J.B. Fletcher."

"He's tied up right now," the girl said, in a bored voice. "Will you hold?" And before Jessica could reply the line went dead.

Ten minutes later Jessica was still "holding." She hung up and asked for the number again. Exactly the same procedure ensued. This time, however, when asked if she would hold, she did manage to get out a loud and peremptory "No."

"Pardon?" said the girl.

"I can't hold any longer. I've been doing so for ten minutes already."

"Very well. Thank you for calling." The secretary hung up.

Jessica was breathing deeply. She put the phone down and went to have a cup of coffee. Ten minutes later she returned to the phone and tried a third time. "Jerry Lydecker, please," she said, when she again heard the secretary's voice.

"He's in conference."

"When will he be free?"

"He's tied up for the rest of the day."

"Can I make an appointment?"

"What was the name?"

"Jessica Fletcher—J.B. Fletcher."

"And the nature of your business?"

Jessica sighed. "I'm the author of *The Corpse Danced at Midnight.*"

For the first time the secretary's voice showed a trace of interest.

"Oh, no," she said.

"What's that?"

"Allan Gebhart's the writer on that project. I'll give you his number and you can speak with him."

"I do not wish to speak with Mr. Gebhart," Jessica said loudly and clearly. "I am the author of the original novel and I wish to see Mr. Lydecker. Now, can you arrange an appointment for me?"

"Well, not today."

"Tomorrow, then?"

"Hang on. I'll look in the book." There was the rustle of pages for a few moments. Then the girl said: "Sorry, he's busy for the rest of the week. He might be able to fit you in for ten minutes at 8:30 A.M. next Wednesday."

"Next *Wednesday?*"

"Yeah. I'll pencil you in provisionally. Better call us Tuesday, though, to confirm it. What was the name again?"

Very gently Jessica put down the receiver.

She sat thinking. Right. She'd made the orthodox approach, without success. She was obviously going to have to gate-crash. She looked at her watch. And now would be as good a time as any. At least she knew Lydecker was at the studio today.

Jessica picked up her purse and went out. On her way down in the elevator, she wondered just what the subject was of the conference Mr. Lydecker was "in."

# Chapter Sixteen

"YOU lied to me, you little tramp." Jerry Lydecker's voice was cold.

"No, Jerry, honey, I wouldn't lie to you."

Eve Crystal stared up at him with big blue eyes. She put her arms around his neck and said coaxingly: "Don't be mad at me, Jerry."

"Eve, I checked with your drama coach. You canceled those extra lessons."

"Oh yeah, I meant to tell you."

He gave a short laugh. "Sure you did. You just forgot."

"That's right. I . . ."

He took her wrists and roughly removed her hands from around his neck. "You're still lying, baby. You're seeing some guy."

She opened her mouth, but before she could speak he put his hand over it. "I don't want to know who it is, Eve. Just stop. Understand?"

He took his hand away. Eve drew a deep breath. "Jerry, I swear to you."

Suddenly, at the top of his voice he yelled into her face. *"I said stop!* You hear me?"

She shrank back, her hands going up, as if to protect herself from some expected blow. But instead he turned abruptly away and stood with his back to her. When he spoke his voice was very quiet. "Get this. When this picture is released, you'll be a big star. I will have made you. You will be mine, body and soul. I'm your future. Don't forget it."

Before Eve could reply there came a sharp rap on the dressing-room door and a voice shouted: "Ready for rehearsal, Miss Crystal."

An expression of relief swept over the girl's lovely but somewhat vacuous features.

"Coming," she answered. Then with one quick nervous backward glance at Lydecker, she opened the door and hurried out.

Lydecker continued to stand quite still for several more seconds. He was breathing heavily, as if he'd been running. There was a glazed look in his eyes. Almost mechanically, he reached into his pocket and brought out a small box. He opened it and took from it a tablet which he popped into his mouth. He hesitated, then added a second. He poured water from a jug on a table and swallowed the two pills.

Gradually, his breathing began to return to normal. He visibly relaxed. A minute passed. Then he crossed to the door and went out. There was now a smile on his lips.

The uniformed guard at the studio gate was adamant.

"Sorry, ma'am. I can't let you in without a pass."

"But I came all the way from Cabot Cove, Maine, to see Mr. Lydecker," Jessica pleaded.

He shook his head. "Too bad. You should have phoned for an appointment. That's how it's done."

At that moment an expensive little foreign car pulled up alongside them. It was driven by an attractive, dark-haired, rather exotic-looking woman of about thirty. Jessica, however, was too preoccupied to pay her much attention. "Listen," she said, "I'm the author of the book that is the basis—supposedly the basis—of Mr. Lydecker's film. I wrote *The Corpse Danced at Midnight.* I'm Jessica B. Fletcher. Now, please."

"Mrs. Fletcher, I have my orders."

"Hold it a second, Paddy."

Jessica turned as the strange voice spoke from behind her. It was the young woman in the car.

"I'll vouch for Mrs. Fletcher, Paddy. Put her down as my guest."

"Sure thing, Miss Quintessa. Seems you're in, ma'am." He retired into his booth.

Jessica said: "This is really very kind. Thank you."

The young woman said, "Just wait till I park and I'll walk you to the set."

Jessica waited while Miss Quintessa drove her car to a parking space, got out, locked it and walked back.

"I'm awfully glad you came along," Jessica told her. "I was beginning to give up hope. But I don't know why you did it, Miss . . . er, Quintessa, is it?"

The girl smiled. "Marta. As a matter of fact, I'm costume designer on *The Corpse Danced at Midnight*—and one of the few people involved with the film to have read your book."

"Oh, I see. Well, thank you again."

"I think it's the very least I could do, considering what we're doing to your novel. Shall we walk."

"Oh, yes, please." She fell in beside the girl. "Does that mean that . . . ? Oh, I don't know how to put it."

"I know what you mean. The answer is I loved the book, which is more than I can say for the screenplay. Jerry has done a beautiful job of trashing it."

"Surely the screenwriter must share the blame for that."

"Not really. Believe it or not, Allan Gebhart *can* write. But he was writing to Jerry's strict instructions. Allan did do his best to retain something of the novel's flavor, but most of that went when Jerry rewrote it."

"I must confess I haven't read the screenplay. No one sent me a copy."

"I have one here."

She rummaged in her shoulder bag and drew out a thick wad of typescript-covered papers, bracketed together, which she handed to Jessica. "You can keep that."

"Thank you." Jessica took the script a little gingerly, as if somehow merely touching the script would give her a shock.

"I only hope you have a strong heart, darling," Marta said. "And a stronger stomach. In here."

She turned aside and led the way into a cavernous building that echoed to the sounds of hammering, voices calling, and the humming of electrical equipment. It was rather dark. People were hurrying about in different directions, some carrying things, nearly all wearing harassed expressions.

Marta picked her way among packing cases, piles of unwanted scenery and cables that snaked about the floor. Jessica looked about her. It was her first visit to a film studio; and she was surprised at how much less interesting it was than she'd expected. But perhaps she was too worried about the fate of her book to appreciate it properly.

Marta suddenly stopped and spoke softly. "Behold and marvel: the star of the picture." She pointed.

Jessica stared. From one of a row of what were presumably portable dressing rooms a girl was emerging. She had long, luxurious blond hair, enormous blue eyes and a perfect figure. She was wearing a loose-fitting terry robe and apparently nothing else. She remained motionless for a second or two, then hurried off in the direction of the set.

"The beautiful and incredibly untalented Eve Crystal," Marta murmured.

"Should I have heard of her?"

"No, not yet."

"She is certainly very lovely," Jessica said reflectively. "I wonder why she looks so desperately unhappy—and frightened."

Marta shrugged. "Probably doesn't know her lines."

"What part is she playing?"

"Jenny."

"Jenny? I didn't have a Jenny in the book. What does the character do?"

"She witnesses the first murder and then is too frightened to talk about it—which of course makes her a target for the killer."

Jessica gave a gasp. "I don't believe it!"

Before Jessica could say any more, Marta pointed again. "There's the man you want to see."

In the doorway of the same dressing room Jerry Lydecker appeared. Jessica's eyes gleamed. "Ah—at last."

"Come on," Marta said. "I'll introduce you. I want to be in on this."

She started to move forward, but before they reached Lydecker, they saw somebody else approaching him from the other direction. This was a tall, rangy man of about thirty-five with curly hair and horn-rimmed glasses.

"Ah, Jerry," he said loudly. Lydecker turned toward him, a resigned expression on his face.

Marta stopped again and whispered to Jessica. "Let's wait here for a minute. This promises to be quite an interesting piece of dialogue. That's Allan Gebhart."

Jessica felt a little embarrassed, for the young woman obviously intended to listen in on the two men's conversation. However, as she made no attempt to conceal either herself or Jessica from view, it could not be described as eavesdropping. So Jessica listened, too.

"You're quite a guy to track down, Jerry," Gebhart was saying. "Why didn't you return my phone calls?"

"Nothing personal, Allan," Lydecker said, in a bored voice. "I don't return anybody's calls."

Allan Gebhart grinned. "Say, that's a good line. I'll use it."

"I'd be surprised if you didn't use any good line you heard someone else say, Allan. What do you want to see me about?"

A slight flush came over Gebhart's face. "It's about my contract," he said stiffly.

"So?"

"It finally came through today. But it's not as we agreed. Those points you promised me for writing the screenplay for less than my normal payment—they got left out. What happened?"

Lydecker gave a casual shrug. "Business affairs."

"What does that mean? You saying it was a mistake?"

"Not really. They said those stipulations were more than you were worth."

Gebhart stared at him. "That's my screenplay you're shooting in there." He pointed in the direction of the set. "Where would you be without it?"

Lydecker gave a sardonic grin. "Tell me about your Oscar nomination when you were twenty-five."

Gebhart's eyes were ablaze with anger. He said: "I'm a damn good writer—and you know it."

"*Were*, Allan, *were*. Now you're just an aging ex-wonder boy."

There was a moment's silence. When Gebhart spoke, his voice was ominously quiet. "Then why hire me?"

"I didn't realize how bad you'd gotten. I had to rewrite your script from page one. Face it, Allan: you're a has-been. You're burned out by booze."

Gebhart was by now almost quivering with rage. "I'm an alcoholic," he said. "I've admitted it. A *recovering* alcoholic."

Lydecker laughed. "Recovering? I don't see much evidence of it. I suggest you stop trying to write anything until the recovery's more obvious."

"There's nothing wrong with that screenplay," Gebhart shouted. "Everybody knows why you rewrote it. You cut every line of Jenny's that called for acting skill, so you could cast your little playmate in the part."

The smile was instantaneously wiped from Lydecker's face. He snapped:

"Right—that's it. You just wrote your ticket off this lot. I don't want you around anymore. Get out."

"That suits me fine," Gebhart said. "But just remember: the picture isn't over till the credits roll."

He stalked off, almost brushing aside Jessica and Marta, but giving the latter a brief nod of acknowledgment as he passed.

"What did I promise you?" Marta said in a low voice to Jessica. "Come on."

They walked forward to join Lydecker.

"Darling, how nice to see you looking so cheerful," Marta said brightly to him.

He gave a grunt. "I was looking for you, Marta. Listen, we got a problem."

She interrupted. "Not for a moment, Jerry. I have a delightful surprise for you. This is Jessica Fletcher, the *original* author of *Corpse.*"

Lydecker shifted his gaze uninterestedly to Jessica. "Yeah? Nice to meet you." He turned back to Marta. "Eve hates that costume for the marching-band sequence."

Jessica took a deep breath and interrupted firmly. "Pardon me, please, Mr. Lydecker, but when it's convenient I would like a few minutes of your time to discuss this picture."

He threw her an impatient glance. "Yeah, sure. Maybe later."

He half turned back to Marta. But Jessica was insistent. "Could you be more exact? This is a matter of some importance to me."

He gave a sigh. "Okay. My office—3:00 P.M."

"Thank you," Jessica said politely.

He took Marta by the arm. "Eve says that glitzy number makes her look like a kid."

"Does she know she's playing a teenager?" Marta asked sarcastically.

He started to lead her away, toward the set. "Make it a bit more sexy. Cut it lower in front and higher on the sides."

"One more cut, darling," Marta said angrily, "and there'll be nothing left but a belt. I refuse to be treated this way, Jerry. That girl knows nothing about costumes . . ."

Their voices faded and Jessica was left alone. She stood uncertainly for a few seconds, then hesitantly followed after them.

Then a voice called loudly: "Quiet on the set, please! Rehearsal!"

Curious, Jessica followed the direction of the voice. She picked her way past the backs of some scenery flats—and suddenly found herself on the edge of a cemetery. It had a decidedly Gothic appearance, with heavily stylized tombstones, bare trees with ghostly branches like the arms of skeletons, and, in the background, a big, dark and somehow forbidding church, with stained-glass windows adding splashes of rich color to the prevailing somber tones.

It was extremely well done and in spite of herself Jessica was impressed. At least Jerry Lydecker didn't cut corners on shoddy sets.

She heard voices coming from her right and turned her head to see Eve Crystal standing with a heavily built, fair-haired, rather untidy looking man of about forty, who was wearing a check shirt. Eve, still clad in her terry robe, was looking puzzled as the man spoke.

"Eve," he was explaining patiently, "Jenny is earthy, sensual, a wild female animal who will do anything for the boy she loves."

Eve puckered her brows in a puzzled frown. "But, Ross, why does he want to do it in a cemetery? That's sick."

"You must remember, Eve, his friends have been horribly murdered. He's defying death with the joy of life."

Jessica, feeling as baffled as Eve was looking, started hastily leafing through her copy of the script, trying unsuccessfully to find the scene they were discussing.

Eve suddenly brightened slightly. "Then he knows the killer is watching?"

Ross ran a hand over his face. "No, sweetheart, he doesn't. It's a *symbolic* act. He's in this cold, grim, dead place, with this live, warm, compliant girl."

Eve sniffed. "Sounds kinky to me."

"Look, honey," he said, "don't worry about it, okay? Just do what the director tells you. And in case you've forgotten, that's *me*. Right?"

She wrinkled up her nose in a grimace. "I'd never have guessed, if you hadn't told me, *Mr.* Hayley."

At that moment they were interrupted by the arrival on the set of an athletic-looking and extremely handsome young man, with a boyish expression and an engaging grin. Like Eve, he was dressed in a terry robe. Eve's face lit up when she saw him. "Hullo, Scott."

He raised a hand in greeting and favored her with a dazzling smile. "Hi, Evey."

He turned to Hayley. "Sorry I'm late, Ross. That stupid makeup man insisted on body makeup. Can you believe it—with my tan?"

Hayley glanced at his watch. "Any questions about this scene, Scott?" he asked shortly.

Scott gave a casual shrug. "Eve and I make love."

"Yeah, and for that neither of you should need any rehearsal. Still, we'd better do it." He raised his voice. "Clear the set."

Jessica, still searching through her script, suddenly felt a touch on her arm. She glanced up. A harassed-looking young man, carrying a walkie-talkie said, "Sorry, ma'am, you'll have to leave."

"Oh," she said, "will I? Why?"

"We're clearing the set for a nude scene."

Jessica's eyebrows shot upward. "Young man, say no more. I'll go at once."

# Chapter Seventeen

JERRY Lydecker's office was sumptuously furnished with a huge real leather couch (the proverbial casting couch? Jessica wondered), a carpet nearly plush enough to touch one's ankles, and a desk the size of a pool table. The walls were covered with photos of incredibly handsome young people who, in Lydecker's world, probably passed for stars, though Jessica searched them in vain for a familiar face.

There were also several posters advertising Lydecker films. These without exception featured well-endowed young women wearing expressions of terror and not much else; various monsters; much blood; and an assortment of evil-looking weapons and instruments of torture and bondage. The poster publicizing *The Corpse Danced at Midnight* included a large photo of Eve Crystal, wearing a very brief drum majorette's outfit, high-stepping through the Gothic cemetery set under a full moon; she was being observed by a hulking, faceless silhouette carrying a scythe, the blade of which dripped blood. Various dead bodies littered the background.

Jessica surveyed this artwork, slowly shaking her head. Then Lydecker, who had been on the telephone ever since she had entered the office, put down the receiver. She turned to face him. He glanced meaningfully at his watch.

"Well, what is it you want to say, Mrs. . . . Fleming . . . er, Fletcher?"

"Tell me, Mr. . . . Liar . . . er, Lydecker, are you proud of that?" She pointed to the poster.

He closed his eyes. "Oh lord, another critic!" Then he opened them and stared at her. "I'll say this once. What I *am* proud of is that a kid who started in this business at seventeen, with a second-hand 16-millimeter camera, is now Hollywood's most successful motion-picture producer. I did that by giving the public the sort of entertainment it wanted. Which is just exactly what De Mille, Goldwyn and Zanuck did in their day. Okay?"

"I have no wish to enter into a discussion on the merits of other people's films, Mr. Lydecker. I'm only concerned with one picture: the one you're basing on my novel. Now, you're obviously free to make what films you like; but you cannot in all conscience call this movie"—she tapped her copy of the script—*"The Corpse Danced at Midnight.* It bears absolutely no resemblance to my book."

"Excuse me, Mrs. Fletcher, but that's nonsense," Lydecker said. "They both deal with a series of inexplicable murders in a small town."

"That's where the similarity begins and ends," Jessica told him exasperatedly. "Take just one example: the character you call Jenny. In my book Jenny was Johnny, the ten-year-old son of a Presbyterian minister. And incidentally, he kept his shirt on for two hundred and twenty pages."

Lydecker grinned triumphantly. "Ah . . . exactly what I thought. It's just the nudity that's worrying you. That's all."

"It is not *just* the nudity," Jessica said angrily. "It's everything: the violence, the sadism, the bad language. The whole tone and style of the picture. You're turning my little mystery into something unbelievably crass and vulgar."

He shrugged. "That's your opinion, Mrs. Fletcher. Mine is that I'm turning your dull little book into an all-time hit picture."

Jessica flushed. "You are at perfect liberty to think my book dull, but I cannot imagine why in that case you wanted to buy the film rights to it."

"I'll tell you why," he said. "I bought the title."

"It happens that my name and professional reputation are attached to that title," Jessica said. "I believe I have a right to protect my interests."

Lydecker shook his head firmly. "Wrong again, Mrs. Fletcher. I *bought* your rights. You can't stop me from doing whatever I want to your story. And that's all there is to it. Now, I've done you the courtesy of listening to you. You used the opportunity to call my work crass and vulgar. That was your privilege." He pressed a buzzer on his desk. "But now I'm afraid I don't have time to listen to any more of the same. So I must ask you to excuse me."

The door opened and his secretary entered, an inquiring look on her face. Lydecker said: "Mrs. Fletcher is leaving, Sunny. Show her out, please. Good afternoon, Mrs. Fletcher. Enjoy your stay in L.A."

Jessica stood up. "Very well. I'll leave you." She marched to the door. Then she wheeled around. "But I warn you, sir," she said loudly and clearly, "I intend to do whatever I have to do to stop you making this picture. Good day."

And she swept past the dumfounded girl and out of the office.

* * *

Jessica lay on the bed in her hotel room. Her eyes were closed and on her forehead was resting a cool, damp, neatly folded face towel. Her head was aching. She wished she were back in Cabot Cove. She wished she'd never written *The Corpse Danced at Midnight.* She wished motion pictures had never been invented. She wished . . .

At that moment there came a tap on the door. Jessica called. "Yes?"

The knocking was repeated. Jessica gave a groan, removed the towel from her forehead, swung her feet to the floor and padded barefoot to the door. She peered through the little peephole set in it, raised her eyebrows in surprise and opened the door.

"Hello, Mrs. Fletcher," said Norman Lester.

"Hello, Norman. Come in."

She stood aside and he entered the room. "Are you all right?" he asked.

"Not really. I have a splitting headache. I hope I didn't look too disappointed to see you, but I was expecting room service with a pot of tea and some aspirin."

"I'm sorry, would you rather I left?"

"No, no, please. It's nice to see a friendly face. Sit down."

She returned to the bed, sat down, and put her shoes on. Norman seated himself on the edge of the room's only chair.

"I just called to see how you were getting on in your campaign," he said.

"Not very well."

"Have you seen Jerry Lydecker?"

"Yes. But I didn't get anywhere. And I'm afraid I lost my temper."

"I hear he has that effect on people."

"Arguments always bring on a headache with me. And I realized afterward I'd handled the interview quite wrong."

"How do you mean?"

"Oh, I went in very aggressively, spoiling for a fight, and started attacking his films generally. I was really very rude. I might have realized I'd get nowhere like that. I should have been more diplomatic and tried to charm him."

"Quite honestly, I doubt if you'd have stopped him going ahead with the movie no matter how charming you'd been."

"I know, and I was silly to try. What I should have done was concentrate on curbing the script's worst excesses; try to persuade him to let me go through the screenplay and trim or cut a scene here and there, rewrite a few snatches of dialogue. After all, the changes in the *plot* don't matter very much. If they want to turn Johnny into Jenny, well, let them. If I'd gone into Lydecker's office and started buttering him up, saying how flattered I was by his choosing to film my book, congratulating him on the set, and so on, then I might have gotten somewhere. He'd have listened to me. I might have convinced him that, if he followed my suggestions, the critics would be kinder. I'm pretty sure that deep down he would really like some favorable reviews for once. But I blew it."

"Well, is it really too late to change your approach?"

"I don't know, Norman. I'm *persona non grata* at the studio right now. I doubt very much if Lydecker would see me again. Certainly not unless I really ate crow."

Norman looked thoughtful. "And how do you feel about doing that?"

"How does anybody feel about doing that? Not good. In fact, I'm strongly tempted to let the whole thing drop: go home, write a few letters to the leading newspapers and literary magazines publicly dissociating myself from the movie, and give the money I earn from it to charity."

"Certainly nobody could criticize you if you did just that."

"Only one thing stops me, and that I suppose you could call pride. I want to see my book filmed. I've been looking forward to it. Only it must be a film I can be proud of—or, if not actually be proud of, at least tolerate."

"So what will you do?" Norman asked hesitantly.

She sighed. "I think I shall have one more go: see Lydecker, apologize for anything I said that was out of place and ask if he's prepared to make just a few changes."

"And if he's not?"

"Then," Jessica said, "I shall just have to admit I am beaten."

After some consideration, Jessica decided not to phone or try to arrange another appointment with Lydecker. She was pretty sure she wouldn't get one, so she planned just to turn up at the studio and hope for the best.

At first she was lucky. After her taxi had dropped her off outside the studio, Paddy, the guard at the gate, just waved her through, obviously assuming she was still a guest of Marta Quintessa. Jessica made her way, rather apprehensively, to Lydecker's office.

She tapped on the door and went in. Sunny, at the reception desk, glanced up with a mechanical smile, which faded quickly when she recognized Jessica.

"Mrs. Fletcher. I didn't expect to see you back."

"I didn't expect to be back. But it's important I see Mr. Lydecker."

"He's not in."

"You mean he's not at the studio?"

Sunny hesitated and Jessica, sensing the girl was considering a lie, said quickly:

"He is, isn't he?"

Rather reluctantly, Sunny nodded. "But he's extremely busy. He went to the screening room, and from there he was going straight to the set."

"Are they still filming?"

"No, they wrapped up for the day. Look, I suggest you call Mr. Lydecker tomorrow."

"What I must do cannot be done on the telephone," Jessica told her. "Excuse me." She went out.

The great sound stage was silent and deserted. Feeling oddly nervous, Jessica made her way toward the cemetery set. She entered the set from behind one of the skeletal trees and stood staring around her. The set was dimly illuminated by a high overhead work light and looked strangely eerie. Jessica shivered slightly. She could almost imagine the monstrous figure with the bloodstained scythe appearing from behind one of the trees and approaching her, murder weapon raised.

Jessica pulled herself together. This was ridiculous. She cleared her throat and called out, "Mr. Lydecker?"

Her voice echoed around the building. But there was no reply. Lydecker obviously hadn't yet arrived from the screening room. Should she wait here or try and catch him there? It was while she stood hesitating that her sharp eye caught sight of something not quite right.

Placed by some of the fake tombstones around the set were a number of metal urns, many containing flowers. However, the urn in front of one particularly large and ornate tombstone was on its side, with the flowers it had contained lying around on the ground. They seemed too scattered to have fallen out if the urn had been accidentally knocked over.

This phenomenon attracted her attention for only a moment, and she would have thought little of it if her eye had not been further caught by something sticking out a few inches from behind the headstone.

Jessica stared. Surely that was a foot. No, it couldn't be. She moved cautiously closer.

Then she stopped dead. It *was* a foot—a man's foot, wearing a brown leather shoe. The toe was pointing upward.

Jessica took a deep breath, stepped resolutely up to the tombstone and peered behind it.

A man was sprawled unnaturally against the back of the headstone. Blood had run down his face from a deep wound in his head. He wasn't breathing.

Jerry Lydecker had produced his last movie.

# Chapter Eighteen

FIGHTING down a rising tide of panic and nausea, Jessica stood quite still. She told herself firmly that this wasn't the first time she had found a body.

But a little voice inside her head murmured, then it had been broad daylight, in the open air, people she had known were close at hand. And no one could have been concealed nearby.

It was once more her keen eyes, together with her insatiable curiosity, which prevented her from running in panic from the scene. On the floor near the body something gleamed. A small shiny object.

Jessica bent and looked at it more closely. It was a button. A gold button with some sort of unusual design on it. She stooped still lower.

It was a bird—yes, an eagle—carrying something—an olive branch?—in its talons.

Jessica reached out a hand to pick it up. She stopped herself just in time. This was a clue. Fingerprints. For a moment she considered picking it up in her handkerchief. No, she decided. Better to leave it exactly where it was for the police.

It was a decision she was to regret before many hours had passed.

Jessica straightened up. Keeping her gaze firmly averted from the dead eyes of the man on the ground—eyes which somehow seemed to be following her every movement—she turned and walked hastily toward the exit.

Or tried to. For within a second or two she realized that she had quite lost her bearings. Where was the door through which she'd entered? It was behind one of those trees. But which one? They all looked alike.

Eventually, after blundering around for a minute or two she found the door she was looking for. She was about to open it and thankfully go through when she heard a noise. It was the sound of footsteps—slow, heavy—and somehow menacing.

Jessica froze. Where was the sound coming from? The other side of the door? Or behind her on the set? She stood quite still, the memory irresistibly returning of standing in her living room, listening to someone coming along the hall, waiting to see if the intruder was in fact Maggie Earl. Then, however, the telephone had been within reach of her hand, with Amos Tupper waiting at the other end of the line. This time she was quite alone. Apart from one other person.

The footsteps had stopped. And she still didn't know from which side of the door the sound had come.

A minute passed in total silence. And Jessica knew she had to do something. She couldn't stand here indefinitely. If the footsteps did belong to the killer, he might have gotten away by now. If not, it was crazy just to wait for him to make the next move. It was much better to take the initiative.

However, that would mean opening the door and going through, and Jessica just didn't think she could bring herself to do that.

Then, while she hesitated, she heard again the sound of a single footstep. And this time she was in little doubt that it came from behind her.

Like lightning Jessica hurled herself at the door, jerked it open and tumbled through.

Too late she realized her mistake. From the corner of her eye she saw a tall, burly figure lunging toward her through the sound-stage door. She gasped and started to run. She heard footsteps, with no attempt now at stealth, clattering after her. Then a hand landed like a vise on her shoulder and she was brought up short.

Jessica screamed as her pursuer swung her around to face him, and found herself staring up at a uniformed security guard.

"Just what are you up to?" he growled.

Jessica nearly fainted with relief. For seconds she couldn't speak. Then she stammered:

"Oh, th-thank heavens. Please—come—quickly—it's . . ."

He cut her off. "Who are you? What are you doing here?"

"Never mind that," she said breathlessly. "There's been a murder."

"Murder?" He stared at her.

"It's Mr. Lydecker."

*"What?"*

"On the set. We must call the police. Quickly."

His grip tightened on her shoulder. "Show me."

He pushed her toward the sound-stage door. For a second she resisted, then, overcoming her natural reluctance, she led him through the doorway.

He looked around. "Where?"

Jessica just pointed. Without slackening his grip, he marched across to the tombstone and peered behind it. He drew his breath in sharply and muttered an oath.

Jessica, who was rapidly regaining her self-possession, said quietly, "I'm afraid he's quite dead. I suspect he was hit with that urn."

He raised his eyes from the body to gaze at her disbelievingly. "You *suspect?*"

With his free hand he reached down and unhooked an object hanging from his belt. She saw that it was a walkie-talkie. He flicked it on and raised it to his lips. He barked into it: "Security! There's a murder on stage three."

There was a moment's pause, then a voice came through. "What's that?"

"Murder," the guard said. He glanced grimly at Jessica. "And I think I got hold of the killer."

Detective Lieutenant Mike Hernandez was to Jessica a new type of policeman. Tall, slim, with rather long, carefully styled black hair and a little mustache, he was dressed in obviously expensive and very trendy clothes. His manner and demeanor suggested someone who modeled himself on the many detectives he had seen on television.

He straightened up now from a cursory examination of Lydecker's body, flicked some invisible dust from the knees of his beige suit and looked at Jessica. She, however, was gazing down at the floor in the vicinity of the body, her eyes darting to and fro.

"Lost something?" Hernandez asked.

Jessica gave a slight start. "Oh, not personally, Lieutenant. But something's missing."

"What do you mean?"

"When I first found the . . . Mr. Lydecker, there was a button on the floor just there." She pointed.

"What sort of button?"

"Gold. With a design of an eagle carrying an olive branch in its talons."

His eyes narrowed. "You sure examined it closely."

"Well, I realized it might be an important clue. But I didn't touch it. I had the feeling I'd seen it before somewhere, but I can't remember where."

"There's no button there now."

"I know."

"Well, how could it disappear?"

"Obviously the killer was still on the set, hiding behind one of the flats, when I found the body. In fact . . ." Jessica nodded thoughtfully. "I must have heard two sets of footsteps: the killer's, and this gentleman's." She indicated the security guard, who was still standing suspiciously by, though he had by now taken his hand from her shoulder. She went on: "That would explain why I couldn't identify the direction they were coming from. Then, when I went out of the door, the killer must have emerged from his hiding place, snatched up the button and got away through one of the other doors before we came back. He would just have had time."

Hernandez glanced at the guard. "Did you see or hear anyone?"

He shook his head firmly. "Only her. I was on my regular rounds, I heard footsteps and thought it was Mr. Lydecker. Then they stopped. Didn't want to be heard. That made me suspicious. So I stopped and waited. Eventually she came rushing through the door, saw me—and tried to get away."

"Don't be silly," Jessica told him severely. "I thought *you* were the killer. I didn't try to get away after I saw your uniform."

" 'Cause I took good care you didn't."

"Oh, fiddlesticks!"

At that moment they were interrupted by the arrival on the set of a positive posse of plainclothes men, bearing cameras and other equipment. On their heels came a tall, thin man, carrying a leather bag and wearing an eager expression, who had "doctor" written all over him.

Hernandez called casually: "All yours, fellas." Then he turned to Jessica. "Let's get away from here."

He took her quite gently by the arm and started to lead her away, saying over his shoulder to the security guard: "Okay, you can go. Talk to you later."

Jessica looked back wistfully at the scene of organized bustle that was developing around the body of Jerry Lydecker. She would have been glad of the opportunity to watch a homicide squad in action. But it wasn't to be.

"Where are you taking me?" she asked.

"Just somewhere we can talk."

They crossed the cemetery set, passed between a couple of flats forming backdrops and after weaving between various large pieces of movie equipment, suddenly found themselves on another much smaller set, which was furnished as a comfortable living room.

Hernandez grinned. "This looks just right. Sit down."

Jessica seated herself in an easy chair. He did likewise, crossed his legs and regarded her thoughtfully. "So you're Jessica Fletcher. J.B. Fletcher, right? Author of *The Corpse Danced at Midnight?*"

Jessica raised her eyebrows. "That's correct."

"Surprised I knew?"

"Well, I only gave my name as Fletcher. You haven't had time to talk to anybody else here to . . . er . . . get a make on me, and I don't know how you'd recognize me."

Hernandez looked pleased with himself. "Well, I knew Lydecker was working on your book. It's unlikely there'd be two ladies called Fletcher connected with the project." Then, a little self-consciously, he added, "I'm sort of in the business myself, so I keep in touch with what's going on."

"The business?" Jessica said, slightly puzzled.

"The movies. I'm T.A. on a couple of cop shows."

"I'm sorry, I don't . . ."

"Technical advisor. I advise the producers on police procedure and so on."

"Oh, I see."

He cleared his throat and said casually, "And I do a bit of writing myself."

"Really?"

"Yeah. Oh, I never actually sold anything, but I got a screenplay out with an agent and there's some interest in it for a TV-movie."

"How nice," Jessica said politely.

"Tell me, J.B., you got an agent?"

"Er, no."

"Don't think much of 'em, eh?"

"Oh, I wouldn't say that. I've just never felt the need for one. My publisher really acts as my agent."

He nodded sapiently. "I suppose that's just as good as hiring an agent. Course, a novelist is in a different situation from a specialist screen-writer."

"No doubt," Jessica said.

"I've thought of trying my hand at a novel. What d'you think of this as a plot?" And Hernandez leaned back and began to regale her with a long and highly involved detective story.

To Jessica, who still felt rather queasy and very much on edge, it seemed to go on for a considerable time.

At last he paused. "What d'you think?"

"Very . . . interesting," Jessica said. "Of course, it would depend on how it was handled."

"Yeah. Course, it'd make a swell movie, too. I was thinking of Clint Eastwood for the part of Rick."

Jessica, however, had had enough and at this she interrupted firmly. "Mr. Hernandez, am I a suspect in this case?"

For a moment he looked puzzled, his mind still obviously on Rick. Then he said: "You? Heck, no."

"My, that's a relief. After what that security guard said, and then your marching me off to interview me."

He shrugged. "Well, *technically,* you have to be on the official list of suspects. Just until we get a proper lead. But I know *you'd* never ice anyone, J.B."

"Why, thank you," Jessica said rather weakly.

"In fact, I was wondering if you had any theories about this case."

"I'm afraid not, Lieutenant. I—"

He raised a hand. "Mike."

"Oh, thank you. I'm afraid not, er, Mike. I prefer to leave theories to the experts. I only *write* mysteries. I'm not a detective."

"So you say, but you've helped in clearing up a couple of murders though, haven't you? I been reading about the Stephen Earl case—and there was that other business in New York."

Jessica sighed. "It's purely chance, Lieutenant. It's not of my making. Or my wish."

"Aw, come on." He grinned. "You love it really, don't you?"

"No, I do *not.* I find real-life crime highly unpleasant—and frightening. I wish I'd never started writing about make-believe crime."

He was about to reply when they heard somebody approaching. A moment later the doctor appeared on the set.

He glanced around. "Well, you've found yourselves a cozy little spot for a tête-à-tête."

"What you got, Doc?" Hernandez asked.

"I've done my prelim. He died between forty-five and sixty minutes ago."

Jessica looked at her watch. "Oh, dear, then the killer probably *was* still around when I found the body."

"Don't let it worry you, J.B.," Hernandez told her. "What else, Doc?"

"Very little, so far. Cause of death was the obvious one: blow on the head—almost certainly with that flower urn. There are bloodstains on it. We'll confirm it's Lydecker's blood when we've run some tests. Oh, and one of your men said to tell you there are no prints on it."

Hernandez grunted. "That figures. It was wiped clean. Okay, Doc, thanks. Let me have your full report soon as possible, will you?"

"Don't I always?" the doctor said, and with a nod to Jessica went away.

"How well did you know Lydecker, J.B.?" Hernandez asked.

"Not well at all. I met him twice."

"So you wouldn't know of anyone who had a grudge against him?"

Jessica hesitated, thinking of the scene she'd overheard between Lydecker and Gebhart.

Hernandez quickly spotted her hesitation. "So you do?"

Jessica came to a decision. It might be her duty to help the police, but that did not entail throwing suspicion on a perhaps entirely innocent person. Marta had listened in on the argument, too, and probably several other people as well. Hernandez would hear about it soon enough.

She shook her head. "I was just going to say, probably a number of people did. I gather he wasn't very popular."

Just then there was another interruption. They heard voices and looked up to see two people coming onto the set. A moment later Jessica recognized them as Ross Hayley and Marta Quintessa. They were approaching from the opposite direction to that of the doctor. They stopped when they saw Hernandez and Jessica. The lieutenant got to his feet.

"Who are you?" Hayley said truculently. "What's going on here?"

Hernandez took his shield from his pocket and held it out. "Hernandez—police. And you?"

"I'm Ross Hayley. I'm directing a picture here. This is Marta Quintessa. She's doing the costumes."

"Let's see some ID."

Jessica said: "I can vouch for Mr. Hayley and Miss Quintessa, Lieutenant."

"Oh, right, if you say so, J.B."

Marta smiled at Jessica. "Thanks."

"Glad to return the favor," Jessica said.

"Look, what *is* going on?" Hayley demanded. "A policeman prevented us from coming in through the main entrance, so we went around and got in through a rear door."

"The officer was obeying orders," Hernandez said curtly. "Do you have important business on this stage?"

"Well, not right now," Hayley said.

"We were in the ladies' wardrobe going over the costumes," Marta added. "We heard the siren and looked out but couldn't see anything, so we went on with what we were doing. Then when we finally came out we saw the police cars in front of the sound stage and came to investigate. Do tell us—has there been an accident?"

"Not exactly," Hernandez said.

"Oh, good. Naturally, we were a bit anxious."

"No accident. A murder."

There was dead silence. Marta went very pale. Hayley stood quite still. Then he stammered: "But wh-who—I mean . . ." He trailed off.

"Jerry Lydecker," Hernandez said deliberately.

*"What?"* Hayley's face showed utter disbelief.

"Oh, no," Marta said quietly. She swayed. Hayley hurriedly put his arm around her and kept her from falling. Jessica leapt to her feet and helped him lower the girl into a chair. Then she started briskly to massage her wrists.

"Breathe deeply, dear," she urged.

Marta followed her advice. Her color gradually returned. "I'm all right," she said. "Thank you."

"Sorry to give you such a shock," Hernandez said. "You and Mr. Lydecker very close?"

"Not . . . not especially. But to hear anybody you know has been murdered . . . It's the sort of thing one just isn't prepared for."

Hayley turned to Hernandez. "Do you have any idea who did it?"

"We're working on several promising leads, Mr. Hayley. Do you know of anyone who might have had reason to kill him?"

Hayley, who seemed to have recovered his composure, raised his eyebrows. "You have to be joking. You'll be asking the suspects to form a double line."

"Don't be idiotic, Ross," Marta said sharply. She looked at Hernandez. "What Mr. Hayley means is that Jerry was not exactly America's sweetheart. He tended to put people's backs up."

"Even yours, Miss Quintessa?"

"Yes, from time to time. Though, on the whole, we got on well enough. But I can't think of anybody connected with the studio who disliked him enough to kill him. Most of the people he fought with would be on perfectly good terms with him by the next day."

"Yes," Hayley said, "because he'd gotten his own way, he'd forget all about it. The other people sometimes had a longer memory. Though I agree—I shouldn't have said what I did. Many people may have felt the urge to kill him, but I can't think of anybody who'd be likely to put it into practice."

Hernandez nodded thoughtfully. "How long were you two in ladies' wardrobe before you heard the police siren?"

They glanced at each other. Hayley said: "I should think a good hour, wouldn't you, Marta?"

"At least. More like an hour and a quarter."

"Together all that time?"

"Yes." They spoke in unison.

"Anybody else there?"

Hayley nodded. "Elinor Riggs, the wardrobe mistress, was with us. We're both in the clear, Lieutenant."

"I'll be checking on everybody, Mr. Hayley."

"I'm sure you will. I don't envy you the job. I think a lot of people will have a sneaking sympathy for the killer and won't want to see him brought to justice. People who might have damaging evidence about others are going to be reluctant to come forward with it."

Jessica, remembering her own refusal to say anything that might implicate Allan Gebhart, felt a tinge of guilt.

"Seems I'm the only one in town who's sorry Lydecker's dead," Hernandez said ruefully. They all looked at him in surprise. "My agent had persuaded him to read my screenplay," he added.

Marta said suddenly, "There *is* somebody who'll be shattered by his death."

"You mean Eve," Hayley said.

"Who's Eve?" Hernandez asked.

"Eve Crystal, the star of the picture. Hasn't she been notified?"

"Not by me," Hernandez said. "She and Lydecker were close?"

Hayley shrugged. "They certainly *were.* Actually, Eve has been—" He broke off.

"Has been what, Mr. Hayley?"

He shook his head. "Forget it. She certainly was in love with Jerry. At least until recently. May still have been. It'll certainly be a tremendous shock to her, as Marta says."

"Where is she now, do you know?" Hernandez asked.

Marta answered. "Probably at the beach house. She left immediately after filming finished today."

"It's Jerry's house," Hayley put in. "Eve's been living there."

"Well, I don't need you anymore for the time being," Hernandez told him. "You're free to go and break the news to her."

Hayley looked at his watch. "I'd like nothing better. Well, I don't mean that, exactly. I mean, I know I ought to, but I just can't spare the time. I'll have to contact the studio brass right away. There'll be a million decisions to make."

Hernandez looked at Marta. "How about you, Miss Quintessa?"

Marta shook her head firmly. "There's no love lost between Eve and me. If I broke it to her, it would only make it worse."

"Oh dear," Jessica said. "I hate to think of her hearing it on the TV news."

Hernandez turned to her. "Okay, J.B., you tell her."

Jessica stared at him. "Me? But why me? I don't know her. There must be somebody around who's a friend of hers."

Hayley shook his head. "I doubt if there's anybody left in the studio now who'd be suitable."

"Surely the police usually take care of this sort of thing?" Jessica said, almost pleadingly.

"Not if we can get somebody else to do it," Hernandez said. "I'd appreciate it, J.B. I can't possibly take time off from the investigation now. I could send a couple of uniformed officers, but frankly, I think you'd do it much better."

Marta nodded. "You do look rather like everybody's favorite aunt, if I may say so."

Jessica sighed. "I'm sure that's meant as a compliment, though it's not one I welcome right now. Very well, I'll do it. How do I get there?"

Hernandez said: "Don't worry. I'll get a black-and-white to take you. I'm sure Mr. Hayley can tell us just where the house is located."

# Chapter Nineteen

IT was a glorious evening; the gentlest of waves were washing the shore with a soft murmur when Jessica rang the front doorbell of the late Jerry Lydecker's beach house. Her heart was in her mouth; she dreaded the task that lay ahead. Nothing happened for about half a minute, and she was about to ring again when the door was suddenly jerked open and Eve Crystal was gazing at her with almost unseeing eyes.

The girl was wearing a man's shirt that reached halfway down her thighs, and below it her legs and feet were bare. Her golden hair was a wild mop, half covering her pallid face. In one hand she was holding a nearly empty whiskey glass. She stared at Jessica without recognition.

Jessica's heart sank. This was going to be even worse than she had feared.

"Good evening, Miss Crystal."

Eve frowned in a puzzled manner. "Do I know you?"

"We haven't actually met, but I did see you on the set today."

Eve's face cleared very slightly. "You work at the studio?"

"No. The film you're starring in is based on a title I wrote. My name is Jessica Fletcher."

Eve made a theatrical bow. "Charmed," she said. She gave a very genteel little hiccup.

"Er, may I come in?" Jessica asked.

"Sure. Open house here." She turned and walked back indoors.

Jessica followed her into an expensively furnished but very untidy living room. Eve plopped down on a sofa, beside a coffee table on which were a nearly empty bottle of Scotch, a number of diet cola cans and a valuable looking silver cigarette box. She pointed to the bottle.

"Have a drinkie?"

"No, thank you."

Eve picked up the cigarette box and held it out. "Then how about one of Jerry's funny cigarettes? Or a pill—any color you like. Jerry's got it all."

"Nothing for me, thank you," Jessica said firmly.

"Hey, why don't you relax? Have fun. That's what it's all about."

She emptied the glass, throwing back her head. Liquid dribbled down her chin. She giggled and wiped her chin with her hand.

"Can't seem to hold my liquor today." She giggled again. "That's a joke."

Then she seemed to see Jessica properly for the first time. "Say, what you doing here?" she demanded abruptly. "Did Jerry send you? Where *is* Jerry?"

Jessica sat down on the sofa next to her. "My dear, I have something very important to tell you."

"Go ahead."

Eve picked up the whiskey bottle and with an unsteady hand refilled her glass, pouring quite a lot of liquor on the table.

"I want to be sure you're capable of understanding what I have to say," Jessica told her.

"S'okay. I hear every single word." She took another swig from the glass.

Jessica shook her head. "This really won't do," she said to herself.

"What's the matter with you?" Eve asked in a loud voice. "Why d'you take everything so serious? You gotta unwind. Hey, wanna go for a swim in the sea? C'mon."

She got unsteadily to her feet and started fumbling with the top button of her shirt.

Jessica also stood up. "Well," she said, "a dash of cold water may be just what you need. But not, I think, the sea."

She took the girl firmly by the wrist. "Come with me."

"Where we going?"

"Where's the bathroom?"

Eve tried to point. Her arm wavered in the air. "Through there. But I don't wanna go to the bathroom."

"Oh yes, you do. Come on."

She led the girl, stumbling and protesting, into a superbly appointed bathroom, took the whiskey glass from her hand, pushed her gently but firmly into the shower and drew the curtains around it.

"Now take off that shirt and throw it out," she ordered.

"I don't want a shower!" Eve wailed.

"You're taking one, whether you want one or not. Now, will you get that shirt off?"

*"No!"*

"Very well, have it your way," Jessica said. She reached in through the curtains and turned the cold water on full blast.

Eve gave a shriek. "It's freezing! You beast!"

She tried to push her way out of the shower, but Jessica ruthlessly thrust her back. "You're staying there for at least half a minute, so make the best of it."

Eve gave a watery sniff. "I hate you."

"I'm going to make some tea," Jessica said. "Join me when you're through."

She went to the kitchen, located a teapot, cups, tea and cream, and switched on the kettle. Five minutes later she was pouring out two steaming cups of tea when Eve came rather sheepishly into the room. She had dried and brushed her hair and was wearing jeans and a woollen sweater.

Jessica smiled at her. "Come and sit down."

"Do make yourself at home," Eve said sarcastically. But she sat down at the kitchen table and took a sip from the cup.

"Thank you. I always enjoy finding my way around other people's kitchens." She sat down opposite the girl. "How do you feel?"

"Okay, I guess." She cleared her throat awkwardly. "I must have been a mess when you got here."

"That's a fair description of your condition."

Eve gave a rueful grin. "I was so tense when I got home from the studio I thought a couple of drinks would make me feel better. Then I couldn't stop. I guess I shouldn't drink alone."

"No, I don't think it's a very good habit to get into."

"Look," Eve said abruptly, "I still don't know why you're here. You waiting to see Jerry?"

"No. I—"

Eve interrupted. "Where *is* Jerry anyway? What time is it? Why isn't he here?"

Jessica took a deep breath. "Eve, listen to me, please. I have something very serious to tell you."

Eve stared at her out of big, puzzled eyes. "Serious? I don't—" She broke off.

"Something happened at the studio, my dear. Jerry was attacked."

Eve drew her breath in sharply. "Attacked? Is he . . . is he badly hurt?"

"Yes. Eve, I'm afraid he's dead."

Eve sat absolutely motionless and silent and for seconds Jessica thought she had not taken in what she'd been told. Then, very quietly, the girl said: "Dead? No. No, he can't be."

"I'm sorry, but yes."

"We had a little argument." Her voice seemed to come from a long way off. Jessica said nothing.

Suddenly Eve's lips started to tremble. Tears came into her eyes. She said brokenly: "I didn't even say goodbye."

She began to sob. Jessica put her arm round the girl and drew her close.

It was very late that night when Jessica arrived back at her hotel. Nevertheless, as she entered the lobby she found herself suddenly surrounded by a swarm of reporters and photographers. Bulbs flashed in her face, television cameras whirred, microphones and miniature tape recorders were pushed under her nose. A babble of questions arose from every side.

"Jessica, what can you tell us about the murder?" . . . "Who did it?" . . . "Are you on the case?" . . . "Any theories?" . . . "What was the motive?"

Jessica tried to ignore the crowd and force her way through, but she then found herself face to face with a particularly determined-looking female television reporter who effectively barred her way.

"Mrs. Fletcher," she brayed loudly, "how are you, a best-selling mystery author, involved in this real-life crime?" She thrust her mike within two inches of Jessica's face.

Jessica regarded her coldly. "How are *you* involved?"

She had the satisfaction of seeing the woman look taken aback. "I'm not involved."

Jessica smiled sweetly. "Do forgive such a stupid question." She raised her hands and managed to bring about a measure of silence. "Ladies and gentlemen," she continued, "I know virtually nothing about this case. I happened, purely by chance, to discover Mr. Lydecker's body. I reported it to a security guard and later made a statement to the police. That is the extent of my involvement. I don't know who committed the murder, or why, nor do I have any theories. I have no intention of making any kind of unofficial investigation. Now, if anybody wishes to ask me what made me take up fiction writing, who my favorite mystery authors are, what my next book is going to be about, or anything like that, I'll be pleased to answer. If not, I'm going to my room."

And she gently but firmly pushed her way through the crowd to the elevator.

Having at last reached her room, Jessica sank down thankfully in the chair and kicked off her shoes. She lay back with her eyes closed for a few minutes. Then she gave a sigh, got to her feet and went to the phone. She lifted the receiver and asked the operator to ring Ethan Cragg's number in Cabot Cove.

It was some minutes before she heard the familiar voice grunt: "Yeah?"

"Ethan?"

"Jess!" He sounded alarmed. "You all right?"

"Yes, fine. Why?"

"D'you realize what time it is here?"

Jessica gave a groan. She looked at her watch. "Oh, Ethan, I'm sorry. I clean forgot. Did I wake you?"

"It's okay. Jess, I heard about that producer guy's murder. You do it?"

"Yes. With my gold-plated, purse-sized flamethrower. Ethan, I just wanted to say it looks as if I'll be staying on here a bit longer."

"I know—the cops have called you in to help them solve the case."

"No! But I have to find out what's going to happen about the film."

"You mean, if they're going ahead with it?"

"Precisely. I just don't know what happens when a producer is murdered immediately after they've started shooting."

"No, I don't suppose it happens very often—even in Hollywood."

"So I'm going back out to the studio tomorrow to make some inquiries."

"I see. Well, best of luck, Jess. And if you want any help you've only got to lift the receiver."

"Thank you, Ethan. I do appreciate it, but I hope it won't be necessary. Anyway, if people ask about me, just explain the situation, will you?"

"Sure. How d'you like L.A?"

"To tell you the truth, I've been too preoccupied so far even to notice it. But I was out at the beach today. And do you know something? The Pacific doesn't look anything like the Atlantic. Maybe it's because it's so big. Smaller oceans are nicer somehow."

He chuckled. "They're just as wet, though. Well, good night, Jess. Keep in touch."

"I will. Good night, Ethan."

# Chapter Twenty

THE next morning Jessica again found no difficulty in gaining admittance to the studios. Paddy, indeed, seemed anxious to talk about the murder. Jessica chatted to him for a minute or so, managing not to say anything of the least significance, and had just turned away when she heard a car behind her. She looked back to see Paddy waving through a sedan with Allan Gebhart at the wheel.

Jessica came to a quick decision, and as Gebhart drove on to the parking lot where Marta had left her car the previous day, she hurried after him. She approached him just as he was walking away from his car.

"Mr. Gebhart?" she called.

He stopped. "Yes."

"I'm Jessica Fletcher."

"Of course!" He held out his hand. "I am pleased to meet you."

Jessica shook hands. "Thank you."

"I want to say how much I loved your book. I'm just sorry more of it isn't in the screenplay. I did try, believe me, but even the material I did manage to incorporate was cut by Lydecker."

"Yes, so Marta was saying."

"Anyway, now perhaps I'll get a chance to restore some of it."

Jessica looked puzzled. "I'm afraid I don't follow."

"Oh, you don't know, of course. Let me see, you were nearby when Jerry gave me the boot, weren't you? Well, guess what: Ross invited me back."

"Ross?"

He snapped his fingers. "Sorry. I keep forgetting no announcement's been made yet. The studio bigwigs have decided to finish *The Corpse Danced at Midnight* with Ross Hayley producing as well as directing."

"Oh," Jessica said. "I see."

He smiled. "Were you hoping the project might be canceled?"

"It did occur to me it might. But I can see now it was very unlikely, with all that money at stake. But I must say I find the motion-picture business terribly confusing. How can a director be a producer?"

"Anybody can be a producer—even a writer."

"Has Mr. Hayley ever been a producer before?"

"No, but he came close once. He had a property of his own he was going to produce *and* direct; which of course is every director's ambition. It was all set, until Jerry decided he wanted Ross to direct *Corpse*. A word in the right ear and the studio dropped Ross' project and reassigned him to Jerry."

Jessica nodded thoughtfully. "Then, in a way, Mr. Lydecker's death was a stroke of good luck for Mr. Hayley."

Gebhart nodded. "With this picture Ross could hit it really big."

"Well, I don't wish him any harm," Jessica said, "but frankly *I* hope the picture is a flop."

"Look," he said, "I understand entirely how you feel. All I can say is I will do my best for you. Ross and I usually agree about things, and I'm sure there will be changes in the screenplay. You still may not actually *like* the finished product, but you should find it less objectionable."

Jessica bowed her head. "Thank you. I appreciate that. But I'm afraid there'll have to be very considerable changes to make me happy."

"Well, let's wait and see what emerges after Ross and I have had a conference."

They had been walking slowly toward stage three all this time and had now reached the entrance.

"You coming in to watch the shooting?" Gebhart asked.

"They're shooting *today?* I thought they might have taken a little time off."

"You mean out of respect to Jerry?"

"Well, yes."

"This doesn't mean he wasn't respected. He wasn't *popular,* and it'd be hypocritical to pretend otherwise. You can imagine how I personally felt about him. But he *was* respected as a good producer. And he certainly wouldn't have expected his successor to keep a whole crew and cast hanging around doing nothing all day. Come on."

They were just about to go inside the building when suddenly a number of people, some in makeup and costumes, started trooping out. Among them was Marta. There was an angry expression on her face, which she didn't attempt to disguise when she saw Gebhart and Jessica.

"Hello. What's up?" Gebhart asked her.

"Eve is. She refused to wear her costume for the marching-band sequence. Says it's not as Jerry wanted it. I told her I convinced Jerry yesterday that it was fine as it was. She as good as called me a liar. Believe it or not, she's demanding a completely new outfit—which I have to spend hours designing. And Ross is poring over the script trying to find some scene he can shoot with the people who are here."

Gebhart said hurriedly: "I'd better go see if I can help." He nodded to Jessica and disappeared into the sound stage.

Marta said: "That girl makes me sick. I try to make allowances for her being upset. But really, I think she likes making my life difficult."

"You mentioned there was no love lost between you," Jessica said.

"I'll probably go on saying it to anyone who'll listen to me. You know, on the first day of shooting we were doing a party scene. For a joke, somebody put real vodka in Eve's glass, instead of water. It's the sort of thing some idiot always does. Eve turned bright red and in front of everybody accused *me* of doing it, to try and ruin her scene! Can you imagine?"

Jessica raised her eyebrows. "Why do you think she picked on you?"

"Well, she thought—or pretended to think—that I was jealous of her."

"But why should a costume designer be jealous of an actress?"

"Oh, my dear, of course you don't know. Well, before Eve wiggled her way into Jerry's heart, *I* used to live in that lovely beach house."

"Oh," Jessica said. Then she added delicately: "When you say *live . . . ?*"

"With all the privileges and fringe benefits. Naturally, Eve thinks I resent her. Actually, by the time she appeared on the scene I was quite ready to pack my bags. Jerry, bless his heart, did tend to pall after a time. As Eve in turn was beginning to find out. Though from the way she's been going on this morning you'd think he'd been some sort of saint. And of course it's common knowledge that lately she's been far from the faithful little companion."

Marta was plainly enjoying the chance to let off steam. Feeling a little guilty, Jessica nevertheless decided to encourage her.

"I see," she said. "You mean she has other, er, interests?"

"Everybody knows she's been seeing Scott Bennett—and I mean *off* the set, as well as on."

"Really?" Jessica was thoughtful for a moment. "And yet, you know, I could have sworn her grief was quite genuine yesterday when I broke the news to her."

Marta looked a little abashed. "Don't get me wrong. I'm sure it was. Eve was in love with Jerry, all right. But there's no doubt he could be a stinker to live with. I think in seeing Scott, Eve was just trying to teach Jerry a lesson; show him he wasn't the only pebble on the beach. In choosing Scott she was being cautious, in an odd way: he plays the field and she probably guessed he wouldn't want a long-term relationship. Apart, of course, from the fact that he's quite a bit younger than Jerry— and very good-looking."

"Well, this is all most interesting," Jessica said. "I wonder what will happen between Eve and Scott now that Jerry is gone."

Marta shrugged. "I guess that after a week or so Scott's going to start finding her a little more clinging than he ever expected."

At that moment there was a noisy interruption. A police car drew up alongside them with a squealing of brakes and Lieutenant Hernandez jumped out.

Jessica turned to him with a smile. "Good morning, Lieutenant. I—"

She broke off when she saw the expression on his face. Then she noticed that a second person was alighting from the car. It was a girl who a moment later Jessica recognized as Jerry Lydecker's secretary, Sunny.

The girl looked cold and hard at Jessica. "That's her," she said loudly. "That's the woman who threatened Mr. Lydecker's life."

Jessica gave a gasp of amazement. She tried to speak, but couldn't get any words out.

Hernandez said: "Can you recall her exact words, Miss Finch?"

Sunny gave a decisive nod. "Yes. She said, 'I warn you, sir, I intend to do whatever I have to do to stop you making this picture.' "

Jessica said incredulously: "But, good heavens, that wasn't a threat to his life! I was just—"

Hernandez raised a hand and cut her off. He addressed Sunny again. "And later, what did she say to you in your office, when you suggested she phone Mr. Lydecker, instead of going to see him on the set?"

There was a pause as Sunny marshaled her thoughts. Jessica noticed uneasily that most of the extras and technicians who had left the stage, and who had been standing around, chatting and smoking, had drawn close and were obviously listening intently.

At last Sunny spoke. "I'll tell you the precise words she used. They were, 'What I must do cannot be done on the telephone.' "

A little murmur went through the crowd of bystanders. "And then she killed him!" Sunny added dramatically, her voice breaking.

"Oh, rubbish!" Jessica snapped.

"Do you deny you said those things, Mrs. Fletcher?" Hernandez asked.

"No, I don't exactly deny . . ."

"And you did go to the set?"

"You know I did."

"And shortly after, you were seen by the security guard hurrying away from the scene of the crime."

"Well, of course. Anyone who found a body would hurry away to raise the alarm."

"When you saw him you attempted to run away from him."

"I explained that. I thought he was the killer."

"You claim there was someone else on the set. But no one else saw or heard a sign of him."

"I can't help that."

"The doctor says the blow that killed Lydecker could easily have been struck by a woman."

"But that doesn't mean it *was!* Lieutenant, this is becoming ridiculous!"

He raised his hand and counted off on his fingers as he spoke. "Means, motive, opportunity. You meet all requirements, J.B. Sorry, but I'm going to have to take you in. Come along."

And he took Jessica by the arm and led her, too dazed with disbelief to protest, to the police car.

The car had been traveling for a couple of minutes before Jessica managed to collect her thoughts enough to speak.

"Lieutenant, haven't you forgotten something?" Her voice was cold.

"What's that?"

"You haven't read me my rights."

"It's not necessary, J.B."

"Oh, it's not? How interesting. No doubt you'll inform the Supreme Court and the Attorney General and Congress and all other interested parties. I mean, it's such a pity, thousands of police officers wasting their time and breath every day reading people their rights, when Lieutenant Mike Hernandez has ruled that it's unnecessary."

He chuckled. "You don't understand. You're not under arrest."

She stared. "You could have fooled me."

"I'm not going to book you, J.B."

"Then what am I doing in this car?"

"I'm throwing the killer off his guard and giving you a chance to do your thing."

Jessica practically gaped at him. "You . . . you mean . . . having someone accuse me of murder in front of all those people was a ploy?"

He shook his head. "No. Sunny Finch is quite convinced you killed her boss. She went to the D.A. He called me in. Said he thought he could get a conviction based on the evidence against you. But I said to him, 'I know J.B. We're fellow authors. She'd never murder anyone.' "

"Don't be too sure of that, Lieutenant," Jessica said frostily.

He ignored this. "Then I figured, might not be a bad scheme to let it be thought you'd been arrested—maybe make the killer relax, let something slip. Also . . . well, I don't like you hanging about the studio with a killer on the loose. You've gotten yourself quite a reputation as a sleuth already, and the killer might well regard you as a threat. Now that's one danger out of the way, for the time being."

"Well," Jessica said with surprise, "I appreciate your concern for my safety, Lieutenant. But I assure you it's not necessary. The identity of the killer is no concern of mine."

"You could make it your concern," he said quietly.

Jessica frowned. "I don't understand. You mean you *want* me to?"

"I don't want you to undertake an active investigation—hunting for clues or questioning people. We do that sort of thing pretty well. I would like you to go back to your hotel, sit quietly and think for a bit. You just might come up with something. And I could use anything. Because frankly I can see this case turning into one of those famous unsolved mysteries."

For the first time Jessica felt a twinge of sympathy for this brash but somehow likable detective.

"It's as bad as that, is it?" she asked.

"Well, look at it like this: we got no physical clues; no eyewitnesses; hardly anybody *liked* the victim, and lots would've been glad to see him out of the way. But I can't find anyone who hated him enough, or stood to gain enough by his death, to kill him. Finally, several thousand people are free to roam around the studio. Virtually any of them could have sneaked onto stage three after Lydecker, bashed him and sneaked out again."

Jessica nodded thoughtfully. "I see your problems. But what good am *I* going to be to you? I mean, the killing may be rooted in some incident way back in the past. Somebody might have been nursing a grudge against Jerry Lydecker for years and now at last have just seized the opportunity to pay it off."

"Yeah, it's possible. But I don't really buy these long-term grudges. People kill either out of sudden passion or for immediate gain. Add to that the fact that Lydecker was killed at his place of work and I conclude that the murder was committed by someone involved with his current project: the filming of your book."

Jessica gazed at him with some respect. "Yes, Mike, that makes good sense. But I still don't see how you expect *me* to get anywhere. I hardly know any of these people."

"In the first place, let's not say I *expect* you to. It's a long shot. But you're smart. It's just possible that if you put your mind to it, something you've seen or heard in the last few days will ring some sort of bell in your brain. That's all I'm asking you to do: just think."

Jessica didn't reply immediately. "Besides," Hernandez added encouragingly, "don't forget what I told you: the D.A. believes we've got enough evidence to bring charges against you. He doesn't know you like I do. But the fact is that if we can't come up with the real killer in a day or so, I may be ordered to arrest you after all."

Jessica gave a sigh of resignation. "Oh, very well. Take me back to my hotel and I'll give the matter some thought. But I'm warning you, heaven help you if this brings my headache on again."

Jessica leaned back and yawned. She picked up the teacup from the table in front of her. But it contained only cold dregs.

The table was littered with sheets of notepaper, all covered with her small, neat handwriting. They comprised summaries of practically every conversation she'd had, and everything she had overheard of others' conversations, since first arriving in Hollywood.

Wearily, she gathered the papers together and read them over carefully. Then she took a fresh sheet and wrote in capital letters at the top:

THINGS TO CHECK

Underneath she wrote:

(1) Eve Crystal's medical history.
(2) Allan Gebhart's battle with alcohol.
(3) Ross Hayley's financial status.
(4) Marta Quintessa's relationship with Jerry Lydecker.

She stopped and was just considering whether anything further should be entered on the list, when there was a tap on her door. She got up, crossed to it and looked through the peephole. Norman Lester was standing outside. She opened the door.

"Hello, Norman. Come in."

"Hello, Mrs. Fletcher." He entered the room.

"To what do I owe this pleasure?"

"Mr. Strindberg had a call from someone at the studio, saying you'd been arrested. He sent me straight to police headquarters."

"To spring me?" she asked dryly.

"Partly. But Lieutenant Hernandez explained you hadn't been charged and were at your hotel."

"What do you mean by *partly?*"

"Well, Mr. Strindberg wants to make a deal. Mrs. Fletcher, thanks to all this publicity, he can get you anything you want, at Warners, Fox, Paramount—anywhere, except the studio where your picture's being made."

"Really? Why is that?"

"Well, I'm afraid that you've been banned from there as a disruptive influence."

Jessica laughed. He looked surprised. "Don't you mind?"

"No, I consider it quite a compliment. And I have no wish to return there, anyway." Then she looked serious.

"Norman," she said, "how would you like to defend me on a murder charge?"

He goggled. "You're not serious?"

"Well, it seems that unless I can come up with Jerry Lydecker's killer, I may well find myself really under arrest."

He stammered. "But Mrs. F-Fletcher, I'm not a real lawyer. I've never f-faced a jury in my life."

"So, it would be a new experience for both of us. I've never been tried for murder. But I wouldn't want anybody but you to defend me, Norman, and I'd tell Mr. Strindberg so. I'd have to have somebody who really believed in my innocence."

"But I c-c-couldn't. Honestly!"

"Well," she said thoughtfully, "there may be a way to avoid it—if you could do something else for me."

"Anything!" he exclaimed. "I'll do anything to stay out of a courtroom. Judges scare me to death."

"All right." Jessica went to the table and picked up the last piece of paper she'd been writing on. She handed it to him. "It'll require some research, but I'd like you to look into these points."

He studied it with an expression of dismay. "I don't know where to start."

"Why not start at the beginning?"

"But surely the police could find out these things better than I could?"

"No, I don't want to give the police ideas and start them digging into matters which may be quite irrelevant to the case. It wouldn't be fair to the people involved. It must be an unofficial investigation. Now, doesn't your firm employ a discreet detective agency from time to time?"

"Well, yes," he said doubtfully. "There is a very good one we use—but they're terribly expensive."

"Don't worry. I'll pick up the tab." She added dramatically: "No price will be too high to clear my name and expunge this foul slur from the reputation of a proud family."

"Are you putting me on, Mrs. Fletcher?" he asked.

"Only a very little, Norman. No, I really do want these facts, so be a good boy and get on with it right away. All right?"

# Chapter Twenty-one

THE next morning Jessica phoned Hernandez at police headquarters.

"Oh, hi, J.B.," he said when he heard her voice. "Any progress?"

"Not so far. Listen, I need some help."

"What's that?"

"Well, I've been banned from the studio."

He chuckled. "I heard about that."

"At first I thought it didn't matter, as I wouldn't want to go there again. But I've changed my mind overnight. I want to take a look at some of the costumes for the movie, and have a word with the wardrobe mistress."

"Elinor Riggs? I've talked to her—had to check Hayley's and Quintessa's alibi for the time of the murder."

"She confirmed it, presumably?"

"Yes. So if that's all you wanted with her . . ."

"No, there were other matters. The point is, can you get me in?"

"Sure; I'm going out there again this morning—trying to check more alibis. You can ride in with me. Nobody will question who I take in."

"Thank you, Lieutenant. That'll be a great help."

"Pick you up in half an hour?"

"I'll be ready."

The plainclothes sergeant at the wheel of the police car pulled into the parking lot at the studios and stopped. Hernandez, in the passenger seat, turned around and regarded Jessica quizzically.

"Know your way to the wardrobe department?"

"I believe so."

"Want me to come with you?"

"No, thank you; I think I'll be better off on my own."

"As you wish. Just remember, I did tell you I wasn't asking you to do any interviewing yourself."

"I remember. But I think this is necessary."

He got out and opened the door for her. Jessica alighted. "You will be around for a while?" she asked.

"Oh, sure. Brody and I'll be here all morning, I expect."

Jessica nodded and trotted off in the direction of the wardrobe department.

Elinor Riggs was a plump, motherly, gray-haired woman in her early sixties. She accepted without question Jessica's assertion that she was "one of the writers on *The Corpse Danced at Midnight,*" and when Jessica asked to see some costume sketches fetched them with the slightest of sniffs and a resigned air. She laid them out on the table.

Jessica thanked her warmly. Then she asked: "Tell me—who gives you the most bother: producers, directors, writers or actresses?"

The woman looked at her in surprise. Jessica smiled and Elinor responded rather diffidently.

"I'm sure we can all be utter pests, right?" Jessica added.

"Well, it depends," the woman said. "The actresses are the worst, I suppose. But anybody's liable to want changes at the last minute."

"It must make life very difficult for you."

"Oh, you've no idea, Mrs. Fletcher."

"Please, call me Jessica."

"Why, thank you. I'm Elinor."

"You know, Elinor, I often think that people at large don't appreciate the importance of the work you do in the success of any movie. Yet they'd soon notice quick enough if the costumes were shoddy—dirty, or with seams coming loose, buttons missing."

Elinor nodded vigorously. "That's very true, Jessica. People *don't* appreciate it."

"In fact," Jessica said, "I've always thought there should be a special Oscar category: Best Wardrobe Mistress."

Elinor gave a hoot of laughter. "That'll be the day."

"Well, if they ever have one I'm sure you'll win the first," Jessica told her.

Elinor looked embarrassed, but definitely pleased. "Why, thank you. I must say it's nice to be appreciated. For once."

"Oh, I'm certain everybody here appreciates what a treasure they have in you, Elinor."

Elinor gave another sniff. "Well, not so as you'd notice."

"What? Why, surely Mr. Lydecker appreciated you, didn't he?"

"Him? Couldn't be bothered to pass the time of day, half the time.

And always wanted everything ten minutes ago—or knew the reason why. Still, mustn't speak ill of the dead, I suppose."

"Then what about Miss Quintessa, for instance?"

"Well, she is a very nice lady, I'll say that for her. Always pleasant—and very appreciative of anything you can do for her."

"That's nice." Jessica lowered her voice a little. "I understand that you and she and Ross Hayley were all together in here at the time it happened?"

"Y-yes." There was the slightest of pauses before Elinor answered.

"That *is* right, isn't it?" Jessica said pleasantly. "I was there when Mr. Hayley was talking to the lieutenant and that's what he said."

"Is that so? You know, Jessica, the costumes for this picture have been—"

"Of course," Jessica interrupted, in the same level and casual tones, "it's very easy suddenly to find yourself lying to the police, to help a friend or colleague. But it's really awfully foolish."

Elinor bridled slightly. "Are you suggesting I lied to the police?"

"Yes," Jessica replied simply.

"Well, really! I don't know why . . ."

"You did, didn't you?"

"Of course not! I would never—"

For the second time Jessica cut in on her. "Elinor, I know how very hard it would have been to refuse to give those two an alibi. Practically anybody would have done the same in your place. But I assure you the police will find out the truth eventually. And then you *will* be in trouble. However, I'm working with Lieutenant Hernandez on this case, and I think—in fact, I'm virtually certain—that if you tell me the truth you'll hear nothing more about it."

Elinor gazed at her, an agonized expression on her face.

Jessica went on: "Now, please do believe me. Tell me what really happened. It's the sensible thing to do. You *weren't* all three here together at the time Mr. Lydecker was murdered, were you?"

Abruptly, Elinor shook her head. And then it all came bursting from her. "Oh, Jessica, I've been so worried. You see I slipped out for about twenty minutes while Mr. Hayley and Miss Quintessa were here. And then later, after they'd left, Mr. Hayley came back and told me what had happened to Mr. Lydecker, and said he and Miss Quintessa had agreed not to say anything about my having gone out, because then I wouldn't have an alibi and I might be suspected. He said he and Marta had been together here all the time I was out and that if we all told the same story, everything would be okay. Well, of course, at first I was so grateful. But then later I got to thinking, whoever would suspect *me* of having killed Mr. Lydecker? The idea was absurd. By then, though, it was too late. I'd already told that police lieutenant that I'd been here all the time. Tell me, Jessica, do you think it will be all right?"

Jessica put a hand on her arm. "Yes, it will. You won't be in trouble with the police."

"But I'll sure be in trouble with Mr. Hayley."

"Well, remember, it was he who suggested lying to the police, so he's not really in any position to make things difficult for you."

"I really am most awfully grateful," Elinor said, relief in her tone.

Then she looked down at the collection of costume sketches on the table, through which Jessica had been rapidly flicking during the early part of their conversation. All except one of these she had now pushed to one side. "You interested in that?" Elinor asked.

Jessica nodded. "Is the actual costume here?"

"Let's go see."

She led Jessica past row after row of costumes, ranging from historical dresses, through Western kits, various types of uniforms and glittering modern ball gowns, to a rack in one corner, which was crammed with a varied assortment of modern costumes.

Elinor indicated them proudly. "These are the ones being worn in *The Corpse Danced at Midnight.*"

Together they went through the entire rack. Then Elinor shook her head. "No, sorry, it's not here."

"Should it be?" Jessica asked.

"Well, yes, technically all costumes should be returned here when they're not being worn in a scene being rehearsed or shot. But the girls tend to leave them in their dressing rooms. And of course I can't be constantly chasing around after them."

Jessica nodded. "I see. Well, they're lovely costumes, anyway, and thank you for showing them to me. And don't worry anymore about the police."

She left Elinor and her beloved costumes, and in a pensive mood made her way to sound stage three again. For some reason there seemed— fortunately—to be no shooting going on at the moment and Jessica entered the building unseen. Following the same route along which Marta had led her that first morning, she soon located the row of portable dressing rooms being used by the cast. She went up to the one with a little card bearing the name EVE CRYSTAL on the door and tapped on it.

There was no reply. Jessica hesitated for a moment, then tried the knob. The door was unlocked. She pushed it open and entered the room.

She looked around. A few odd garments were lying here and there, but on the whole the room was reasonably tidy. There was no sign of what she was looking for. Her eye lighted on a large clothes closet at the end of the room. She moved toward it and reached for the door handle.

Her fingers had actually started moving it, when without the least warning the door was violently thrown open from inside.

Jessica gave a strangled gasp as the figure of a man loomed up in front of her.

With one arm raised to hide his face he shoved fiercely at her with the other hand. She staggered back and fell heavily up against the wall, as the intruder, head down, lurched across the room, knocking a chair flying, yanked open the door and ran out.

Shaken and with her heart pounding, Jessica hauled herself to her feet and staggered to the door.

She heard the clatter of the intruder's footsteps receding, and as she stuck her head out of the door caught a glimpse of a running figure disappearing along the pathway leading to the sound-stage exit.

At the top of her voice, and to nobody in particular, Jessica yelled, "Stop that man!"

Then she hurled herself in pursuit.

The man disappeared from her sight round a corner, but the next moment she heard a muffled shout, another set of footsteps, a crash and then panting, cursing and the sound of a blow.

Jessica rounded the corner and in an open space twenty yards ahead of her saw two figures rolling over and over on the floor.

As she ran toward the two men, one got the upper hand. He pulled himself up to a kneeling position, pinning the other man facedown onto the ground. The next moment she recognized the victor as Sergeant Brody.

Jessica ran up. "Oh, well done, Sergeant!"

Brody didn't answer immediately. He was too busy twisting his captive's arms behind his back and snapping handcuffs onto his wrists. The man was coughing and wheezing, obviously too breathless to speak.

Brody looked up at Jessica. "Hope you knew what you were doing when you called out, ma'am," he panted.

He clambered to his feet, hauled the other man up and spun him roughly around.

Jessica found herself looking into the face of Ross Hayley.

*  *  *

At last Hayley managed to speak. He glared at Brody. "How dare you treat me this way! Don't you know who I am? I'll have your badge for this."

Brody glanced rather apprehensively at Jessica. She spoke calmly. "Ask him why he was hiding in the closet in Eve Crystal's dressing room."

"Well?" Brody growled.

"I don't have to answer to you for my actions here. I'm the producer of the film that's being shot here."

"Yes," Jessica said, "he is, Sergeant—thanks to the timely demise of Jerry Lydecker."

Before Hayley could reply they heard footsteps approaching. Jessica looked up to see Hernandez hurrying toward them. His eyes darted between the three of them. "What's going on?"

"I'll tell you what's going on, Lieutenant," Hayley said savagely. "This tame ape of yours just set on me, knocked me down and put handcuffs on me. And I'd be obliged if you'd tell him to take them off!"

Brody said succinctly: "He was running. She yelled to stop him. I did."

Hernandez glanced at Jessica. "That right?"

Jessica nodded. "It was very lucky Sergeant Brody happened to be nearby."

"He didn't happen to be nearby," Hernandez said dryly. "I told him to stay as close to you as he could without your seeing him all the time you were here. Why did you want Mr. Hayley stopped?"

"I didn't know it was Mr. Hayley. He was hiding in the closet in Eve Crystal's dressing room. He knocked me down and ran out. Hardly the action of an innocent man."

"Good heavens!" Hayley said angrily. "I had a perfect right to be in Eve's dressing room. I was on the set, trying to work out some camera angles for the next scene we're shooting when I found I'd temporarily mislaid my copy of the screenplay. I thought Eve might have left her copy in her dressing room and I could borrow it. I was rummaging in the closet when I heard somebody coming in. I looked up and saw that it was *her.*" He jerked his head at Jessica before continuing.

"The last thing I'd heard she'd been picked up on suspicion for Jerry's murder. I thought she might be intending to knock off anyone who tried to produce this film of her book. And for all I knew, she might have been armed. So, before she glimpsed me I drew the closet door shut. Then I heard her coming toward me. She started to open the door. I wasn't going to stand there and be shot. I decided to go on the offensive. And that's it. If she got knocked down, it's her own fault."

Hernandez cocked an eye at Jessica. "Sounds reasonable, J.B."

Jessica regarded Hayley appraisingly. "Oh, it *sounds* eminently reasonable. But why didn't he answer when I tapped on the door?"

"I didn't hear you tap!" Hayley shouted. "I had my head down in the back of the closet."

"Looking for a copy of the screenplay?"

"Yes!"

"Did you really think she'd put her copy away in the closet? Why should she? Surely she'd leave it on the dressing table, or somewhere within easy reach."

"Yeah, but it wasn't anywhere in sight. There was a chance she'd shoved it in the closet. It was worth trying."

"Why was it worth trying?" Jessica persisted. "There's a row of dressing rooms there. Why not try one of those?"

Hayley tossed his head in exasperation. "Oh, this is impossible!" He took a deep breath. "I'm sorry I knocked you down. Okay? But to suggest I killed Jerry is crazy. For one thing, I have an alibi."

"No, you haven't," Jessica said quietly.

Hernandez looked at her sharply. "What's that?"

"Well, it's possible Marta Quintessa will still give him one. But it wasn't true that the two of them and Elinor Riggs were all together at the time of the murder."

Hernandez's eyes gleamed. "The Riggs woman lied to me?"

"At first, yes. But she's told the truth now. And, incidentally, I've promised her you won't be taking any action against her. I hope that was in order."

"Sure, sure." Hernandez waved this aside as an irrelevance. He stared at Hayley. "Well?"

Hayley opened his mouth, then thought better of it. He swallowed before saying defiantly: "I have nothing to say."

Hernandez shrugged. Then he snapped an order at Brody. "Search him."

"You can't search me!" Hayley yelled. "I didn't do anything."

"You knocked me off my feet," Jessica put in.

Hernandez nodded. "Felonious assault. Search him."

Brody started running his hands over Hayley's clothes and delving into his pockets. He brought out a number of items, which he passed to Hernandez: a wallet, several pens, a comb, a pack of small cigars, a lighter, a diary, a penknife, a bunch of keys, a handkerchief, an assortment of loose change—and finally a small round object that gleamed golden in the sergeant's beefy hand.

Brody handed it to the lieutenant. It was a button. Hernandez held it up for Jessica to look at.

"Is this what you saw lying next to Jerry Lydecker's body?"

Jessica peered at it closely. "It has the same design," she said.

Hernandez gave a satisfied nod. "That's good enough for me. He was trying to plant this in Eve Crystal's dressing room when you caught him in the act. Brody, read him his rights."

"And that's just about all of it, Norman," Jessica finished up. "They took Ross Hayley away, I returned briefly to Eve's dressing room and then came back to my hotel."

"Gee, that's terrific, Mrs. Fletcher!" Norman said excitedly. "You did it! Uncovered the real killer and got yourself off the hook. Congratulations!"

"Thank you."

"And it all ties up with the information I've uncovered."

He reached into his pocket and brought out some sheets of folded paper. "Listen." He unfolded the papers and started to read aloud:

"Ross Hayley mortgaged his house to buy the screenplay, which the studio later abandoned. He is overextended in every direction and deeply in debt."

He looked up. "Bingo! Hayley knew he had a hit on his hands with *Corpse.* But he needed to make it *his* picture—to get all the credit for it; plus, of course, the extra money which would come with being the producer."

Jessica nodded. "Yes." There was a faraway look in her eyes. "Yes, he certainly *did* have a motive—for killing Jerry Lydecker."

Norman said: "I don't suppose you're interested in the rest of this stuff now?"

Jessica came abruptly back to the present. "Oh, is that the information on the other three?"

"Yes."

"Then please let's hear it," she said. "I'm not going to spend all that money for nothing."

"Oh, right." He consulted the papers. "Allan Gebhart," he read. "Calls himself a recovering alcoholic, but really there's no such thing. You've either kicked the habit or you haven't. Gebhart's position is that he's continually going on the wagon, stays dry for a while, then has a relapse and goes on a real bender—usually during periods of stress. Often doesn't remember anything about them afterward."

"I see. Go on."

"Eve Crystal. You asked about her medical history. Haven't been able to get much. But she is a diabetic. Takes oral medication. That's about all on her, I'm afraid."

"That's okay. What about Marta Quintessa?"

"She used to be Jerry Lydecker's mistress. But it seems she was too possessive for him. He was a man who liked his freedom. Marta once threatened to kill him for fooling around with younger women. She has quite a temper."

Norman looked up. "That's about it, Mrs. Fletcher. Not a lot for your money."

"It's as much as I expected. More, really."

"And anyway, it doesn't really matter now, does it?"

"Oh, information is always useful to a writer."

He grinned. "And to a detective."

"I am *not* a detective. However, I'm very grateful, Norman. Thank you."

"You're welcome." He stood up. "Mrs. Fletcher, can I buy you a drink? You've cracked the case and that calls for a celebration."

Jessica gave a sigh. "Frankly, Norman, I don't feel much like celebrating. I haven't achieved my main aim in coming to Hollywood: preventing that film from being made."

"Do you think they'll still go ahead with it?"

"I don't see why not. They've bought the rights; they have a screenplay —a cast—the sets are built—the costumes are made. They've actually started shooting—and the murder's given them a tremendous amount of free publicity. From a financial angle they'd be crazy to cancel it now."

"Yes, I suppose you're right. I'm sorry. So, what are your plans? Home to Cabot Cove?"

"Not just yet. I hate to leave things unfinished."

"What more can you do?"

"I don't know. But at the very least I ought to say goodbye to all the friends I've made here. Perhaps I'll give a little party."

He stared at her in surprise. "A party?"

"Yes; after all, you're quite right—I *do* have something to celebrate: I'm no longer under suspicion of murder. Now, I wonder if I can persuade everybody to come? It might take quite a bit of tact—and organization—to get them all."

"Mrs. Fletcher, if you can't arrange it, nobody can."

"Thank you, Norman. And now let's go downstairs. I want to see about a room for my party. And then I'll let you buy me that drink, after all. Frankly, I could use one."

# Chapter Twenty-two

JESSICA looked around the room with satisfaction. Her party was in full swing. And all the guests she'd invited had turned up.

In one corner, Allan Gebhart, a glass of diet cola in his hand, was chatting to Martin Strindberg, who like most of the others present was sipping from a glass containing a very good and expensive champagne.

In the center of the room the tall, athletic figure of Scott Bennett stood happily acting out some anecdote, with a wealth of gesture, to an audience consisting of Eve, Norman and Elinor Riggs—who was systematically emptying a plate of canapés.

In another corner Marta Quintessa, a resigned expression on her face, had been buttonholed by Mike Hernandez. As Jessica looked at them she heard his voice, raised slightly. "I was thinking of Clint Eastwood for the part of Rick."

Jessica smiled to herself. This party had taken a lot of arranging, several days of irritating delay, dozens of phone calls and all her powers of persuasion to get everyone here. However, it seemed to be working.

Of course, she hadn't actually needed *all* these people. But it would have been awkward just to ask the ones she really wanted; she'd had to make the affair look like a genuine party. Even now, the numbers were a bit thin. She almost wished she'd hired a few extras from Central Casting to stand around, chatting and smiling. But that would perhaps be going just a little too far.

And, after all, nine was quite a reasonable number—under the circumstances. Moreover, it was still early and most of those present no doubt expected other guests to be turning up as the evening wore on.

"Mrs. Fletcher?"

Jessica turned to see Sunny Finch at her elbow.

"Yes, my dear?"

"I wanted to apologize."

"Oh, what for?"

"Well, you know—making the police think you'd killed Jerry."

"Oh, I realize that was just a misunderstanding," Jessica said. "And I have to admit that my words that day could easily have been misinterpreted."

"Thank you for being so nice about it. And for inviting me. It's not often a secretary gets to be asked to the same party as the stars."

They looked across to where Scott was still acting out his story.

"He's certainly very handsome," Jessica observed. "Tell me, Sunny, in confidence, just how good an actor is he? I've never seen him perform."

"Well, *I* think he's very good."

"But other people don't?"

Sunny shrugged. "You know how people are. I suppose it's just a matter of opinion."

"Mr. Lydecker must have thought highly of him, though?"

For a moment Sunny hesitated. Then she said: "I—I believe so."

"You don't sound very certain," Jessica said.

"Well, yes, he did at first, of course." The girl was plainly embarrassed.

Jessica eyed her keenly. "You mean he'd *stopped* thinking so highly of him?"

"Really, I don't think I ought . . ."

Jessica drew her a little to one side. "My dear, do you want Mr. Lydecker's killer brought to justice?"

Sunny stared at her in amazement. "But he has been!"

"Ross Hayley has been charged with the crime," Jessica said. "He hasn't been convicted. And he strenuously denies the charge. Now, anything I can find out may help secure a conviction."

Sunny gazed at her without speaking. Jessica went on. "You thought a lot of Jerry Lydecker, didn't you?"

The girl's chin went up. "Yes, I did. I know he wasn't popular with everybody, but he was very good to me. And, no, we weren't lovers. He never even made a pass."

"Well, certainly anybody who can generate that sort of loyalty among his employees can't have been all bad," Jessica said. "So won't you please tell me what you know about Scott?"

Sunny took a deep breath. "Well, Jerry was planning to fire him from the movie."

Jessica's eyebrows went up. "Really? For what reason?"

"The reason he was going to give was that Scott was unreliable—turned up late, didn't know his lines, things like that."

"And was that true?"

"I wouldn't know, Mrs. Fletcher. I didn't get onto the set very often. I only know about it at all because the day he was killed Jerry had me type a memo to the head of the studio, explaining his reasons for dropping Scott."

"And did he send that memo?"

"I believe not. He put it in his pocket when I gave it to him."

"Did you make a copy?"

"No. He specifically said he didn't want one."

Jessica was silent for a moment. Then she said: "Thank you, Sunny. You've done the right thing in telling me." She paused: "Now, there's a young man over there who wants to meet you. Excuse me a moment."

She went over to where Scott had just finished his anecdote and touched Norman on the arm.

"Norman, there's a young woman who wants to meet you over here."

She led him across to Sunny, performed hasty introductions, picked up a bottle of champagne from the makeshift bar and returned to Scott and Eve. (Elinor, she noticed, had wandered over to the buffet table and was contentedly refilling her plate.)

"My dears," Jessica said, "your glasses are empty. Let me fill them."

Eve put her hand over the top of her glass. "No more for me, thank you."

"Oh, come on," Jessica urged. "Just one more glass. Or don't you like champagne?"

"Oh, it's not that. It's very good champagne, but . . ."

Scott started to interrupt her. "But you . . ."

"But you know what I get like when I drink," Eve finished. "Tonight I'm severely rationing myself."

"Well, no doubt you're wise," Jessica told her. "Scott?"

"Yeah. Please."

Jessica filled up his glass.

"Thanks." He emptied it in one go. "This imported?"

"Oh, yes; the wine waiter told me it's a very good vintage."

"Scott wouldn't know. It goes past his taste buds too fast to leave a flavor."

It was Marta who spoke. She was standing at Jessica's elbow with an empty glass. "May I?"

"Of course." Jessica poured some champagne into her glass. "You seem to be getting on famously with Mike Hernandez."

"It's extraordinary," Marta said. "Today he's treating me like his oldest friend. Yet a couple of days ago he was tearing into me for not contradicting Ross' statement that Elinor Riggs was with us when Jerry was killed."

Jessica smiled. "He's off duty now. I suppose that changes things."

"He was trying to make me admit that Ross went out for ten minutes during the crucial time."

"And what did you tell him?"

"What I'll continue to tell him—and everybody else; that we were together every second."

"I see."

Marta regarded her with slight amusement on her face. "Don't you believe me, Jessica?"

"I'm sure normally you're a very truthful person, Marta." Jessica paused before adding: "I'm also sure you're a very loyal one."

Marta smiled. "And you're a very diplomatic one."

Scott said: "Hey, we gotta keep talking about murder? I thought this was supposed to be a party!"

"It's pretty hard not to talk about it," Marta said. "After all, nearly everybody in this room knew Jerry. He brought most of us together. If it weren't for him, we wouldn't all be here tonight. We may not have found him the easiest of guys to get along with, but he *was* a personality and we won't forget him in a hurry. In fact, I'd like to drink a toast to him."

Sunny approached. "I'll second that."

Allan Gebhart came up, holding out his glass. "If I'm going to have to drink to Jerry Lydecker's memory, I'm going to need something a bit better than cola in my glass, or I might choke." He took Eve's glass from her hand. "If we're doing it, let's do it properly. Jerry would have hated being toasted in anything except champagne."

Jessica looked somewhat dubious, but nevertheless filled both the glasses. Gebhart handed Eve's back to her. Jessica meanwhile crossed to Hernandez and added some champagne to his glass. As she was doing so, she spoke to him in a low voice, unheard by anyone else. He listened, then shook his head.

Jessica went to each of the other guests, topping up their glasses where necessary. Then she replaced the almost-empty bottle on the table and said to Marta: "Go ahead, my dear."

Marta looked a little embarrassed. "I didn't want to make anything too formal of it. So I'll just say: to Jerry Lydecker . . . wherever he is."

Somewhat self-consciously, they all drank. There was a rather awkward silence for a few seconds. Then Jessica spoke:

"Now I'd like to offer a toast, if I may."

Everyone looked at her. She raised her glass.

"To a man who has been wrongfully accused: Ross Hayley."

She sipped from her glass. But nobody else moved. Their expressions were blank. At last Marta said: "Hear, hear. To Ross Hayley." She drank.

Norman Lester muttered, "T-to Ross Hayley," and took a sip.

Jessica looked calmly around the circle. "Dear me, I seem to have caused some surprise."

"Of course we're surprised," Scott said. "Ross *must* have killed Jerry."

Jessica raised her eyebrows. "Must? I think not."

She put her glass down. "Several other people had a motive for the murder—all of them in this room now. And according to Lieutenant Hernandez, none of you has a cast-iron alibi—that is, one vouched for by unimpeachable, independent witnesses."

"Look," Allan Gebhart said angrily, "what is this? Some sort of trial?"

Jessica ignored his question. "You, for instance, Mr. Gebhart. You had a motive. Jerry Lydecker had insulted you, humiliated you, scorned your screenplay and barred you from the studio. It's a well-known fact that you have a drinking problem—and go through periods of which you have no memory afterward. Can *you* be certain you didn't murder Jerry Lydecker?"

Gebhart had gone white. "You're crazy!" he exclaimed harshly.

"You're wrong, Jessica," Marta said quietly. "Allan couldn't kill anybody."

Jessica turned to gaze at her. "Well, what about you, Marta? Could *you* kill? You did threaten to murder Jerry Lydecker once. Is the reason you're sticking by Ross Hayley's story of your being together at the time of the murder because, if that story were disproved, you wouldn't have an alibi either?"

"No," Marta said, her voice still low. "The reason I'm sticking to it is because it's true."

"Aw, let's drop all this garbage," Scott said loudly. "Ross killed Jerry —period."

"Why are you so keen to stop the discussion?" Jessica asked him.

"Why? Because I don't like it."

"I'm not surprised. For you had the strongest motive of all."

His jaw dropped. "What are you talking about? I didn't have any—"

Jessica broke in, her voice hard. "What about the fact that Lydecker was going to drop you from the film?"

Again there was dead silence. Scott drew his breath in sharply.

*"Drop me?* That's a lie!"

"It's no lie."

"What reason would he have had?"

"Jealousy. The fact that you were having an affair with Eve."

Scott gave a shout of laughter. "He'd sack me for that? I'd have sued him for every cent he had—and he knew it."

"Ah, but that wouldn't have been his official reason. He was going to claim you were unreliable as an actor, turned up late, didn't know your lines."

"Prove it!" Scott sneered.

"Sunny here typed a memo to the head of the studio from Jerry Lydecker on the day of his death, saying he was dropping you, and giving those very reasons."

Jessica looked at the secretary. "Tell him."

Sunny hesitated, then gave a quick, jerky nod. "It's true."

Scott Bennett licked his lips. He was very pale. "And where is this precious memo?"

"It can't be found."

"Because it never existed!"

"Oh, but it did. Lydecker had it on him at the time of his death. But I've checked with the lieutenant. It was not found on his body. Someone stole it."

Her voice rose. "Which makes you the murderer, Mr. Bennett. Nobody but you had a reason for stealing that memo. You knew if it was made public, it would have a devastating effect on your career. You met with Lydecker on the set and had an argument about Eve. He showed you the memo he had ready to send. You lost your temper, picked up the urn and hit him with it. Then you took the memo, forgetting that somebody else knew about it: the person who had typed it."

Beads of sweat had formed on Scott Bennett's brow. "This is a frame-up!" he shouted.

Jessica turned to Hernandez. "Well, Lieutenant, it's all yours. I've gone as far as I can go."

Hernandez stepped up to Scott. But before he could speak a shrill scream rent the air.

Everyone in the room gave a start. The scream had come from Eve. All eyes swung to her. Her face had gone deep red. She was sobbing.

"No—no—he didn't do it."

"The evidence is conclusive, my dear," Jessica said softly.

Tears were running down Eve's cheeks. "It's not conclusive. Scott is innocent."

"How can you be so sure?" Hernandez snapped.

Eve turned an anguished face to him. "Because . . . because I killed Jerry."

# Chapter Twenty-three

"THE first point to bear in mind," Jessica said, "is that Eve Crystal is a very good actress indeed—and a potential box-office star. Jerry Lydecker and Ross Hayley were both well aware of that. However, I was put off the track by some words Allan Gebhart spoke when he had that row with Jerry Lydecker and was banned from the studio—something to the effect that Eve was utterly incompetent as an actress and had only been given the role because she was the producer's girlfriend."

It was fifteen minutes after Eve's dramatic confession. Hernandez had read her rights to her and taken her away. Martin Strindberg had accompanied them, so he could at least temporarily act as her attorney. A shaken Allan Gebhart and a plainly devastated Scott Bennett had both slipped quietly away shortly afterward. When the initial shock had worn off, those remaining—Marta, Norman, Sunny and Elinor—had demanded explanations.

"Gebhart's claim was completely untrue and uttered in pique. It infuriated Lydecker, not, I think, because it was insulting to Eve, but because it was a slight on his professional integrity. And it's true that, in one sense, as Gebhart later admitted to me, Lydecker was a very good producer. His films had high production values—excellent sets, costumes, special effects and so on—and they always made huge profits. In fact, it was inconceivable that he would jeopardize the financial prospects of any film by casting an incompetent actress in the lead, whatever their personal relationship. However, I didn't realize that at the time."

Jessica looked sternly at Marta. "You didn't help, either: you referred to Eve as being incredibly untalented. But you, too, were letting your personal feelings run away with you. You were very jealous of Eve. Because, in fact, whatever you may have said about Jerry, you were still carrying a torch for him."

Marta gave a rueful shrug. "Perhaps you're right. Sorry if I misled you."

"It didn't matter in the long run. In the end you helped me a lot."

"How? And why was the fact Eve was a good actress so important? Do you mean just the fact she was able to feign grief so well?"

"Yes, but not only that. I was convinced she was genuinely shattered that day by the news of Jerry's death. I was also in no doubt that when I arrived at the beach house she had been there, drinking on her own, for a considerable time. So at first I never seriously suspected her at all."

"When did you first suspect her?" Sunny asked.

"It was over that business of the gold button."

Norman grinned. "The f-famous gold button."

"I was sure, when I spotted it by the body, that I'd seen it before. Actually I hadn't! But I had seen a picture of it. I'd sat in Jerry Lydecker's office for several minutes, staring at a large poster, which featured a very prominent photo of Eve, wearing her drum-majorette costume, and the buttons on it were quite distinct. As soon as I remembered that I began to have doubts about Eve. But could I have been fooled about her grief and her drunkenness that day? Well, one thing had been odd: she'd apparently been mixing good Scotch whiskey with diet cola. I'm no expert on liquor, but even I know that's something no real drinker would ever do."

Marta said: "That was hardly conclusive, though, was it? I mean, if Eve *wasn't* a *real* drinker she might not know that—and would probably get even more drunk."

Jessica nodded. "Precisely. Though, in fact, she did use the expression 'I shouldn't drink alone'—implying it was something she did habitually. However, it was there that your help came in, Marta."

"I can't think how," Marta said.

"You mentioned that once when someone replaced Eve's soft drink with vodka, she 'turned bright red.' Now, that often happens when people who take a certain medication for diabetes drink alcohol. I had Norman check, and he discovered that Eve *was* a diabetic. That clinched it: she wasn't a drinker, or only a very rare one, and certainly hadn't been drinking that day at the beach house. She was actually pale that day. That's the reason I tried to press champagne on her this evening: I wanted to see how she'd react. In fact, she pretended she'd already had some—said that it was good—when in fact she'd only been drinking diet cola. Scott nearly gave the game away by starting to say, 'But you haven't had any,' before she cut him off. No doubt you all noticed how red her face was at the end—after she'd been more or less forced to drink champagne."

"So once you realized she'd fooled you, what did you do then?" asked Norman.

"First of all, I wanted to look at the drum-majorette costume and confirm that a button was missing from it. Elinor and I looked for it together in the wardrobe department, but it wasn't there. So then I went to Eve's dressing room to look for it—and got knocked down by Ross Hayley. However, I went back after he was arrested; the costume wasn't there, either."

"Where was it?" Elinor asked.

"No doubt hidden at the beach house. Or burned, or dropped in the ocean, wrapped around a rock. Eve was wearing it when she killed Jerry. He probably made an instinctive, convulsive grab at her as he was falling and pulled off the button."

Elinor gave a decisive nod. "It would sure take something like that. No costume *I* was in charge of would go before the cameras with buttons that would come off easily. And if the cops had asked *me* about that button I could have told them where it came from."

"Yes," Jessica agreed, "one should always go to the expert. Anyway, Eve must have run out and driven home, still wearing the costume. When she got home she no doubt discovered the button was missing. It was a very unusual design, so she couldn't just replace it. Therefore, she had to find some excuse for not wearing it again, and that's why she kicked up the fuss about Jerry having wanted it redesigned—requiring Marta to start on a completely new outfit."

There was silence for a few seconds, before Sunny asked, "What was Ross doing in Eve's dressing room that day? Presumably he wasn't really trying to frame her?"

"No, of course not. I never did believe that theory. Everybody agreed that this film was desperately important to Ross. He would have been crazy to try and frame his leading lady on a murder charge! She was very important to the picture. If she were arrested, even if they found a suitable replacement, there'd certainly be considerable delay and extra cost. And Ross Hayley was now not only director, but also producer."

Sunny pressed for an answer. "So why was he rummaging about in her closet?"

Norman's face lit up. "I know! He was hoping to replace the button."

Jessica beamed at him. "Precisely. Like me, he was looking for the drum-majorette costume, doubtless intending to sew the button back on. I'd wager that if the police had searched him really thoroughly that day they'd have found a needle with a length of thread attached stuck in back of his lapel."

"So, it was Ross you heard on the set just after you'd discovered the body?" Norman said.

"It has to have been. He must have arrived a minute or so after me, discovered the body while I was trying to find my way out, recognized the button, realized who the killer was and taken the button to protect his leading lady. He probably also wiped the urn. Then he got away while I was talking to the security guard."

She looked at Marta. "Don't worry, my dear: Ross' part is of no importance, now that Eve has confessed, and I won't say anything about that part of the case outside this room."

Marta smiled. "Thanks."

Sunny persisted. "I still don't know *why* Eve killed Jerry."

"She killed him to protect Scott. Her motive was exactly the motive I imputed to Scott. You see, Eve has been in love with Scott for some time."

Marta frowned. "I thought she was just fooling around to make Jerry jealous."

"I know. It may have started like that. But it had become much more serious, for her at least. I think she'd become positively frightened of Jerry. I remember the look on her face the very first time I saw her, coming out of her dressing room, just having left him. Well, Jerry wasn't going to have her ditch him for her leading man. He decided to get rid of Scott—a good actor, but not all that important to the picture. However, he had to disguise his real reason for sacking him. So he had you type that memo, Sunny. Perhaps he never intended to send it, but just use it as a lever to make Scott resign from the picture. Then, though, Jerry met Eve on the set and couldn't resist showing the memo to her—taunting her and telling her he was going to send it. Eve was horrified. She knew that if the memo was sent it could set Scott's career back years, perhaps ruin it. And it would be her fault. She snatched up the urn, hit Jerry with it, perhaps not even intending to kill him, grabbed the memo and ran."

"Did you know all this before the party?" Norman asked.

"I'd worked out a lot of it, but I still didn't know why Eve should have killed Jerry just when she did. I was hoping to get people a little drunk, get them talking about the crime, perhaps play on them a little, and try to squeeze a lot of facts into the open. But then, Sunny, you told me about that memo, and everything clicked into place."

"One thing more," Elinor said, "if you knew Eve was guilty, why did you accuse Scott?"

"I think I know," Marta said quietly. "You wanted to give her a chance to confess, didn't you?"

Jessica nodded. "I knew things would go much easier for her if she did confess. And I knew that if she'd confess for any reason it would be to save Scott. Maybe I'm wrong, but I do feel rather sorry for that child. Now I believe that with a good lawyer, and provided she gives a good performance on the witness stand, she'll get off fairly lightly."

"I-did-it-all-for-love," said Marta dryly.

"Something like that."

"And," Sunny said, rather coldly, "suppose she does get off lightly—and then one day kills again?"

"Then I'll have been very wrong. But I won't feel guilty; because *I* won't be the one to have let her off lightly. *I* trapped her—and just made the one concession of letting her confess."

Marta gave a grin. "It was pretty hard on poor old Scott."

"That young man has a very high opinion of himself," Jessica said. "This won't have done him any harm—and may well help make him a better actor. I was also hard on Allan Gebhart, but that was deliberate. I believe for a few seconds he actually realized that during one of his blank periods he just might do something terrible and not remember it. That could have a salutary effect. I felt more sorry that I had in various ways caused you four embarrassment—telling Hernandez that you'd given Ross a false alibi, Elinor; making you talk about that memo, Sunny; getting you to work for me, Norman."

She looked at Marta. "And suggesting in front of everybody that you might be the killer."

"I could tell from your eyes that you didn't really mean it," Marta said.

"And I could tell by *your* eyes that you knew I didn't."

"Well," Norman said, "speaking for myself, it was a privilege to help you."

"I'll second that," Sunny added.

"I'm just relieved to have got that lie off my conscience," Elinor told her.

Marta took Jessica's hand. "You cleared Ross. That's the important thing. What if you did have to be a bit sneaky?"

"Well, thank you all," Jessica said. "I must say it's a very satisfying sensation. I can go home feeling I have achieved something. Even though . . ." She trailed off.

"Even though what?" Elinor asked.

"Oh, nothing, Elinor, nothing," Jessica said.

# Chapter Twenty-four

IT was nearly noon the following morning. Jessica was just finishing her packing when there came a tap on the door. She was expecting the bell-hop, so she called out:

"Come in."

The door opened to reveal Ross Hayley standing on the threshold. In his hands was a huge bunch of flowers.

"I've come to say thank you," he said.

Jessica gave an exclamation of delight.

Then he saw the suitcases and his face fell. "Oh, you off already?"

"Very shortly."

He came right into the room. "Then I'm afraid these are a rather impractical gift. However . . ." He handed them to Jessica, giving a slight bow. "With my deepest gratitude."

Jessica took the flowers. "Oh, thank you so much. They're lovely."

"But hardly something you'll want to carry from the West to the East Coast by plane. I'm sorry."

Jessica eyed the flowers dubiously. "Well, it might be a little inconvenient. I'll tell you what." She handed the flowers back to him. "Why don't you give them to Marta? You have a very good and loyal friend there."

"Don't I know it! She's been great. But are you sure? I mean . . ."

"Quite sure. But thank you very much for the extremely kind thought."

"Well, if you're certain . . . Er, you don't think Marta might get the wrong idea?"

"She'll certainly get *an* idea. But need it be the wrong one?"

He suddenly gave a broad smile. "Jessica Fletcher, you're fantastic! Not only do you see things other people don't see. But you make them see things right under their noses that they've never noticed before."

"Good, I think you'll find her quite receptive. But remember, she's been hurt once. Don't let it happen again."

"You can rely on me." He scratched his head. "Only trouble is now I haven't anything to give you."

"You've no call to give me anything."

"Except perhaps this." He put the bunch of flowers down on the bed, reached into his inside pocket and brought out a thick wad of paper. He held it out for Jessica to see that it was the screenplay of *The Corpse Danced at Midnight.*

"Oh, thanks," she said, "but I don't want . . ."

Before she could finish, he took the script in both hands, and tore it into two sections.

Jessica stared. "What *are* you doing?"

"Performing a purely symbolic act."

He crossed the room and dropped the script into the wastebasket. Then he turned.

"I've just spent a couple of hours with the studio top brass. And I have to tell you that the film has been finally and irrevocably abandoned."

Jessica gazed at him in delighted disbelief. "You really mean it?" she breathed.

"Cross my heart and hope to die."

She sat down slowly on the bed by the flowers. "Oh, Ross, you couldn't have brought me a better present. It's wonderful. I did hope, when Eve was arrested, that perhaps it might put an end to the project. But then I thought that so much money's been spent on the picture already, and they'll probably have some other young actress on their books, who's just been waiting for a good part."

"They have. By name, Emerald Love. And for a while it was touch and go. But it seems that the top-grossing picture at the moment is one about sex-crazed teenagers on a cruise. So they're going to put Emerald in one about sex-crazed teenagers on safari—co-starring Scott Bennett. It's based on a Hemingway short story."

Jessica shook her head. "Poor Ernest. Are you going to direct?"

"No way. They've decided also to resurrect *my* project—the one they shelved when *Corpse* came along. I'll have virtually a free hand."

"Oh, I'm so glad. Congratulations."

"And to you. And again, many thanks." He looked at his watch. "I must run."

She picked up the flowers and held them out to him. "Don't forget these."

"Oh, thanks. Well, goodbye, Jessica. Safe journey." He then crossed to the door.

Just before reaching it, he turned. "By the way, you must have gained something from this business—some great material for your next murder mystery."

Jessica shook her head decisively. "No. I'm not writing any more murder mysteries."

He looked at her in amazement. "You're not?"

"No. Ever since I started them, *real* murders have followed me around. And I've had enough of it. It's very wearing."

He came back into the room a little way.

"It must be. But you obviously have a talent for it—for which I for one am very grateful. And remember the other people you've gotten out of trouble. Besides, what makes you believe that just because you stop *writing* murders you'll stop being involved with them? Think about that. Bye."

He went out.

It was not in fact until the plane bearing her homeward soared into the California sky, and Los Angeles shrunk to a toy town below her, that Jessica really had time to think.

She lay back in her seat and closed her eyes. Those few days had been quite an experience. Though everything had really turned out remarkably well in the end.

Could what Ross Hayley said really be true? Did she genuinely have a talent for solving mysteries? Was her success due to more than simple luck? Either way, it was certainly true that her gift had helped several people out of very nasty situations: Ross himself . . . Nan Earl . . . her own nephew Grady . . . as well as all the people connected with them.

She paused in her train of thought. That word *gift*. It implied something God-given. And such gifts were meant to be used. So perhaps she had a duty to continue to use it whenever the opportunity came along.

Jessica sighed. If so, she'd just have to accept the fact, not fight it.

Though, naturally, this did not mean that she had to go on writing murder mysteries. The authorship and the detection weren't connected. On the other hand, if it hadn't been for her books, she wouldn't have been involved in those cases . . .

Anyway, did she truly *want* to write any more mysteries? *Could* she write any more? Would the ideas keep coming?

Of course, she couldn't really make a story out of the Lydecker murder. Or of the Earl case. Somebody would surely sue her if she did.

Mind you, there might be certain elements in them she could use . . . take the basic stories, twist them around a bit, change the identities of the killers. In anything she based on the Earl case, now, she wouldn't make the Maggie character into the murderer. But who, instead? Well, there had been one rather shadowy figure in the background of that affair, a person whom Jessica had somehow always been expecting to turn up: Grace Earl's estranged husband. She might bring him into it.

And what about the Lydecker case? Again, the fictional murderer would have to be somebody quite different from Eve Crystal.

Jessica opened her eyes suddenly. How about the lady mystery writer? That would surely fool everybody. But would readers believe such a dénouement? Probably not. She smiled. After all, everybody knew that mystery writers were good people.

Should she stick to her original resolve and forget about writing any more whodunits? Yes. Much the best plan.

Though perhaps it wouldn't do any harm to jot down a few ideas. Just in case.

Jessica reached into her bag and took out a notebook and pencil. She thought for a moment, her eyes staring out of the window. After a few seconds her head was bent. Her pencil moved over the paper, slowly at first, and then with gathering speed.

# LOVERS AND
# OTHER KILLERS

# Prologue

"BUT, Inspector, we know Haskell was shot in the temple. The bullet exited at the base of the skull. A *downward* trajectory. Nell Foster was in a wheelchair. Haskell would have had to be on his knees for her to have shot him from a sitting position."

The Inspector smiled grimly. "Well, why not?"

*"Why not?"* The Sergeant stared. "You saying he got on his knees, begging her not to—"

The Inspector shook his head and drew on his pipe. "Not at all. But he was blackmailing her, right? This was a payoff. Or so he thought. She has the money in an envelope. But instead of handing it to him, she hurls it contemptuously on the floor at his feet. He bends to pick it up—and at that moment she brings the pistol from under the rug on her knees and shoots him."

The Sergeant stared. "But that's brilliant, Inspector—"

Jessica Fletcher stopped writing. Oops! She couldn't have the Sergeant staring again already. She thought for a moment, and changed the second *stared* to *whistled*.

Then she read the page over. She crossed out *grimly* after *smiled*. That was a cliché. People were always smiling grimly in novels. Yet she couldn't ever remember seeing anyone do it in real life. Apart from that, the page seemed okay.

Though, was the Inspector being all that brilliant? Was the point, on the contrary, just a little elementary?

Jessica sighed. It was so difficult to tell what would fool mystery buffs and what wouldn't. Sometimes what you considered your cleverest twists passed unnoticed, while points that seemed to you quite ordinary were picked out as being especially ingenious.

At that moment there came a sharp and familiar rat-tat on the back door. With relief—anything to stop work for a few minutes—she called: "Come in, Ethan."

The door opened, and Ethan Cragg entered the room. He was a tough-looking, weather-beaten man in his mid-fifties who had been a friend of her late husband Frank, and who, since Frank's death, had been a good friend to his widow.

Now he grinned. "Somehow, I thought I'd find you working at the kitchen table as usual, Jess. What happened to that smart writing room you were going to get fixed up?"

Jessica looked around the kitchen. "Oh, I don't know. I've certainly got plenty of spare rooms, but somehow I work so well in here. Perhaps because, before I started writing, the only creative work I ever did was done at that stove."

He nodded at the pile of typewritten papers on the table. "New story coming along all right, is it?"

She shrugged. "Well, I am getting there—slowly. Somehow, though, I don't think it's much good."

"At least that's an improvement on your other books. In the past, you've been quite *sure* they're no good—until they've been published and sold millions."

"Oh, don't exaggerate, Ethan. My books don't sell in *millions.*"

"They do pretty well, though, don't they?"

"I suppose you could say that."

"You're a best-selling author."

She pursed her lips. "I just about qualify."

"And those critic guys like you."

"Most of them seem to."

"So of course this book's good. Quit worrying."

She smiled. "You're a great comfort, Ethan. Somehow, though, I can't help worrying."

He eyed her closely. "You don't look well, Jess. Reckon you've been working too hard. You need a rest."

"Some hope."

"Listen: you've published three books on the trot, you're working on a fourth—and the only breaks you've had you've spent solving real-life murders."

She nodded thoughtfully. "Life has been a bit hectic, I agree. But I wanted to capitalize on the success of *The Corpse Danced at Midnight* while it was still fresh in people's minds."

"Okay, but now you're established. You're not short of cash. So why not take a vacation?"

"I have to finish this book. I've got a deadline."

"Then right after you've finished it."

"There'll be so many other things to do."

"Tell me, when did you last take one—a real one?"

"Oh, I don't remember exactly. It was with Frank."

"There you are, then. That's too long. So how about it?"

"I'm not good at doing nothing, Ethan. But . . . well, I'll think about it."

He raised his arms in despair. "I give up. I've done my best."

As his arms rose she noticed that he was holding a bundle of letters in one hand.

"What are those?" she asked, pointing.

"Oh, sorry—nearly forgot. They're yours. I met the mailman at your gate."

He handed the letters to her.

"Thank you."

She started shuffling through them, discarding the bills and the obvious junk mail. She was left with two letters, both addressed in hands that looked familiar but which for the moment she couldn't place.

She held them at arm's length, one in each hand, and gazed at them.

"Now, who are these from?"

"Why not open them and find out?"

"Ethan, one of the chief pleasures of getting letters is not opening them —trying to guess who they're from."

"Strange letters worry me till they're open: I always expect it to be bad news."

"You're a natural-born pessimist. And you tell *me* not to worry."

She peered at the slightly blurred postmark on the letter in her right hand. "Seattle, Washington. Oh, of course, it's from Edmund."

"Edmund."

"Edmund Gerard. You remember: an old friend of mine, Gwen Gerard, died a few months back?"

"Oh, yeah—you were upset at having to miss her funeral, I remember."

"Yes, it was unavoidable. Edmund was her husband. He's dean of students at Sequoia University. I wonder what he can be writing to me about."

As he opened his mouth, she raised her hand to forestall his comments. "All in good time, Ethan."

Then she squinted at the postmark on the other letter.

"Kentucky: Can't read the town. I don't think I know anyone in Kentucky." She held the letter out for him to see. "A woman's writing, this one, wouldn't you say?"

Ethan laughed. "I wouldn't know, Jess. Anyway, I got to be going."

"Oh, wait and see who this one is from now. You've earned that."

Quickly she ripped open the envelope and drew out the letter. She glanced at the first page, frowned, turned to the back and looked at the signature. Then her face cleared.

"Oh, it's from Abby."

"Well, dang my hide!" Ethan slapped his thigh with the palm of his hand in mock amazement. "Abby! Who'd have thought it?"

Jessica laughed. "Sorry, Ethan. Abigail Freestone, my cousin. She's British."

"What's she doing in Kentucky?"

"That's what I'm trying to find out." She was scanning the letter. "She's at some place called Langley Manor." Her eyes ran on. "Oh, horses, of course."

"What do you mean?"

"Horses are Abby's life. She was one of the best trainers of show jumpers in England. Seems this man—er, Denton Langley—keeps lots. He's put Abby in charge of schooling them. My, she'll love that."

"That's fine. Well, I really must be getting along—"

"Hang on, Ethan, this'll please you."

"What's that?"

"She wants me to go and stay with her."

"Great, I hope you go."

"Listen." She read aloud: " 'I have a very cosy little cottage on the estate, quite close to the big house. I say little, but there's plenty of room for a guest. I've told the Langleys about my cousin Jessica, the famous writer, and they're all longing to meet you. I do hope you'll come. One small word of warning though: you will be expected to come hunting.' "

Ethan's brow puckered. "Not much of a hand with a rifle are you, Jess?"

Jessica smiled. "I think she means fox hunting."

He looked alarmed. "What—on horseback?"

"That is the conventional way, I believe."

"Say, that's dangerous. I don't trust those critters."

"Foxes?"

"No—horses."

"There speaks the true sailor."

"You ever ridden?"

"A little—at one time."

"Well, they say it's something you never forget."

"That I believe to be a myth. However, I suppose I'll find out."

"You mean you're going?"

"Well, you know, Ethan, I very well might . . . after I've finished the book. It's a lovely part of the country, I believe, though I've never been there. And I'm very fond of Abby. She's a sweet girl—if a trifle dotty. Well, I say girl, because that's what she's always seemed to me, but she must be nearly forty now. I'd like to see her again."

"Then go and enjoy yourself."

"If I can fit it in, I will. Anyway, let's see what Edmund has to say."

She tore open the letter with the Seattle postmark and started to read. After a few seconds she gave a sudden gasp.

"Oh, I couldn't possibly!"

Ethan glanced at her sharply. "Couldn't what?"

"Lecture." She looked up at him, her face a study. "He wants me to lecture—to the students *and* the faculty."

"What about?"

"The crime story."

"Well, why not? You know enough about them, don't you?"

"I'm not at all sure I do." She glanced down at the letter again. "I mean, he suggests three lectures over a week: one on the history of the genre—which means I'd have to go back to Poe, and Wilkie Collins and Conan Doyle; another on the crime story's place in literature; and another on the technique of writing them—how I set about it."

"So what?"

"Well, I'm not at all sure I know how I set about it. I just sit down and think—and then write."

"Then tell 'em that."

"Fine lecture that would make! No, I shall write back and politely decline."

"You won't."

"What do you mean?"

"You're not one to duck a challenge like this, Jess. Besides, you might do your profession a bit of good."

"I don't understand."

"Well, weren't you saying the other day that the highbrow students of literature at the universities don't take the mystery story seriously enough?"

"Yes, I was."

"Well, maybe this is your chance to make some of 'em sit up and take notice."

"Certainly somebody should do that. But I don't think I'm the one to do it. I've had no experience."

"You've been a teacher."

"I've taught high school. There's a big difference between that and a university."

"Principle's the same, I reckon."

"Perhaps . . . up to a point. But aside from that, there's my deadline."

"When's this Edmund fellow want you?"

Jessica consulted the letter again. "He suggests the fifteenth. That's just over two weeks—a week this side of my deadline."

"Can't you speed up—finish the book before then?"

"I doubt it. I'm not good when I try to speed up. I'm a slow, careful, finicky writer. I rewrite a lot. I like to get everything as good as I can make it."

"You're too much of a perfectionist."

"I shall never achieve perfection—but I always aim for it." Jessica sighed. She was looking the picture of misery.

Ethan said, "Well, it's up to you. I'll lay odds now, though, that you will go; and you'll be a hit—just as you'll wow 'em down in Kentucky."

He chuckled suddenly.

"What's the matter?" she asked.

"I was just thinking: for years you didn't leave Cabot Cove. Since you wrote *Corpse* you been to New York City, Los Angeles—and now it's going to be Seattle and Kentucky. Talk about all points of the compass."

"I haven't been yet, Ethan."

"You will, Jess, you will."

He turned for the door. "Well, so long. See you later."

"Bye, Ethan. And thanks for being such a morale-booster."

After he'd left, Jessica returned to the exploits of her brilliant, pipe-puffing Inspector. But she found it difficult to concentrate. What on earth would she say to all those eggheads? And how, after all these years, would she manage on a horse?

# Chapter One

THE taxi drew up outside the fashionable apartment block. The driver glanced over his shoulder.

"Hey, lady, we're there."

The woman in the back opened her eyes and looked around.

"What?"

"You're home."

"Oh? What time is it?" Her speech was slightly slurred.

He glanced at his watch. "Eleven-thirty." Then, ironically, he added: "P.M."

"What am I doing home as early as this?" She glanced sideways, as if expecting to see somebody. "And why am I on my own?"

"Don't ask me, lady. I only brought you here. You hailed me outside the Ninety-Nine bar, if that's any help. You were alone then."

The woman nodded slowly. "Oh yes, I remember now. I was stood up. Would you believe that, cabbie? Me—Alison Brevard—was stood up." She frowned. "Or should that be *I?* Would you stand me up, cabbie?"

He sighed. "Look, lady, I'm a happily married man. I only been married six months. And I'd like to get home to my wife. Okay?"

"I don't drink normally, you know. But it's a shock to the system, a thing like that. A girl needs a bracer after a thing like that."

"Yeah, sure. Listen, let me give you a hand inside—"

"No, no." She raised her hand in negation. "I can manage. How much?"

"Six-fifty."

"Okay." She fumbled in a small silver evening bag, took out a bill, squinted at it, then passed it to the driver. "How much is that?"

"Twenty bucks." He started to delve in his pocket.

"All right—keep it."

"Gee, thanks."

She eyed him more closely. "Say, you're cute. Come up and have a drink."

"Lady, I explained—"

"I know—you're a mappily harried . . . I mean happily . . . say, that's good: mappily harried. I like that. What they call things like that? Something to do with spoons, isn't it?"

"Listen, Mrs.—Miss—Ms.—"

"Brevard. But you can call me Alison."

"Listen, Alison, why don't you go indoors, go up to your apartment, and go straight to bed? What you need is a good night's sleep."

"You mean go to bed at eleven-thirty?"

"That's right."

"On my own?"

"That's what I'd recommend."

She gave a little giggle. "Well, it would certainly have novelty value. You know, I might very well try out your suggestion, Harry."

"Name's Bill."

"What's that?"

"Skip it." He got out hastily and opened the rear door.

Alison Brevard emerged slowly, staggering a little as her feet touched the sidewalk. Bill caught her by the elbow.

"Thanks, Harry. You're a real gentleman. How much I owe you?"

"You paid me. You going to be all right now?"

"Oh, sure. I live here, you know. You like it?"

"Yeah . . . swell. Well, good night."

"Night, Harry. See you around."

She stood watching him rather wistfully as he climbed back in his cab and drove off.

As the car disappeared down the street, she called out suddenly: "Spoonerism. That's what you call it when you mix your words . . ."

She turned, went slowly through the revolving doors and crossed the lobby to the elevator, swaying ever so slightly as she walked.

Alison Brevard was in her late thirties. She had dyed blond hair, was tall, and thin almost to the point of gauntness; her face, high-cheekboned and once beautiful, now looked haggard. Her large and lovely gray eyes had the lost, slightly glazed expression of the habitual drunk. She was wearing a stunning black evening dress and a mink cape.

She entered the elevator and stabbed jerkily at the fifth-floor button. The car ascended. On the fifth floor, she weaved along the thickly carpeted corridor to her apartment. She reached out toward the bell, then remembered that her maid was on a few days' vacation. She swore under her breath and began to grope in her purse for the front-door key. She found it at last, aimed it at the lock, and lunged. She missed the opening by about half an inch, and tried again.

It was the sound of Alison's key tapping against the lock and sliding back and forth across its brass surface that alerted the man who was at that moment in the act of rifling the antique walnut bureau in Alison's living room.

The intruder gave a muffled gasp and for a second froze. Then he quickly extinguished the flashlight in his hand. The only illumination in the room was now the dim glow of the city from the windows, over which the drapes had not yet been drawn. This gave the man just enough light to snatch up a bulging canvas bag and flit silently to a tall closet in the corner. He slipped inside, drew the door almost shut after him and stood—motionless and silent as a statue, only the wild beating of his heart seeming, to him, likely to give away his presence.

Alison eventually got her front door open and, muttering crossly to herself, she entered the apartment. She flapped vainly at a wall switch, letting her cape fall from her shoulders to the floor as she did so. Then she lost interest and, leaving the living room unlit, made her way, as purposefully as her condition and the darkness allowed, in the direction of the kitchen. She went in, and this time was successful in switching on the light. She crossed to the refrigerator, opened it and took out a half-filled pitcher of martinis. She reached into a cupboard above the refrigerator, picked up a glass and poured a stiff drink. She downed it in one go, and as she lowered the glass her eye fell on a snapshot that was tacked onto a cork bulletin board next to the wall phone. It was a picture of her, smiling at a dark, slim, good-looking young man of about twenty-five.

Alison's expression changed, became harder. She slammed down her glass, stomped across to the phone, picked up the receiver and, after several fluffed attempts, eventually managed to dial a number. She stood with the receiver to her ear, listening to the ringing tone.

"Come on, come on, you creep," she muttered. "I want an explanation from you."

But the ringing remained unanswered, and after a minute, Alison angrily replaced the receiver. She turned to face the living room, and stopped dead. The kitchen light behind her showed, on the floor by her desk, an upturned drawer, with its contents spilled out over the carpet.

Alison's heart missed a beat. Then she stepped into the living room and switched on the light. She stood, staring, her still befuddled brain trying to take in what her eyes were seeing.

The room was in a shambles. Every drawer had been pulled out and turned upside down on the floor; the papers in her bureau had been scattered everywhere. Objects had been swept from tables and shelves. And—

Alison swung toward the wall on her right. In the center of it, the door of the safe hung wide open. Even from here she could see that her jewel box was missing.

Sheer anger overwhelmed Alison. She stamped her foot in almost childish temper.

"Damn you!" she said out loud. "Damn you, damn you!"

She then stood quite still for a few seconds, letting the scene of desolation sweep over her and into her.

Then she turned again and marched determinedly back to the kitchen. The shock had done something to sober her up—enough to know what she had to do. Again she lifted the receiver and dialed.

After a moment she said, "Police—I want to report a break-in."

Hardly were these words out of her mouth when she heard a strange rushing sound behind her. She swung around to see a slim figure in black sweater and pants and wearing a ski mask dashing across the room toward the front door. The intruder was carrying a canvas bag.

Alison gave a gasp of pure fury. If the figure had come toward her, she would probably have screamed, but the sight of the burglar trying to get away seemed to increase her anger. She dropped the receiver and started in pursuit.

If she hadn't been so imbued with Dutch courage, she'd never have tried it. But, although partly sobered up by the shock, her system was still full of alcohol—impaired in mind and body.

She caught up with the man just inside the door and flung herself on him—clawing, beating with her fists and kicking. The intruder managed momentarily to throw her off and tried to open the door. But again Alison came back, this time not striking at him, but clinging tight, attempting by sheer brute force to stop him.

It was a crazy ploy, and if she had been sober, Alison would have realized this. However, for a few moments it worked. Although thin, she was wiry, and tall for a woman; the burglar was slim and of no more than average height. They remained locked together, swaying from side to side, as the intruder attempted desperately to dislodge her. At first he did nothing but try to pry her loose and push her off, but as the seconds passed and still Alison clung to him, he clearly began to panic.

His breath started to come even faster, and he began to make little noises—half grunts, half whimpers—in his throat. Alison felt a surge of triumph. She was winning! If he'd just let go the bag, she'd release him—

give him a chance to get away. She managed to gasp, "Drop it!" But he continued to cling to it like a limpet.

The end came suddenly. They barged into a small table just inside the door, on which stood a heavy bronze statuette. The man's eyes fell on it, and almost instinctively, he snatched it up with his free hand, raised it and crashed it down with all his force on Alison's head.

Like a puppet when the strings are released, she crumpled instantly to the floor. She lay quite still, not breathing.

For a moment the man was as motionless as his victim. Then he let the statuette fall from his gloved hand, carefully stepped over Alison's body and again approached the door. He bent, picked up her cape from the floor and stuffed it into his bag.

Next, he went right up to the door and put his ear against it. All was silent outside. He switched off the light, opened the door a crack and peered out. The corridor was deserted. He thanked his lucky stars that these swank places were solidly built and almost soundproof. Also that the rich kept to themselves.

He took a deep breath, slipped into the corridor and closed the door silently.

Around the ugly wound in Alison Brevard's temple the blood was already congealing. In the kitchen the telephone receiver swung slowly at the end of its cord and the martinis grew tepid in the pitcher.

# Chapter Two

DR. Edmund Gerard was a soft-spoken, introspective man of about fifty-five. But he looked older than that, thought Jessica: he'd aged a good deal since she'd last seen him—before his wife's death. His hair was now gray. But it quite suited him; he looked much more like a distinguished academic than most of the other academics of her acquaintance, who often could be taken for farmers, prizefighters or gangsters.

He'd met Jessica at the Seattle-Tacoma airport in his own car and insisted on driving her to her hotel. He was apologetic about the hotel.

"I'm sorry I can't put you up at home, Jessica," he said as he eased his dark blue sedan out of the airport parking lot. "But the fact is, most of the house is shut up. I have no live-in staff—just a cleaning lady who comes in a few mornings a week—and I hardly ever eat at home. So it wouldn't be very pleasant for you. Still, I think you'll be quite comfortable at this hotel—and it *is* close to the campus."

"Frankly, Edmund, I'll be happier at a hotel. If I stayed with you, we'd spend far too many hours rehashing the old days."

"Probably true, but why shouldn't we?"

"Because, unfortunately, I have to work while I'm here."

"Work? You mean writing?"

"I'm afraid so. I have just about a week to finish my book."

She explained about her deadline. "I'm afraid there's not going to be much time for sightseeing," she ended.

"Oh, Jess, I'm sorry to drag you away at an awkward time. You should have explained it wasn't convenient to come right now."

"I very nearly did. But my vanity got the better of me. I couldn't throw away the chance of lecturing at a major university. But, of course, composing my lectures has put me even further behind with the book."

"I hate to think of your spending all your time here slaving away alone in a hotel room."

"Well, not all the time, and probably not alone. I think that for the first time in my life, I need a secretary. If I can get a girl to do the typing for me, three hours a day should enable me to meet the deadline. Do you think the hotel will have a secretarial service?"

"Probably, but I imagine it'll be quite expensive."

"Can't be helped, I'm afraid."

"Suppose we have a word with my secretary, Amelia Browne? I doubt she could spare the time personally, but she may be able to find someone for you. She's incredibly efficient herself, so I'm sure she wouldn't recommend a dud."

Jessica nodded. "Very well. Thank you."

"We can stop by the university and see her now if you like—before going to the hotel."

"Suits me," she said.

They found Amelia Browne in the anteroom to Edmund's office, seated at her desk, surrounded by dozens of bills, statements, credit card receipts and the like—all stacked into tidy piles. She was soberly dressed, her hair drawn into a neat bun. Her features were rather plain, but she had a pleasant, kindly expression.

Edmund introduced Jessica and explained her requirements.

Amelia nodded comprehendingly. "I'm sure we can help you, Mrs. Fletcher."

"I'd be very grateful. But I don't want to put you to any trouble. You seem to have your hands rather full." She indicated the paper-covered desk.

Edmund smiled. "Amelia handles all my accounts—for which I am eternally grateful. It's not part of her official duties, of course."

"It's my pleasure," Amelia said. She picked up a credit card receipt and held it up for Edmund to see. "By the way, Dr. Gerard, did you really order an inflatable raft from the White Saddle Sporting Goods Company?"

Edmund looked a shade embarrassed. "Just an impulse buy, I'm afraid. I had thoughts of taking a camping trip later in the year."

Amelia shook her head in mock despair. "It's a wonder he keeps any of his money," she said to Jessica.

Edmund chuckled. "You see, Jess, there she goes, acting like a wife again."

Jessica was looking at the secretary as Edmund said this, and she didn't miss the faintest flicker of distress which appeared for a moment in the woman's eyes. Then it was gone and Amelia was saying briskly: "I'll put the word out about the secretarial job. Some grad student will jump at it, believe me."

* * *

As they were walking through the campus on their way back to Edmund's car, Jessica asked, "Has Amelia been your secretary long?"

"Ten years, nearly eleven."

"You must find her invaluable."

"I don't know how I'd manage without her."

"You *do* realize she's in love with you?"

He stopped short. *"What* did you say?"

"Amelia's in love with you."

"Oh, don't be silly, Jess."

"There is none so blind as he who won't see."

"Stop quoting Jonathan Swift at me. No, Jess, you've got it wrong. She's fond of me, I think, and looks indulgently on my inefficiencies. But she tends to mother me, more than being in love with me—even though I must be ten years her senior."

"No doubt you know best, Edmund," Jessica said quietly, in her most convincing meek-little-woman manner.

He eyed her suspiciously for a moment, but her expression was quite innocent.

Jessica found she had been allotted a very pleasant, spacious room, with a private bathroom and a patio that gave an excellent view of the city.

Edmund, who went up with her to inspect the accommodation, was quite anxious she should feel happy with it.

"Now, are you sure this is a room you can work in, Jess?" he asked. "If not, I can have you moved into a suite."

"This'll be fine, Edmund. Honestly." She turned to the bellhop. "I'd like a typewriter, if that can be arranged."

"Sure thing, ma'am. I'll see to it right away." He left the room.

"I'll leave you to get settled in now, Jess," said Edmund. "I hope you'll have dinner with me tonight."

She shook her head regretfully. "Not tonight, Edmund, thank you. Tonight I'm going to bed early. I'm still on East Coast time, remember."

"Of course. Tomorrow, then?"

"I'll look forward to it. I shall enjoy it more, too, having got my first lecture out of the way."

He eyed her keenly. "You're not really nervous, are you?"

"Petrified."

"There's no need, I promise you. We're always very nice to visiting lecturers at Sequoia."

"I'm sure you are. That almost makes it worse. I can imagine everyone politely clapping afterward and whispering to each other, 'What on earth possessed Dean Gerard to invite this old fool?' "

Edmund chuckled. "You'll be fine, Jess. Now, as you know, it's scheduled for five tomorrow afternoon. Shall I pick you up here?"

"No need. I'll make my own way there. A good, bracing ten-minute walk before the lecture may be just what I need."

"As you like. Come straight to my office and I'll take you to the lecture room."

"If I don't chicken out on the way."

"You won't." He went to the door. "Good night, Jess."

"Good night, Edmund. And thanks for inviting me. I do appreciate it —whatever I may have said."

After he'd gone, Jessica unpacked her things, including her manuscript and notebooks, together with some typing paper (she always had the irrational feeling, whenever she traveled away from home, that she would be unable to buy things like this anywhere else). By the time she'd completed her unpacking, the bellhop had returned with a typewriter.

When he'd departed, well-tipped, Jessica phoned Room Service for some coffee and sandwiches, then took a shower. She'd finished by the time the waiter had arrived, and she watched TV while having her supper. Then, she decided, it was time for bed. She went to the bathroom, cleaned her teeth, came back—and suddenly realized that she felt completely alert and wide-awake. Really, how irritating! What should she do? Switch the TV on again, locate the most boring program she could find and rely on its soporific effect to send her to sleep? Or work? She didn't really enjoy working late at night (and on her personal time-clock, it was late). On the other hand, the more she could get ahead of her deadline, the better; and five hundred words down on paper tonight would mean she could take it a bit easier tomorrow.

She went to the table where she'd laid out her work things, sat down and picked up her pen.

It was half an hour later, and she was making slow but fairly satisfactory progress toward the Inspector's *dénouement,* when there came a loud knock on the door. Jessica looked up in surprise. She stood up, went to the door and called out: "Yes?"

A man's voice answered. "Mrs. Fletcher?"

"That's right."

"I'm here from the university."

Of course! They'd canceled her lecture. She'd expected something like this all along. With an emotion halfway between letdown and relief, and keeping the chain-lock in place, Jessica opened the door and peered out.

Standing in the corridor was one of the most handsome young men she had ever seen. He was about twenty-five, with black wavy hair and blue eyes. He smiled engagingly at her, showing two rows of pearly white teeth. While not especially tall, he was slim and lithe-looking.

Jessica was wondering if this was somebody kept on staff especially for the purpose of breaking bad news to visiting lady lecturers, when he said: "I've come about the job."

"I beg your pardon?"

"The secretarial job."

Jessica stared. "Oh . . ."

"My name's David Tolliver. I've brought a note from Miss Browne."

He handed her an envelope. Jessica took it, tore it open and read: *The bearer may not be exactly what you had in mind, but I'm sure you won't find anyone better in the whole of Seattle. However, if you're not satisfied, I'm certain there'll be plenty of other applicants. A.B.*

Jessica looked up from the note and studied the young man for a few seconds. Then she said, "You'd better come in."

She closed the door, unhooked the chain and opened the door again. David Tolliver strolled easily into the room. "Thank you." He glanced around appreciatively. "Nice room."

Jessica said: "Mr . . . er—"

"Tolliver."

"Mr. Tolliver, I was expecting . . ."

He smiled. "Someone in a skirt? Surely, Mrs. Fletcher, you're not going to hold my gender against me?"

"It's not that. I'd need to think about it. Actually, I wasn't expecting anybody so soon."

"Yes, I'm sorry about the hour. But I wanted to beat the crowd; and believe me, Mrs. Fletcher, they'll be lining up to work for you."

"Then in fairness I oughtn't to take on the first person who applies. I should give the others a chance . . ."

She trailed off as he walked casually across to her worktable and looked down at the papers strewn on it.

"That sounds fine," he said, "except it looks like you could use a typist right now."

"You mean you want to start tonight?"

"Why not? Look, let me give you an example of my skills." He picked up a page of her manuscript and handed it to her. "Have you finished polishing this?"

"Yes, I think so," Jessica said a little weakly.

"Good."

He sat down at the table, deftly inserted a sheet of paper into the typewriter, glanced at the page of writing and commenced typing with what seemed to her incredible rapidity. Then, without a pause in his typing, he said, "I don't mind competing as long as I'm given an equal footing. You'd be surprised how prejudiced some people can be—although it's more noticeable among male employers. Not that I've worked for that many men. I don't usually get the chance. Most of the time I end up working for women."

"I wonder why," Jessica said dryly.

He ignored this. "The question I'm most often asked is where I went to secretarial school, and of course, I didn't. I'm self-taught, but I promise you, Mrs. Fletcher, I'm fast and accurate. As a matter of fact, as you can see, I can even talk and type at the same time."

"Remarkable."

"I don't have to, of course. I *can* type in silence."

He continued to do so for another minute, then stopped, tugged the paper from the machine and handed it to her with a flourish.

Jessica read it through and gave a nod. "Excellent. I congratulate you."

"I do one hundred and fifty words a minute shorthand, too."

"I wouldn't need that. Tell me, do you intend to make your living as a stenographer?"

He laughed. "Lord, no. I'm studying to be a journalist. But typing is sure a better way to raise tuition fees than slinging hash."

Jessica eyed him for a second or two.

"I only charge five dollars sixty an hour," he said hopefully.

Jessica smiled. "Believe it or not, that wasn't what I was thinking about. It's simply that I've never worked with a secretary of either sex yet, and I just feel I'd be more comfortable with a woman. . . . Of course, we won't be working together, as such. The typist will be working on stuff I've completed—and a lot of the time I won't be here . . ."

She suddenly came to a decision. "All right, Mr. Tolliver, you've got the job."

He looked pleased, but by no means surprised. She then realized that he'd never been in any real doubt that she would hire him.

"Great," he said. "Shall I start now?"

"No. Tomorrow morning."

"Not tonight? I can put in a couple of hours—"

"No, thank you," she said firmly. "Ten A.M. tomorrow will be fine
. . . that is, if you don't have classes or anything."

He stood up. "Not tomorrow. I'll be yours to command."

"Very well. Ten o'clock it is."

She led him to the door and opened it. "Good night."

"Good night, Mrs. Fletcher. You've made a wise choice."

"I sincerely hope so," she said.

He strolled out, and she heard him go down the corridor, whistling
softly to himself. She closed and bolted the door. A most self-confident
young man. Overconfident, perhaps? But masses of charm. And certainly
a first-rate typist—as Amelia had said. She only hoped he was reliable.
And punctual.

Jessica went back to the table and sat down. But she suddenly found
that she couldn't pen another word that night. What she had just written,
plus what she'd done on the plane, made up a pretty good day's work,
under the circumstances. And she was now sleepy.

She quickly tidied the papers on the table, and ten minutes later was in
bed and asleep.

# Chapter Three

JESSICA was up the next morning at six-thirty, and working on her book by seven. By ten o'clock she'd done another thousand words—a thousand good words, she thought.

David Tolliver was late. But only by two minutes, which didn't really count. He seemed eager to chat, but she put him immediately to work on typing what she'd written the previous day and this morning. The weather was fine and mild, and in order to get away from the clatter of the typewriter, she retired to a wicker chair on the patio to continue with the book.

He came out twice in the next two hours, to check on points of typography and punctuation; but by one o'clock she had, to her great satisfaction, completed her schedule for the day. She could knock off work now with a clean conscience.

David completed his typing at about the same time, and presented it to her with modest pride. She glanced through it quickly. "Oh, that seems excellent, David. Thank you. I'll proofread it later."

"There's no need," he said airily. "That can go straight to your publisher as it is."

"No doubt you're right, but I shall proofread it nonetheless. Now, about this"—she indicated the work she'd done in the last three hours—"can you come and do it this afternoon?"

" 'Fraid not. I have to study. But I could come in at about five-thirty and do it. It shouldn't take me very long. Will that be all right?"

"That'll be fine. I won't be here myself, of course, but I'll tell them at the desk to let you have the key."

"Oh yes, your lecture. What time will you be back?"

"Not till fairly late. I'm going out to dinner afterward. Which means I won't see you again today; so I'd better pay you now." She started for her purse.

"No, please. I don't want any money until the job's done."

"Are you sure? It'd be no trouble—"

"I prefer it that way."

"As you wish. I'll see you tomorrow, then."

"Sure. Well, best of luck with your lecture." He made for the door.

"David?"

He turned. "Yes?"

"You hadn't been thinking of coming to the lecture, had you? I wouldn't want to stop you."

"Actually, no. I'm not really into mystery stories. My taste in literature runs more to Vonnegut and Hesse."

Jessica raised her eyebrows. "Detective stories and serious literature aren't mutually exclusive interests, you know. In fact, the genres often overlap."

"I realize that. But crime fiction just doesn't grab me. I've seen a little of the real thing, you see."

"I'm not without experience of it myself," Jessica said dryly.

"Yes, I know. Sorry. Didn't mean to be rude. But I believe in the complete truth always. Do forgive me."

"I should think you're incapable of being rude, David."

His face broke into a smile of devastating charm. "Thanks. You'll find all that stuff done when you come in tonight. And I'll see you tomorrow. 'Bye." He went out.


Jessica spent the early part of the afternoon going over her lecture notes—cutting, adding, amending and polishing. She had decided not to follow precisely Edmund's suggested program. He was quite happy about this.

At four-thirty she had a cup of tea in her room, changed, did her face and hair, and set off on the short walk to the campus. She felt just as she had at fourteen, going to school on the day of an important exam.


Jessica sat on a hard upright chair and fought the impulse to count the number of people in the room. Nearly a hundred, she guessed—more than she'd expected—and including at least half a dozen faculty members in the front row. Oh dear!

Edmund, at the rostrum, was introducing her. As far as she could tell, it was a very nice introduction—complimentary without being too flowery—but she was finding it hard to concentrate on his words.

At last, far too soon, she heard Edmund saying: "And so I'll take up no more time, but simply say, ladies and gentlemen—Jessica Fletcher."

He stepped back from the rostrum, smiled at Jessica and sat down. She stood and moved forward. There was a polite ripple of applause. She placed her notes on the rostrum, cast a brief glance down, took a deep breath and began.

"I was talking earlier to a young man who told me that crime fiction just didn't grab him. And I thought, if that is true, what a lot of great literature he's cut off from. For crime—and especially murder—has been a dominant element in world literature from time immemorial. It seems to be, along with sex and money, a subject of never-ceasing fascination. In fact, the three subjects are inextricably linked in fiction as in real life.

"The oldest murder story of all appeared in the fourth chapter of Genesis, where is recounted the murder of Abel by Cain. It's a short story, but one that contains all the vital elements: motive, crime, discovery and retribution. Certainly it lacks some of the later subtleties of the genre: the murderer makes no attempt to cover his tracks, sets no false alibi, doesn't try to throw the blame on anyone else or make a desperate last-minute attempt at escape. Although his only words of exculpation have passed into the language as a proverb, one feels that he never really expected to get away with it—perhaps because the investigator in the case was a more formidable opponent than Hercule Poirot, Philip Marlowe, or even Sherlock Holmes."

A faint but decidedly warm chuckle eddied around the lecture room, and Jessica began to feel a little more confident. She continued.

"Maybe the Cain and Abel story lacks dramatic tension because it's true. Many people would deny this, but I feel that a story so brief, so bald, cannot be anything but true: no fiction writer could hope to get away with a tale so completely devoid of twists. Perhaps, therefore, *The Abel Murder Case* has no place in our lecture today and we should move on to what is undeniably fiction. I shall, in fact, jump centuries of ancient literature—a discussion of murder in classical Greek literature alone would require a whole series of lectures—and come to more modern times. I am tempted, I must admit, to begin my discussion of mystery fiction proper with the man who is probably the greatest crime writer of all time, William Shakespeare. I have never tallied the number of murders in Shakespeare. No doubt some savant has, and has published his findings, together with a full list of weapons used, types of poison employed, and a breakdown—in tabular form—of the various motives involved. If so, I haven't read it and I don't intend to. However, if anybody present does know the exact Shakespearean body count and would care to supply it, I'd be pleased if he'd do so now."

Jessica paused and glanced with raised eyebrows along the row of academics in the front. There was an amused shaking of heads, which was followed by a guffaw from the student body. The laughter was entered into by at least one of the faculty members. This was a big, blond, ungainly-looking young man in his mid to late thirties, wearing a sports jacket and old jeans; although he sat with the staff, he looked more like an elderly student. He was already giving the strong impression of immensely enjoying the occasion. Jessica warmed to him.

To her great surprise, she was even beginning to enjoy herself. She took a sip of water and went on.

'"I will, though, resist the temptation to discuss Shakespeare at length, merely digressing long enough to point out that a murder is the key event in many of the tragedies: the murder of Desdemona by Othello, and of Duncan by Macbeth, for instance. *Hamlet* has good claim to be regarded as one of the . . . well, I was going to say one of the first whodunits. That isn't quite correct—although in the early part of the play we don't *know* that Claudius murdered Hamlet's father, or, if so, whether Gertrude was an accomplice. It would be truer to call it one of the first of the how-will-he-be-exposed sub-genre of crime stories. In setting out to bring the truth to light, Hamlet himself becomes one of the first amateur detectives—and in being both of noble birth, and a scholar, may be regarded as the direct literary ancestor of Lord Peter Wimsey.''

Jessica broke off and again glanced at the faculty members. "Now, there's a brand-new examination question, or essay subject, which I offer free of charge: 'Discuss the influence of *Hamlet* on the detective fiction of Dorothy L. Sayers.' ''

She again waited for the laughter to die down before resuming.

"However, you are not here today to learn about a writer who no doubt has been discussed in this very room a great many times by people far better qualified than I. Before I leave the subject of Shakespeare, though, let me add that I am not, naturally, claiming that *Hamlet* and the other great tragedies are *merely* crime fiction. But then, *no* good crime fiction is *merely* crime fiction.

"Ellery Queen, of course, was well aware of this fact, when over thirty years ago he published his anthology *The Literature of Crime*—a book which elevated the prestige of the genre, containing as it did crime and mystery stories by, among others, authors as diverse as Sinclair Lewis, Galsworthy, Steinbeck, Faulkner, Hemingway, Twain, Huxley, Stevenson, Wells, Kipling and Charles Dickens.''

She had read this list from her notes and now looked back at her audience.

"Yes, it makes you sit up, doesn't it? It did me when I first came across it. And perhaps you now understand more fully what I meant when I said that in taking no interest in crime stories, my young friend was cutting himself off from a considerable amount of great literature. Now, let us look at some of that literature more closely . . ."

Three-quarters of an hour later Jessica arrived at her closing remarks. "Well, I hope I have demonstrated that the crime story occupies an honorable and important place in literature and that those who sneer at it only succeed in exposing themselves as possessed of an extremely provincial outlook. We have looked today at crime fiction of every kind. In many of these stories the identity of the criminal was known from the start; some of them in fact have been written from the criminal's viewpoint. Novels such as *A Gun for Sale* and *A Kiss Before Dying* contain little actual mystery element. Next time I plan to examine the development over the last century of the pure puzzle story—the whodunit—and I hope to prove that in the hands of a master this branch of fiction can provide a greater degree of intellectual stimulation in a single volume than a whole library of experimental or *avant-garde* novels. Thank you."

She stepped back and sat down. The applause broke out. Several students whistled their approval, while the faculty members clapped particularly warmly. Jessica got to her feet and gave a little bow. Then she sat down again.

Sitting beside her, Edmund was looking pleased as punch. As the applause finally died down, he turned to her with a grin.

"There you are, Jess. I knew you could do it."

At that moment the young lecturer from the front row came bustling up. "Mrs. Fletcher, my congratulations. That was fascinating."

"Why, thank you, er—"

Edmund said: "This is Professor Todd Lowery, Jess."

Lowery held out a big hand, which practically enveloped Jessica's. "I'm with the English department, Mrs. Fletcher," he said. "You've given me a fresh insight into crime fiction. I really think we ought to introduce a study of it into our curriculum."

"That would be very exciting."

"These things take a long time, of course, but I shall certainly push for it. Anyway, I look forward to the next lecture."

"Well, that will be more specialist and rather less literary."

"Then my wife will probably enjoy it even more. She's a great fan of the pure puzzle story. She wanted me to tell you how much she's enjoyed your first three books."

"Thank you. Is she here?"

"Emily? She was." Lowery glanced toward the door, where the crowds were milling out. "I don't see her right now. She's probably left."

"I'd like to meet her. No author can hear the words, 'I enjoy your books,' too often."

He smiled. "I'll tell her. I'm sure she'd love to speak with you next time. She's not one to push herself forward. I, of course—"

Various knots of people were still standing about the lecture room chatting; and, while speaking, Lowery had been glancing around, apparently still searching for a glimpse of his wife. Now he suddenly broke off. Jessica followed his gaze. Standing near one of the exits, and staring coolly and frankly at him, was a girl. She was an extremely attractive blue-eyed blonde of about thirty, with a quite stunning figure.

Lowery turned back to Jessica and got his train of thought under control with what was plainly something of an effort.

"I, of course, never have any inhibitions." He glanced at his watch. "Well, if you'll excuse me. . . . Can't wait for the next lecture. Good-bye."

He moved off toward the door by which the girl was standing.

At the same moment Edmund, who for the last minute had been engaged in urgent conversation with another faculty member, turned back to Jessica. They spoke together.

Edmund began: "Jessica, I'm afraid—"

Jessica said, "Edmund, that wouldn't be—"

They both stopped. "After you," said Edmund.

"That wouldn't be Emily Lowery, I suppose?"

For a second he looked blank. "Who? Where?"

"The playmate of the month—standing by the door."

He stared in the girl's direction. "Good Lord, no. That's Jack Schroeder's wife. Lila, I think her name is. Emily's rather a demure little creature."

At that moment Lowery reached the door and walked straight out into the corridor without glancing sideways at the girl. She, on the other hand, kept her eyes fixedly upon him; and as soon as he was through the door she turned and followed him out.

"Who's Jack Schroeder?" Jessica inquired.

"The swimming coach. I believe they're living apart now."

"She's not studying English, I suppose?"

"Oh no. Hardly the type, I'd imagine. I'm surprised to see her here, actually. What is this, Jess?"

"Oh, nothing, Edmund. What were you going to say?"

He looked a little awkward. "I'm terribly sorry, but I'm afraid I've got to let you down."

"How do you mean?"

"I've just been told we have a crisis. Nothing that need concern you. But we have to hold an emergency faculty meeting. I'm afraid I can't take you to dinner after all."

"Please, Edmund, no apologies necessary."

"But what will you do? I'm sure I could find someone who'd be delighted to escort you—"

"No, please don't think of it. I'll be delighted to have a quiet meal in my hotel room, watch TV for an hour or two, and turn in early. I've had a long day."

"Well, if you're sure. Can I get you a taxi?"

"Don't go to the bother. I'll be glad to walk."

"Okay. I'll be able to make it tomorrow for sure."

"I'll hold you to it."

"Thanks for your understanding, Jess. I'll call you."

He hurried from the room. Jessica noticed for the first time that a number of students were hanging around a few yards away, eyeing her diffidently. She smiled at them, and they came near her. A few were holding copies of her books, which they wanted autographed. She remained with them for about a quarter of an hour, discussing mystery novels and answering their questions. (Though she was, as always, unable to answer the most persistently repeated inquiry: how she thought up her plots. A weak and rather apologetic "they just come" was about the best she could do.)

When the students dispersed—all promising to attend the next lecture—Jessica made her way back to her hotel. She felt physically drained and was rather relieved not to be going out with Edmund. Though she did feel quite elated about the lecture. It had gone much better than she'd anticipated, and she was far happier now about the other lectures. If this one had been a flop, it would have been awful having the prospect of two more hanging over her.

She reached her hotel and asked at the desk for her key. To her surprise she was informed that Mr. Tolliver had not yet returned it. The work must have taken him longer than he'd anticipated, she thought as she went up in the elevator.

However, when she entered the room, the typewriter was covered and beside it lay a neat little pile of typescript. She went over and glanced at it. Yes, it was this morning's work. But there was no sign of David.

Then she noticed that the patio lights were on. She went out.

David looked up at her with a slow, lazy smile and got to his feet. In his hands was a copy of *The Corpse Danced at Midnight.*

"Hi," he said.

"Hello, David. I didn't expect to find you still here."

"Well, don't worry. I'm not charging for my time now. I had to hang on and find out how the lecture went."

"Quite well, I think—thanks partly to you."

"Me?"

"Your remarks about crime fiction gave me an idea for a new opening. Then I was able to spend a good part of the hour shooting you down in flames. There was quite a big audience and they seemed to enjoy it."

He looked hurt. "That was a bit severe, wasn't it? I'll be the laughing-stock of the campus tomorrow."

"Don't worry. I didn't mention your name."

"Well, that's a relief. Guess I'd better come to the next lecture."

"I thought you weren't into crime fiction."

"I am now."

"Since when?"

"Since I started this." He held up the book. "It's really good."

"Thank you." Her voice was a little cool.

"No, I mean it: these characters are real. They're alive."

"So a few people have said—including one or two eminent critics."

"Oh, I never read book reviews. I prefer to make up my own mind. And about this book I have. I want to apologize for what I said earlier. It must have sounded pretty pompous."

Jessica smiled. "Just a little."

"The work's all done," he said.

"So I noticed. Very nice."

"I didn't expect you back yet. I thought you were going out to dinner."

"I was stood up."

"Shame!"

"No, not really. Dr. Gerard had an emergency meeting. He offered to find a substitute."

"But no one measured up to your standards. Would I?"

She blinked. "I'm sorry, I—"

"Would I measure up? Would you have dinner with me?"

"Oh, David, that's very sweet of you; but really, there's no need for you to be kind to a middle-aged woman. I'm sure you have a nice girl waiting somewhere."

"No, honestly, I haven't. I'd like to take you to dinner. I'd like to talk. Truly."

Jessica looked at him thoughtfully, then glanced at her watch. It was after seven, and she'd eaten nothing since a very light lunch at one.

"Well, actually I was going to have something sent up. And frankly, I don't think my digestive tract could handle pizza and beer—or whatever it is you young people eat nowadays."

"*Those* young people eat pizza and beer. But I'd prefer a Châteaubriand anytime. How about it?"

Jessica's eyebrows went up. "David, are you sure you can afford that?"

"Quite sure I can't. But you can."

She stared at him speechlessly for a moment. He grinned back. In manner, he reminded her very much of her nephew Grady, who could always twist her around his finger. She suddenly laughed.

"Go downstairs and wait for me in the bar. I have to change."

"Great." He seemed genuinely delighted—though probably only at the prospect of getting a free meal. "I'll phone for a reservation somewhere. I think I know just the place."

The *place* he knew, Jessica guessed, was probably the most expensive restaurant in Seattle. It had the lot: thick carpets; exquisite linen and silver; fine china; quiet, rapid and highly obsequious waiters. It also possessed a very romantic atmosphere, with candles and soft music. The rest of the clientele, in fact, seemed to consist almost exclusively of obviously rich young lovers.

Seated at a corner table with David, Jessica felt decidedly out of place. While they were sipping their aperitifs, she said as much. "I keep thinking everyone's staring at me."

"Well, you're famous."

"My face isn't. And I guarantee none of this crowd was at the lecture."

"I guess not. They're probably staring at *me*—with envy in their hearts."

"Oh, David, that's not just transparent; it's corny."

"Only the words, not the thought."

"Don't be silly."

"Okay." He put down his glass. "Let's say I *was* being silly. Those guys are not particularly envious of me—because, truth to tell, they probably haven't given us a thought. But they ought to be. Quite frankly, most of the girls in here are *stupid.* They can't talk. The truth is, I have a middle-aged psyche bottled up in this twenty-five-year-old body. I don't enjoy the company of my bubble-headed female contemporaries. I do enjoy yours. I can't remember when I've had such a good time."

"I'm sure that's not true."

"It is. Honestly." He raised his glass. "Jessica, thank you for coming. To you."

He drank. She said, a little awkwardly, "Thank you."

He lowered his glass. "Do you mind if I call you Jessica?"

"Not at all."

"I just can't think of you as 'Mrs. Fletcher.' I already feel so close to you—as though I've known you for years. And getting to know you has really meant a lot to me. I want you to believe that."

She took a deep breath. Something had to be said. "David, this is beginning to sound a bit silly. I'm old enough to be your—"

He put his hand on hers, effectively cutting her off. "To be my friend," he said softly. "Why don't we leave it at that?"

At that moment, rather to her relief, the waiter appeared with their food.

The meal, if not outstanding, was acceptable, though Jessica didn't enjoy it as much as she might have. She continued to feel uncomfortable and to imagine that eyes were on her. Seeming to sense this, David turned the conversation almost immediately to her books. On this topic he displayed a lively interest. His questions were intelligent; he never once asked her how she thought up her plots; and she gradually lost her self-consciousness and was eventually chatting fluently.

Too fluently, she suddenly realized when they were drinking their coffee. "Now, that's more than enough about me and my work," she said. "I know very little about you—apart from your plans to be a journalist. Tell me more about yourself."

He shrugged. "There's little to tell. It's all very dull, I'm afraid. For the last several years it's mostly been a question of long hours of hard work."

"Parents?"

"Both dead, for many years."

"I'm sorry. Girl friends?"

"I told you I don't often seek the company of young girls."

"Ah, but that can't always have been the case. You had to discover you didn't like their company, didn't you?"

"That's true. There have been girls, of course. But nobody I want to talk about, if you don't mind."

His voice had gone suddenly cold. Jessica suspected he was in the throes of getting over an unhappy romance, perhaps a broken engagement. Had a girl treated him badly? That would account for his contempt for what he'd called his female contemporaries. In which case it was no doubt a very temporary phenomenon.

She changed the subject. "One thing you said interested me."

He smiled. "Only one? Oh dear."

"One thing in particular. That you'd had a bit to do with real-life crime. What exactly did you mean?"

"Oh, that. Don't get me wrong. I didn't mean I've had much personal involvement. It's just that I spend quite a lot of time down at the courthouse. I listen to the cases, take a shorthand notebook and try to write an interesting report of the case. It was a special-studies project in the first place, but it seemed such good practice that I kept on with it. I even got permission to talk to some of the prisoners. I've written up some of my interviews with them and tried to sell them. Without luck so far."

Jessica nodded. "I see. Must have been interesting. I'm afraid I was imagining—"

"That I'd been involved in some horrible crime . . . suspect in a murder case, or something?"

"Something like that, yes."

"Nothing so dramatic. As I said, I've lived an extremely dull life. Until tonight, that is."

"David . . . !"

"Sorry—sorry. I was forgetting you don't like people to say nice things about you, however true they happen to be."

"I wouldn't go that far. What I don't like is flattery."

He looked hurt. "That wasn't flattery. This is quite a thrill for me. I'm enjoying myself enormously. Don't spoil it for me."

"I'm sorry. No doubt I'm oversensitive. Forgive me."

He smiled. "Nothing to forgive."

At that moment the waiter sidled up and discreetly laid their check on the table next to David. Jessica reached out for it. "I'll take that."

"No, you don't," said David, scooping up the check. "I was only joking. You didn't really think I'd let you pay, did you?"

"David, you must. I can afford it. You admitted you couldn't."

"I can't afford lots of things that I do all the time."

He took out his wallet and extracted a hundred-dollar bill. She couldn't help noticing that there were several others in the wallet. He handed the money, with the check, to the waiter, saying with a grin, *"Don't* keep the change."

"No, monsieur."

The waiter departed, and David looked back at Jessica, returning his wallet to his pocket as he did so. "I never claimed to be starving."

"No, I know."

"Fact is, I allow myself one meal in a good restaurant each semester. This has been the one for this semester."

"All the same, I'm not happy about it. I would never have come if I'd known you were going to pay for me."

"Well, of course, if you'd like to return the compliment later in the week, I'll be happy to let you pick up the tab."

"That won't help to restore your bank balance."

"No, but it'll do wonders for my digestion. And yours, if I may say so. I bet you live on snacks most of the time. It's not good for you."

"Now don't *you* start mothering *me.*" She glanced at her watch. "If you don't mind, I think I'd like to go now. It's been a long day."

He looked disappointed. "Sure you wouldn't like to go somewhere? I know some good night spots. One where the local mobsters hang out. Might give you some material."

"Thank you, no. I don't write about mobsters, anyway. I write about nice, polite middle-class murderers."

A few minutes later, outside, David opened the passenger door of his car for Jessica to get in. It was a long, low red sports model. Jessica surveyed it. She was not greatly interested in automobiles; earlier in the evening the only thing that had struck her about it was how very difficult it was to get out of. Now she realized that it must be a pretty expensive model.

"This is a very nice car," she said.

"A reflection of the man."

He bowed and held the door wide for her. She was about to enter when a large black sedan came along the street and drew up within a couple of inches of David's front fender. He looked annoyed. "He might give me a bit of room to—"

He broke off as two men emerged from the sedan and approached them with a purposeful air. They were tall and burly, dressed in dark suits. The slightly older one was black, and it was he who spoke.

"David Tolliver?"

"Yes."

"I'm Lieutenant Andrews, Seattle P.D." He flashed some identification. "Sir, would you mind accompanying us to headquarters? We have a few questions we'd like to ask you."

David was looking bewildered. "Yes, I would mind. Questions about what?"

Andrews shot a quick glance in Jessica's direction. "It won't take long, Mr. Tolliver."

"Look," David said, "if you've got something to ask, ask it, so I can get this lady back to her hotel. Tell me what this is about."

Andrews gave a slight shrug. "All right. It concerns the murder of Alison Brevard."

David drew his breath in sharply. "Why do you want to speak to me about that?"

"You were . . . er, acquainted with the lady."

"Yes—but so were dozens of other people."

"You had a date with her the night she was murdered."

"No." David gulped. "Well, yes . . . I mean, originally I did. But I wasn't able to keep it. I canceled."

"Did you, Mr. Tolliver?" Before David could answer, Andrews went on: "My information is that you knew the lady well. She had your picture in her apartment. Now, are you prepared to come with us, or do I have to put you under arrest?"

"Seems I have no choice," David said bitterly. "What about my car?"

"You can drive it to headquarters. The sergeant will ride with you."

"But I can't just leave this lady—"

"She can come if she wants to, or we can get her a cab now."

David turned helplessly to her. "Jessica . . ."

He suddenly seemed very young: helpless, forlorn and rather frightened. Jessica came to a rapid decision. "I'd like to come."

He looked grateful. "Are you sure? It won't be very pleasant. . . ."

"I've had some experience with police stations."

"Okay," Andrews said, "get in the car."

"Lieutenant, you may not have noticed that Mr. Tolliver's car is a two-seater," Jessica said. "If the sergeant is riding in it, there won't be room for me. I'm afraid I shall have to travel with you."

He hesitated, then gave a curt nod. "As you like. Let's go."

# Chapter Four

FOR the first couple of minutes Jessica and Andrews traveled in silence. It was she who spoke first.

"My name is Fletcher—Jessica Fletcher."

"Pleased to meet you." Then the name seemed to strike a chord. He said, "The writer?"

"Yes."

He gave her a quick sideways look. "And amateur detective?"

"No," she said firmly.

"I thought . . . I mean, surely you've been—"

"Other people keep regarding me as an amateur detective. In fact, on three separate occasions—in New York, in Maine and in Los Angeles—I have been asked by police officers to help them. I didn't want to, but I really had no choice."

"Well, I'll tell you one thing, ma'am. You won't be asked to help in Seattle."

"Good. I wouldn't have time, anyway. I have to deliver two lectures at Sequoia University *and* finish a novel in less than a week."

"Fine. Then we understand each other." He paused; then: "How d'you think up your plots?" he asked.

Jessica sat on a bench in the waiting room at police headquarters for over an hour. People came and went around her. Nobody spoke much. Some faces were bewildered, others anxious, most merely blank. One old man slept solidly, snoring quietly now and again. At last for the twentieth time the door opened and Jessica, glancing wearily toward it, saw David standing there. He looked tired, but was smiling. She got to her feet and went to him.

"David, are you all right?"

"Fine—and free to go."

"Oh, good."

They went out. "Jessica," he said, "thanks for waiting. I'm terribly sorry to put you through this. Now let's get you home, pronto."

In the car he said, "It was just routine, really. They're talking to everyone who knew Alison. I think I was number forty-eight on a list of fifty."

"You knew her well?"

"Not really. I was just one of the dozens of men friends she had."

"But you had had a date with her the night she was killed."

"Well, we'd dine together once in a while. She liked to talk. That was all there was to it. This time I'd had to cancel—pressure of work."

"You *did* know she'd been murdered?"

"Only what I read in the papers. Seems she surprised some burglar in her apartment. Jewelry and a mink were stolen. She must have put up a struggle: the police found black wool threads under her nails—probably from his sweater."

"I see. How was she killed?"

"Hit over the head with some sort of statuette. Must have died almost instantly."

"It must have been a shock when you heard about it."

"Of course. But somehow . . . well, it wasn't all that much of a *surprise,* if you know what I mean. Alison was one of life's victims, I'm afraid. Anyway, I'm out of it now, thank God."

Jessica didn't speak. There were dozens of questions she wanted to ask, but she resisted firmly. It was really nothing to do with her. Nothing at all. . . .

Ten minutes later David dropped her outside her hotel. She refused his offer to escort her to her room, and stood on the sidewalk watching his sports car as it roared away. As it did so, a black sedan—very similar to that driven by Andrews—which had pulled up fifty yards down the street as she alighted, started moving again and sped off in the same direction.

Jessica went indoors. She was almost certain the sedan had been behind them when they drove away from police headquarters. Somehow she doubted very much if David Tolliver was "out of it," after all.

The next day Jessica again started work on her book early and, with just a short break for lunch, kept hard at it all morning and afternoon. By six o'clock, to her intense satisfaction, she'd got well ahead of her schedule: the end of the book was now just a few days off, and she could afford to take it a bit easier, as a couple of hours' work a day should see her finished in time.

Edmund had phoned to confirm their dinner engagement, but she had no other appointments before then; and as David was not coming for another typing session until the next day (he was so fast he could easily catch up with her), she was rather surprised, while rereading her day's work, to hear a tap on the door. She went across and opened it, keeping the chain in place. Lieutenant Andrews was standing outside.

"Why, good evening, Lieutenant." She unhooked the bolt. "What can I do for you?"

"I'd like a word, ma'am, if it's not inconvenient."

"Come in."

She stepped back and he came into the room.

"What's this about?" she asked.

"David Tolliver."

"Don't say he's been arrested?"

"No . . . not yet."

"Not yet? Surely you don't really think he killed that woman?"

"I can't comment on that, Mrs. Fletcher."

"Why are you here, Mr. Andrews?"

He hesitated. "Frankly—to give you a bit of advice."

"Oh? And what's that?"

"Stay away from David Tolliver."

Jessica's eyebrows nearly disappeared into her hair. "Really—isn't that rather presumptuous?"

He shrugged. "Maybe. Sometimes it's our duty, though, just to give a friendly warning. Now, I know he's a good-looking, charming young guy; and I'm sure to a lady like you it's very flattering to have someone like that being attentive, paying compliments, making you feel—feel, er—"

"*Young,* Lieutenant? Is that the word you're groping for?"

"Let's say *younger,* ma'am."

Jessica took a deep breath. "Just what do you imagine is the relationship between David and me?"

"It's hardly for me to say."

"Well, I'll tell you. I arrived in this city two days ago. I hired him to type my manuscript—he's a marvelous typist. Yesterday evening Dean Gerard of Sequoia University had to beg off our dinner engagement. David offered to take his place. And that is the extent of our relationship."

"Naturally, I accept that, Mrs. Fletcher. But I assure you that's not all Tolliver has in mind. And he's bad news. I'm just warning you—for your own good."

"I think I'm old enough to look after myself, thank you."

"I hope so, ma'am."

"Lieutenant," Jessica said slowly, "I'm not a bad judge of people. David has his faults: rather too much self-confidence and a tendency to flattery. But I like him. Now, it's quite obvious you suspect him of murder—I saw the police car tailing us last night. But I am sure of one thing —that he is incapable of beaning somebody with a statuette. And I'll wager you ten dollars that he did not kill Alison Brevard."

Andrews gave a slow smile. "I might take you up on that, if I didn't figure it was kind of unethical: the thought of such riches might make me press too hard for a conviction."

She sighed in exasperation. "I cannot understand why you suspect him —as obviously you haven't any *firm* evidence, or you'd never have let him go. He didn't know the woman well. She was just a casual acquaintance."

Andrews uttered a snort of derision. "Casual acquaintance, my foot! Mrs. Fletcher, they were lovers. She was paying his tuition fees. She bought him that sports car he took you out in last night."

Jessica stared at him. "Are you sure?"

"Sure I'm sure."

She rallied. "In that case, why would he want to kill her?"

"Who knows? Maybe she wouldn't come across with enough dough and he decided to help himself to her jewels. Remember, he had made a date with her. That way he'd be sure of getting her out of the apartment. But he didn't turn up for the date. Where was he? He says studying in his room, but there's no confirmation of that."

"He canceled the date in advance."

"That's not our information. According to a bartender, and a cabbie who drove her home, she said she'd been stood up—her date hadn't shown. And at first she was hopping mad about it. Then she had a few drinks and became maudlin."

Jessica was thoughtful for a few moments. Then she said, "Well, Lieutenant, maybe I've been deceived by David. He has tremendous charm, and perhaps I let that fact blind me to all his faults. He *could* be a bit unscrupulous where money or women are concerned. He could be a fortune-hunter. But I'm still certain that he couldn't commit a violent murder."

"Even if she caught him robbing her apartment and was going to call the police? So he could see his whole future life being ruined?"

"I don't believe so, no. I think his reaction in that situation would be to run."

The lieutenant shrugged again. "Well, we'll see. Anyway, I've done what I felt I had to. You're a distinguished visitor to our city, Mrs. Fletcher. I wouldn't want any harm to come to you."

"I appreciate your concern, Lieutenant, and I assure you I shall take every precaution to avoid coming to harm."

"You do that, ma'am." He moved to the door. "I'll say good night."

"Good night, Mr. Andrews. And thank you. And by the way—"

"Yes?"

"You can still have that bet, if you want it."

Andrews gave a grin. "I'll pass this time, thanks."

He went out.

Jessica sat down slowly. Her mind was in a whirl.


"Edmund," Jessica said, "How well do you know David Tolliver?"

"Well, it's impossible to get to know many of my students as well as I'd like to. I suppose I must say *not very.*"

They were just finishing dinner. The restaurant was by no means as posh as the one David had taken her to, but the food was considerably better and the atmosphere far more comfortable. They had been chatting as only very old friends could chat for an hour, but at last Jessica dredged up the subject which had been constantly at the back of her mind since Andrews' visit. Now she said: "Well, from what little you *do* know, what do you think of him?"

Edmund considered. "He's bright, intelligent; a good student, certainly —though I'm not sure he works quite as hard as he should."

"What about his character—I mean his moral character?"

"Well, he's never been caught cheating in exams. That's about all I can tell you. Why do you ask?"

"You know Amelia sent him along to do my typing?"

"Yes, she mentioned it. Isn't he satisfactory?"

"As a typist, very. I think I'd better tell you the whole thing."

She did so. Edmund listened closely. When she'd finished, he shook his head slowly. "David Tolliver a murderer? I can't believe it, Jess."

"Neither can I. But there are things that worry me."

"Such as?"

"That evening we were talking about crime. He'd mentioned earlier that he'd had a bit to do with it. I asked him what he meant, and he told me about his journalistic exercises—reporting court cases, interviewing prisoners. He more or less specifically stated he'd never been personally involved in a crime."

"Well, he hadn't then, had he? It was only after that the police took him in."

"But surely it would be natural, almost inevitable, when we were talking like that about crime, to mention that an acquaintance of his had just been murdered?"

Edmund looked pensive. "Not necessarily. I can think of two reasons why he might not."

"What are those?"

"Suppose he *had* stood the woman up that night, and that as a result she'd gone home alone much earlier than expected—and been murdered. Don't you think he might be feeling terribly guilty about it?"

Jessica nodded. "He certainly might. All I can say is that he didn't seem to feel the slightest guilt."

"He may be a very good actor."

"Oh, I'm sure he is. What's the other reason?"

"Embarrassment. If he was being more or less kept by an older woman, he might well have hoped to keep the fact quiet."

"But he'd realize that was impossible. The police always dig up things like that."

"I'm not suggesting he hoped to keep it from the *police.*"

"Just from *me?*"

"Yes. It was very bad luck that they happened to pick him up for questioning when he was actually with you."

"Why?"

"Well, wouldn't it be likely to make you less inclined to, er . . ."

Jessica was never slow on the uptake. "You mean he's looking for another meal ticket?"

"In a sense, perhaps. And if you knew that the last meal ticket had been murdered in circumstances which might throw suspicion on David, you'd probably—or so he'd imagine—want to steer clear of him."

"But he couldn't possibly cast me in the role of meal ticket. I'm only in town for a week."

"I said meal ticket *in a sense.* David will be looking for a job soon. He might hope—if he made himself very useful to you while you were here, and was extremely charming and attentive—that you'd take him on as a full-time secretary."

"But he wants to be a journalist."

"Maybe he doesn't. Maybe he just wants to write. And being secretary to you, Jess, would be a lovely job for a would-be writer. You wouldn't be a hard taskmaster, you'd read his work, advise him, introduce him to your publishers. It would be a perfectly legitimate aspiration—but one which would make him very wary of mentioning any association with Alison Brevard and the circumstances of her death."

Jessica nodded thoughtfully. "Yes, Edmund, that all makes very good sense. It was a possibility that hadn't occurred to me."

"Does it make you feel a bit better about him?"

"Oh, yes. Though I still find the idea of his living on that woman highly distasteful."

"Well, it's purely his business, I suppose. Now . . . let's talk about something else."

"Like what?"

"Like you. And your books. You know, we've hardly mentioned them."

"It's been a nice change not to."

"Oh, then I won't press the topic. But just tell me one thing, will you?"

"What's that?"

"How on earth do you think up your plots?"

Jessica opened the door of her hotel room and stopped abruptly. The light was on inside. Surely, she hadn't left it on. The next second she heard the rattle of the typewriter. She went right in. Seated at the worktable, his hands racing over the keys, was David.

He looked up, stopped typing and gave a grin. "Hi."

"David, how did you get in here?"

"The maid let me in. She knew I was working for you."

"I thought you weren't coming today."

"I found I had an hour or two to spare. I figured I'd make a start."

"It's very late." She crossed to the table and glanced at the papers on it. Her eyebrows rose. "You don't seem to have done very much."

"No, unfortunately, the typewriter's been playing up. I've been fiddling with it for ages with my little pocket screwdriver." He produced this. "I think the machine's okay now."

"You shouldn't have bothered. I'm sure the hotel would provide a replacement."

"I didn't realize it would take so long. I suppose you don't want me to keep at it?"

"Hardly. I'm going to bed as soon as possible. So I think you'd better leave right away."

He frowned. "Jessica, you seem quite different tonight. Very cool. Why?"

"Well, for one thing I don't like people coming into my room uninvited."

"I'm sorry. It seemed like a good idea at the time."

"Very well. We won't say any more about it."

He stood up. "There's more to it than that, isn't there? Jessica, have the police been talking to you about me?"

"Why should you think that?"

"Something that lieutenant said. He more or less warned me to keep away from you. I made it obvious I wouldn't, and he talked about 'taking steps.' "

"As a matter of fact, he did come to see me."

"To warn you I was a danger to the entire female populace of Seattle?" He spoke bitterly.

"He didn't go quite as far as that."

"Jessica, I didn't kill Alison Brevard."

"I never thought you did. But you did lie to me about your involvement with her. For one thing, she bought you that car."

He gave a groan. "Is that what he told you?"

"Isn't it true?"

"Technically it's true. But it's thoroughly misleading to put it like that. What he didn't tell you is that Alison had wrecked my old car."

Jessica frowned. "She was driving it?"

"No, it was parked at the curb. She slammed into it head-on. It was a total write-off. That was the first time I met her."

"Was she hurt?"

"No, just badly shaken. And very drunk. She begged me not to notify the police or the insurance people, and swore she would replace my car. I found out later she had quite a record of accidents and couldn't afford another one. Eventually, I agreed. Her car wasn't too badly damaged, and she was in such a state I drove her home. The next day that sports car was delivered to me, fully paid for. I nearly fell over. Of course I went straight over to thank her. Our friendship started there."

"I see." Jessica nodded slowly. "Well, it certainly puts a new complexion on the story. But Mr. Andrews also says Alison was paying your tuition fees."

"No!" He was vehement. "She loaned me four hundred and fifty dollars. My final tuition payment was due and I was broke. I paid it back three weeks ago—out of money I earned typing other students' theses."

Jessica gazed at him. His face was flushed, and it was almost impossible not to believe him. She said, "If those are the facts, I was misled and I apologize. I take it your financial situation is now improved?"

He looked blank for a moment, then smiled. "Oh, you mean my loaded wallet the other night? Well, only very temporarily. Fact is, I had a hot tip on a horse. I scraped twenty-five bucks together, and my choice romped home at twenty-to-one. That's the only day for years I've had that much cash on me. Our dinner was a celebration. I just thought you wouldn't approve if you knew where the money came from."

Jessica smiled too. "I've put the odd dollar on a horse from time to time myself." Then she asked, "Why do you think the police suspect you?"

He shrugged. "Who knows? She had my picture in her apartment, but it was only a snapshot somebody took of us together; she pinned it up by the phone in her kitchen. I suppose people had seen us together, too. But there was nothing to it. We weren't in love. I liked her. She could be delightful company. When she was sober, that is. Which wasn't very often. We had dinner a few times; that was the extent of it. She'd had dozens of male friends. I'll admit I think she liked me. I grew fond of her. But I wouldn't have gone on seeing her if I hadn't been rather sorry for her—and, second, felt I owed her something in return for the car and the loan."

"Did you stand her up the night she was killed?"

"No. I phoned the day before, telling her I had to work and couldn't make it."

"Why do you think she *said* she'd been stood up?"

"Probably forgot I'd called. She was definitely tipsy at the time. I suppose I should have called again, to make sure the message had sunk in; but there'd have been no guarantee of catching her sober." He paused. "You do believe me, don't you?"

"That you didn't kill her? Yes, I do. But I can see the police point of view. It's a shame you don't have an alibi for the time of the murder."

"But not surprising. It's far from unusual to find a student studying alone in his room at night."

"Well, David, I told the lieutenant you could never kill somebody in that way, and I stick to that. And I'm sure you have nothing to worry about. After all, if a person hasn't committed a crime, there's no way the police can prove he did."

"Maybe, but unless they find the real guy, there'll always be that suspicion hanging over me."

"I'm sure they'll find the murderer."

"I wish I was. Jessica, would you help? You've trapped a few killers already."

"Oh, David, what could I do? I was personally involved in those cases. I knew the victims. And I was asked to help by the police. Andrews has already made it quite clear I won't be asked to help here."

"Well, will you take an interest? Read about the case, talk about it, and *think* about it? You just might come up with an idea."

"Yes, David, I'll do that. I'll do anything I can to help clear you, though I'm sure it won't be much."

He gave her his devastating smile. "Thanks, Jessica, I do appreciate it." He looked at his watch. "Now, if you're sure you don't require my services, I'll be off."

"Quite sure, thanks."

"Tomorrow morning?"

"That'll be fine."

"Good night, then."

"Good night, David."

He left the room. Jessica went to the door and bolted it. Then she sat down on the bed and stared thoughtfully at the floor. She just didn't know what to make of the boy. She didn't believe he was a killer. But she still wasn't at all sure, in spite of his explanations, that Alison Brevard hadn't been keeping him. She thought he would be capable of exploiting a woman for his own ends.

Further, why had he been in her room tonight? Had he come to work, and was the story of the broken typewriter true? Or had that just been an excuse? What could he have wanted here? He knew she'd be out.

Jessica's eyes wandered around the room—and suddenly alighted on her attaché case. It was on the floor between the bed and the dressing table. And one of the catches was open. She was sure—*almost* sure—she hadn't left it like that. Had David been snooping? He wouldn't have found much of interest—mostly work notes, letters from her publisher; one from Edmund regarding this trip; another from Abby confirming her visit to Kentucky; a few other items. But had a search through her things been the sole purpose of his visit? If so, to what end? Was he simply one of the types who liked to store up information about people, just hoping it might come in useful? She could hardly believe it of David.

Perhaps she had left the catch improperly fastened. She didn't really think so, but she had to give David the benefit of the doubt.

Jessica sighed, put the whole thing out of her mind and went to bed.

# Chapter Five

JESSICA'S second lecture was just as successful as the first. Word about her performance had got around, and the seats were packed. "We'll have to find a larger room for your third," Edmund murmured as he surveyed the audience. She got to her feet with more confidence this time, and at the end felt reasonably pleased. The applause certainly was highly enthusiastic.

Afterward there was a surprise. She discovered the faculty had prepared a reception for her. About thirty staff members were present, and she was amazed to find how much interest there was in the mystery genre, even from the science faculty. At the beginning Todd Lowery was present with his wife—a quiet, shy little woman—but they left together for home fairly early.

The reception was drawing to a close when someone tapped her on the shoulder and told her she was wanted on the telephone. She was taken out and led to a pay phone in the corridor.

She picked up the receiver. "Hello?"

A woman's voice said, "Mrs. Fletcher?"

"Yes."

"Look, you don't know me, but I'm a friend of David Tolliver, and I can prove he didn't kill that woman."

"Who are you?" Jessica asked sharply.

"My name's not important. Now just listen. We have to meet."

"You know where I'm staying?"

"No. We can't be seen together. Get this: there's an abandoned warehouse—Number 33—down by the Harbor Island docks. I'll meet you there at ten o'clock tonight."

"Whoever you are, I have no intention of—"

The voice cut in. "If you care at all what happens to David, be there. And be alone."

There was a click and the line went dead.

Jessica stood unmoving, the receiver still in her hand. She blinked.

How utterly absurd! This was the stuff of thousands of bad thrillers: the mysterious message, the lonely rendezvous (an empty warehouse, of course) at night, and that final touch of melodrama, the ominous instructions to come alone. It was really unbelievable.

She put down the receiver. Was it a joke, a student hoax aimed at the visiting mystery writer? She thought not. The voice had been too sincere. A professional actress might have achieved that degree of verisimilitude, but not a student. The question in that case was what was she to do? Notify the police? Tell David? Seek Edmund's advice? Or ignore the whole thing?

Or go?

It would be quite insane, of course, a ridiculous risk. How many times had she read of thriller heroes or heroines going off on perilous nocturnal missions of this kind—and wondered why they were such fools. She had even sent her own heroine once—though in that story had made sure the girl really had no choice.

Jessica certainly had a choice. But for the first time she realized why the protagonist of a mystery story really couldn't be allowed to turn down such an invitation. It was a dare, a challenge. You could never afterward feel quite the same about someone who backed down. And you could never feel quite the same about yourself if *you* backed down. Besides, she had promised to do all she could to help David. Moreover, no one involved in this case could have any possible motive for wanting to kill her.

Could they?

It would be untrue to say that Jessica didn't feel nervous as the taxi weaved its way through the maze of streets leading to the docks of Harbor Island. In fact, she felt very frightened. A dozen times she opened her mouth to tell the cabbie she'd changed her mind and to drive her to police headquarters instead; and a dozen times she closed it. She was about to open it a thirteenth time, when he said: "This is it, lady."

Jessica stared out the window. She could see very little: a high, faint moon being the only illumination. To her left, somewhere, was the ocean; to her right (a mere darker patch against the sky), a large, forbidding building, apparently one of a row of similar ones. Jessica peered toward it dubiously. Then she looked at the luminous dial of her watch. It was two minutes to ten. Quickly, before she had time to change her mind, she opened the door and got out.

"How much?" she asked the driver.

He was looking worried. "Say, lady, you sure you want to be dropped here?"

"I'm quite sure I *don't*. But I've got to be."

"You a cop?"

"No."

"Spy?"

She managed a smile. "No. I just have to meet someone."

"Look, lady, any guy who gets a dame to meet him at a dump like this ain't worth it, believe me."

"Thanks for the warning. But it's nothing like that. And I'm not up to anything illegal, believe me."

"I never figured you was. You got respectable written all over you."

"I hope that's a compliment."

"You want I should wait?"

Jessica thought. It would be very comforting to have this nice little man within reasonable distance. She said, "Could you drive a few hundred yards, park, wait ten minutes and then come back?"

"Sure."

"Thanks. Then do that, will you? Here." She handed him ten dollars. "Take that for now, and we'll settle up properly later. Drive away now, please."

He shrugged. "You're the boss. But I don't like it." He looked at his watch. "Ten minutes it is."

Jessica stood still, watching the taxi as it drove off. Then she turned and surveyed the vast bulk of the deserted warehouse. Everything was deathly silent. There was no wind tonight, and she couldn't even hear the water. She wished she'd never come. She wished she were back in her hotel. Or, better still, home in Cabot Cove.

She opened her purse, took out a flashlight, and walked toward the warehouse, the sound of her footsteps echoing back to her as she did. Outside the entrance, she stopped and took a deep breath. Then she went inside.

It was now totally dark. Jessica switched on her flashlight and swung it around and up. The cavernous reaches of the building stretched far beyond the range of the beam. Apart from a few piles of empty packing cases, the place seemed quite empty. She shivered, licked her lips and called out, "Hello?"

Her voice seemed to come back at her from all sides, but there was no response. She tried again, slightly louder. "Hello! Anybody here?"

Still the silence was total. Jessica stood, uncertain as to her next move. She wanted very much to leave. She'd done what had been demanded of her. She could be expected to do no more. And there certainly seemed to be nobody here. But, if there was no human being present, there might well be rats. She felt she would almost prefer her flashlight's beam to fall on a masked man with a gun than on the beady red eyes of a rat. Oh dear!

Then she heard a sound. She froze. What was it? Footsteps? Something being dragged? Fighting down a rising panic, Jessica called out again: "Who's there?"

She shone her flashlight around frantically—and nearly screamed out loud as the beam alighted on a human figure.

It was a woman. And she was staggering toward Jessica, dragging her feet. Her face was ashen, her expression ghastly. She seemed for a moment to be wearing a dress with a garish abstract pattern of scarlet patches. Then Jessica saw that the scarlet was blood.

As Jessica took a step toward her, the woman raised one despairing hand; then her knees buckled and she fell forward to the floor.

Momentarily forgetting all possible risk, Jessica ran to her and knelt down. She turned the woman over and shone the light into her face. Then she picked up the woman's limp wrist and groped for her pulse. There was nothing.

Jessica got shakily to her feet and for five seconds stood quite still. Then she turned and ran.

She ran as she had not run in years, out of the warehouse and in the direction taken by the taxi, her flashlight's beam making a crazy, jumping path before her. She prayed the cabbie hadn't changed his mind and gone. She was just beginning to think he had when at last she saw the cab.

She staggered up to the driver's window. He turned a startled face to her as she gasped out, "Get on your radio—quick! There's been a murder!"

For a moment he stared at her. Then without a word he reached for his microphone.

The black-and-white was there in ten minutes, though it seemed an hour. Jessica heard the siren long before she saw the car. She jumped out of the cab where she'd been sitting, breathless and speechless. She stood, waving her arms. The car screeched to a halt in front of her, and two reassuringly large uniformed policemen got out. Jessica hurried up to them, pointing behind her.

"Along there, about two hundred yards. Warehouse thirty-three."

One of the officers stepped back and opened the rear door of the car. "Get in. Show us."

Jessica did as she was told.

Half a minute later, the police car pulled up outside the warehouse and the two officers went inside, Jessica at their heels. Both had drawn their revolvers and one was carrying a powerful flashlight.

For a moment Jessica had a horrible fear that the body would have disappeared. But no: it was still there.

One officer knelt down by it while the other stood, shining his flashlight around. After a few seconds the first one got to his feet. "She's dead, all right." He looked at Jessica. "You know her?"

She nodded. "I've never spoken to her, but I know who she is. Her name is Lila Schroeder. She's the wife of the swimming coach at Sequoia University."

# Chapter Six

"IT was a damn fool thing to do, Mrs. Fletcher," Lieutenant Andrews growled.

"I know," Jessica said.

"You should have phoned me as soon as you received the call."

"Yes. But if I had, she might not have been willing to talk."

His face creased into a sudden, unexpected smile. "I certainly give you top marks for guts."

Jessica looked surprised. "Thank you, Lieutenant."

It was an hour later, and they were in his warm, brightly lit office at police headquarters. Jessica had told her story and was now gratefully sipping at a steaming cup of coffee.

Suddenly Andrews was serious again. "Well, she didn't talk, anyway."

"No, she never had a chance."

"This so-called proof she was going to give you, that Tolliver couldn't have killed the Brevard woman—do you have any idea . . . ?"

"None whatsoever. I've told you all I know."

He grunted. "Well, we'll see if he can throw any light on it soon. I've given orders for him to be picked up."

"You don't suspect him of this murder too?"

"Let's just say I want to know where he's been for the last few hours."

Jessica put down her coffee cup. "But, Lieutenant, wouldn't it be awfully stupid for him to kill off his own alibi?"

"What I'm thinking, ma'am, is that we're dealing with a very clever young man who might have set this whole thing up to make us *think* he had an alibi; and then eliminated the girl before she could say anything—hoping we'd fall into the trap of thinking just as you are."

Jessica shook her head. "Really, Mr. Andrews, that does seem to be a scheme of quite incredible, almost unbelievable, subtlety."

He shrugged. "Maybe. We'll see. Now, we'd better do something about getting you back to your hotel."

\* \* \*

Probably as a result of nervous reaction, Jessica slept like a log that night and was late getting up the following morning. She turned the radio on first thing. The murder of Lila Schroeder was the lead item on the local news. It was reported that her husband Jack had been taken in for questioning. The murder weapon had been found about twenty yards from the body: an old longshoreman's hook that might have been on the premises for years. An unpremeditated murder—or a clever attempt to make this seem the case? No mention was made of David—or, Jessica was pleased to note—of her own part in the affair.

Immediately after breakfast she started work. However, she had only just got under way when there came a tap on the door. She gave a sigh and went to answer it.

It was David. He looked terrible—pale, haggard, and red-eyed.

Jessica stood back and let him in. "I didn't expect to see you today," she said.

"I told you I'd be here, didn't I?"

"Yes, but I heard last night that the police were going to bring you in for questioning."

"They did. I was there for hours. Do you mind if I sit down?" He did so, then looked up at her. "Oh, Jessica, I just can't believe Lila is dead."

She was amazed to see tears in his eyes. "Were you so very close?" she asked.

He nodded and his eyes dropped.

"David, she told me on the phone she had proof you couldn't have killed Alison. Was that true?"

"She could have given me an alibi." He looked up at her again. "The night Alison was killed Lila and I were together—the whole night."

"Oh," said Jessica. "I see."

He managed a faint smile. "You don't approve?"

"She was a married woman, David."

"In name only." He got to his feet. "She and Jack had been living apart for months. She wanted a divorce. He drove her to it with his insane jealousy. She only had to smile at a man and he'd accuse her of having an affair. And he'd go crazy with rage. He threatened to kill her a dozen times. She had to leave him."

"It seems his jealousy might have been justified."

"No!" He shook his head sharply. "There was nothing between Lila and me until after her marriage had broken up."

"But had her marriage broken up—finally?"

"As far as she was concerned, yes. Jack, of course, had been hounding her to go back to him, but there was no way she would have."

"If she could have given you an alibi, why didn't she?"

"I wouldn't let her. Jack would have had to find out about it. And I was scared what he'd do if he discovered she'd been with me that night."

"Scared what he'd do to her? Or to you, David?"

"To her, of course. He just wouldn't accept they were through. He said if he couldn't have her, nobody would. He meant it; she believed it. Why else would she choose to meet you down at that damn warehouse?"

He suddenly put his head in his hands and gave a groan. "Oh, why did she have to do it? I warned her not to."

"Why did she do it?"

He stared. "To clear me. She felt she couldn't go on any longer—"

"No, I mean why *me?*"

"Oh, she was at your lecture the other night. I guess it was the first lecture she'd ever been to. And she was bowled over by your brain-power. She was convinced that if she put the whole story to you, you'd think up a way to solve everything."

He gave a twisted grin. "Poor little Lila. She was the sweetest person you could imagine. But in some ways she was really incredibly dumb."

On the last word David's voice broke and he turned away for a moment. Then he looked back at Jessica. "I'm sorry. I didn't mean that like it sounded."

"I know what you meant," Jessica said softly.

David brushed a hand quickly across his eyes. "Well," he said briskly, "better get to work."

"David, how much sleep have you had?"

"Oh, not a lot."

"Any?"

"Well, I guess not, now you come to mention it."

"Then you hurry straight home and go to bed."

"Oh, I couldn't—"

"You could and you will. Now scoot. I have no work for you today, anyway."

"Well, if you're sure . . ."

"Be here early tomorrow."

When he'd gone, Jessica went on to the patio and stared out over the city. In the distance, through mist and fog, she could make out the Space Needle. Slender, solitary, and a little spooky.

Jessica sighed. Much against her will, she was being inexorably drawn into this case. It was a nuisance. But she remembered the decision she'd reached at the end of the Lydecker case: that if such events came her way again, she wouldn't fight, but rather use her gifts in any way that seemed necessary. And her book was near enough finished for her to take a break from it today.

She sat down, got out a notebook and spent ten minutes writing in it. Then she rose and put on her hat and coat. She needed some information, and probably the best person to supply it was Edmund.

Jessica tapped on the door leading to Edmund's office. Amelia Browne's voice called, "Come in," and Jessica opened the door.

Amelia looked up from her typewriter in the anteroom. There was the beginning of a smile on her face. But it froze ever so slightly at the sight of Jessica.

"Oh, good morning, Mrs. Fletcher."

"Good morning, Amelia. How are you?"

"Very well. I'm afraid Dr. Gerard isn't in just now."

"Oh. Do you know when he will be?"

"I really couldn't say." Her manner was decidedly cold.

"Well, it's rather important I see him. Do you mind if I wait?"

"If you wish." She indicated a chair, then turned away and started typing quickly. Jessica sat down.

Five minutes passed. Then, when Amelia stopped typing to change the paper, Jessica said suddenly, "Amelia, despite what you think, I am not a rival."

Amelia's head jerked up. "I—I beg your pardon?"

"Edmund and I are dear friends and nothing more, believe me."

Amelia's face slowly went red. "Mrs. Fletcher," she said, "you misjudge me, really—"

Jessica spoke impatiently. "Oh, Amelia, for heaven's sake, only a blind person could misread your feelings for Edmund. I think he must be in desperate need of a good optometrist."

She smiled, and suddenly, a little awkwardly, Amelia smiled too.

"That's better," Jessica said. "Now please, let me be your ally, because I'm certainly not your enemy."

"I wasn't aware my feelings were so transparent. I was very fond of Mrs. Gerard, I really was, and she was good for him. Then when she died . . ." She broke off and shrugged. "If patience is a virtue, I'm the most virtuous of women."

"All he needs is some gentle nudging," Jessica told her. "Not from me. From you."

"I'm working up to it."

At that moment the door opened and Edmund came in.

She stood up. "Hello, Edmund."

"Hello, Jessica. I didn't expect to see you today."

"Can you spare me a few minutes?"

"Of course. Come on through."

He took her into his private office and they sat down. She wasted no time. "Have you heard about Lila Schroeder?"

His face clouded. "Yes—on the radio. And Jack Schroeder taken in. Terrible—terrible."

"Did you know that I was the one to find her?"

"No." He stared. "Good Lord!"

She told him the story of the previous night. When she'd finished, he shook his head in disbelief. "My word, Jess, what a risk you took! If she was alive when you got there, it means the murderer was almost certainly still nearby."

"I know. But I didn't come here to talk about my own exploits. Edmund, you said *the murderer.* Does that mean you don't think it's her husband?"

He shook his head helplessly. "I just don't know. I can't really believe it of him."

"Is it true he was insanely jealous?"

"Jealous, yes. I don't know about *insanely.* But, of course, Lila was a very beautiful young woman. It's natural, I suppose, he should think other men were after her."

"Does he have a temper?"

He paused for a moment. "Yes, he does."

"Violent?"

"He's been involved in fights. I don't think he'd use violence against a woman. Lila certainly never complained of that; their fights were purely verbal affairs, I believe. But, of course, I don't really know. You say the police had David Tolliver in for questioning, too?"

"Yes."

"It's beginning to look black for him, Jess—two women he knew, both murdered."

"The other night at dinner, you were arguing against his being a killer."

"I know, but one has to face facts. And, of course, as I explained, I don't know him well. I'm beginning to fear I was wrong about him."

"But Lila told me she could prove him innocent of Alison's murder."

"So you said." He looked thoughtful. "I wonder how. Were she and Alison friends, perhaps? Did Alison tell Lila about some *other* man she was afraid of? And then did Lila see them together, or something like that?"

"Oh no," Jessica said. "I should have explained; David came to me this morning. Lila was going to give him an alibi. They were together all through the night Alison was murdered."

Edmund stared. "Lila said that?"

"She was going to, according to David."

He shook his head. "I'm sorry, Jess. I can't swallow it."

"Why?"

"Well, isn't it very convenient for him that she should say that just before dying? Suppose he forced her to call you and say what she did—and then killed her before she could recant?"

Jessica sighed. "You're as bad as Lieutenant Andrews. But I just don't believe it. If she'd called the *police* and said what she'd said to me, I might credit it. But I'd still have great difficulty in believing David could hit Alison over the head with a statuette, or kill Lila with a longshoreman's hook. I'm *certain* he's not a violent type."

Edmund smiled. "Well, you're the expert."

"I'm no expert. I just have feelings. And that's a very strong one. But, Edmund, it doesn't have to have been either Jack or David, does it?"

"Of course not."

"In fact—and this is what I principally wanted to ask you about—I do have an idea about someone else who might have had a motive."

"Who's that?"

She didn't answer directly. "Lila was at my first lecture, remember?"

"Yes, it was rather surprising."

"I don't think she really came to hear me. I think she wanted to see Todd Lowery."

Edmund eyed her sharply. "What makes you think that?"

"The way she was looking at him. The way she followed him out. And he didn't like it. He did his best to avoid her. But she wasn't having any."

Edmund was looking at her with admiration. "You're remarkable, Jess, you really are. Well, it's true—and please, this is between you and me: Lila did have a brief affair with Todd. But it's over."

"Are you quite certain it's over?"

"I couldn't swear it on oath, but I believe so."

"Who ended it?"

"He did."

"Suppose Lila didn't want to end it? Suppose she was in love with him, wanted to marry him, and was threatening to tell his wife?"

"You're suggesting Todd would kill her to stop her? No, Jess, I find that hard to believe. Besides, there's absolutely nothing that I know of to link Todd with Alison Brevard."

"Of course not. But, Edmund, there doesn't have to have been any connection between the two murders. Lila needn't have been killed because of anything she was going to tell me about the Brevard case."

He pursed his lips. "Bit of a coincidence, otherwise, isn't it?"

"Yes. But coincidences do happen. Or somebody might be using the first murder as a sort of smoke screen for the second."

"I suppose that's possible. But, Jess, you're wrong on one point: there *is* a known connection between the two cases."

"What's that?"

"David Tolliver."

Jack Schroeder was released by the police for lack of evidence at noon that day. That development was reported on the lunchtime news, and at two o'clock that afternoon Jessica was ringing the front door bell of the neat suburban home which, until a few months ago, Schroeder had shared with his wife. There was no reply, and after about fifteen seconds she rang again. A voice from inside called roughly: "If that's another reporter, you can clear off. I got nothing to say."

"It's not," Jessica called back.

There was a pause, then the door was yanked open.

"Well?" Jack Schroeder said.

He was a tall, lean, lithe man with the well-developed shoulders of the athlete. His dark hair, brushed back, was receding slightly and his face was thin, almost gaunt. He was in need of a shave.

"I'm Jessica Fletcher," she said.

"Oh, the murder lady. What d'you want?"

"You may have heard that it was I who found your wife. Immediately after the—the attack."

"So?"

"Well, I just wanted you to know that she didn't suffer for any length of time. One second she was on her feet; the next she'd collapsed. She died almost instantly."

"Well, thanks for telling me. Is that all?"

"Mr. Schroeder, can I speak to you privately for a few minutes?"

"What about?"

"About your wife."

"Look, if you're thinking of ripping off Lila's death for your next book, forget it. She's dead. Let her rest in peace."

"I have no intention of writing about her. I *am* interested in who killed her. I thought you might be, too."

"How d'you know it wasn't me?"

"I don't."

"Taking a bit of a risk, then, aren't you?"

"You wouldn't be such a fool as to kill me here and now, in your own home, in broad daylight. Besides, I have nothing, er, on you that might give you a motive."

"Ah, but I got an uncontrollable temper, don't I? Or so the cops say."

"I shall do nothing to provoke it."

He hesitated, then said, "Oh, you might as well come in, I suppose."

He turned and went back into the house, leaving Jessica to follow him in and close the front door.

The living room in which she found herself had obviously not been cleaned for a week. Empty coffee mugs and beer cans were dotted about; items of clothing were on every chair; and the place smelled stale. She ached to get busy with a Hoover, duster and polish, but there were more important matters on hand.

"You probably think I'm just being nosy," she said.

"Aren't you?"

"No. I tried not to get involved. Your wife involved me herself. It seems there's no firm evidence—forensic-type evidence—as to who might have killed her. Which could mean the case will never be solved. And unsolved murders are bad for everybody involved—particularly the surviving spouse. A shadow of suspicion always lurks over them. Now, of course, it may be you did kill her and don't want the truth to come out. But if you didn't, it would be advisable to talk with me. If we put our heads together, we just might get somewhere."

He stared at her for a moment. Then he grunted. "Better sit down."

He indicated a chair by snatching a dirty shirt off it. He tossed the shirt into a corner. Jessica sat. He pulled out an upright chair from the table, swung it around and sat astride it, his hands resting on the back.

"Could be I'm talking because I want you to *think* I'm innocent."

"Of course," she replied.

"What did you want to ask?"

"Did you threaten to kill Lila?"

"I guess so. I also threatened to win an Olympic gold twelve years back. I didn't even make the team. I'm real bad at follow-through."

"You know, Mr. Schroeder, if this was your manner at the police station, you can't have done yourself much good. Why so flip, so apparently callous? I believe you loved your wife very much."

There was a momentary hesitation, a sudden look in his eyes, and Jessica knew she'd hit a nerve. Then the look was gone and he was saying: "So did a lot of other guys."

"Naturally. But did she love them?"

"Depends what you mean by love."

"You're saying she was just a tramp."

"No!"

The word came out like a gunshot. He got suddenly to his feet, nearly knocking the chair over. He turned away, groping for words, then spun around to face her again.

"It may have seemed like that. It did to me at one time. But I figured it out. The problem was, she could never get enough love. She craved affection, a sense of being wanted. Maybe it was something she missed as a kid. All I know is that I wasn't enough for her."

"And you found that hard to take?"

"Sure I did. Wouldn't anybody?"

"Only if he loved his wife. If he didn't, he'd just get a divorce and start over."

"Okay—so I loved her." He said it defiantly, as though he was admitting something shameful.

Jessica changed tack. "You know she called me, saying she could clear David Tolliver of suspicion of Alison Brevard's murder?"

He stared. "No. I didn't know that."

"He claims she was going to give him an alibi for that whole night."

"Bull!"

Jessica raised her eyebrows. "Are you saying they weren't lovers? Wasn't he one of the men you were jealous of?"

"Jealous of Pretty-Boy? No way. Lila knew him. But that's all. He'd have been too young for her. She liked men a few years older than herself."

"Such as Professor Lowery?"

There was silence. Jack looked away. "At one time."

"But not currently?"

He turned back. "Mrs. Fletcher, I don't know. Lila and I were living apart. I have a job. I couldn't follow her around. I couldn't afford a private detective. So I just don't know who she'd been seeing. And that's what I told the police. If I had any clue about her present lover, do you think I wouldn't say?"

"No; obviously you would." Jessica stood up. "So there's nothing else you can tell me?"

He shook his head. "Except that I didn't do it."

"I see. Well, thank you for your time, Mr. Schroeder. I'm sorry to have—"

He interrupted. "Maybe there's one thing."

"What's that?"

"The cops told me—asked if I could explain something. I couldn't. They found her purse behind one of those crates. There was a thousand dollars in an envelope inside it. She didn't draw it from the bank, and there was nothing she could have sold to raise it. Somebody must have given it to her. But they don't know who. Or why."

# Chapter Seven

"I THOUGHT that for my final lecture," Jessica said, "I would look at the technique of *writing* detective stories—the particular problems which face the mystery author. And there are problems which are unique to this genre, which give it, for the author, both a fascination and a frustration all its own.

"For example, a so-called straight novelist can write one chapter about character A, a second about character B, and so on. The author doesn't normally have to concern himself with what B is doing at precisely the same moment that A is having the adventures in chapter one. The mystery writer, on the other hand, frequently has to consider not only the movements of B at this same time, but also those of C, D and perhaps half a dozen others. They all have to be worked into an extremely intricate pattern, sometimes before you even put pen to paper. And the reason, of course, is that it must be possible for a number of different characters to have committed the crime. It's no good finding yourself in a situation where at the time of the second murder, one of your potential suspects is lecturing at a university and several of the others are in the audience—thereby leaving only one person without an alibi. And, therefore, the guilty party.

"It's necessary, in fact, for the author to put himself—or herself—into the mind of the murderer. Let's take a specific but imaginary crime. A young woman is unhappily married to a jealous and perhaps violent husband. She needs love and affection. He cannot provide them. A perfect recipe for the murder of passion. The young woman is found dead. The suspects are legion."

Jessica stepped down from the rostrum and stood immediately in front of the first row of spectators.

"Now, what's our first problem?"

She let her eyes run along the row of students. One said, "Check out the alibis."

Jessica shook her head. "Not exactly. That's thinking like a detective:

an admirable exercise sometimes. But in this case we're not *solving* a murder. We're setting it up. So again: what's our problem?"

A familiar voice said, *"Create the alibis."*

It was David. He was sitting relaxed and easy in his seat three rows back.

Again Jessica shook her head. "Closer, but still not quite correct. Writers can fairly easily create alibis for their characters: A is lunching with a bishop, B playing golf with a Supreme Court justice, C being interviewed on television, and so on. But that's too easy. As I was trying to indicate, if the writer is to baffle his readers, he must put himself in the shoes of the murderer—who has to *take advantage of non-alibis.* He must time the killing for maximum effectiveness. He chooses . . . a weekday. Evening. Say ten o'clock. He knows A *will* have an alibi. But B won't. C will—but won't be able to reveal it, for fear of letting somebody else down. D's alibi will be provided by, let's say, his mother—so will be worthless."

Jessica had continued to walk slowly along the row and now came face-to-face with Todd Lowery.

"Who's the obvious suspect in this case?" she asked.

She looked at the professor, almost forcing him to answer.

"The husband, naturally," he said.

"Why?"

He grinned. "Because you haven't yet identified A,B,C or D."

There was laughter in the room, in which Jessica joined.

"Fair enough," she said, "then let's identify them. Take A—"

David called out: "Don't bother with him—he's got an alibi." There was more laughter.

"Then we'll make it . . . let's see . . . D," Jessica said. "D is a youngish professional man. He's in love, or has been in love, with the victim. But he has a major problem: he's married. Now, do you suppose his wife knows about his relationship with the victim?"

Again she looked at Lowery.

He gazed at her coolly. "I'd say no."

"Good. Because if she *did* know, we'd have to add her name to the list of suspects, and we wouldn't want to do that, would we, Professor?"

"It's your scenario, Mrs. Fletcher."

"Oh, come, come, Professor, this is give-and-take. Tell me about his alibi for the time of the woman's death. Remember that D had the alibi that was worthless."

"I suppose he could have been with his wife."

"And would she swear to that?"

"Yes."

"I suppose now we say this character is B—who, remember, didn't have an alibi at all: he was out somewhere—and alone. Will his wife give him a false alibi—will she *lie* for him?"

Lowery shifted in his seat. "I don't know."

"Do make a guess, Professor. Come on—would she lie for him?"

"She might."

Jessica nodded. "Yes, of course, that is the most any murderer can ever say. The writer, on the contrary, is omniscient, and knows exactly what everybody is going to do and say. Which is why authorship is a much more pleasant activity than homicide can ever be."

She moved on from Lowery and addressed the room at large.

"Now let's turn to another of the author's problems: the search for original motives . . ."

At the close of the lecture, as the applause broke out, Todd Lowery got hurriedly to his feet and, without a backward glance toward Jessica, walked to the door and went out. She eyed him for a moment thoughtfully, then the students were around her again. There were half a dozen in the front who had attended all the lectures and were full of questions. They begged her to come and have coffee with them, and she hadn't the heart to refuse.

Just then Edmund touched her shoulder. She turned.

"Jess," he said, "I have to see somebody in my office now. Could you come along when these young savages release you? I'd like to talk."

She smiled. "Of course."

"Good. Must rush." He hurried off.

There were some more books to autograph, and the students who had invited her to coffee moved in a clump to one side while she did the signings. When she'd finished, she looked up and saw David standing a few feet away, smiling.

"Hello, David," she said. "You coming for coffee?"

He moved a little closer. "No, thanks. I'm not one for entering into undergraduate discussion groups. I prefer to talk to you on your own. Look, I have a bit of time to spare. I thought I'd go to the hotel and do some more typing. Would you mind?"

"Not at all."

"Oh, I thought, after what you said, that perhaps you wouldn't want me there on my own."

"By no means. As long as you arrange it with me in advance."

He grinned. "Fine. See you later, then."

He stuck his hands in his pockets and strolled out.

\* \* \*

The students were bright, keen and extremely knowledgeable, and within a very few minutes Jessica found herself completely involved in an animated discussion on crime fiction. So involved that when she happened to glance at her watch, she was amazed to find she'd been with them for nearly an hour and a half. She speedily said her goodbyes and thanks and left them.

She hurried along to Edmund's office. As she walked up to the door, it opened and he came out. He looked relieved to see her.

"Ah, Jess, good."

"Sorry, Edmund, I got caught up with those students. Have I kept you waiting?"

"It's all right, I had some dictating to do. But I'm afraid I have to dash now. Another meeting. And I did want a serious talk with you. Jess, what are your plans? I suppose, now the lectures are over you'll be leaving Seattle for Kentucky tomorrow?"

"No, actually I thought I'd stay on till I've at least finished the book. I'm quite settled at the hotel now, and I don't want another disruption of my routine until the manuscript's been mailed to my editor. I can go to Abby's anytime. So I'll be around for a few more days."

"Oh, I *am* glad." He sounded genuinely pleased. "Look, can we get together again tomorrow night? We've seen so little of each other, really —just the one dinner and a few fleeting conversations."

"Yes, tomorrow evening will be lovely."

"That's fine. Would you like to go to the same restaurant, or try another one?"

She smiled. "Well, do you know what I'd really like? A home-cooked dinner. I always get the urge after about a week of restaurant and hotel food."

He looked dismayed. "Oh dear, I'm afraid I can't manage that."

"No, but I can. Tell me, Edmund, how long since *you* had a home-cooked dinner?"

"Oh, I don't know. I get invited to somebody's house now and again, but I don't often go."

"Then suppose I cook at your place tomorrow?"

His eyes widened. "Would you really like to do that?"

"I'd love to. I enjoy cooking."

He smiled delightedly. "Well, if you're really sure, that would be wonderful. It'll make the things I want to say to you very much easier, too, than in a restaurant."

He glanced at his watch. "Oh, Lord, I really must fly." He pulled the office door closed behind him. "I'll call you tomorrow at your hotel, Jess. All right?"

"Right, Edmund. Good night."

"Night, Jess." He hurried away down the corridor, turning to say over his shoulder: "There are no groceries at the house."

"Leave all that to me."

He waved a hand and was gone.

When Jessica got back to her hotel room, she expected to find David typing. But in fact there was no sign of him. Then she spotted a note propped up on the typewriter. It read: *Jessica—I had to go out. Sorry. You had a call from Prof. Lowery. Wants you to meet him at his office at nine this evening. Says it's urgent and confidential. Regards, David.*

Jessica slowly lowered the paper. This was most interesting. Her little verbal duel with Lowery must have had some effect. She wondered what he wanted to say. Would he be very angry? Well, she'd soon find out.

No doubt Edmund would be extremely cross if he knew she was going to another nocturnal rendezvous. But visiting the university was quite different from going to a deserted dockside warehouse: there would be people about. And Lowery, if he was guilty, would certainly not be such a fool as to do her harm in his own office, especially after having phoned and passed on a message through a third person.

Of course, there was the trip back to the university. But this time she would take a cab.

The taxi drew up outside the building which housed the English department, and Jessica got out. She looked up. There plainly weren't many people around, but half a dozen windows were lighted. She paid off the driver and made her way inside. Two students passed her and went out, laughing together. Then, apart from her, the big entrance hall was empty. She consulted a wall directory and found that Lowery's office was on the third floor. She crossed to the elevator and pressed the button. Nothing happened. Impatiently she jabbed at it again. Still, there was no response.

Jessica groaned inwardly. Either it was out of order or the power was turned off at night. Probably the latter. She walked resignedly to the stairs and started to climb.

She reached the second-floor landing and paused. It was quite deserted up here and very quiet. Suddenly she felt nervous. She hesitated, then reached into her purse and took out a small cylinder of Mace. She was probably being ridiculously nervous, but it wouldn't do any harm to be on the safe side. Clutching the cylinder in her hand, she walked to the next flight of stairs. Her heels were loud on the marble floor, and the sound echoed back from the high ceilings.

Jessica arrived on the third floor and again paused, both to get her breath and to peer at a couple of nearby door numbers and try to discover which was the way to Lowery's office.

Then from somewhere, from nowhere, a shapeless black figure suddenly materialized at her side. She started to swing around, but at the same instant she was shoved violently in the chest. She had no hope of saving herself, and fell back—straight down the stairs.

The world spun crazily. Lights shot like rockets across her field of vision. She heard herself giving an utterly involuntary scream. For what seemed an age she was conscious of no pain—only a mad whirl of movement. Then she felt an agonizing blow on the front of her head and everything went black.

# Chapter Eight

"YOU'RE a very lucky woman, Mrs. Fletcher," the doctor said. "The X rays show nothing's been broken, and the wound to the head is quite superficial."

"Does that mean I can go?" she asked hopefully.

He shook his head firmly. "You've had a nasty fall and been badly shaken. I'm keeping you in overnight for observation."

Jessica sighed and lay back on the pillows. "Well," she said, with a slight smile, "perhaps I'm not altogether sorry. I could use a rest, and it will give me a chance to think."

"Good." Then he looked a trifle embarrassed. "Incidentally, the paramedic who brought you in says that when you came to in the ambulance, you murmured something about being pushed. Is that right?"

She opened her mouth to speak, then thought better of what she'd been going to say. She paused. Then: "If that's what he says, I'm sure he's right. But I must have been delirious. I just fell."

He gave a satisfied nod. "That's what I thought. Now, is there anybody you'd like notified?"

"No; I'd rather not have any visitors."

"Right, then I'll leave you. That was a sedative I gave you just now. It'll start to take effect any moment. You should get a good night's sleep." He crossed to the door.

"Thank you, doctor. Good night."

"Good night."

He went out, switching out the light. Jessica lay with her eyes closed. *Lucky,* he had said; he didn't know how lucky. That had been a deliberate attempt on her life. Not that there would have been any point in telling him, or in reporting it to the police. She couldn't give them the slightest clue as to the identity of the man who had done it. And it might be better to keep him in suspense about how much she knew or suspected.

But who had it been? Lowery was the obvious suspect. Too obvious?

Or would he rely on her thinking that? Was he pulling a sophisticated double bluff? It was just the sort of thing that might appeal to an academic who was also a mystery buff. Or was she fooling herself, avoiding the only logical answer as to the identity of her attacker: the only other person who knew she was going to be at the English building . . . ?

But why? Why should he want . . . ? What harm could she do . . . ?

Jessica slept.

It was half past two the following afternoon when Jessica again ascended to the third floor of the English building. This time, however, she took the elevator.

She located the office of Todd Lowery and tapped on the door. A voice called loudly: "Come in."

She entered. Lowery was alone in the office, working at a big desk that was covered by papers. He looked surprised to see her (just surprised, she noted; not guilty or shocked), and got to his feet.

"Mrs. Fletcher! I say, what have you been doing to yourself?"

Jessica fingered the bandage on her head. "Oh, hadn't you heard, professor? I had a fall."

"Not too bad, I hope."

"Bad enough. I was in the hospital overnight."

"Really? Where did it happen? Oh, please sit down."

"Here." Jessica sat.

"Here?"

"In this building. I fell down the stairs from this floor to the second. I'm told that a research student, working late, heard me and called an ambulance. I was on my way to keep our appointment. I expect you wondered why I didn't show up."

He looked blank. "Our appointment?"

Jessica stared. "Are you saying you *didn't* call and leave a message asking me to meet you here at nine last night—on an urgent and confidential matter?"

It was his turn to stare. "I most certainly did not."

"I see." Jessica looked at him thoughtfully.

"What sort of urgent and confidential things could I have to speak to you about last night?"

"That's what I was wondering. I imagined . . . Lila. Professor Lowery, I said I fell down the stairs. Actually, I was pushed."

"My God! Are you sure?"

"Quite sure."

"Have you reported—" He broke off. Suddenly he'd gone pale. "Mrs. Fletcher, I hope you're not thinking that I—I lured you here to—to attempt . . ." Again he left the sentence unfinished.

"Well, it certainly would have been extremely foolish." She paused. "Or extremely ingenious."

"Mrs. Fletcher, I give you my word: I was at home all yesterday evening. As it happens, I made no calls at all. My wife can vouch—"

He stopped short, then gave a slow and rather feeble smile. "Of course —the worthless alibi. And I may as well admit right now that the same thing applies to the time of Lila's murder. My wife and I went straight home from the reception and stayed there—alone."

"I haven't accused you of murdering Lila, Professor."

"No . . . but you think I might have pushed you downstairs, don't you? But I ask you, what reason could I possibly have?"

"I don't know. Except that I realize you *were* quite angry with me yesterday, after the lecture."

"I admit it. I was."

"I feel rather embarrassed about that now, to tell you the truth."

"Don't be. Your little charade knocked some sense into me. I realized how ridiculous I'd been. My wife and I were up all night, talking. She's a very understanding woman. She believed me when I told her my fling with Lila was over a couple of months ago. To my great relief, as a matter of fact. Anyway, Emily and I are going away for a week, just the two of us, to try to put it back together. So, I have no cause to wish you harm. You can see that, can't you?"

Jessica nodded. "Yes. I can see that." She did not add, as it was on her mind to: "I can see you have no cause to wish me harm—*now.*"

After leaving Lowery, Jessica want back to her hotel. She found she was still quite shaky on her feet. She lay down on her bed for an hour, and at the end of that time felt much better. She was just about to call Room Service for some tea when there was a knock from the corridor. She put down the phone and opened the door. It was Edmund. He looked immensely relieved to see her.

"Jessica, are you all right?"

"Fine, Edmund, thank you."

"I've been trying to reach you all day. I called the hospital early, as soon as I heard about your accident from the research student who found you; but you were still sleeping. I called again later and they said you'd been discharged. Immediately after lunch I phoned here and they told me you'd gone out. Then I ran into Lowery on campus, and he told me about your visit to him. Jess, he says you claimed you were pushed down those stairs. Is that true?"

"Yes, Edmund, quite true."

"Great Scot!" He'd gone pale. "What's this place coming to?"

"Sit down and I'll tell you about it."

She returned to the phone, ordered tea for two, and then narrated the whole story of the previous evening.

When she'd finished, he shook his head incredulously. "I feel responsible," he said slowly. "If I'd never invited you here . . ."

"Oh, that's foolish, Edmund. How could you possibly know what was going to happen? Besides, I wasn't seriously hurt, and by tomorrow—apart from a few minor bruises—I should be quite all right."

"Well, thank heaven for that. Jess . . . you don't really suspect Todd Lowery, do you?"

She spread her hands helplessly. "I honestly don't know. He could have done it. He could have killed Lila—to prevent his wife and the university from finding out about their affair. On the other hand, his wife seems to have taken the news of the affair very well; and *you* knew about it anyway. In addition, I have to admit there isn't a shred of hard evidence against him."

"My dear," he said quietly, "you know who it has to have been, don't you? David Tolliver."

"But *why?*" She got to her feet and took two or three indecisive steps around the room.

"I don't know," he said. "But I believe he killed the Brevard woman. And I also believe he bribed Lila to supply him with a false alibi that night. Then he got cold feet—realized that if she had second thoughts and reported the bribe to the police, he'd almost certainly find himself under arrest for the murder of Alison. Perhaps Lila was already getting attacks of conscience and was threatening to back down. So he killed her before she could, but not before she'd told you she could prove him innocent."

"But, Edmund, that still doesn't explain why he should attack *me!*"

"I can only assume he's frightened of you. He knows of your reputation as an amateur detective and that you're interested in this case. It's quite possible that during all the conversations you've had with him, he's given himself away—slipped up by saying something that implicates him in the Brevard murder."

Jessica shook her head firmly. "He hasn't. I'm sure of it."

"Then he *thinks* he has. And he's terrified that you're suddenly going to put two and two together. Jess, when a killer who's murdered twice believes his security is threatened in any way, he'll kill again at the drop of a hat."

"I know, I know. I just can't picture David as a killer. Not of that type, anyway. He may be weak. He may be unscrupulous where money or women are concerned. But after a lifetime's study of human nature, I'd stake a lot on my belief that he's not capable of violence. And remember there's no hard evidence against him, either. He hasn't been caught out in any lies about his movements—"

Edmund interrupted. "He has." His voice was harsh.

Jessica stared. "But the police have questioned him at length—"

"I don't mean by the police. But he claimed Lila was with him the night Alison was killed."

"You don't *know* that wasn't true."

"I do. You see"—he took a deep breath—"that night Lila was with *me.*"

There was a long silence. Then Jessica said softly, "I see." She sat down slowly.

"You don't seem surprised. You hadn't guessed?"

She looked at him. "No. I hadn't. I didn't think that. But it was at the back of my mind that you knew Lila better than anyone thought. You said something about her never complaining that her husband used violence against her. It seemed strange. She'd hardly complain to you about that—not unless you were quite close friends."

"I'd like to explain about—" he started.

Just then there was a tap on the door. It was a waiter with the tea things. When he'd gone and Jessica was pouring the tea, she said, "Edmund, there's no call for you to explain anything. Whatever went on between you and Lila is your business, not mine."

"Jess, nothing went on. Not really. Please, I'd like to tell you."

"Very well." She handed him a cup of tea. He took it, but didn't drink."

"Several months ago, Lila came to me to ask if there was any work for her at the university. I think really she was just bored. Well, she wasn't exactly the academic type, but I happened to know that Todd Lowery was looking for someone to help with the indexing of a book he's nearly finished on Jacobean poetry, and I put them in touch. That's how their affair started.

"The first I knew about it was a month or two later, when Lila came and told me. She was in an awful state. She was terrified of her husband. He suspected what was going on and had threatened to kill her. Also, she was full of guilt about possibly breaking up Todd and Emily's marriage. She was still in love with him, but didn't know what to do. You know the sort of thing."

Jessica nodded.

"Well, I talked to her like a Dutch uncle. I told her she should give Todd up, make a clean break, and so on. Nothing very original or wise. To make a long story short, she did break with Todd. Unfortunately, though, that didn't improve things with Jack. He didn't believe the affair was over. She continued to come and see me, pouring out her troubles. At last I began to take Todd's place in her affections. Though I really believe I was always more of a father figure to her than anything else. I admit I was attracted to her. I was lonely, she was young and very pretty. It happens."

"Edmund," said Jessica, "honestly, there's no need—"

He raised a hand. "Please, Jess, let me finish. The upshot of it was that we started going out together. There was never anything more to it than that. All the same, she *was* married to one of the university employees, and I did feel guilty about it. I used to take her way out of town, to a little place called the Lumberjack Inn. Nevertheless, we both felt terribly furtive about it. I kept imagining somebody seeing us there and telling Jack—being cited in their divorce. The works."

He gave a wry grin. "I got so neurotic, I remember that after the first few times I even stopped paying the bill by credit card—just to make it harder for anybody to prove I'd been there. It was all very stupid."

He stopped and sipped at his tea. Jessica just waited. At last he looked up and continued. "However, I've gotten away from the main point. Which is that on the night Alison Brevard was killed, Lila and I were at the Lumberjack Inn until past midnight. We didn't get back to Seattle until nearly twelve forty-five in the morning. So you see, when Tolliver said Lila could give him an alibi for the night of Alison's death, he was lying."

Jessica didn't speak for several moments. She drank some tea, then put her cup down before asking, "Are you certain you haven't mistaken the date?"

"Quite certain. It was the last time we went to the Lumberjack. And it was the night Lila believed someone had followed her home and tried to run her down. I called her—"

"Tell me about that."

"Lila was sure this car was following us when we were on our way back. She was terrified it was Jack. I told her the driver just happened to be going to Seattle by the same route as we. Anyway, I dropped her in town and put her in a taxi; I never took her all the way home, of course—just in case. When I called her the next day, she told me she was sure the same car had tailed the cab to her address. Then when she got out and was crossing the road, it came roaring up and very nearly knocked her down. She had to run for the sidewalk. She said to me on the phone that there were very nearly *two* women murdered in Seattle the previous night. So, you see, I couldn't have mistaken the date."

"You've never mentioned this before, Edmund."

He hesitated. "No. I'd more or less forgotten it. I assumed it was just a drunk driver who'd nearly run her down, and that she'd imagined the part about being tailed. Are you saying there's a connection between that and her murder?"

Jessica shrugged. "Who knows? The fact remains, she *has* been murdered since. I suppose she didn't get the car's license number?"

"I'm sure she didn't. She would have said."

"Or a description?"

"She just said a car."

"You didn't see it?"

"I just saw the lights of *a* car in my rearview mirror. I'm not even sure it was the same car all the time. Lila kept looking back, and swore it was."

"Who else knew you were at this Lumberjack Inn with Lila that night?"

"Nobody, as far as I'm concerned. And I'm sure she didn't tell anybody, in case it got back to her husband. Jess, I don't think there's anything in this."

"Don't you? Well, I think one can be pretty sure when an attempt's been made on one's life. It's a sort of gut certainty." She smiled. "And I should know."

"Maybe you're right. But in Lila's case it would be impossible to prove it—after all this time."

"Oh, I know. But if it's true, it proves something else, doesn't it? That at least half of your suspicions of David are unfounded."

He frowned. "I don't see that."

"It would mean that there must have been *two* murderers around that night. The one who killed Alison couldn't at the same time have been following you and Lila from the inn and attempting to run her down. So, even if David was one of them, he couldn't have killed both women, as you suspected."

"Oh, I see. Unless, of course, somebody else entirely tried to kill Lila *that* night, which is stretching coincidence too far, I agree. No, I don't believe there *was* a deliberate attempt to run her down. Jess, I told you this story—although it makes me look very foolish—because it serves one useful purpose: it exposes David Tolliver as the liar—and killer—he is."

Jessica looked at him. "You're very sure, aren't you, Edmund?"

"Yes; and if we were talking about anybody but him, you would be, too."

Jessica sighed and stood up. She shook her head slowly. "I don't know. Maybe you're right, Edmund, maybe you're right."

"I'm sure I am." He too stood up. "Anyway, I must go. I've said what I came to say. Oh, about tonight—"

"Do you mind if we postpone it until tomorrow, Edmund? I think I'd enjoy it more then. I'd probably cook better, too."

"Yes, of course, that'll be fine. Get some rest now. I'll call you tomorrow."

"Yes, do that."

He said goodbye and went out. Jessica sat down again. She really did feel terribly tired. The hours of work on the book, the added mental strain of the lectures, and now this fall, had all combined to exhaust her. At the moment she was aching all over. Probably the best thing she could do was go to bed.

There was a tap on the door. The waiter for the tea things, she thought. She hadn't bolted the door after Edmund had left, so she called: "Come in."

The door opened and David entered.

He grinned. "Hi."

Jessica stared at him. She got slowly to her feet. "David, what are you doing here?"

His eyebrows went up. "I work for you, don't I?"

"I never expected to see you again."

"Why?"

"After the lie you told me."

"What do you mean? I never told you any lie."

"You told me Lila could give you an alibi for Alison's murder. That wasn't true. I know who *was* with Lila at that time. It wasn't you."

He'd gone pale. He said: "Oh, Lord . . ."

"Why, David? Why?"

He ran his fingers through his hair. "Why do you think? I'm in a jam, Jessica. I have no alibi for Alison's murder. I thought if I could get Lila to give me one I'd be off the hook. It's as simple as that."

"But that doesn't make sense! Why have her approach me? Why not the police?"

"She wasn't willing to lie to the police—make an official statement, perhaps go to court and swear on oath. But I thought if she could convince you I was innocent, it wouldn't be so bad. The cops might still suspect me, but as I didn't do it they could obviously never prove I did. And if you were batting for me . . . Well, you're a well-known person, a person of integrity. You've had experience with this sort of thing, you've cleared other people who were falsely accused. . . . If you were convinced of my innocence, then perhaps you'd nail the real killer."

He paused. "Besides, our friendship, your good opinion, means a lot to me. I couldn't bear to think of you believing me a killer."

"I never believed you were a killer," she insisted. "But I must admit that now I'm having doubts."

He looked at her in dismay. "Why? The evidence against me is no stronger now than it ever was."

"Innocent people don't normally bribe witnesses to prove their innocence."

"I didn't bribe her. I just persuaded her to do it as a favor to a friend."

"But what about the money in her purse?"

"I don't know a thing about it. Where would I get a thousand dollars?"

"Who said it was a thousand dollars?"

For perhaps five seconds he didn't answer. Then: "Andrews told me."

Jessica threw her hands up in despair. "Oh, David, I don't know. I want to believe you, I really do. But then there's that business of the phone call. Professor Lowery denies categorically having made it."

He said vehemently, "Jessica, I swear the call did come in. The caller said: 'This is Todd Lowery. Will you tell Mrs.'—"

Jessica cut in. "Hang on. You didn't say: 'Lowery's lying.' Your words were: 'The *caller* said.' "

"That's right."

"Does that mean you doubted it *was* Lowery?"

David frowned. "Not consciously at the time."

"But?"

"Well, thinking it over, the voice was odd. Of course, I don't really know Lowery. I've never been to his lectures; but I remember thinking the voice was strangely gruff. Naturally, I had no reason to believe there was anything wrong . . ."

"Strangely gruff: you mean as though it was disguised?"

He nodded. "Yes. It was—I don't know—unnaturally gruff."

# Chapter Nine

THE next morning Jessica phoned Lieutenant Andrews. She detected a slight air of weariness in his voice as he answered. "Yes, Mrs. Fletcher, what can I do for you now?"

"I won't keep you a moment, Lieutenant, and I'm not interfering, but I may have some information on the Brevard case for you. However, first will you answer me one question: did you tell David Tolliver that Lila Schroeder had a thousand dollars in her purse when she died?"

"No, I didn't."

Jessica's heart sank. "That's what I feared," she said. "Then I do have something to tell you."

"Before you go on, Mrs. Fletcher, I should tell *you* the Brevard case is closed."

"I beg your pardon?" Jessica thought she had misheard.

"We've got our man."

Her heart missed a beat. "You've actually made an arrest?"

"Yep. And charged him."

"Well, who is it?" she asked excitedly.

He hesitated. Then he said: "Oh well, you may as well know. It'll be in the afternoon news in a couple of hours. His name's Eddie Griggs."

"Who?" Jessica exclaimed.

"He's a professional burglar, with a record of resorting to violence when cornered."

Jessica felt her theories about the case being turned upside down. "How did you get on to him? May I ask?"

"Burglary Division got a lead on some of the jewelry stolen from Alison Brevard's apartment. They backtracked from the fence to Griggs. When he was questioned, he suddenly broke down and made a full confession."

"Why should he do that?"

"Neurotic sort of guy. Never killed before. Riddled with guilt. He's confessed to a string of other burglaries, all from middle-aged rich women living alone—widows, divorcees. This job went wrong, and he just couldn't live with it."

"Forgive me, Lieutenant, but could there be any doubt? I mean, I know you often get false confessions, don't you?"

"Not in this case. There's no shadow of doubt. Griggs knew far too much about the incidental details of the case. Take my word for it."

"Oh, I do, Mr. Andrews."

"Of course, the Schroeder case is still wide open. Griggs didn't kill *her*. So if you have any info that ties in with that, please spill it."

Jessica didn't answer immediately. Her mind was working quickly. At last she said, "I don't."

"Are you sure, Mrs. Fletcher? Anything might be useful."

"I have nothing at the moment. I may later. I need to do some heavy thinking. I'll get back to you."

"Just keep it to thinking, will you? Don't go for any more nighttime prowls in empty warehouses. Or empty universities."

She said sharply, "You know about my accident?"

"I know about the attempt on your life, Mrs. Fletcher. And I'm warning you: take care."

Jessica spent the rest of that morning putting the finishing touches to her book. She typed the last few pages herself, packed up the manuscript, took it to the hotel post office, and mailed it. She felt then as if a great burden had been lifted from her. She also felt at a bit of a loose end, and didn't quite know what to do next.

She'd told Andrews she would do some serious thinking about the murder. But it was no use just sitting down, staring at the wall and hoping that enlightenment would strike. She needed to do something—something mechanical that would let her mind roam freely. Of course! She had shopping to do for the dinner she was going to cook at Edmund's that night.

She made her way to the nearest supermarket.

As she wandered along the aisles making her selection, it occurred to her that it might have been a bit pushy of her to suggest cooking a meal in Edmund's house. Perhaps he wouldn't want her there—in Gwen's kitchen. Too late to back out now.

Of course, on the other hand, he might well be looking forward to her visit. Surely he must get tired of constant restaurant meals. She reflected that his restaurant bills over the course of a year must be tremendous. Though very likely, if asked just how much, he wouldn't have a clue. She smiled. One would have to ask Amelia. It wasn't as though he patronized cheap restaurants, either. The one he'd taken her to the other night, though not as expensive as the one she'd gone to with David, must nevertheless have set him back a good few dollars. And the Lumberjack Inn, where he'd taken Lila, sounded like quite a swanky place, too. However, Edmund would probably regard those outings as special occasions.

Jessica reached out casually for a packet of flour. And as she did so she froze. She stood unmoving, aghast at the thought which had struck her.

Oh no . . . Impossible.

But even as she told herself this, she knew it was far from impossible. It was hideously possible.

Jessica's legs felt suddenly shaky. She continued to stand quite still. It took a woman's voice, whining irritably, "Pardon me," to bring her to her senses, and make her realize she was blocking the aisle with her shopping cart.

She moved away hastily, trying to pull herself together. She could hardly face the possibility that this idea might be true. But it all fitted— fitted with a beautiful kind of coherence and logic. And obviously she couldn't just forget it. Once a murder had been committed, others would probably follow. Indeed, an attempt at a second had almost certainly already been made. She was going to have to do something about it.

But what?

Jessica walked slowly but resolutely along the marbled corridor. There was a gnawing inside her, and her heart was beating like a steam hammer. It was not that she was frightened—she was pretty sure she faced no personal danger—but to accuse *anyone* of murder was a horrible thing, let alone someone who . . .

Jessica came up to a door and stopped. She drew a deep breath, then tapped on it. The name on the door was Dr. Edmund Gerard.

A voice called, "Come in."

Jessica entered. Amelia looked up from her desk with a smile. Without any preliminaries, Jessica asked abruptly, "Amelia, is the Dean in?"

"No, he's not."

Jessica didn't know whether to be glad or sorry. "Where is he, do you know?"

"Not exactly, right now. Is it important?"

"Yes," Jessica said. "Very important."

Amelia eyed her keenly. "Mrs. Fletcher, you don't look at all well."

"I don't *feel* well," Jessica said. She managed a weak smile. "Do you mind if I sit down?"

"Of course not." She got to her feet. "Can I get you some water?"

"No, I'll be all right if I can just sit here for a moment."

"What exactly is the trouble?" Amelia sat down again slowly.

Jessica looked at her. She hesitated. Then she gave her a helpless shrug. "It's no good. I have to tell somebody." She moistened her lips. "Amelia, the police believe Edmund killed Lila Schroeder."

Amelia went white. "You—you can't be serious."

Jessica nodded dumbly.

"But why—I mean what . . . ?" She trailed off. "But he hardly knew her."

"Yes, he did," Jessica said. "He's been seeing her secretly for a couple of months."

Amelia gave a gasp. "I don't believe it!"

"I'm afraid it's true. He used to take her to that place outside of town —the Lumberjack Inn. You know?"

Amelia shook her head blankly.

"Oh, surely you must," Jessica insisted.

"I tell you I've never heard of it!" She spoke sharply.

"How odd." Jessica's tone was suddenly cold.

"What do you mean?"

"Well, you pay Edmund's credit card bills, don't you? It was what you were doing the first day I met you. And you check them all very carefully."

"So?" Amelia's voice had taken on a higher pitch.

"So I know for a fact that the first couple of times he went there he paid by credit card. You couldn't have missed those bills. Edmund told me no one knew he took Lila there. But you did."

"No—I—you're wrong," Amelia said vehemently.

"You're the only one who *could* have known, Amelia," Jessica said quietly. "When you came across those bills, you could probably tell from their totals that they covered dinner for two. And you must have realized Edmund was seeing another woman surreptitiously; after all, if the thing was aboveboard, why should he take his guest all that way out of town, at least two times? I think you became obsessed with discovering who this woman was. So much so that you started following Edmund around to try to find out. One night you followed when he took the girl out to the Lumberjack again. And you followed them back to Seattle afterward. Perhaps you still hadn't got close enough to identify her; so when Edmund and she separated, you followed her cab. Then when she got out and started crossing the road, you tried to run her down." She paused. "I'm right, aren't I?"

Amelia said nothing. She seemed dazed, bemused, almost hypnotized by Jessica's low-level voice and steady gaze.

Jessica waited for several seconds, then continued remorselessly. "You missed on that occasion. But you had at last seen her face and knew who she was. You were horrified. That Edmund should take up with an empty-headed little tramp like Lila Schroeder . . . and you were eaten up with jealousy. You started following Lila around instead of Edmund. You knew you had to get rid of her, not only for your own sake, but for Edmund's: you couldn't let her mess up his life as she had other men's. It was almost a duty to save him. You only had to wait for the right opportunity. And it came the other night when she drove out to the docks. Alone. You probably thought she was going to meet Edmund. You followed her into the warehouse. When she heard you coming, she no doubt thought you were me. She came toward you—and you struck at her with that longshoreman's hook. Then you heard my taxi approaching, ran to your own car and got away just before I arrived."

Again she stopped. Amelia was still staring speechlessly at her. Her eyes were wild; guilt was written all over her face. Jessica realized the tremendous pressure the woman was under, the almost irresistible urge to talk—to tell someone about her crimes. Yet, still she resisted. Jessica knew that if she came through this crisis, her resolve would be strengthened and she would probably never confess. And, with the evidence against her as flimsy as it was, she might never even come to trial.

Jessica called on all the persuasiveness of her command. She spoke softly but compellingly. "Amelia, you did all this for Edmund. Don't let him suffer now because of it. Tell the truth. Think how much better you'll feel after. No more lies. No more concealment. . . ."

For long seconds she waited. The muscles of Amelia's face were twitching. And then suddenly it all came bursting out.

"I didn't plan it," she gasped. "I didn't go there meaning to kill her. I thought she'd gone to meet Edmund again. I had to know. I followed her into the warehouse and she spotted me. She guessed why I was there. She started to laugh—jeer at me. She called me a frustrated old maid. She said she was going to tell Edmund. I couldn't take it. I snatched up that hook thing and lashed out at her. She . . . she stopped laughing."

She stared pleadingly at Jessica. "If I'd planned to kill her, I'd have taken a weapon with me, wouldn't I? I wouldn't have relied on finding something just lying around."

Jessica didn't answer. She felt physically and mentally drained. She raised her voice.

"You can come in now, Lieutenant."

The door, which she'd left an inch ajar behind her, swung wide open and Andrews and his sergeant stood there.

Amelia looked at them. She didn't seem at all surprised to see them. "I suppose you want me to come with you?" she asked quietly.

"If you please, ma'am. Read her her rights, Lou."

The sergeant took a card from his pocket and read out the familiar words. When he'd finished, Amelia whispered, "I understand. My coat, please."

She pointed to the back of the door. Andrews turned away to get it, and as he did so Edmund pushed his way into the room and between the two policemen. His face was flushed. He stared at Amelia.

"You heard?" asked Amelia.

He nodded. "They made me wait outside. Amelia—*why?*"

"Because I loved you."

He shook his head helplessly. "I had no idea."

"No." Her voice was bitter. "None at all. Even after all these years. Even after Gwen died. I was an adjunct to your life—only a little more useful than a piece of office furniture."

"That's not true. I valued your friendship deeply."

"So you took up with that girl."

"Amelia, Lila meant nothing to me. It was a passing thing. I could have handled it."

Andrews held out Amelia's coat and she slipped into it. She stared coolly at Edmund.

"Are you sure?" she said. Then she added: "And what about her?" She nodded at Jessica.

"There's nothing like that between Jessica and me," he said.

"So she told me. And for a while I believed her. Then I heard you talking outside that door the other day: saying you wanted a serious talk with her; arranging for her to come and cook dinner at your house. I asked you to have dinner at my place twice after Gwen died. Or, I said, I'd come to you. You turned me down."

"So for that reason you lured her to the English building by pretending to be Todd Lowery and pushed her down the stairs?" He was incredulous.

Amelia didn't answer. After a moment Andrews touched her on the shoulder. "Let's go."

The sergeant led the way out of the room. Without a backward glance, Amelia followed. Andrews went last, closing the door behind him. Three seconds later he opened it again.

"Mrs. Fletcher?"

She glanced up wearily. "Yes?"

"Thanks."

He closed the door a second time. Edmund and Jessica remained in silence—he standing, she sitting—for about half a minute. Then he stepped across to her.

"Jess, you look dead beat."

She raised her face. There were tears in her eyes. She spoke with intensity.

"Edmund, I hate this, I hate it!"

"It is pretty horrible."

"People mustn't be allowed to get away with it," she said. "Because they're unhappy or frightened or worried or jealous or can't control their tempers, they mustn't be allowed to get away with murder. I know that. Yet every time, the temptation to let them—just to keep quiet—is tremendous. I feel so cruel."

He smiled. "You, cruel? You're joking, of course."

"I don't feel like joking." Then she took a deep breath. "Anyway, let's not talk about it anymore. At least for now."

She got to her feet. "Edmund, will you come to the supermarket with me? If I'm going to cook you that meal tonight, there are things to buy. I started earlier, but I had to break off."

He frowned. "Supermarket? Is that one of those places where you help yourself to goods from the shelves?" Then, as she stared at him, he smiled again. "Jessica, I live in an academic ivory tower, remember? I wouldn't know about such things."

# Chapter Ten

JESSICA sat reading in the airport departure lounge, waiting for her flight to Kentucky to be called. Edmund, who had a full day's engagements, had been unable to come and see her off. She was not sorry, because she preferred not to be waved off at railroad stations and airports. They had said their goodbyes the previous evening, after she had at last prepared for him his home-cooked dinner.

"Jessica, I've caught you," a voice said breathlessly.

Startled, she looked up. Standing smiling down at her was David.

"I phoned the hotel and they told me what plane you were catching. I thought I wouldn't make it."

She looked up at the clock. "I have just ten minutes."

"Fancy leaving without giving me a chance to say a proper thank-you."

"For what?"

"Without you I might have been convicted of murder."

"Oh, I doubt that."

He sat down next to her. "Jessica, we haven't much time, so can we cut out the polite repartee? You know how I feel about you."

"No, I don't; and I'm not sure I want to."

"Well, the truth is that you're a fascinating woman and I'm enormously attracted to you."

"The way you were attracted to Alison Brevard?" she asked.

He looked hurt. "Oh, that's not fair! I've explained how things were between Alison and me."

"And the others?"

"What others?" His expression was blank.

"David, stop pretending."

He shrugged. "All right, there've been a couple of others. Look, I can't help it, but I find myself attracted to mature women, particularly if they're bright and funny—"

"And rich?"

He flushed. "That has nothing to do with it. The most important thing is intelligent conversation. And I like a woman I can learn from. I mean, take the way you've opened my eyes about crime fiction: it's a whole new interest for me now."

He put his hand on hers. "Jessica, I've read all your books in a week. I'm crazy about them. I'd just love to be involved with your work."

"As my typist?"

He spread his hands. "Sure! You know I'm good. But I'd hope not to be exclusively a typist, for always. Jessica, I'm sure there are dozens of ways I could be useful to you."

She regarded him appraisingly. "Well," she said, "I'll tell you what I do lack: somebody I can try my ideas out on before I even start writing. There's nobody in Cabot Cove whose literary judgment I can really rely on."

He grinned. "Well, I'd be perfect for that. I'm a good judge of literature."

"Very well," she said slowly, "let's have a test. Let me try out a scenario on you. Tell me what you think of it."

"New?"

"Yes."

"Great. But is there time?"

"Oh, it'll only take a few minutes. Right, let me see. The principal character of this story is a young man. Very good-looking. Talented. Charming. And highly attractive to women."

"Lucky guy."

"Older women especially find him almost irresistible. He soon learns how to use this . . . this gift. There are many lonely, wealthy older women around; and being of an unscrupulous nature, he exploits this situation for all it's worth. Such women are usually generous, and the young man starts doing pretty well for himself. But not quite well enough. For our protagonist is greedy.

"Now, he is a student journalist and spends a lot of time at the courthouse, reporting cases, interviewing prisoners. In this way he meets a man who is shortly to be paroled after serving a term for burglary. And he gets a brilliant idea. He cultivates the acquaintance of this man—let's call him Teddy Briggs—and finds out all he can about him. He learns that Briggs is insecure, slightly neurotic, has a tendency to panic in an emergency and to use violence. But his technique as a burglar is first-class. And he's extremely loyal to his associates. It's a perfect setup, and eventually the two go into partnership. Our charming young man cases the homes of his wealthy lady friends—finds out what valuables they keep there, their safe combinations, details of security devices installed. Perhaps our protagonist is even able to make impressions of their front door keys. Then, on a particular evening he takes the lady for a long night out—out of town. When she returns in the early hours she finds her home stripped.

"This extremely lucrative racket continues for some months. The ladies don't suspect our young charmer of involvement—or, if they do, they keep quiet about it. Most of them are rather embarrassed about their friendship with a younger man and so don't tell the police whom they were out with on the night of the crime. Also, they don't talk about the relationship to their friends—and he's thus able to string several women along at the same time.

"However, after a while things start to go wrong. He takes up with a woman—we'll call her Alice—who isn't embarrassed by the relationship. She talks about it. She even pins his photo up in her apartment. Moreover, she's clinging: she demands more and more of his time. Worst of all, she's an alcoholic. She becomes a real pest—and a potential threat. Because she makes it clear that, in spite of her infatuation with him, she doesn't really trust the young man. He knows he can't afford to take any risks where she's concerned. At the same time Briggs is harassing him—keeps demanding the information he needs to burglarize Alice's apartment. The young man begins to get desperate. He wants to be rid of both Briggs and Alice. But how?

"Then he has an idea. Briggs has used violence in the past. The young man could never use violence himself. But he has no objection to others using it. He couldn't actually organize it or order it. But with this scheme he doesn't have to. All he has to do is give Briggs the information he needs about Alice's apartment, arrange a date with Alice one evening, notify Briggs—but then not turn up for the date.

"Of course, it's a hit-and-miss plan. He doesn't know what will happen. Perhaps nothing. But it's likely Alice will go home early and catch Briggs in the act. Then . . . who knows? She might call the police and Briggs might be arrested. Or Briggs might kill her. It's just possible Briggs will kill her *and* be arrested. So there's a fair chance our young man will get either Alice or Briggs off his back—perhaps even both of them. Anyway, he's a gambler. It's worth a try. And the beauty of it is that he doesn't have to do anything, just stay at home studying and leave the outcome to fate.

"Well, his plan works—to an extent. Briggs does kill Alice. But he gets away. However, his nerve is broken and he has to lie low for a bit. No more jobs. Our young man thinks his troubles are over. The one possibility, though, which in his conceit had not occurred to him, was that he himself would be suspected of Alice's murder . . ."

Throughout this recital David had remained perfectly silent and still. His eyes were fixed on Jessica's face. The only signs of emotion were some beads of sweat on his upper lip. And his body was tense.

"Well, what do you think?" she asked.

He made a clearly conscious effort to relax. He smiled. But it was a travesty of his old smile.

"Fascinating," he said. "Though a little farfetched, don't you think?"

Jessica shrugged. "Perhaps. Of course, it's all merely a product of my imagination." She cocked her head. "Ah, that's my flight being called."

She picked up her purse from the seat and her attaché case from the floor and got to her feet.

"Well, goodbye, David." She started to turn away.

"Jessica!"

She stopped. "Yes?"

"What happens to the young man?"

"I don't know, David. You decide."

And Jessica walked briskly away in the direction of the departure gate.

# Chapter Eleven

ABBY Freestone's compact foreign car drew to a halt outside the big iron gate. Jessica, in the passenger seat, expected her cousin to get out, or at least sound the horn, but for about five seconds Abby just remained behind the wheel. Then the gate slowly opened. It did not swing wide, but slid back like an elevator door, with a rumbling of rollers on metal tracks. Abby drove through the gateway, raising a hand in acknowledgment as she did so.

Jessica looked sideways at her in bewilderment. "Who did you wave to?"

"Barnes, the security guard. Or his assistant."

"I didn't see him."

Abby laughed and stopped the car. "Look back—out the window."

Jessica did as instructed, craning her head around. "I still don't see anyone."

"Have a look up that tree to the right of the gate."

Jessica squinted upward. Through the foliage her eyes spotted something black and angular. "Is that a camera?" she asked.

"That's right. Closed-circuit TV. Sometimes one has to use the intercom to call up the security room; but if Barnes is watching his monitor, it's usually not necessary."

Jessica drew her head back into the car. "Well, goodness me."

"Surely you've seen security cameras before?" Abby got the car moving again.

"Yes, of course—in department stores, banks, offices, even apartment buildings in big cities. Here it seems wrong somehow. Out of place."

She gestured around. The wide graveled drive was curving between large close-cropped paddocks enclosed by immaculate white fencing. Elegant, glossy-coated horses grazed or frisked. The sun shone brilliantly. Birds sang. Somewhere in the distance a dog was barking. It was all very rural and peaceful.

Abby gave a nod. "I know what you mean. But believe me, it's very necessary here."

Before Jessica could ask her what she meant, the car rounded a clump of trees and Abby announced: "Langley Manor. What do you think of it?"

The house gleamed a vivid white in the afternoon sun. It was colonnaded and seemed to have spread itself luxuriously over the ground with a confidence born in an earlier age's sense of limitless space and limitless money.

"It's lovely," Jessica said softly.

Abby drove around the back of the house and through a stable yard lined by stalls; over the closed lower half-doors, the heads of several more horses eyed them curiously.

Abby drew up in front of a snug-looking, picturesque little cottage beyond the stable yard and they both got out. Abby marched to the rear of the car, opened the trunk and heaved out the larger of Jessica's suitcases.

"Oh, Abby," Jessica said hastily, "that's too heavy!" But her cousin ignored her.

"Bosh," she said cheerfully. "I'm the hearty, outdoor member of the family, remember? You're the indoor, bookish type. You take the little one."

"I'm nothing of the sort," Jessica told her indignantly. "I'll have you know I jog every day at home—and cycle everywhere."

But Abby had disappeared into the house. Jessica picked up the smaller case and followed.

A moment later she was looking with pleasure around the low-ceilinged living room of the cottage. There was a big open fireplace, cretonne covers on the easy chairs, chintz drapes at the windows, horse brasses on the walls. The table and the dining chairs were of dark polished mahogany.

"It looks very English, Abby," she said.

"Well, I've tried to make it a home away from home. However olde-worlde it may be, it's got all modern conveniences, even indoor plumbing. Come on, I'll show you your room, then you can freshen up while I make some tea."

Fifteen minutes later Jessica was seated deep in one of the comfortable old easy chairs, gratefully sipping a cup of steaming Earl Grey and nibbling at a cake. Abby poured herself a cup, sat down opposite, kicked off her shoes and tucked her legs up under her. She drank some tea and gave a sigh. "Ah, I needed that!"

Jessica regarded her with an expression of slightly amused affection. In spite of her forty years and athletic build, there was still something very schoolgirlish about Abigail Freestone. Her round, rosy-cheeked, well-scrubbed face, apparently completely devoid of makeup, glowed with health. Her shiny light brown hair was tied back in a loose bun. She was wearing a shirt, a sleeveless pullover and corduroy trousers. She looked utterly relaxed and contented.

"Abby," Jessica said, "I feel very guilty. Ever since you met me at the airport, I seem to have been talking about myself—my books, my adventures. I've hardly asked a thing about you."

"But your life is so much more exciting than mine, Jess. I was dying to hear about everything."

"Well, I want to hear about you now. I must say you look very well and happy."

"Oh, I am. This job's a dream come true. Denton gives me a completely free hand with the horses. And the facilities are super."

"How did you happen to land the job?"

"I met Denton years ago when he came to England as an official with the American show-jumping team. Then about a year ago I had this letter, out of the blue, asking me to take over the training of his horses. I was staggered. Of course I jumped at it. Oh, Jess, he's a marvelous man. He doesn't treat me like an employee at all: just like—" She broke off.

"One of the family?" Jessica finished.

"No, not really. Better."

Jessica raised her eyebrows. "Really? Doesn't he treat his family well?"

"My dear, it's not his fault. They're awful, they really are. They've got no interest in the stables or the estate. If you ask me, they're just waiting for him to die so they can sell everything and carve up the loot."

Abby's eyes flashed. Her expression was suddenly angry. Jessica surveyed her thoughtfully. Then Abby looked a little abashed.

"Perhaps I'm being a bit hard. I don't suppose they actually *want* him to die. But they can't wait to get their hands on the dough."

"Who do *they* consist of?" Jessica asked.

"Well, there's Spenser. He's the son. About my age, or a bit younger. He's one of these sharp operators—only interested in the fast buck. Always seems to be involved in some scheme I can't understand, but which definitely sounds shady. At the moment he's in some sort of PR work, I think—lobbying on behalf of one of those Arab organizations. Denton says they're nothing but terrorists. Spenser's got a lot of charm when he wants it, but it's all quite spurious. I think he's just a glorified con man. He really ought to have been a Mississippi riverboat cardsharp about a hundred years ago."

Jessica smiled. "Right, that's Spenser very succinctly summed up. Who else is there?"

"Two daughters. Morgana and Trish."

Jessica frowned. "Trish Langley. That seems to ring a bell."

Abby nodded meaningfully. "The Hollingsworth case. Trish was the other woman."

"Oh, of course." Jessica remembered the acrimonious and highly publicized divorce of the multimillionaire Jeremy Hollingsworth and his high-society wife several years earlier.

"Hollingsworth dropped her like a hotcake afterwards," Abby went on, "and according to her, she didn't get a penny out of him. She still looks on herself as one of the smart set, though: it's casinos and nightclubs half the year, running through her allowance; and then home the other half, sucking up to Daddy and hoping to cadge another few thousand dollars to keep her in strong liquor and weak men. She throws herself into everything when she's home—even comes hunting. But you should see the expression of utter boredom on her face sometimes!"

Abby helped herself to a cake from a plate on a low table between them and bit into it hungrily.

"And the other daughter . . . Morgana, did you say?"

Abby nodded, swallowed a lump of cake, and swigged some tea. Then she said, "Mrs. Morgana Langley-Cramer. She's divorced. Morgana's harmless enough, but quite loopy."

"Oh, in what way?"

"She's into all that supernatural stuff: spiritualism, fortune-telling, astrology—you know."

"Yes, I know," Jessica said, "I've met people like that."

"She just floats around in a sort of daze, mumbling about astral projection and the great pyramid—all that sort of thing. Though I sometimes get the impression she may be just a little more astute than she seems on the surface. Not that Echo seems to think so; she treats Morgana with a kind of pitying condescension."

Jessica's eyes widened. "Who or what is Echo?"

"Morgana's daughter."

"You did say *Echo?*"

"Yes; priceless, isn't it?"

"Does she keep coming back?"

Abby gave a chortle. "She does, actually. But only because her mother insists: she's the only grandchild and Morgana won't let her risk getting cut out of the will. She's a punk."

Jessica laughed. "Really?"

"Yes, though at the moment she's going through a conservative phase: she's got her hair cut very short and dyed snow-white, not green or mauve this time. And she hasn't got a safety pin through her nose, or anything."

"That must be a relief to everyone."

"Actually, I rather like Echo," Abby said. "She's honest; doesn't attempt to disguise her boredom or her contempt for her Aunt Trish and Uncle Spenser. And, believe it or not, she has a very good seat on a horse. In the blood, I suppose. I think she could be a fine rider—if she could just forget that horses typify all the conventional upper-class values she despises."

"You're becoming quite a psychologist, Abby."

Abby looked rather embarrassed. "Gosh, no. I understand horses and dogs better than people, really. You'll probably tell me I'm quite wrong about them all when you meet them."

"They're all here now, are they?"

"Yes, they're not often all present at the same time, but it's a special occasion on Thursday. Denton's birthday. There's going to be a meet here to celebrate it."

"A meet of the hunt?"

"Yes, there'll be the traditional hunt breakfast first, complete with a punch bowl."

"Should be fun," Jessica said. "Perhaps they'll be able to use the television cameras to locate the fox."

"Oh, Jess, you must say that to Denton. He'll love it."

"I've been meaning to ask you: what did you mean when you said all this security was very necessary here?"

"The paintings, of course."

"Oh, does Denton have a collection?"

"My dear, they're valued at over three million dollars."

"Indeed?" Jessica looked impressed.

"Are you surprised? I thought you realized he's very well off."

"Oh, I did. I just didn't associate him with art treasures."

"Now, don't get it wrong, Jess. There's none of this modern abstract nonsense. The pictures are good old-fashioned country scenes: animals, birds, horses. But first-class. All the experts say so."

"I see: Landseer, Munnings, people like that?"

"Very probably."

Jessica concealed a smile.

"Anyway," Abby continued, "you'll see them all tonight and be able to judge for yourself."

*"Tonight?"* Jessica stared.

"Yes. Denton's invited us both over to dinner. Didn't I tell you?"

"No, you did not." Jessica spoke a trifle grimly.

"Sorry." Abby sounded quite unapologetic. "Of course, I've been boasting so much about my cousin, the famous author, and he's longing to meet you. So's Tom and—"

Jessica interrupted. "Whoa! Tom?"

"Tom Cassidy. Oh, you'll love him. He's Denton's oldest friend. Farms six hundred acres next door. Then again, Mr. Boswell says he's got some ideas for you—real-life cases he's come across that he says would make super mystery stories."

Jessica raised a hand. She spoke ominously. "And who is Mr. Boswell?"

"Oh, Marcus Boswell—Denton's lawyer."

Jessica closed her eyes. "Abby," she asked quietly, "are all these people coming to meet me?"

"I don't know what you mean by *all:* only Tom and Mr. Boswell are coming specially. The others would be there anyway."

"I'm guest of honor, aren't I?" Jessica's tone was exasperated.

"It's not going to be anything as formal as that," Abby said defensively.

"But that's what it amounts to?"

Abby wriggled awkwardly. "Well . . . sort of—"

"Oh, really, Abby! I came here to get away from all that sort of thing."

"I say, do you mind awfully? I'm sorry, Jess. Denton has his heart set on it. There are only going to be nine of us. And it's given me a lot of clout with Spense and Trish, having a famous cousin. Until now they've looked on me as just a country bumpkin."

Jessica relented. She laughed. "No, I don't really mind, Abby. I suppose it's flattering. It's just that I could have done with a day or two to rest up and settle in before going on display."

"All right, then, I'll ask Denton to put it off for a bit."

"No, no, I wouldn't hear of it. If I could just lie down for an hour or so first? I always find air travel so exhausting, and I don't think I've completely recovered from that fall I told you about."

"Yes, you do that. I've got to go and look at a couple of the horses anyway." She got to her feet. "We'll get a jolly good blowout up at the big house, anyway. Much better than I could knock up in my little kitchen. So count your blessings, old girl."

# Chapter Twelve

"WELL, there you are, Mrs. Fletcher, that's about the lot. What do you think?"

Denton Langley spoke with just the faintest tone of pride.

"I'm very impressed indeed, Mr. Langley," Jessica said.

And it was true. The paintings covered nearly every spare foot of wall space in the hallway and main staircase of Langley Manor. They included two Landseers, a small, early Constable and a Whistler, as well as a host of works by somewhat lesser artists, which were nonetheless of first-rate quality.

"Well, I don't claim to be an expert on art," Langley said, "but I do know these fellows' *subjects*. And the one thing they have in common is that they've gotten their subjects just right. That's my criterion. And the art experts seem to agree with me."

"I'm sure one could spend hours studying them with great pleasure."

"Well, feel free to stop by anytime and browse as long as you're here."

"Why, thank you, Mr. Langley."

"And call me Denton, please. Nothing makes a man of my age forget his years like hearing a young woman call him by his first name."

"And nothing makes a woman of my age forget her years like hearing a man call her young."

"You're young to me, my dear. I bet I could give you twenty-five years."

"Oh, I'm sure that's not true."

"How old do you think I am?"

"Well, really, I couldn't say." Jessica was a little flustered.

"Eighty this week."

She gazed at the tall, soldierly figure. Denton Langley's hair was white, but his face was unlined and his eyes bright. His back was ramrod straight, and he moved with a speed and suppleness that would have done credit to a man of sixty.

"I find that hard to believe," she said truthfully.

He looked pleased. "You must spend as much time as you can here, Mrs. Fletcher."

"Jessica."

"Well, Jessica, if you've seen enough of these for now, let's go and have a drink."

He gave her his arm and escorted her across the great square hallway and into the beautifully proportioned and elegantly finished living room. Here Abby was standing, clutching a glass and chatting somewhat uneasily with a man whom Jessica had already met briefly before Denton had swept her off on a tour of his art collection. This was her host's son, Spenser.

As she approached him now, Jessica appreciated afresh the aptness of Abby's likening him to a Mississippi cardsharp. Spenser Langley was as tall as his father, but less erect and somehow softer looking. His face was pale, high cheek-boned, and his light blue eyes had a transparent quality. He wore a strangely old-fashioned narrow mustache. His movements were slow and graceful. His smile came quick and often.

"Ah, tour over, Mrs. Fletcher?" he asked.

"For the moment."

"What can I get you to drink?"

"Could I have a dry sherry?"

"Coming up."

He glided over to a drinks cabinet against one wall. Abby looked slightly relieved, and relaxed a little.

Denton addressed Jessica. "I must admit I'm not much of a literary man, but Abby loaned me a couple of yours, and I enjoyed 'em no end."

"Thank you, sir."

"Tell me one thing." Jessica braced herself. "How on earth do you think up—?"

But fortunately, at that moment there was an interruption. Three women entered the room through the big double doors at the far end.

Denton turned toward them. "Ah, girls, come and meet our guest of honor."

The three advanced across the expanse of carpet. The first was about thirty. She was petite, slim and very attractive, with long blonde hair that gave no indication of being dyed. She had the same high cheekbones as Spenser. But her movements were quick and jerky, and her eyes, also blue, were constantly on the move, seeming never to alight on anything for more than a second.

"My daughter Trish," Denton said.

Trish's face lit up—just too much. "Darling," she drawled, "it's wonderful to meet you at last! I just adore your gorgeous little books."

She held out a rather clawlike hand with bloodred nails. Jessica took it somewhat gingerly. But she'd hardly touched it before Trish was turning and saying to her brother, who had just approached: "Spense, give me a big, big martini. At least a treble."

Spenser handed Jessica a glass of sherry, glancing sardonically at his sister as he did so. "Thought you said *big,* Trish. Surely you don't consider a mere treble big?"

She made a face at him. "Oh, funny, funny. Just start pouring and shut up."

Meanwhile Denton was saying, "And this is my elder daughter, Morgana."

A shorter woman pushed herself close up to Jessica and peered at her out of narrowed eyes. She had a pleasant, good-natured, rather stupid face. Her makeup was carelessly applied, and her hair a mass of untidy curls. Cheap-looking, chunky jewelry dripped from her: heavy drop earrings in the form of signs of the zodiac, a big scarab brooch, several charm bracelets and about eight rings—also bearing zodiac emblems. She gripped Jessica's hand tightly, pressing the rings painfully into her flesh. She gave a beatific smile, her gaze shifting to a spot about six inches above Jessica's right shoulder. "You have a very strong aura, my dear," she said.

Jessica smiled weakly. "Oh, have I? That's good."

Morgana cocked her head, as though listening, before continuing. "Running Elk says you are a true medium."

Jessica thought rapidly. "Your spirit guide?" she hazarded.

Morgana looked pleased. "Precisely. He's right behind you. You can hear him?"

Resisting a strong impulse to glance over her shoulder, Jessica said, "I'm afraid not."

"You will. Give it time. Don't worry."

"I'm not worrying." Jessica told her.

Morgana peered again into Jessica's face. "Gemini?" she asked abruptly.

"Er, actually, no. I'm—"

Morgana cut in. "Don't tell me. Let me think." She closed her eyes.

For the last few seconds, Denton had been making impatient harrumphing noises under his breath; he sounded rather like an anxious horse. Now he said hastily, "And this is my granddaughter, Echo."

He almost brushed Morgana to one side and tried to usher forward the girl who'd been standing in the background. But Echo didn't budge. She just glowered.

"How do you do?" Jessica said brightly.

"Hi." Still Echo didn't smile. With her short, spiky white hair, she had affected an almost equally white pancake makeup, and big scarlet lips. But at least she had no abstract designs painted on her cheeks, and her dress was quite plain, almost drab.

Jessica held out her hand, virtually forcing the girl to step forward and take it. Echo cast a glance at her mother, who had moved away to join Spenser and Trish. She then said defiantly, "Mother's not insane."

"Echo!" Denton spoke sharply.

"I never assumed she was," Jessica assured her.

"Oh, but all that about Running Elk—you must have thought—"

"If your mother can see a Red Indian standing behind me, who am I to say there's no one there?"

A glimmer of a smile started on Echo's face, but just then there came another interruption as the butler from the doorway announced: "Mr. Cassidy!"

A big, lumbering, jovial-looking man in his sixties bustled across the room. He had a red face and thinning sandy hair.

"Ah, Tom," said Denton in a relieved voice.

Tom Cassidy grinned. "Hi, Dent."

"Tom, meet the famous Jessica Fletcher."

Tom stuck out a huge brown hand and enveloped Jessica's in it. "So you're little Abby's cousin," he said. "We've sure heard a lot about you."

He was as tall as the Langley men, but broader in the shoulders, and altogether beefier. He still had a look of sheer physical strength about him. Jessica found herself wondering if all the men in this part of the world were tall.

The question was answered a few minutes later when Marcus Boswell, the lawyer, was shown into the room. He was a short, stocky, dapper man with small regular features, slicked-down black hair, and the air of somehow being busy even when making small talk over a cocktail.

It was after they'd all been doing this for a further fifteen minutes that the butler announced dinner and they trooped into the dining room.

The meal, as Abby had forecast, was substantial and good. Jessica noticed that, for one so spiritually-minded, Morgana had a surprisingly healthy appetite; that Echo merely played with her food; and that Trish ate little more than her niece, but compensated for this by drinking at least eight glasses of wine during the meal. She also observed that Spenser seemed definitely nervous and looked to be worried about something.

After dinner they returned to the living room. They were chatting quietly over their coffee when they were interrupted by the sound from the hall of an eager and impatient barking.

"Oh, there's that damn dog!" Denton exclaimed. "Sorry. Robert'll shut him up in a moment. He's got to learn he can't come in when I have guests—especially eminent lady novelists."

"Oh, please don't keep him out on my account," Jessica said hastily.

Denton looked gratified. "You sure?"

"Quite sure. I like dogs."

"Oh, very well. Echo, my dear, will you let him in?"

Echo went toward the door. "Really, Father," Trish said testily, "he'll be jumping up all over everyone."

"Not now, he won't. Abby's been working on him."

Echo opened the door and the dog came in excitedly. He was a young bright-eyed beagle, about six months old. He went frisking across to Denton, whose eyes softened as he bent down to fondle the dog's head.

"Hello, Teddy, old boy, how are you?" he murmured.

Teddy gave a little yelp and wagged his tail hard.

"Come on, boy, meet a new friend," Denton said. He led the dog to Jessica's chair and said, "Sit."

Teddy sat in front of her. "Shake, boy," Denton ordered, and the dog raised his right front paw.

Jessica put out her hand and shook it solemnly. "How do you do, Teddy? I'm pleased to meet you."

Teddy gave another little *wuff.* Next he suddenly spun on his tail, ran to Marcus Boswell, briefly thrust a nose into his hand, scampered from him to Abby, looked at her, then sat up and begged.

Denton chuckled. "He wants a reward from his trainer. Here." He took a sugar lump from the bowl on the table and handed it to her. She fed it to the dog, who crunched it up with relish.

"I never thought he'd remember me," Marcus Boswell said. He sounded quite touched.

"Teddy was a present from Marcus after my old dog died last year," Denton explained to Jessica. He patted the dog's head.

"You've done wonders with him, Abby," Tom Cassidy told her.

She shrugged. "All by kindness. Actually, he's a remarkably intelligent dog and very easy to train."

Teddy obviously knew he was being talked about and thoroughly enjoyed being the center of attention. He gazed around the circle proudly, his tail thumping the floor. Jessica could have sworn he was smiling.

However, when the conversation became general again, he lay down with a disgusted air and went to sleep.

Tom Cassidy said, "Understand you'll be coming out with us Thursday, Mrs. Fletcher."

"Oh, I don't really think so," Jessica said diffidently.

Denton looked disappointed. "Come, come, Jessica; Abby told us you'd be sure to want to join in. Mustn't be modest, you know."

Jessica cast her cousin a withering look. "It's just that I haven't been in the saddle for so many years . . ."

"Oh, that's nothing. We'll soon get you back into the swing. Abby can put you up on one of the old mares tomorrow and take you hacking gently around the estate. In a day you'll be rarin' to go, and on Thursday you'll be leading the field over the fences."

"I'm afraid there's no chance of that, at all. If I trot sedately around at the back of the field, that'll be the extent of it."

He chuckled. "We'll see, we'll see." He glanced her up and down appreciatively. "I know a natural horsewoman when I see one."

"Let's hope the horse does, too," Jessica replied.

Jessica spent the next day quietly. She slept late, read for a while, and then watched her cousin schooling some of the horses. Abby introduced her to an elderly, placid mare called Doughnut (named from her having, as a foal, devoured a bag of them left carelessly lying around by a stable boy; it was a name that somehow suited her).

Jessica also made the acquaintance of the hitherto invisible Barnes, who proudly showed her his security room, with its bank of television screens, intercom system and row of buttons operating the various gates leading on to the estate. Later she met his assistant, a somewhat taciturn individual named Smedley.

Later in the afternoon Abby persuaded Jessica to don a riding habit (a number of spare outfits were kept around the place for visitors) and mount Doughnut. They then went for a quiet amble on horseback around the estate. It felt strange, after so many years, to be on a horse again, but she soon found herself regaining the feel of it.

At one stage they came upon Echo. She was sitting on the grass under a tree, smoking a cigarette. When she spotted them, she hastily thrust the cigarette down into the soil at the foot of the tree. Jessica frowned. That cigarette hadn't looked entirely normal. As a former high school teacher she was unfortunately all too proficient at recognizing marijuana. She wondered if it was her duty to tell someone. But whom? It would surely be pointless to inform Morgana. Besides, the girl wasn't a child. And

Jessica was sick of interfering in other people's lives. She would *not* let herself become a busybody.

Abby broke in on her thoughts. "Come on, let's try a canter."

"Oh no," Jessica said quickly. "Really, I don't think I'm quite—"

But Abby just reached over and gave Doughnut a slap on the flank. The mare broke into a canter and suddenly Jessica found herself clinging on for dear life.

# Chapter Thirteen

BY that evening, Jessica, though stiff and sore, was feeling much more confident on horseback; and was beginning to think that—provided she didn't try anything too spectacular in the jumping line—she might get through Thursday morning unscathed.

When the day actually came, much of this confidence seemed, however, to have deserted her. She was feeling quite nervous when, smartly attired in her riding habit, she walked over to the manor house for the traditional hunt breakfast. She was on her own, as Abby had been up and working since five-thirty.

Outside the house swarmed a hive of activity. People on horseback, on foot, even on bicycles, milled excitedly among the dozens of parked cars —mostly Cadillacs, Mercedes and Jaguars—which were parked everywhere. More were arriving all the time. Jessica went indoors.

The breakfast was being held in the fine, spacious ballroom, which was already crowded with guests. The tables were loaded with food and drink, including a huge punch bowl, and the complexions on some of the faces present indicated that quite a few stirrup cups had already been quaffed.

Jessica slipped in unobtrusively, looking about hopefully for a coffeepot. The first familiar face she spotted was that of Trish, who was standing very close to a thin, nervous-looking young man. She was clinging to his arm and smiling up at him. As Jessica watched, she whispered into his ear. He flushed, and she gave a raucous laugh that turned several heads in her direction.

A moment later the tall, elegant figure of Spenser elbowed his way unceremoniously through the crowd and addressed the young man. "Anthony, we're awfully sorry your wife couldn't make it today." Then, looking pointedly at his sister, he added: "Aren't we, Trish?"

Trish's eyes flashed. Then quietly, but in extremely impolite terms, she invited her brother to depart. Jessica could not hear the words, but the movement of the girl's lips clearly indicated the phrase used. An expression of disgust appeared on Spenser's face and he turned abruptly away.

Just then Jessica became aware that Echo had drifted up to her. "Hi," the girl said shortly.

Jessica was pleasantly surprised. Echo had until now shown not the slightest sign of wishing to be friendly. So she smiled more broadly than usual in response. "Good morning, my dear."

She was just reflecting that, with the punkish hairdo topping the strictly conservative riding gear, Denton's granddaughter certainly stood out from the crowd, when Echo jerked her head over her shoulder. "The pits, aren't they?" she said.

Jessica was startled. "Er, who—what—?" she began incoherently.

"Spense and Trish. My revered uncle and aunt."

Jessica frowned. "Whatever your personal opinion of them, Echo, you really shouldn't ask me to share it."

She was sorry the moment the words were out. They had sounded censorious and schoolmarmish. As a guest here, it was no business of hers to teach Echo manners. She should simply have ignored the remark.

Echo went slightly red, and for a moment Jessica thought she was going to give an angry retort. Then, plainly making an effort, she swallowed. "Sorry, don't mind me. Can I get you a drink or something?"

Determined to make amends, Jessica answered effusively. "That's very sweet of you. But what I'm really dying for is a cup of coffee."

"Oh, sure. Okay, wait here." She turned away, saying as she did so: "I remember how you take it."

Jessica eyed her back thoughtfully. She was remembering the cigarette she had seen Echo smoking. Had the girl suspected her of recognizing it for what it was? And was she now ingratiating herself, in the hope of stopping Jessica reporting the incident to Morgana or Denton? Jessica smiled. She had firmly decided to say nothing of what she'd seen. But it wouldn't do the girl any harm to sweat for a bit.

A moment later Echo returned with coffee. "Oh, thank you, my dear. You've saved my life." Jessica sipped gratefully at the steaming cup. The girl stood by a little awkwardly. She seemed unable to make small talk. Then she glanced up, over Jessica's shoulder, muttered, "Excuse me," and edged away.

The next second Jessica realized that it was the approach of Denton that had driven her off. He came up, beaming. "Good morning, Jessica. Enjoying yourself? Quite an occasion, isn't it?"

"Yes, it is. In more ways than one. May I give you my very best wishes on your birthday?"

"You may indeed."

"Abby says that's *all* I'm allowed to give."

"Correct. Some people wanted to make quite a thing of this—birthday cake, even a kind of presentation. But I put my foot down. At my age a birthday isn't anything to be particularly proud of. Or to be ashamed of either, of course. I told everybody I'd accept their good wishes privately, but if they gave me anything more substantial, or tried to make a formal speech, I'd turf them out." He chuckled. "I usually get my own way."

"I'm sure you do," Jessica replied.

"That's coffee you're drinking? How about some punch?"

"No, thank you. This'll be fine. As a matter of fact, I hadn't realized a hunt breakfast required so much of the other kind of liquid refreshment."

He gave a grunt. "Only way to get most of these milksops over the first fence." He took her by the elbow. "Come on, my dear. At least let's get you something to eat."


No more than fifteen minutes later the imposing figure of the Master of the Hunt strode in through the big double doors and announced stentorianly: "Ladies and gentlemen—to horse!"

There was an immediate movement. Jessica's heart sank a little. This was it. She just hoped she didn't make too big a fool of herself. She emptied the glass of punch, with which Denton had eventually persuaded her to finish off her breakfast, and followed the crowd outside.

She saw Abby, who was already mounted, and who beckoned and pointed to where a stable boy was holding the already saddled Doughnut. Jessica walked across and, aided by a leg-up from the boy, got into the saddle with greater ease than she would have thought possible a few days previously. She walked Doughnut across toward Abby, but had to rein in sharply as a riderless horse veered across her path. Then she saw that Trish was clinging to the animal's bridle. She was red-faced and muttering angrily to herself as she tried to control it. "Keep still, damn you!" she hissed.

She took a grab at the saddle with one hand and started to raise her left foot to the stirrup. Again the horse, sensing something wrong with the rider, blundered sideways and Trish nearly fell.

Abby slipped from her saddle, handed her reins to a bystander and ran across. She grabbed the bridle of Trish's mount. As she patted and soothed the beast, she said calmly, "You know, you shouldn't be riding in your condition. It's dangerous to the horse."

Trish ignored this. With Abby holding the horse's head, she made a great effort and managed to lift herself into the saddle.

Abby tried once more. "Trish, look, why don't you think again? It's—"

Trish shot her a dirty look. "Oh, clear off! Go kiss up to father—while you've got the chance."

Abby's mouth dropped indignantly. "Because the day he goes, honey," Trish continued bitingly, "so do you!" She emphasized the last words with three pokes toward Abby with her riding crop. Then, giving a vicious jerk on the reins, she virtually pulled the horse's head from Abby's grasp, spun it around, kicked her heels into its sides and cantered off, scattering people and dogs before her.

Abby stood staring after her, her face white. Then she strode back to her own horse and remounted. Jessica rode up to her. "Ignore her, my dear," she said quietly.

Abby looked at her. "You know, Jess, around here all the *real* beasts walk on two legs."

Before Jessica could reply Denton trotted up. He was on his regular mount, a steady and reliable old gray called Sawdust. Teddy, keeping himself aloof from the main pack of hounds, was frisking around the horse's feet.

"All ready, Jessica?" Denton asked.

"As ready as I'll ever be, Denton."

"I'll stick close to you."

"Oh no, I'll be at the rear. I'm sure you'll want to go ahead."

"There's no way I'll persuade this old nag to keep up with the pack. He hasn't broken out of a trot for years."

The Master of the Hunt came up to them. "We're ready to move, Denton."

"Right." Denton walked Sawdust over to an intercom mounted on a post near the front steps. He spoke into it. "Barnes? We're ready to go. Open the gate."

There was a momentary crackle, then the security guard's voice was heard. "Very good, sir."

The hunt set off down the drive.

Jessica soon found herself enjoying the ride very much. It was a glorious day. Doughnut was in fine fettle, and with Denton riding one side of her and Abby the other—ready to help in case of emergency—Jessica never felt in the slightest danger. Moreover, they were soon so far behind the pack and the leading riders that there was fortunately no possibility of her being in on the kill.

She did, however, feel a bit guilty about holding Abby back. Her cousin was a superb horsewoman and ought to have been leading the field. At last she said as much. Denton backed her up.

"Yes, catch up with the leaders, Abby. And, Jessica, I suspect you're holding yourself back, too. Why don't you both go ahead? It can't be much fun poking along with an old man."

"I assure you," Jessica said, "I am perfectly happy just where I am."

"And I wish you'd stop calling yourself old, Denton," Abby put in. "In every way that matters you are in your prime."

"Thank you, my dear. Ah, if I were thirty years younger . . ." He winked at Jessica as he spoke, but she could tell he was pleased.

At that moment they heard galloping hooves from behind, and a second later Echo flashed past them. They'd come upon her, dismounted and tightening a girth, some minutes before, and now she was obviously intent on catching the pack. Her face was flushed and her eyes sparkling. She raised a hand in salute as she came level, but she didn't pause or speak.

Denton gave a grunt as Echo drew ahead. "That granddaughter of mine looks almost normal—"

He never finished the sentence, for just then something seemed to come over Sawdust. It was as if the sight of Echo's horse had awakened in him some long-dormant instinct against being overtaken. He tossed his head and whinnied. His eyes rolled and his ears went back.

Denton said sharply, "Steady, boy!" He reached out a hand to stroke the animal's neck. But before he could do so, Sawdust launched into a gallop.

"Whoa!" Denton roared. He pulled on the reins. But the horse took no notice. He had the bit between his teeth and was going like a champion three-year-old. Teddy, who had stuck close to Denton from the start, gave a yelp of protest and chased after him.

Abby uttered a gasp. "What's come over him?" She gave her own mount a tap with her crop and set off in pursuit. Jessica took a deep breath, gave Doughnut a gentle kick, and the old mare broke into a lumbering canter. But she had no chance of catching up and Jessica was a fairly distant spectator of what ensued.

Sawdust was already rapidly closing on Echo's horse. The girl heard his hoofbeats, looked over her shoulder and then in amazement saw her grandfather shoot past.

Abby was only thirty yards behind. "What's he playing at?" Echo yelled to her. "Is he crazy?"

Abby didn't answer. She drew level, then overtook the girl. But she was making no inroad into Denton's lead.

At the far side of the field they were crossing was a stone wall, over six feet high. For a moment Abby was relieved at the sight of it, for it would surely bring Sawdust to a halt. She waited for the horse to slow. It was now less than forty yards from the wall. Still Sawdust was at full gallop. Thirty yards. Twenty. Abby's heart gave a leap of horror as she suddenly realized the horse was going to jump it.

It seemed that Denton had given up trying to stop the old gray. He was bending forward over his head, in the manner of one whispering encouragement to his mount.

Man and horse reached the wall. Sawdust gave a magnificent jump. He soared up—up—up. As he cleared it, with an inch to spare, Denton's voice rang out in a cry of triumph.

"Tallyho!"

Then he disappeared from Abby's sight. There came a horrible dull thud, and the sound of receding hoofbeats. But now they sounded different—lighter, as though the horse had been relieved of a burden.

Abby galloped up to the wall and reined in sharply. Fear at what she might see held her heart in an icy grip. She forced herself to edge her mount close to the wall and peer over. Then her stomach lurched. Denton Langley was sprawled on his back on the grass. He wasn't moving and his head was lying at an unnatural angle to his body. Teddy, who had somehow found a way over or through the wall, was licking his face and whining.

For what seemed a long, long time—but was in fact only seconds— Abby just sat numbly staring down. Then she was recalled to her senses by the sound of hooves as Echo came thundering up. Her face was white.

Abby spun around and held up her hand. "Stay there, Echo!"

The girl whispered, "Grandfather—is he . . . ?"

Abby just shook her head. Then, without getting down from her horse, she pulled herself directly on to the top of the wall and dropped down onto the grass on the far side. She knelt down by the inert figure, gently pushed the agitated and bewildered Teddy aside and felt Denton's heart. She was just getting heavily to her feet when Jessica's face appeared over the wall.

Their eyes met. Abby slowly shook her head.

"Oh no . . ." Jessica's voice was a whisper.

Abby clambered back over the wall. She looked up at Echo. "I'm afraid he's dead, my dear."

Echo's face was bewildered. She seemed unable to comprehend what had happened. It was, Jessica thought, probably the first time she had come in contact with violent—or perhaps any—death.

"Can't—can't we do anything?" Echo sounded suddenly like a very young child.

"Yes, you can." Jessica spoke briskly. "Ride back to the house and tell them what's happened. Get them to send for an ambulance. Are you up to breaking the news to your mother?"

The girl nodded silently.

Abby said suddenly, "Get somebody to call the sheriff as well, Echo."

There was something so strange about her voice that Jessica glanced at her sharply. But Echo didn't seem to notice anything different. She just said wonderingly, "He was really enjoying that last gallop. When he passed by me he was—he was laughing."

Then she abruptly wheeled her horse and galloped off like the wind.

Jessica and Abby were left. Abby's face was very white, and for a moment Jessica thought she was going to faint. She wished she had some brandy or whiskey, but the best she could do was say: "Abby, why don't you sit down? Come along, lean up against the wall."

She took her cousin's arm, but Abby shook it off. "I'm all right, Jess."

"As you wish." She paused before adding: "Abby, I'm so terribly sorry. I know how you felt about him."

Abby looked at her. There were tears in her eyes. "He was a wonderful man, Jess. I—I admired him so much."

"I know."

"And he was so unhappy underneath all the jollity and charm. Because of *them.*"

Jessica didn't need to ask whom she meant by *them.* Groping for words of comfort, she said, "Still, there are many worse ways to go. He died quickly and without lingering pain, doing what he liked to do best. He was enjoying himself: you heard what Echo said."

Abby nodded. "Of course—once he knew it was inevitable, he'd make the best of it. As soon as he realized that, whatever he did, Sawdust *was* going to take this wall—then he stopped trying to rein him in, but gave him every encouragement. It was brilliant. And I daresay he did relish the challenge of the jump—even though he must have known that he faced a terrible spill."

She took a handkerchief from the pocket of her jodhpurs and blew her nose hard.

Jessica said, "Abby, what made Sawdust take off like that? I thought he was so reliable."

"He was. He *is.* He will be again—if he hasn't injured himself and we get him back safely." She paused. "Once he gets the drug out of his system."

Jessica let her breath out slowly. "You're suggesting the horse was deliberately interfered with?"

"Yes."

"But, my dear, are you sure? I mean, couldn't it have been some sort of fit?"

Abby shook her head. "I've spent all my life around horses, Jess. I've never seen or heard of any natural cause that would have that effect. Just think of the speed he was going! I wouldn't have believed it possible. But I do know there are drugs that can have the most incredible effects. Normally, of course, they're given in small doses—just to improve an animal's form slightly, without it showing too much. But if a really big dose were given . . ." She trailed off.

"Abby, you know what you're suggesting is murder?" Jessica's voice was grave.

"Of course. Denton was an extremely rich man, Jess. He was also extremely fit. I believe his father lived to well over ninety. There was no reason why he shouldn't have done the same."

Her voice suddenly broke. "If—if it hadn't been for those greedy murdering swine." And she burst into tears.

Jessica put her arm around her. She didn't really know what to say.

# Chapter Fourteen

A KNOCK came at the door of Abby's cottage. Jessica went to answer it. A tall, rather gangling, fair-haired young man was standing outside. He tipped his hat.

"Afternoon, Miss Fletcher."

"Oh, good afternoon, Mr. Roxie. Do come in."

She'd met Will Roxie shortly after Denton's death and had taken to him immediately. He was slow-spoken and friendly, seemingly more like a farm boy than a law officer. Though she suspected he was considerably shrewder than he seemed on the surface.

She wished she could have felt the same about the sheriff, Gus Millard, a burly, bull-necked, red-faced man who gave every indication of being even less shrewd than he looked.

She led the way into the living room. "Abby, it's the deputy."

Abby came in from the kitchen. "Oh, hello, Will."

"Miss Freestone, thought I'd drop by and let you know we've received the vet's report on those tests you wanted us to do on Sawdust."

"And?"

"Negative."

She made a gesture of irritation. "Predictable. It was hours before they found him. Besides, there *are* drugs that leave no trace."

Will shrugged. "Maybe. But there's no evidence they were used in this case."

"Will, the horse bolted like a mad thing, straight at that wall. Yet now he's perfectly normal—go and see him. How do you account for that—unless he was drugged?"

"Maybe you were mistaken, Miss Freestone."

She stiffened. "What do you mean?"

"Suppose he didn't bolt? Suppose it was Mr. Langley had a rush of blood to the head? Maybe he got fed up with plodding along at the back of the field and decided to jump that wall."

"Oh, nonsense!"

"Miss Echo says he was laughing when he passed her. *You* said he called out *tallyho* as he took the jump."

"I'm not saying he wasn't enjoying himself by then. But first of all, he was startled. He tried to stop the horse. It wouldn't stop. Yet there'd been nothing to spook it. And it's one of the quietest and most reliable animals in the stables."

He shrugged again. "Well, I don't say you're not right. There's just no proof. So that's it."

"What does that mean, exactly? No further investigation?"

"Afraid not. Sheriff says it goes down as an accident. Of course, there'll be an inquest. But we won't be putting forward any evidence to suggest foul play. Sorry."

Abby uttered an explosive noise that sounded like *tscha!* Then: "He was murdered," she said.

"Bring us some evidence, Miss Abby, and we'll investigate it. *I'd* be pleased to. But with nothing to go on . . ." He didn't finish the sentence.

After Will had left, Abby sat down wearily. "It's all wrong, Jess. One of those three's getting away with murder."

Jessica didn't answer. Abby looked at her sharply. "You do agree? You saw the way that horse behaved."

"Oh yes."

"Then one of them must have done it. Perhaps all of them."

*"Must* is a strong word, Abby. I wouldn't want to commit myself to it yet. I agree it does look highly suspicious."

Abby suddenly reached out and put a hand on Jessica's arm.

"Jess—you investigate it!"

"Oh my dear, I couldn't possibly!"

"But why not? You've done it before."

"In those cases the circumstances were quite different. Either somebody I knew, a friend or relative, was a suspect. Or I was myself. Or I was asked by the police to help. Nothing like that applies here. I have no standing, no opportunity to investigate, nothing to go on—aside from your belief that Sawdust was doped. What would I do? Where would I start?"

"Talk to them."

"Who? The family? My dear, I'm *your* guest. Denton made me welcome up at the house. They haven't—and they're not about to. If I started snooping around, cross-examining them, they'd have me off this estate double-quick. You as well, I expect."

Abby slumped back in her chair. "They'll have me out anyway, as soon as they can legally do so."

"Not necessarily. Somebody's got to be in charge of the horses."

"Oh, they'll sell them off, for sure. None of them is really interested. Besides, I wouldn't want to work for a crook, a bitch, or a fool."

"I'm terribly sorry, my dear. You were so happy here."

"Oh well, all good things must come to an end. And I suppose I have a couple of weeks' grace, at least. We'll know the exact position after the reading of the will tomorrow. And you will stay on for a bit won't you?"

"Well, I was invited for a holiday."

"I know. It's just that there's not going to be much of a holiday atmosphere around the place. But I'd feel terrible on my own now."

"I'll stay as long as you want me to." She paused. "And Abby—if I get a chance to . . . well, talk, ask questions, find out things—then I'll do my best."

"Oh, thanks, Jess, that's super!"

"Now, it won't be what you call an investigation. Just conversation. So don't expect too much."

# Chapter Fifteen

IN the living room at Langley Manor, the atmosphere was both tense and gloomy. Spenser stood by the mantelpiece, nervously taking long, deep pulls on his cigarette. At the coffee table Morgana was gazing fixedly into the bottom of a teacup. Echo was staring moodily out the window. Trish, at the bar, was pouring herself a vodka. Abby and Tom Cassidy sat side by side on the sofa. Her face was pale and drawn, while he just looked sad. The only utterly relaxed figure in the room was Teddy, who was fast asleep on the hearth rug. Nobody was talking.

Spenser suddenly threw his cigarette half-smoked into the fireplace and walked across to the bar. He pointed to his sister's vodka glass. "Add some orange juice, and you can call that breakfast."

Trish didn't seem to hear this. "Where's Boswell?" she said impatiently. She looked at her wristwatch. "He should have been here three minutes ago."

"Perhaps he's kindly postponing the evil hour for us."

"Don't be silly, Spense." She spoke sharply. "It's going to be all right."

He raised his eyebrows. "Wish I was so confident."

"Oh dear. Oh my."

They turned to see Morgana stumbling toward them. She was carrying the teacup and was positively trembling.

Spenser gave a sigh. "What now, Morgana?"

She thrust the cup toward them. "The tea leaves! Look!"

They glanced into it. "So?" Trish said in a bored voice.

"But don't you see?"

"See *what?* Oh, Morgana—"

It was at that moment the front door bell chimed. Instantly every head swung to face the big double doors. Half a minute passed before they opened and the butler announced: "Mr. Boswell."

Marcus Boswell bustled into the room. He was wearing a suit of English tweed and was carrying a briefcase. He crossed to Spenser, holding out his hand.

"Spenser, please accept my heartfelt sympathy. This place won't be the same without Denton Langley."

"Thank you, Marcus. We are devastated by our loss."

Boswell made as if to shake hands with Trish and Morgana; met Trish's cool glare and Morgana's distant, troubled gaze, thought better of it, and gave a series of hurried nods to include everyone in the room. He cleared his throat nervously and said, "Ah . . . yes. Well, as Denton's attorney, I'd best get down to business."

"What a brilliant idea," Trish drawled.

Boswell flushed slightly. He put his briefcase on the table, opened it, and to everyone's surprise drew from it a videocassette.

"What's this?" Trish asked. "Home movies?"

"No, Trish, it's the latest in will technology."

"You mean *that* is father's will?" Spenser pointed to the cassette.

"In a sense. Not his legal will, of course—that's all down in written form." Boswell tapped the briefcase. Then he held up the cassette. "This is Denton's message to you all, in which he explains his testamentary dispositions. He recorded it just over a month ago."

"A voice from beyond the grave." Morgana spoke in hollow tones.

"Exactly. So, if I may . . . ?"

"Go ahead," Spenser told him.

Boswell crossed to the television set, switched it on, inserted the cassette into the VCR that stood next to it and pressed the Play button.

The screen flickered into life—and there before them was Denton Langley. Trish drew her breath in sharply, Morgana gave a little moan, Spenser muttered something. Tom Cassidy and Abby leaned forward in their seats.

Denton had been photographed sitting in his favorite chair. He looked relaxed and happy. One hand was holding a brandy glass; the other rested on the head of Teddy—the dog was draped over the arm of the chair. Denton raised the glass and smiled into the camera.

"Greetings, friends and kinfolk. I went to a lot of trouble getting this little show together for you all. Hope you enjoy it."

At the sound of Denton's voice, Teddy had sat up. He was staring at the screen, his head to one side. He was plainly puzzled. Abby momentarily wondered how far, with no sense of smell to guide him, he was able to recognize the image on the screen as his master. And what did he make of the strange dog sitting by him? Then she concentrated on the television screen.

"Since I know you're all there, waiting breathlessly," Denton said, "I think I'll prolong the suspense with a parting word to each of you. Spenser—it's too bad they keep blowing up your clients. But I never thought lobbying for Arab dictators was a decent job for you." He paused. "But then, what would be? I've never figured out an answer to that one."

Abby glanced at Spenser. His jaw had tightened, but otherwise he displayed no reaction at all.

"As for you, baby Trish," Denton went on, "you always were your mother's spoiled child. I'm glad she can't see you now—guzzling martinis the way you used to suck up root beer, and collecting men instead of dolls. Find a nicer hobby, honey. This one's not only unseemly. It's dangerous."

Abby cast a quick glance at Trish. The girl had gone pale and was chewing at her lip. Denton had stopped to take a sip of brandy. Now he resumed.

"Morgana. You're not a bad woman. But you've got no common sense. Come out of that fantasy world and face your problems."

Morgana was smiling gently and beatifically at the screen.

"Because you do have problems, you know," Denton continued. "Such as that mixed-up daughter of yours. Suggest you pay a bit more heed to her. She could use it."

He smiled. "You there, Echo? I expect so. Is there anything stirring under that unique haircut of yours?"

"You'll never know, old man," Echo said loudly.

Denton shifted slightly in his chair. "Well, so much for fond farewells. Now to business. Boswell's got the usual 'sound mind' claptrap written down someplace. So—this is how it goes. There are some charitable donations that I won't go into now, also small bequests to various distant relatives and old friends, such as Robert Hawkins, my broker, who won't be here when this is played. There's a cash gift for each of the staff, and Barnes gets something extra for guarding the paintings. Now, here's the part you all came for. I'm sure my old friend Tom is watching. Tom—you get my shotguns and all my fishing tackle. Enjoy 'em—and mind you look after 'em."

Tom Cassidy blew his nose suddenly, but Abby hardly noticed, for she heard her own name.

"Abby, my dear, you've trained practically every animal on the place. In a few months I figure you'll have my Guernseys jumping through hoops. You've done wonders with the horses. I want you to have one. Any one. It's your choice. If you take my advice, you'll pick Silver King; but it's up to you."

Abby gave a gasp of amazement. Her face was a study of delight. Then she suddenly felt tears pricking at the back of her eyes and raised her hands to her face. She had to force herself to concentrate as Denton's image continued: "Next, the paintings—the art collection, as Marcus insists on calling them. They're going to the National Gallery."

Simultaneously, exclamations of horror came from Spenser and Trish. Denton, with perfect anticipation of their reaction, was nodding. "That's right, children. A fast three million in oils—on their way to Washington. As for the rest of my estate, built with my brains and my sweat, it comes to about fifteen million dollars. It takes a sound mind and good judgment to handle that much money. Maybe even a good nature. So, who meets those requirements?"

There was a breathless hush in the room. Nobody stirred. Trish was biting her nails. Slowly Denton shook his head.

"Sorry, children, none of you do. I therefore leave you the sum of fifty thousand dollars each. The remainder I bequeath"—Denton paused and looked down—"to my faithful companion, Teddy. Goodbye, folks."

The camera zoomed in on the head of the dog and the screen went blank.

For an instant there was a stunned silence in the room. It was broken by the principal beneficiary, who, hearing his name spoken, uttered an enquiring: "Woof!"

The next moment the room broke into a medley of sound. Denton's family turned on Boswell in fury. They all talked at once. Trish grabbed his arm. Abby could pick out odd sentences.

"Of all the dirty tricks!"

"This is insane! Teddy's a *dog!*"

"I may faint."

"Boswell, we'll break that will."

This last was Spenser, and here Boswell managed to get a word in.

"You'd be advised not to try it, Spenser. It includes a clause stipulating that, if you challenge it, you're cut out completely."

"Marcus." Trish spoke in a voice of low venom. "I'll never forgive you for what you've done. I'm warning you—I'm going to get even."

"I was only carrying out your father's instructions, Trish."

Spenser was staring malevolently at Teddy. Boswell seemed to read his thoughts. "And don't even think of harming that animal. If he dies of anything but natural causes, every dime goes to the ASPCA."

"Well, well, well," Jessica said slowly, "how very remarkable."

Abby hugged herself. "Isn't it gorgeous? Oh, Jess, you should have seen their faces! Trish seems to blame poor old Marcus. Never forgive him, going to get even, and so on."

"And what's your position now, Abby?"

"Well, I'm employed by Teddy! But, of course, Marcus Boswell is trustee or executor or administrator, or whatever it's called. He made it quite clear he wants me to stay on."

"That's marvelous. And you've got a fine horse of your own in the bargain. I suppose you *will* choose Silver King?"

"You bet! I introduced you to him, didn't I?"

"I think it would be more accurate to say you presented me to him. I felt from your buildup I ought to curtsy."

"Sorry. But really, Jess, he is the most magnificent beast! A potential Olympic champion. Never did I dream of owning such a horse. You know, one day I laid out the toughest treble I could devise: it consisted of a—"

Jessica gently interrupted. "Yes, my dear, you told me. And at the moment I'm really more interested in *you*. Do you think you're going to be happy here, under the circumstances? Feeling as you do about the Langleys? And as they feel about you? Wouldn't it perhaps be better just to take Silver King and go?"

Abby shook her head decisively. "Oh, no. I'm not leaving here until I —until *we*—get to the bottom of Denton's death. That's the beauty of the new situation. We can make whatever inquiries we like. There's not a thing they can do about it."

She leaned back in her chair and clasped her hands behind her head. "You know, Jess, I think I'm going to enjoy myself in the days to come." She smiled a contented smile.

But Jessica wasn't smiling. She had promised to help Abby. But *she* anticipated no enjoyment in what lay ahead. She suspected that Abby, in the hope of arriving at the truth, was going deliberately to needle Denton's family. Which could lead to a very nasty situation at Langley Manor in the not too distant future.

# Chapter Sixteen

THE trouble Jessica had anticipated began the very next day. She and Abby were sitting in the sun after breakfast reading their papers when there came a whinny from the stable yard. It was followed by the sound of hooves on concrete.

Abby dropped her paper and got suddenly to her feet. "What's going on?" she exclaimed. And she hurried off in the direction of the sound.

Jessica hastily followed, and was on Abby's heels when she entered the yard. They saw Trish in the act of saddling up a chestnut gelding that Jessica knew her cousin had been intending to put through his paces that morning. Abby marched angrily over to the girl.

"Just who gave you permission to take that animal from his stall?" she demanded.

Trish gazed at her coolly. "I gave myself permission."

"Well, you can just put him back."

"I shall do no such thing."

Abby stepped closer. "I would remind you that I am in charge of these stables. Nobody takes out a horse without my permission. Especially not you."

An expression of fury came over Trish's face. "Now listen, Miss Stable Nanny, *I* would remind *you* that you are an employee of this estate. A servant."

"And you aren't even that. You don't own this estate. You have no rights here at all."

"Well, we're here—Spense, Morgana and I—and we're staying. Marcus Boswell had sense enough not to try and cheat us out of our family home. So you'll have to get used to our being around."

"And you'll have to get used to *my* being around. Just remember that these stables are my domain—officially."

Trish sneered. "For the time being, maybe. Just until we get this crazy will overturned. Spense has already been in touch with a lawyer from

D.C. who specializes in these cases. He's flying down to see us very soon."

Abby regarded her contemptuously. "Never give up, do you? Your first scheme to get your hands on your father's money failed, so—"

Trish interrupted. "Just what do you mean by that?"

"You know very well what I mean." Abby was shouting now.

Jessica touched her gently on the arm. "Abby, I think perhaps enough has been said."

"No!" It was Trish's turn to shout. "Let's have this out. I know you—both of you—have been going around saying Sawdust was doped. It's pretty obvious what you're implying. Well, I warn you: it can be very dangerous to make accusations of that sort."

"Is that a threat?"

"Take it any way you like."

A voice called urgently: "Trish!"

It was Spenser. He was striding toward them, an angry expression on his face. "For heaven's sake," he snapped. "You can be heard halfway across the estate."

Trish swung around to him. "She's just accused me of murdering Father."

Spenser stared. "Is that true, Miss Freestone?"

"No."

Trish gave a gasp. "Why, you lying—"

Abby cut in. "I didn't accuse your sister *personally,* Mr. Langley. I say *somebody* murdered your father. Somebody who had a good motive. Or believed he had."

Spenser when white. "Meaning me?" he asked very quietly.

Abby shrugged. "I repeat: I make no personal accusations."

Spenser struggled to control his temper. He took several deep breaths before replying: "I would be careful what you say, Miss Freestone. Very careful."

"Don't worry about me, Mr. Langley. But thanks for the warning."

Trish said suddenly, "Oh, come on, Spense. She's not worth fighting with." She dropped the reins of the chestnut and strode off to the house.

Abby sighed. "Typical! Leaves me to put the horse back in his stall."

"Oh, here!" Spenser grabbed up the reins. "I'll do it."

"No, it's my job."

Abby reached out to take the reins from him. But Jessica decided it was time she intervened. She again took her cousin by the arm, more firmly this time.

"Let him do it, Abby."

"But—"

"Let him do it!" Jessica turned her and began to lead her, still resisting, back in the direction of her cottage, calling over her shoulder: "Thank you, Mr. Langley."

"Jess, really," Abby muttered, "there's no need—"

"There is every need. That had gone on quite long enough."

"You really *should* be careful, you know, Abby," said a voice.

They stopped. It was Morgana who had spoken. She was emerging from the shadow of an empty stall, though Jessica could not imagine how she had gotten there without being seen, unless she had been there since before the fracas started. She was wearing a long black dress covered with exotic emblems, and many strings of beads. She was shaking her head and giving her beatific, unearthly smile.

They both stared at her for a moment, then Abby pulled herself together. "I'm not afraid of Spenser," she said.

"I was thinking of Trish," Morgana said. "Her Gemini is in the ascendant, your Capricorn is at low ebb, and last night three owls were seen in a black oak tree."

Abby stared at her, hands on hips. "Do you really expect to frighten me with that gibberish?"

Morgana was unabashed. She shrugged. "The signs are there for the reading."

Before Abby could speak again, there suddenly came the terrified whinny of a horse from behind them. They spun around to see the chestnut, saddle askew, bolting out of his stall. At the same time they heard a ferocious growling and barking from inside the stall. Abby broke into a run, back the way they had come. Jessica and Morgana followed her.

Abby arrived at the stall and peered in to see Spenser backed into the corner, a terrified expression on his face. In one hand he held a bucket and in the other a riding crop, and with them he was trying to ward off a viciously snarling dog. It was Teddy. His teeth were bared, his hackles up. He was making aggressive little darts forward, trying to get at Spenser.

Abby gave an angry exclamation. "What have you been doing to that dog?"

Spenser threw her a furious glance. "Call the brute off!" he yelled.

Abby was about to respond angrily again, then thought better of it and addressed the dog in a special high-pitched command voice that she used on animals.

"Teddy! Good boy! Down, Teddy! Sit!"

The dog glanced up at her and whined. For a moment it seemed he was going to disobey, but then he backed away from Spenser and settled down on his haunches.

Spenser dropped the bucket and strode out of the stall. His face was red with fury and embarrassment. He positively snarled, himself, as he addressed Jessica and Morgana.

"That damn dog has got to be destroyed!"

Morgana gasped. "Spenser, what happened?"

"He just started attacking me—the vicious brute."

Abby came out of the stall. Teddy, head lowered, panting and looking chastened and very tired, was at her heels. "You must have done something to provoke him," Abby said calmly.

"I did no such thing!" Spenser shouted. "I didn't even know the crazy creature was there until I heard him snarling behind me. I was concentrating on the horse. The dog obviously hates me."

Abby calmly bent and tickled Teddy's ears. "Yes, he's a sensible animal."

"Now, look here—" Spenser burst out, but Abby interrupted sharply. "Did he bite you?"

"N-no." The admission came almost reluctantly. "But he damn well would have if I'd given him the chance."

"What about the horse?" Abby was still bending over the dog. Her hand was fingering his collar.

"Oh, no," Spenser sneered, "you wouldn't train him to attack one of your precious horses. Only me."

Abby ignored the gibe. "What's the matter, Abby?" Jessica asked.

Abby looked up. Her face was troubled. "There's blood on his collar."

"You see!" Spenser's voice was triumphant. "I knew it! The animal's dangerous. He'll have to go."

At that moment Teddy slumped down onto his side and closed his eyes. Abby knelt down by him and felt his heart. Then she put both hands under his body and effortlessly got to her feet, the dog in her arms. Teddy lay limp and unresisting.

Spenser's eyes lit up. "Is he—is he dead?"

"No such luck, Spenser. He's been drugged. I'm taking him to the vet. Jess, will you drive?"

"Yes, of course." Jessica hurried ahead to the car and opened the doors.

Abby spoke over her shoulder. "Better finish the job, Spense. Catch that horse and put him away. He probably doesn't like you either, but try not to cry about it."

\* \* \*

"So you were right," Jessica said thoughtfully.

"I was never in any doubt," Abby said.

They were on their way home from the vet's, Abby now at the wheel; Teddy, still exhausted, stretched out in the back.

"What did the vet say the stuff was called?"

"Search me. I'm only interested in its effects. Jess, who'd want to do that to Teddy? I can understand them wanting to poison him—if it wasn't for that clause in the will. But what's the point in drugging him? It's obvious why they did it to Sawdust."

"The vet said he found no trace of that substance in the horse."

"So, he made a mistake or they used different stuff. Sawdust was drugged—to kill Denton. But whom did they expect Teddy to kill? *Me?* Did it backfire on them when he attacked Spenser instead?"

Jessica shook her head. "No, I don't think that was the plan. I don't believe your life is in danger. Not at the moment."

"Then why? Do you have any ideas?"

"I have a vague idea of what somebody may be up to. But I'm not sure it would work. It would depend on the exact wording of Denton's will."

"What do you mean?"

"Well, suppose Teddy were destroyed officially—by order of the court? It wouldn't be strictly natural causes. But it wouldn't be the result of foul play against him either. So what would happen to his inheritance then?"

"You mean—they gave him something that would drive him to attack people, so that he'd be put to sleep without their laying a finger on him? Why, that's fiendish! You know, those people are absolute scum. Oh, wait till I see them again! I'll tear them off such a strip—"

"Abby, I think that would be very ill-advised."

"Why? You're not saying they're innocent, are you?"

"I'm saying that I cannot believe in a full-scale family conspiracy to kill their father. They're not *all* guilty."

"Then you find out who *is* the guilty one, and I'll apologize to the others."

Jessica sighed to herself. It seemed impossible to argue with her cousin in this mood.

Abby suddenly chuckled. "You know, the really delicious thing is Teddy turning and attacking Spenser. He knows who his real enemies are."

"I'm not so sure of that," Jessica said. "Remember the blood on his collar. It seems he did attack somebody else first."

"And I know who they're going to claim it was, too." Abby pointed through the windshield.

For the last minute or so they'd been traveling up the drive and had just turned into the stable yard. Parked in the middle was the sheriff's car. Standing near it were Millard, Spenser, and a scraggly, balding, middle-aged man wearing a tattered old checked shirt with the sleeves rolled up. His left arm was heavily bandaged, and he seemed to be remonstrating with Spenser while the sherrif tried to calm him down.

"Potts!" Abby muttered between her teeth: "I might have guessed!"

"Who is he?"

"He's a farmer. His place abuts the estate. He's a drunk, a liar, a cheat, and he treats his animals abominably."

She drew up near the three men. Potts immediately peered into the back of the car. Then he pointed at Teddy and turned to Millard.

"That's the dog, Sheriff. That's the dog that attacked me."

Abby and Jessica got out of the car. The sheriff tipped his hat. " 'Morning, ladies. I'm here on official business. Mr. Potts claims that there pooch bit him."

Abby regarded Potts coldly. "Do you have any witnesses?"

"Witnesses? What do I need witnesses for? Just take a look at my arm! Think I bit it myself?" Potts started trying to undo his bandage.

"There's no need for that," Spenser said. "No one's denying you were bitten."

"But what evidence is there that Teddy did it?" Abby demanded.

"Oh, for heaven's sake, Miss Freestone," Spenser said irritably. "What's the point in denying it? You saw how the animal went for me."

"He didn't bite you."

"Understand there was blood on his collar, though, Miss Freestone," the sheriff put in.

Abby glared at Spenser. "Thank you very much, Mr. Langley. Determined to put the boot in, aren't you?"

Spenser shrugged. "Wouldn't be right to withhold information from the police."

Abby turned to Millard. "Sheriff, that blood on the collar could be anything. Teddy might have killed a rabbit or a rat."

"Our lab boys can easily find out, Miss Freestone."

"Oh, all right, take the collar and run your tests."

"I will, but I'm going to have to take the dog in, too. Reckon there's a *prima facie* case against him." He pronounced the Latin phrase carefully.

"Listen," said Abby, "we've just come from the vet's. He confirms

Teddy was drugged with some stuff that would make him behave viciously. If Teddy did bite Potts, he couldn't help himself."

"Maybe so, Miss Freestone. But being under the influence of drink or drugs is no defense to a criminal charge—though it may be an extenuating circumstance when it comes to sentencing. Especially if the stuff was forcibly administered. However, that's a matter for the judge. Whatever the cause, the animal's dangerous. I gotta put him where he can't do any harm. So I'd be obliged if you'd move him into the back of my vehicle."

"I'll ride to town with him," Abby said with resignation. "He has to know he's got one friend." She turned to Jessica. "Jess, will you ring Marcus Boswell? Tell him what's happened and ask him to put the wheels in motion to get Teddy sprung as quickly as possible."

Jessica nodded. "I can't imagine he'll need much persuading. After all, I don't suppose he has many millionaire clients, and it must be extremely rare for one of them to be arrested. Particularly for biting somebody."

# Chapter Seventeen

IT was after lunch the next day that the phone rang in the cottage. Abby answered it.

"Abby?"

She recognized the voice. "Yes, Mr. Boswell."

"Well, it's taken my entire bag of legal tricks, but I've arranged to have Teddy released on his own recognizance."

"Oh, that's marvelous!"

"I'd like to have you look after him most of the time from now on. Okay?"

"Yes, of course—great."

"Good. And times when you can't keep an eye on him, I suggest you put him in Barnes' care. He's a reliable man."

"Will do."

"In fact, it might be an idea to let him or his assistant have the dog in the security room at night. No one can get into it from outside, so he'd be perfectly safe there and you could relax."

"Good idea," said Abby.

"Then that's settled. You can pick up Teddy at the sheriff's office as soon as you like."

"I'll get down there right away."

"Now, Abby, I'm afraid that *was* human blood on Teddy's collar— same type as Potts'. So for heaven's sake make sure he stays out of trouble from now on in. If anything like this should happen again . . ." He left the sentence unfinished.

"I'll take good care of him."

"I'm sure you will. Oh, by the way, you'll be happy to know he wasn't rabid."

"Are they sure?"

Boswell laughed. "Positive. Potts hasn't died." He hung up.

Abby put down the receiver.

"Good news?" Jessica asked.

"Very. Teddy's coming home." She relayed all that she had been told. "I'm going to collect him now. Coming?"

Jessica nodded. "I'll get my coat."


It was after they had picked up an ecstatic, and completely recovered, Teddy from a reluctant sheriff and were on their way back to the car when Abby suddenly stopped and touched Jessica on the arm. "Enemy sighted." She pointed.

Jessica looked across the street and saw, emerging from an office building, Spenser, Trish and Morgana. Accompanying them was a tall, sleek, prosperous-looking man in a dark business suit.

"The lawyer from D.C., do you suppose?" Abby murmured.

"I wouldn't be a bit surprised."

"Marcus Boswell has his offices in that building. Shall we try and find out what's been going on?"

"Oh, do you think we should interfere?"

"Surely, as Teddy's official guardian, I have a right to know if there's any chance of him losing his inheritance. Come on."

Gripping Teddy's lead firmly, she started purposefully across the street. Jessica hesitated for a moment, then followed.


Marcus Boswell's suite of offices was luxuriously equipped with oak paneling and real leather furniture. Obviously valuable antiques abounded. The receptionist announced Jessica and Abby over the intercom and they heard Boswell say: "Oh, send them right in."

He met them at the door of his private office. "Ladies, do come in. I see the prisoner's been released."

At that moment the phone rang. The receptionist answered it, listened, covered the mouthpiece and said, "Bob Hawkins. Third time he's called today."

"Tell him I'm tied up."

Boswell ushered Jessica and Abby through the door, closed it and ensconsed them in deep and very comfortable chairs. Teddy lay down on the thick carpet and went immediately to sleep.

Boswell sat behind a massive oak desk and regarded them benignly. "To what do I owe this pleasure?"

"Sheer nosiness, I'm afraid," Abby said. "We saw the Langleys leaving."

"Oh."

"That man with them: Trish said they were consulting a big-shot lawyer from Washington. Was that him?"

Boswell nodded slowly. "One Gary Deems. His specialty is breaking wills."

"Can they do that?"

"They can try."

"But what about that clause, cutting them out completely if they do?"

"Well, you know, a well-drawn will can stand up to fire, famine and pestilence. Denton's was well drawn, but it's always possible to find some loophole."

"And Mr. Deems has found one?" Jessica inquired.

"More like a rathole," Boswell said.

"Can we know what it is?" asked Abby. "I *am* an interested party."

"I don't see why not. We're all on the same side, after all. Well, Deems' angle is the question of sound mind."

Abby gave a snort of derision. "Nonsense! Denton Langley's mind was as sound as a bell!"

Boswell shook his head. "You misunderstand me. He's not thinking of Langley's mind."

Abby frowned. "Then whose . . . ?"

For answer, Boswell pointed down at the sleeping dog on the carpet.

"Teddy!" Abby gasped. Without waking, the dog wagged his tail.

Boswell nodded. "If a court were to declare the dog mentally incompetent—"

"But that's ridiculous!"

"I know it is. But it might take a lot of years in court to prove it. For instance, if a dog had a reputation for attacking people, would that be evidence of insanity?"

Abby glanced at Jessica. "Now we know why he was fed that dope."

Boswell raised a hand. "Abby, you must watch it. It's safe enough to say that sort of thing in your lawyer's office; but get in the habit of saying it, and you may find yourself in court."

"I know. But it's all so beastly! I hate to think of those people getting their hands on Denton's estate, after all."

"Now, don't worry. I may be a country boy, but I know a few legal tricks myself."

At that moment the intercom on his desk buzzed. He sighed. "Excuse me, ladies."

The voice of the receptionist said, "I'm sorry, Mr. Boswell, but it's Bob Hawkins again. Says it's vital he speak to you."

"Okay, put him on." He addressed the women. "Sorry, ladies, seems I just have to take this call."

"We must go," said Jessica.

She got to her feet, and Abby followed suit. "Thanks for your time, Mr. Boswell." She gave a tug on Teddy's lead, and he jumped up eagerly.

"Anytime, Abby," Boswell told her. "Remember what I said—don't worry—and keep a sharp eye on that VIP—which stands for 'very important pooch.' "

Abby was silent driving home in the car, and responded to Jessica's remarks shortly. Jessica sensed that for some reason she wasn't at the moment on her cousin's good side. But it wasn't until they were back at the cottage and having a cup of tea that she plucked up courage to ask directly: "Abby, have I done anything to offend you?"

Abby looked at her. "No, certainly not."

"I'm glad."

"But to be quite frank, Jess, I'm rather disappointed you haven't done anything yet."

"Done anything?"

"About the case."

"Oh, Abby, what can I do? If the Langleys—or one of them—drugged Sawdust, the deed's over and done with. I don't see any way to prove it. The police might be able to trace the purchase of the drug to them, but there's no way *I* can."

"I know that. But you did say you'd try to help."

"I was thinking of conversation. I do have a sort of knack for drawing people out. And then I sometimes get an idea. But the way your relationship with the Langleys has deteriorated makes conversation of that kind with them impossible. You call them the enemy; no doubt that's how they think of you. And from their point of view, I'm firmly in the enemy camp. So just tell me, what *can* I do?"

Abby sighed. "Oh, I don't know. Sorry, Jess. I suppose I'm being unreasonable. I was thinking of you as a miracle worker."

"Which I'm most definitely not."

"Well, perhaps it's a good thing, in a way. It means I'm on my own. I can plan my own campaign. And I don't have to be as cautious as you, or Marcus Boswell. I can be a little more drastic in my methods." There was a strange note in her voice.

"What do you mean, Abby?" Jessica spoke sharply.

"What?" Abby blinked. "Oh, nothing, Jess. I haven't got anything definite in mind. I was just thinking. More tea?"

# Chapter Eighteen

SEVERAL days passed. By tacit consent, the topic of Denton Langley's death was dropped. Jessica spent her time reading, walking on the estate, doing a little gentle riding on Doughnut and planning the main outline of her next book. Abby was busy with the horses. She kept Teddy with her at most times, but on the occasions she was not able to watch him, she followed Boswell's suggestion and had Barnes look after him. The guard was clearly fond of him, and seemed pleased to have the dog's company at night.

Marcus Boswell visited regularly to check on his client's welfare, and himself took Teddy for several long walks.

Jessica and Abby saw little of the Langleys, who confined themselves mainly to the house. Twice, according to Barnes, Gary Deems called, and remained over an hour on each occasion.

For a while Jessica worried about her cousin. She'd seen a tremendous change come over her during the short period since Denton Langley's death. The cause was not hard to find. Abby had hero-worshipped her employer. He had been her benefactor, giving her the sort of position she had dreamed of all her life. Perhaps he had been a father figure to her. Perhaps, in spite of the difference in their ages, she had been—maybe unconsciously—in love with him. But then had come the tremendous shock of Denton's death. This had been followed by the discovery that he had remembered Abby so magnificently in his will. Her feeling of indebtedness had deepened still further. Linked with this had been the conviction—possibly, but by no means certainly, justified—that he had been murdered; and the growing suspicion that nobody else shared her conviction or was going to do anything about it.

However, her cousin's presence must have been a comfort. Given Jessica's reputation as a private detective, Abby had no doubt felt that she could have no better ally in her fight to establish the truth. But Jessica had let her down—or that, at least, was how Abby must have seen it. The famous solver of mysteries had failed even to investigate this one. When

Jessica had at last pointed out the impossibility of taking action, Abby must have felt very much alone.

Jessica herself was highly conscious of the situation; she felt guilty about it. While her logic told her that everything she had said to her cousin was true, her conscience constantly nagged, telling her there was surely something she could do.

But much as she racked her brains, she couldn't think of anything.

However, as the day's passed, Abby's manner seemed gradually to return to normal. She brooded less, stopped giving forth streams of invective against the Langleys and talked no more about drastic methods. It was a relief to Jessica, who began to feel that when her vacation ended she would finally be able to go home with an easier mind about her cousin.

That, though, was before the second murder.

# Chapter Nineteen

IT was one A.M. In the security room Barnes yawned. Four hours before Smedley would take over for him. This was the boring shift. Nothing ever happened.

He glanced down at Teddy, who was fast asleep in his basket. "Fine company you are tonight, pal," he said out loud.

Teddy gave a snore, but didn't wake up. Barnes grinned and glanced at his watch. Time to make some coffee.

He was just going to get to his feet when he saw movement and light on one of his monitors. He stared closely at the screen, which was the one that showed the area of the main gate. The headlamps of an approaching vehicle were illuminating the scene; and as Barnes watched, the car itself drew up just outside the gate. He couldn't see much detail, but it had surely halted in a queer position, as if one wheel had mounted the pavement; the lights were shining at an angle across the road. Barnes felt the stirrings of suspicion, and his hand inched toward the phone.

Then he relaxed as a human figure moved from the darkness into the glare of the headlights in front of the car—a figure wearing a full-length fur coat and a head scarf, and staggering slightly as it moved.

Barnes shook his head disgustedly. "Trish," he muttered. "Drunk again. I might have guessed!"

He saw the figure reach out to the intercom on the gatepost, and a second later a buzzer sounded loudly in the security room. It woke Teddy, who sat up with a jerk.

"Relax, feller," Barnes said. "It's no friend of yours."

He reached out and pressed a button marked MAIN GATE. On the screen he saw the gate start to roll back and the buzzer stopped. Teddy was now sitting up and staring at the screen with every indication of interest, ears cocked and head on one side.

"Go on, girl," Barnes muttered. "Get back in your car. The gate's open."

However, the next second he stiffened, as without warning the figure on the screen suddenly swayed, fell heavily onto the road and lay still.

Barnes groaned. "Passed out."

He got wearily to his feet. Teddy looked at him hopefully and gave a little yelp.

"Sorry, boy, no walks tonight. More than my job's worth to let you out."

He checked his gun, picked up a flashlight, walked to the door and opened it. Then he turned.

"Okay, Teddy, mind the store while I'm gone, okay?"

He went out, closed the door and carefully locked it with one of a bunch of keys that hung from his belt. Then he started walking briskly across the grass in the direction of the main gate.

It was a still, dark night, and the only sound to break the silence was the single call of a mockingbird, which rang out just as Barnes got his first direct sight of the main gate. The car lights were the only illumination, but by them he could see an inert human form still lying near the side of the drive.

The next second, Barnes stopped dead. He stared in amazement. The gate, which could be operated only from the security room, had started to move. It was closing.

He gave an exclamation. "Now, how in tarnation—"

The words died in his throat. With utter horror he had suddenly realized that Trish Langley was lying on the rails, directly in the path of the gate. Her head was just inches from the massive concrete gatepost.

Barnes broke into a run, at the same time yelling at the top of his voice: "Miss Langley! Look out!"

The girl didn't move. Barnes continued to sprint and shout, but he was still forty yards from the gate when he realized that he was going to be too late.

The grinding of metal on metal was a sound that was to remain in Barnes' mind for years to come. So was the sight of the gate, inexorably closing, moving nearer and nearer to Trish Langley's head.

At the very last moment Barnes stopped running and shut his eyes. There was nothing to be gained by watching. He only wished he could have shut his ears to that final sound of Trish's head being driven up against the gatepost. . . .

# Chapter Twenty

"NOW, let's get this straight," Sheriff Millard said. "You're saying the gate can only be closed from inside that security room of yours."

Barnes nodded vigorously. "The only way it can be closed electronically, yes. It can be hauled across manually in an emergency, of course, but it certainly wasn't closed manually tonight."

"And you say you locked the security room behind you when you left?"

"Sure did."

"And there was nobody there then?"

"Nope."

"How many keys are there?"

"I've only ever seen one. I hand it to Smedley when we change shift."

The sheriff stared at him belligerently. "Seems to me you're putting your own neck in a noose. You're saying no outsider got into the security room, yet someone pressed the button. We only got your word the gate started to close when you were on the drive. What's to have stopped you closing the gate on Miss Langley before you left the room?"

Barnes' face went red. "Why, you great—"

Marcus Boswell, whom Barnes had telephoned soon after finding the body, and who had driven straight over, laid a restraining hand on his arm. "That's ridiculous, Sheriff. What motive could Barnes have had for murdering Trish?"

"You never know what sort of motives are going to come to light till you start digging."

"Look, if Barnes was guilty, it would be easy for him to say he forgot to lock the security-room door, so somebody could have gotten in and pressed the button. But he didn't. He's told you the truth."

Millard scratched his neck. "Okay, Mr. Boswell, what's your suggestion?"

"Well, how about an electrical fault of some kind—a short circuit, causing the gate to close of its own accord?"

The sheriff shrugged. "Possible. We'll have it checked, of course." He looked at Barnes. "Any signs of that?"

Barnes stared back. "No," he said defiantly, "and the whole system has regular maintenance checks."

Millard gave a grunt. "Okay, you can go. But don't leave the estate."

Barnes gave a disgusted mutter and ambled off.

"Well, guess I'd better go talk to the family," said Millard.

"Mind if I tag along? I'm not the Langley lawyer, but I am an interested party—as the legal representative of the owner of the estate."

"Reckon I can't stop you, Mr. Boswell, if you want to be there. Come on."

In the living room they found Morgana and Echo, both in their robes; Spenser, in shirt and slacks; and Jessica and Abby, who were both fully dressed. Abby was sitting on the couch, petting Teddy, who somehow sensed something was wrong.

As the two men entered the room, Morgana turned and came fluttering toward them. Boswell was reminded of a dazed moth making for a candle. She moved close up to Millard and clutched him by the sleeve.

"Sheriff, my brother and daughter say I mustn't tell you this, but I have to. You'll say I'm crazy. But I really saw it!"

The Sheriff drew a sharp breath. "You saw the accident?"

Morgana shook her head impatiently. "No! I saw my dear sister's ghost rising up from her earthly form and crying like a mourning dove."

"My mother's a little upset, Sheriff," Echo said dryly from across the room.

Morgana swung around to her. "Of course I'm upset! Wouldn't you be if you'd just seen Trish's spirit take wing?"

Millard narrowed his eyes. "Just what you saying, Mrs. Cramer?"

She turned back. "I was looking out of my window—"

"At one o'clock in the morning? May I ask why?"

"I had woken suddenly. I don't know why, but no doubt the sudden destruction of my sister's earthly vessel had set up psychic vibrations that had acted adversely on my—"

"Never mind all that. Tell me what you saw."

"I got out of bed. I often do if I wake at night. My aura thrives on moonlight. It seems actually to feed—" Morgana saw Millard's expression changing and broke off before going on: "Well, I went to the window and looked out. My bedroom is the only one with a view of the main gate through the trees. I saw this figure lying lifeless on the drive. And then, before my eyes, she rose and—and—disappeared." Then, plainly feeling this was an insufficiently mystical expression, Morgana amended it to:

"Was absorbed into the ether." She took a deep breath before going on hurriedly. "I ran to tell Spenser. I knocked on his door, but he didn't answer."

"I'm a heavy sleeper," Spenser said irritably. "You know that."

"Tell me, Mrs. Cramer: was the gate open at the time?"

Morgana looked a little taken aback. "Er, yes. That is, I think it must have been."

"Well, your sister was killed by the gate closing, ma'am. It stayed closed till I arrived. If it was open, Miss Langley was still alive. You must have been mistaken."

Morgana gave a helpless little flap of her hands. "It's not fair," she said tearfully. "My first real ghost, and no one will believe me."

Millard cleared his throat and addressed the room at large. "There's some questions I've got to ask."

But at that moment he was interrupted. A young deputy hurried into the room and whispered excitedly into his ear.

Millard's face suddenly changed to an almost ludicrous extent. His jaw literally dropped. He gazed at the deputy in disbelief, then said hoarsely, "They—they sure?"

"Absolutely, Sheriff."

Millard stood, staring blankly in front of him, as though trying to grasp some concept too abstruse for human comprehension. Seconds passed before Spenser asked tersely, "Sheriff, what's happened? We have a right to know."

"What? Oh." Millard gave a little shake of his head. Then he said, "Well, folks, seems we got our killer."

There was an instant hush in the room. Everyone stared at him with bated breath.

"That button in the security room that closes the front gate *was* pressed deliberately. Our boys have found a print on it."

"A fingerprint?" Boswell asked.

"Nope. Near as we can figure, it's a paw print."

It was Spenser who reacted first. "Teddy? *Teddy* murdered my sister?"

"He pressed the button," Millard said.

"That damned dog!" Spenser hissed the words. "First he attacks me, then Potts, now he kills Trish."

"He's evil," Morgana whispered. "He's possessed." She backed across to one corner of the room, her eyes fixed with a horrified expression on the dog.

Teddy, once more realizing that he was the center of attention, uttered a little *woof* and wagged his tail.

Morgana gave a muffled scream and began to mutter rapidly under her breath in a strange language. It was, Jessica guessed, some sort of incantation.

Meanwhile, Spenser had turned on Boswell. "Marcus, that cursed animal has got to go!"

"Oh, and wouldn't *that* be convenient, Spenser," Boswell said sarcastically.

"This is utterly absurd!"

The voice, shaking with emotion, was Abby's. She was on her feet, Teddy in her arms. "Sheriff, you cannot possibly believe a *dog* is capable of murder!"

"Of course he can't," Boswell snapped. "Sheriff, it was obviously just a tragic mischance. Teddy happened to step on the button."

"That won't wash, Mr. Boswell. You've seen the inside of the security room. That hound-dog must've jumped up on Barnes' chair and pressed his paw on the one button out of all of them that'd close the front gate—just at the crucial moment Miss Langley was lying there. Couldn't't've been accidental."

"You don't seriously mean to tell me that you believe a dog could work all that out for himself?" Boswell's voice was incredulous.

Millard shrugged. "He did it."

Abby spoke again, her tone one of despair. "But he'd have to be trained. . . ."

The next second she froze, her mouth still open, suddenly realizing the import of her words. Every eye in the room was on her. Teddy turned his head up and tried to lick her chin. She gulped. "Well, I mean—"

"I think we know quite well what you mean, Miss Freestone," Spenser said. He turned to the sheriff. "That woman has hated my sisters and me ever since she came here. She's practically accused us of murdering Father. She verbally attacked Trish on several occasions. She's been in charge of Teddy—and she's a professional animal trainer. If you don't arrest her, you're an even bigger fool than I thought you were until now."

These last words were a mistake. Millard flushed angrily.

Jessica took the opportunity to speak for the first time. "Mr. Langley, are you really implying that Teddy could be trained to recognize your sister on a small black-and-white television screen; realize, when she tripped, that she was in the path of the gate; and seize his opportunity to leap up on the chair and press the button?"

Spenser looked a little taken aback. "Well, no, of course not. I mean—"

"Well said, Mrs. Fletcher," Boswell broke in.

"The sheriff realizes perfectly well," Jessica went on, "that Teddy could only be trained to respond to a direct order—to press the button when he was told to. Anybody can speak to the security room through one of the intercoms scattered around the estate, and that's how the command must have been given. Am I right, Mr. Millard?"

"Yeah." Millard nodded vigorously. "Yeah, that's the way I figured it out."

"And I'm sure your next question of Mr. Langley was going to be: does he believe my cousin stayed up in the grounds until one A.M., on the off chance that his sister returned home late and just happened to fall and lie unconscious in the path of the gate—and we have Barnes' testimony that that's what happened—so giving Abby the chance to relay the order to Teddy?"

The sheriff looked at Spenser. "Well, what about it, Mr. Langley?"

Spenser shrugged. "According to your own scenario, Mrs. Fletcher, *somebody* did just that—even if it wasn't Miss Freestone. What's your explanation?"

"I don't have one," Jessica said frankly. "I agree, it seems wildly unlikely. But it's certainly *less* unlikely that it should be done by somebody who was conversant with Miss Langley's plans for earlier tonight, and who knew roughly what time to expect her home. I'm quite certain Abby wasn't such a person. I imagine even Mr. Langley would concede that his sister wouldn't have confided in *her.*"

Millard chewed the end of his pencil. He was clearly quite out of his depth. Spenser turned away with a gesture of hopelessness. Abby gave Jessica a mute little nod of thanks.

Jessica looked at her watch. "It's nearly two o'clock," she said, "and if you don't require me any longer, Sheriff, I think I shall leave."

He nodded. "That's okay."

"Thank you." She looked at Spenser, Morgana and Echo in turn. "My deepest sympathy in your loss."

Spenser muttered, "Thanks."

Jessica moved to the door. "Coming, Abby?"

Abby stood up. "Is that all right, Mr. Millard? Or am I under arrest?"

"No, no, you can go. But don't leave the estate."

"You've got to be joking," Abby said. She followed Jessica to the door and they went out, Teddy close behind them.

In the hall, Abby drew a deep breath. "Whew, let's get out of here."

"In a moment. Abby, which is Morgana's room?"

Abby raised her eyebrows. "Why on earth—?"

"I'll explain later. Quickly."

"I'm not sure. Let me think." She screwed up her eyes. "I think you turn left at the top of the stairs and it's at the far end of the corridor."

"Right. You go on home. I'll join you shortly."

Jessica hurried up the stairs. Abby looked at her uneasily for a moment, then left the house by the front door, Teddy at her heels.

A few minutes later Jessica arrived back at the top of the stairs and peered cautiously down into the hall. It was clear. Good. It would be highly embarrassing having to explain to the family why she'd been roaming about the upper floors of the house—even though it was for a quite innocent purpose.

She started down the stairs, then stopped as the front door opened. The deputy, Will Roxie, entered. He was carrying a partly folded full-length mink coat and a plastic bag. As she watched, he started trying to roll the coat into a compact bundle and stuff it into the bag. However, it soon became clear the coat was too bulky to go in easily.

Jessica remained motionless for about ten seconds. Then she continued down the stairs. After all, Will Roxie didn't know she wasn't free to wander all over the house whenever she pleased. As she neared the bottom she said brightly, "Here, Will, let me help you with that."

He looked up. "Oh, hi, Mrs. Fletcher. Thanks. I think this could use a lady's touch. It's just a mite too big for the evidence bag. Thought if I came indoors in the light I'd manage better, but it hasn't really helped."

"I think we'd better start from scratch."

She took the coat from him and shook it out. Will gave a whistle of admiration at seeing it full-length in good light. "Say, my wife sure would give her eyeteeth for this."

"It was taken off the body?"

"Yes, ma'am."

She was staring at the inside of the coat. "Could it have been torn when they were getting it off?"

"Oh no, Mrs. Fletcher. I helped. We were most careful."

"Well, it *is* torn. Look."

She turned the coat inside out for him to see. "This coat's nearly new, I'd say, but the seams are split like my old car coat. Yet I can't imagine Trish Langley wearing it like that for long, can you?"

He frowned. "Meaning it was torn tonight?"

"Well, certainly very recently. Make a note of those splits, Will. They could be important."

"Yes, ma'am. Will do."

He spoke politely, but she fancied he was humoring her. She smiled, helped him fold the coat into a neat and tight bundle and insert it in the bag, said good night, went out and made her way to the cottage.

She found Abby in the kitchen, making a pot of tea.

"As I expected," Jessica said. "Under stress the English always head for the teapot."

"Want a cup?"

"Please."

Abby poured two cups and they went into the living room and sat down.

"Now, why the search of Morgana's room?" Abby asked.

"Oh, not a search. I just wanted to find out exactly what she could see out of her window at night."

"But why? You surely don't believe that crazy story?"

"Well, Morgana's certainly got some weird beliefs, but has there ever been any indication she actually suffers from hallucinations?"

"Not that I know of."

"And I can't think of any reason why she should lie about such a thing."

"You mean you *do* believe her?" Abby's voice was incredulous.

"Not that she saw Trish's spirit leaving her body; of course not. I wanted to find out if she could have seen *anything*—while there were still headlights shining down by the gate and people moving around."

"And could she?"

"Just very small figures. They all look the same height, and naturally you can't see anything of the faces at all. But you can just make out roughly what they're doing."

Abby looked at her curiously. "What are you getting at, Jess?"

"I don't know. I just like to have as many facts as possible." She took a sip of tea. "Abby, how would you go about training Teddy to press that button?"

"Jess! I hope you're not suggesting—"

"Of course not. I'll change the question: how would *one* go about training *a dog* to press it?"

"A simple voice command would suffice. Something like: *Teddy— push!* You'd repeat it over and over, lifting his paw onto the button, until he got it, rewarding him when he did."

Jessica shook her head. "I think it would be too risky to use one's voice. Someone might turn on the intercom and recognize it."

Abby shrugged. "Any sort of sound would do, so long as the dog learned to associate it with the action and respond. A snap of the fingers or a whistle."

"A whistle," Jessica nodded. "That's more like it. Would it take long?"

"Not with a bright young dog like Teddy. He picks things up very quickly."

At that moment there came a knock on the front door. They glanced at each other, then Abby stood up and called, "Who is it?"

"Marcus Boswell."

Abby gave a sigh of relief, crossed and opened it. Boswell came in.

"Thank goodness it's you," said Abby. "I had a horrible feeling that was the sheriff come to arrest Teddy. I was surprised he let me walk out with him."

"Millard doesn't know what he's doing tonight. You were out of the room with the dog before he really noticed. Where *is* Teddy, by the way?"

"Locked in my bedroom. I wasn't taking any chances."

"Good. Though I think we can expect Millard to take Teddy in tomorrow. He'll probably call it protective custody."

Boswell's glance fell on Abby's nearly full teacup on the table.

"Would you like a cup of tea?" Abby asked. "Or something stronger?"

"Tea will be fine. I'd love a cup."

Abby crossed to the kitchen. "Please have a seat," she said.

"Thanks." He lowered himself into an easy chair, stretching his legs out toward the fire.

Jessica noticed that the inside of his right trouser leg, near the bottom, was badly marked with dark stains. She pointed it out to him.

He looked down and gave a grimace. "Oh, great! I had a flat on the way over. Must have got some grease off the jack. I was working more or less in the dark."

Jessica's expression was pensive. "Something wrong?" he asked.

"What? Oh no. Er, where was this?"

"Where I had the flat? About half a mile away."

Abby came in with Boswell's tea. She too noticed the expression on Jessica's face. "What's the matter, Jess?"

Jessica smiled. "Probably nothing. But tell me, Mr. Boswell, do you have many flats?"

"No, very few. Why?"

"It's just that I don't like anything even slightly unusual happening in the vicinity of a murder. It just occurred to me to wonder whether your puncture may have been, er, induced."

They both stared at her. Boswell said, "I don't get it."

"Oh, no doubt it's just a coincidence. But suppose the killer wanted to make sure nobody passed the main gate at the time of the murder. I mean, if a car came along at the crucial moment and the driver saw the gate closing on Trish, he might have had time to stop and pull her clear. Some tacks, say, sprinkled across the road half a mile away might have ensured no car *did* come along. Of course, by the time you arrived, the murder had been done, but I don't suppose the killer would have bothered to go back and sweep them up in the interim."

Boswell nodded slowly. "Well, it's a possibility. I must admit it hadn't occurred to me."

"As I say, there's probably nothing to it, but perhaps you could humor me and show me tomorrow just where it happened?"

"Of course, be glad to."

Abby asked, "But, Jess, what will it prove if you do find some tacks?"

"Not a lot. Except that it would be proof positive we're dealing with a highly ingenious and farsighted murderer who carefully planned this murder in advance, down to the smallest detail. It would tell us a lot about his—or her—character; and the better you know your adversary the better your chance of catching him."

Abby smiled to herself. She liked that word *adversary* coming from Jessica. At last, it seemed, her cousin was well and truly involved in the Langley affair.

# Chapter Twenty-one

"AS far as I can remember," Marcus Boswell said, "it was just about here." He pulled into the side of the narrow country road.

"Excuse me," Jessica said, "but if you did go over a tack or something similar, you wouldn't have stopped the same second, would you? I imagine you'd have been going pretty fast. It would have taken fifty or a hundred yards before you realized what had happened and pulled up."

"Yes, you're probably right." Boswell drove on another hundred yards and again stopped. They both got out.

"Suppose we take different sides of the road?" Jessica suggested.

"As you like."

He crossed to the other side, and they began slowly making their way along the highway, heads bent, peering down at the surface. A minute or so passed, and then Boswell jerked his head up sharply at a triumphant cry from Jessica: "Eureka!"

She was kneeling down, her fingers scrabbling at the ground. He hurried across to her. She stood up and proudly held out her hand to him. Lying in the palm were three inch-long, large-headed shiny new tacks.

"Good grief!" Boswell took one of them, an expression of complete amazement on his face.

"You didn't think much of my idea, did you, Mr. Boswell?"

He took a deep breath. "Actually, Mrs. Fletcher, no."

She smiled. "Frankly, Mr. Boswell, on reflection, neither did I. However . . ."

"However, you were right. Congratulations. Are there just the three, I wonder?"

"There seem to be. No doubt the killer *did* come back after and cleared the others away."

"Well, there's no chance of his having left any tire tracks on this road surface."

"In fact," she said regretfully, "it really gets us no farther forward. I'm sure these tacks can be bought in any hardware store, and even if it was possible to find a suspect who'd bought some recently, it would be absolutely no proof he's the murderer. Even if we showed these to the sheriff, I'd be very surprised if he bothered to follow it up."

"I'm afraid you're right. However, it must be very satisfying to have your theory vindicated."

"I do feel quite pleased."

During the latter part of the conversation they'd been retracing their steps to the car. Now Jessica suddenly got down on her hands and knees and stared up at the two front tires. Then she rose, went round to the rear and repeated the procedure.

Boswell looked amused. "A guess: you're wondering if any of my other tires picked up a tack."

"I was, yes. But there's no sign of anything. All the tires look exactly the same. Of course, I couldn't see every section."

"Don't worry, I'll get the garage to check them over."

"Perhaps we could take a look at the wheel you removed last night and see if there's a tack embedded in the tire?"

"Sorry, it's in my garage back home, waiting to be taken in for repair. The one in the trunk now is a second spare I usually keep in the garage. I'll take a look at the other when I get home."

"Good. I'd be interested to know."

"I'll keep you informed. Now, Mrs. Fletcher, I'd better take you back to your cousin's."

When Boswell and Jessica drove up to Abby's cottage, the familiar sight of Sheriff Millard's car met them.

"Uh-uh, I expected this," Boswell said.

They got out and went inside the cottage. They found a tearful Abby confronting a belligerent Millard, while an embarrassed-looking Will Roxie stood by.

"Look, Miss Freestone," Millard was saying, "either you go upstairs and bring that dog down, or we go up and break down your bedroom door. Now which is it to be?"

"What's going on?" Boswell asked coldly.

"They want to take Teddy," Abby explained. "I told them I wasn't letting him go till you got back."

"Mr. Boswell," Millard said, "I've gotta have that dog. I don't know whether he's a suspect or a material witness or an accessory or a clue or an exhibit, but he's sure one of them. He's gotta be kept in protective custody till we clear this business up."

"That means for the rest of his life," Abby snapped.

"I don't think it's any good fighting it, Abby," Boswell told her. "It's probably for the best. We know Teddy will be safe there. And I'm sure we can arrange visiting rights. Better go and get him."

"Very well, if you say so." Abby left the room.

Jessica went after her. They climbed the stairs; Abby took a key from her pocket and opened her bedroom door. Teddy came bounding excitedly out. Abby picked him up and petted him. "Poor old boy. Having to go to prison, just because he does what he's been taught to do."

Jessica spoke on the spur of the moment. "Abby, it won't be for long. I promise you."

Abby stared at her and her eyes widened. "Jess," she said incredulously, "you've solved the case, haven't you?"

"I'm not sure. I'm pretty certain I know how Trish's murder was arranged, but—"

Abby gave a squeal. "Oh Jess, you're wonderful! I knew you'd do it!"

And with Teddy in her arms, she turned and hurried down the stairs. At the bottom she rushed into the living room and Jessica heard her voice raised elatedly.

"It's all right! You can stop worrying. My cousin's solved the case."

Jessica closed her eyes. Under her breath she murmured, "Oh, no." Hastily she descended the stairs herself. When she entered the living room, every eye was on her. She smiled weakly.

Abby regarded her with pride. "Tell them, Jessica."

"Really, Abby!" Jessica spoke with vexation. "I'm not ready yet."

"Jess, you must talk now, or you'll get bumped off yourself. You know that's what always happens to people who keep silent."

"Yes, do please spill everything, Mrs. Fletcher," Millard said sarcastically. "I'm all ears. This should be a real lesson in police work."

Jessica sighed. "I just have a theory, that's all."

"Better and better. Theories are so much more exciting than boring old facts."

"Sheriff," Boswell snapped, "if you want to hear what Mrs. Fletcher has to say, why don't you just shut up and let her talk? Go on, Mrs. Fletcher."

Jessica took a deep breath. "The problem until now, it seems to me, has been this: even if the killer got Trish drunk, how could he—I'll say *he* for brevity—how could he possibly ensure that she fell right across the path of the gate? Yet the business of training Teddy to press the button proves that that *was* his plan. My idea solves that problem, and explains two other pieces of evidence: what Morgana saw from her window and the fact that the seams of Trish's mink coat were split."

Millard groaned. "Mrs. Fletcher, Morgana's a weirdo. She saw nothing that anyone else would have seen. Trish's coat could have gotten torn anytime."

"Maybe you're right. But I don't think so. Let's look at Barnes' testimony. He saw Trish's car pull up outside the gate at one A.M. Somebody dressed in a fur coat and head scarf got out and pressed the intercom buzzer. Barnes opened the gate, the person fell and Barnes went down to help. Then Morgana looked out of her window and saw the person who'd fallen rise up and, as she put it, disappear. Actually, the person merely moved into the darkness behind the car."

"But she didn't, Mrs. Fletcher!" Millard spoke with exasperation. "Unless Barnes is lying, Trish was still flat on the driveway when he got in sight of the gate."

"What I'm questioning, Mr. Millard, is the word *still*. I don't believe that when Barnes was on his way down from the security room she *was* lying there. I think she'd only been there a matter of seconds when he arrived on the scene."

"Bull! He saw her fall minutes before on his TV screen."

Jessica shook her head. "He saw *somebody* fall. But was it Trish? I think not."

There was a pause. Then Will Roxie suddenly snapped his fingers. "He saw the killer! Dressed in Miss Langley's fur coat."

Jessica beamed at him. "Exactly, Will. Coat and scarf, I think."

Will concentrated. "Miss Langley was very slim and slight, and when the killer put the coat on, it was too small and the seams got split."

"Right."

"But where was Miss Langley then?"

"Lying unconscious—knocked out or drunk or drugged—in the back of the car. I think it was the killer, dressed in Trish's coat and scarf, who drove the car up to the gate. He deliberately slewed it sideways, to suggest drunk driving, got out and staggered to the intercom. But he didn't speak into it—just pressed the buzzer. Barnes could only see a figure outlined against the headlights. He assumed it was Trish and opened the gate.

"The murderer then deliberately fell across the path of the gate, knowing that Barnes would see and come down to help. He gave him a minute to get clear of the security room, then got up, hurried to the back of the car, lifted Trish out, put her things back on her, carried her to the gate and laid her down in the same position he'd been lying himself. Then he used the intercom to give Teddy the command to close the gate. The whole thing must have taken him rather longer than he'd anticipated, because Barnes nearly got there in time to pull Trish clear. However, in the end the plan did work."

There was silence for several seconds before Will Roxie said softly, "Gee, that's brilliant."

Millard shot him a dirty look.

Boswell spread his hands. "Mrs. Fletcher, for once I'm speechless."

"What about it, Sheriff?" Abby asked pointedly.

Millard had taken out his pencil and was engaged in his favorite hobby of chewing the end. At last he gave a reluctant shrug. "Well, I suppose it makes sense, in a screwy kinda way. But tell me, Mrs. Fletcher, what sort of signal d'you figure he'd give the dog?"

"I don't think he'd use his voice, for fear of it being overheard and recognized. I suggest possibly a whistle."

Millard reached into his pocket and pulled out a short silver chain from the end of which dangled a shiny whistle. "Something like this?"

"Yes, I imagine so."

He put the whistle in his mouth and blew. None of the people in the room heard anything, but Teddy pricked up his ears and gave a bark.

"It's one of them ultrasonic jobs," Millard said. "Only dogs can hear them. We found it in the grass at the edge of the road, about ten yards outside the gate."

"Well, there you are," Jessica said excitedly. "That's it, for sure."

"Glad to hear you say that, Mrs. Fletcher, because it's got some initials on it."

He looked down and read out slowly: "A.B.F." He stared straight at Abby. "Your middle name's Benton, isn't it, Miss Freestone?"

"Yes." Abby had gone very pale.

"That's all I wanted to know. I'm taking you in. Suspicion of murder in the first degree. Read her her rights, Will."

Looking unhappy, Will took a card from his pocket and approached Abby.

Millard turned to Jessica. "Thanks for fingering her for us, Mrs. Fletcher."

Jessica gave an indignant gasp. "I did no such thing! Sheriff, this is ridiculous! The fact the killer used Abby's whistle doesn't make Abby the killer."

"In my book it goes a long way toward it, Mrs. Fletcher."

Boswell said, "But what conceivable motive could Abby have for murdering Trish?"

Millard shrugged. "There's been bad blood between them. Everybody knows that. Besides, you can never tell—"

"What sort of motives are going to come to light till you start digging —I know, I know." Boswell spoke irritably. "Sheriff, Trish might have had a motive for killing Abby, after the accusations Abby's been making about Denton's death. But not the other way around!"

"And what *about* Denton's death?" Jessica put in. "Isn't it rather a coincidence that there have been two violent deaths in the Langley family in so short a time?"

"Not really. Not if they were both murder."

Jessica gasped. "But you've refused all along to believe Denton was murdered!"

"There was no real evidence of murder. Trish's death changes things. We now know there's been a killer at large."

"You're . . . you're not suggesting my cousin murdered *Denton* too?" Jessica said incredulously.

"Why not? She had a good motive. That horse, Silver King, must be worth thousands of dollars."

"But, Sheriff," Boswell said wearily, "Abby didn't know Denton had left her the horse."

"Can you be sure of that, Mr. Boswell?"

Boswell looked at Abby. "Tell him, will you?"

Before she could answer, Millard interrupted. "Never mind what she says. Could you, Mr. Boswell, swear Denton Langley didn't tell her?"

Boswell hesitated. "Well, I suppose I couldn't actually—"

"There you are, then. And remember, if Sawdust was doped, this young woman had the best chance of anyone to do it."

Jessica stared at him in disbelief. "But it's Abby who's been insisting, against you and the Langleys, that that's what happened. If she'd done it herself, it would be insane to draw attention to it!"

Millard shrugged again. "Could be a sophisticated double bluff."

Jessica threw her hands in the air. "If you believe that, you'll believe anything."

"Fact is, Mrs. Fletcher, you're kin. You don't want to believe she's guilty. Now, I'm not saying Miss Freestone will be charged with Denton Langley's murder—that'll be up to the DA. But we got enough on her to nail her for Trish's death. And well you know it."

He turned to Abby. "Get your coat, Miss Freestone."

Jessica made one last attempt. "Sheriff, please, give me—"

But she was interrupted. For the last several minutes Abby had been silent. She had merely stood, fondling Teddy, seeming to be only half listening as Jessica and Boswell sought to defend her. There appeared to be a slight smile on her lips. Now, however, she spoke.

"It's all right, Jess. I don't mind. I'm sure you and Mr. Boswell will look after my interests very well. And it means Teddy's going to have a friend with him in the slammer, doesn't it? We can keep each other company."

# Chapter Twenty-two

"WHY, Mrs. Fletcher, this is a surprise. Do come in."

Tom Cassidy stepped aside, and Jessica entered the house.

"Thank you."

"Go into the den."

He ushered her through a door on the right. She found herself in what was very much the room of an unmarried outdoor man. Sporting trophies lined the walls; stuffed fish were mounted in glass cases; photographs of horses and dogs and groups of men with rifles and fishing rods were dotted about. There was a big open fireplace of undressed stone; deep, shabby but comfortable-looking leather armchairs; bearskin rugs on the floor. There were no flowers or ornaments or anything of purely decorative value.

"Won't you sit down?" Cassidy asked.

Jessica lowered herself into one of the armchairs, sinking so deeply into it that she began to think she would never stop descending.

Cassidy was looking at her as if he didn't quite know what to do with her.

"Can I get you a drink?" he asked abruptly.

"No, really. Thank you."

"Coffee? Tea?"

"Nothing at all, thanks."

"Oh." He fidgeted a little from foot to foot.

"Mr. Cassidy," Jessica said gently, "do forgive me saying this in your own home, but won't you please sit down?"

"Oh, sure." He took a seat opposite her. He cleared his throat. "I heard about Abby. Very sorry."

"She didn't do it, you know."

"Never thought she did. Millard's a fool."

"You know most people in this neighborhood pretty well, I imagine," Jessica said.

"Sure do. Lived here all my life."

"They look up to you, I'm sure."

He looked embarrassed. "Don't know about that. It was Denton who carried the weight around here."

"But Denton's dead."

"What you getting at, Mrs. Fletcher?"

She paused before asking. "First of all, how well do you know Deputy Roxie?"

"Will? His pa worked for me for thirty years. Will could have, too, if he hadn't decided he wanted a bit more excitement in his life. He's a good boy."

"And rather more intelligent than Sheriff Millard."

"You can say that again. But I don't follow—"

"Well, you see, I'm pretty sure I know who killed Denton and Trish Langley."

He sat up with a jerk. *"You do?"*

"Yes. But unfortunately I have absolutely no proof. I need some help —from someone in a position to make a few inquiries, ask a few questions, take a look at some of the evidence in this case. From somebody in the Sheriff's Department. It's hopeless to ask Millard. Will Roxie seems the obvious man to approach. But I'm an outsider here. Furthermore, I'm Abby's cousin. I think he might be loath to act unofficially, at my request. However, if *you* were to ask him . . ." She left the sentence unfinished.

"Well, of course, I'll do all I can. And I think probably I can persuade Will to do me a favor. I gave him a character reference when he first applied to join the department, so he owes me."

"Oh, that's wonderful."

"What do you want him to do?"

"I'll come to that in a moment. But next let me ask how well you know the coroner?"

"Charlie Harrington? One of my oldest buddies. We've played poker together 'most every Sunday night for the last twenty years."

"Better and better. And he's not, er, hidebound?"

"Not at all. Why?"

"Well, I may want to take part in Trish Langley's inquest. As *amicus curiae.*"

"Friend of the court, if I remember my Latin. Rather unusual, isn't it?"

"Yes, but not unheard of. A coroner is allowed a lot of latitude in the way he conducts an inquest. So I'm wondering if you could sound him out on the possibility."

"Yes, of course, if you think it's important."

"I believe it's very important, if we're going to nail the killer."

"Then I think I can guarantee Charlie will play ball." Tom Cassidy chuckled. "I know about one or two things he did in his younger days that he wouldn't want shouted around the town now . . ."

"Oh, I'm not asking you to go in for blackmail."

"There'll be no specific threats, Mrs. Fletcher. But Charlie'll understand. I'm quite adept at arm-twisting when it's really necessary."

Jessica smiled. "I'm not unskilled at it myself. Now, there are a couple more things I want to ask. You've known the Langley children all their lives, I take it."

"Of course."

"Would you give me your impressions of Spenser?"

Cassidy's face clouded slightly. He didn't answer. He reached for a pipe that was resting on a table near his elbow, then withdrew it.

"Please do smoke," Jessica said.

"Oh, thanks."

He filled the pipe from his pouch, lit it and sucked fiercely to get it well glowing. It was a slow, leisurely process, but Jessica did not attempt to hurry it. She knew Tom Cassidy needed the time to straighten out his thoughts. At last he spoke.

"Must say I've never taken to him."

"May I ask why?"

"Something shifty about him."

"He's a bit of a crook?"

"Well, he doesn't have a criminal record. I don't know anything specific. But I've heard things. And I know Denton was very unhappy about some of Spenser's business deals." He hesitated. "Look, I'm probably being unfair. These are rumors only. I *know* of nothing personally against him."

"I didn't expect you to. I only asked you for your impressions. Has he ever been violent?"

Cassidy glanced at her sharply. "Not that I've ever heard—or seen. Frankly, I doubt he'd have the guts."

"You mean he'd be afraid it would come back on him?"

"Right."

"I see." Jessica was thoughtful for a moment. Then she looked up and spoke more briskly. "Now: what about Morgana?"

Again, Cassidy let several seconds pass before speaking. "Meeting her now, you'd think she was just batty, wouldn't you? But she wasn't always like that. In fact, she was a highly intelligent young woman. She was always interested in the paranormal. But in those days the interest seemed more scientific. She retained some skepticism. Then, after her marriage broke up, she gradually changed. It was as if she began to swallow all that stuff—hook, line and sinker. She seemed to become . . . oh, I don't know, almost a caricature of an occult buff. D'you know what I mean?"

Jessica nodded. "Very well. From the first it seemed to me to be over-done. Spiritualism, astrology, divination, portents—it was just too much."

"That's it. Must admit I found myself wondering once or twice whether it was all genuine. Though for the life of me I can't figure out what reason she could have for pretending."

"Well, you know, in certain circumstances it might suit an intelligent person to be regarded as a bit crazy; not to be taken too seriously; to stand around smiling vaguely, gabbling on about astral projections and auras and spirit guides; and all the time to be listening—picking up all sorts of information other people imagine is going straight over your head. I can conceive of someone getting a kick out of that—secretly laughing all the time at others' gullibility."

He gazed at her in admiration. "Yes, I guess that makes sense. I hadn't seen it that way. You know, Mrs. Fletcher, I understand why you're a successful author."

"Because I have such a vivid imagination?"

"Not really. Because you understand how other people's minds work —you can put yourself in their shoes."

Jessica smiled. "It's not always a fortunate ability. Sometimes I try to put myself in the shoes of a murderer, and, really, I often begin to feel quite murderous. But to revert, what do you know about Echo?"

"Not a lot. Haven't seen much of her. She hasn't been here a great deal. What I've seen I rather like. She's a cheeky young minx, but she's got spirit. I feel a little sorry for her, though. . . . Mrs. Fletcher, you say you think you know who killed Denton and Trish. So may I ask just what's the point of these questions?"

"You're wondering if it's just pure nosiness? Well, no. I admit that not everything I've asked is relevant to the identity of the murderer. But I want to tie up all the loose ends before I make my presentation in court, and an independent opinion on the character of some of the people in-volved should be a help. I promise you that everything you've said will remain quite confidential. I may be inquisitive. But I'm not a gossip."

"I never thought you were, ma'am."

Jessica opened her purse and took from it a folded piece of paper. "Now, these are the points I'd like you to have Will check out for me."

Cassidy took it and read it through slowly. The expression on his face changed from blankness to mystification and finally to anger. He looked up.

"If this points the way it seems to—"

"There's no proof as yet," she said. "That's why those things are so important. Particularly the first. That should be followed up immediately; otherwise it could be too late. It's a long shot, but it could provide proof positive."

Cassidy stood up. "I'll get on to it right away. And if Will can't do it, I'll check it out myself."

Jessica also rose. "Thank you very much. Will you call me as soon as you find out anything?"

"Sure will."

"Good. And now you can do one more thing for me: tell me how to get to Asa Potts' place. I have to see a man about a dog bite."

Asa Potts' farm looked a mess. Paint peeled from the woodwork, a window was boarded up. The gate into the yard, which was littered with junk, hung crookedly from its post. A shed looked on the verge of collapse. A few scrawny-looking hens pecked listlessly about.

It was a depressing sight, Jessica thought, as she gazed at it from the shelter of a clump of trees. There was no sign of human life. However, the next moment there came the sound of a power saw from the far side of the house.

Jessica glanced around, then left the trees. She made her way up to the crooked gate and entered the yard. She crossed it and peered cautiously around the side of the house.

Asa Potts, in scruffy old jeans and a checked shirt with the sleeves rolled up, was cutting logs. His back was to her, and Jessica was able to eye him at leisure for several seconds. She paid particular attention to his arms. They told her all she needed to know; and she was about to turn away when a voice from behind her nearly made her jump out of her skin.

"Is this just a social call, Mrs. Fletcher?"

She spun around. Spenser Langley was standing about six feet away. His face was cold and hard.

Jessica rallied. "I might ask you the same question, Mr. Langley."

"Potts is a neighbor of mine. The properties adjoin. Naturally, we have common interests."

Jessica nodded. "Yes, I'm sure you have."

The sound of the saw had stopped and she heard footsteps behind her. She turned again to see Potts staring suspiciously at her. In his hands was a shotgun.

"What you doing here?" he growled.

"I came to see how you were recovering."

"Recovering?"

"From that very bad bite you received from Teddy. I must say your healing process is quite remarkable. There's not a mark of any kind on your arm, not the slightest sign of a scar."

"You fool, Potts," Spenser said viciously.

Potts' complexion went red. "Less of the fool, mister. This was your crazy idea. I should never have listened to you."

Jessica looked at Spenser again. "Did you really expect to get away with drugging Teddy and having this man fake an injury?"

For a moment it seemed Spenser was going to deny the charge. Then he obviously realized the futility of this.

"Having the dog destroyed seemed the surest way to break the will," he muttered.

"Where did the blood on Teddy's collar come from?"

"Potts pricked his finger and we smeared it on."

Jessica nodded. "I see. That was before Boswell put the dog in Abby's full-time care, so you had easy access to him. Then you drugged him to make him attack you. You pretended to stop Potts' showing his wound to the sheriff that day. I suppose you figured that with Potts' blood on the collar, witnesses to testify the dog *had* attacked *you,* plus Potts' artistically bandaged arm, no one would think to question that he had actually been bitten by the dog."

"But *you* did, of course, Mrs. Fletcher," Spenser sneered.

"Oh, I'm sure if the case ever came to trial, Mr. Boswell would demand medical proof of the bite."

Spenser grinned. "That could have been forthcoming—if needed."

"Ah, I see." Jessica nodded comprehendingly. "Yes, Mr. Langley, you would be the sort of person to be acquainted with a certain type of amenable doctor."

Spenser bowed. "I take that as a compliment."

Suddenly Potts' gave a yell. "Shut up this gabble!" He glared at Spenser. "You're playing into her hands—admitting everything. You call *me* a fool!"

"She knows!" Spenser snapped. "Once she'd seen your arm, there was no point in denying it."

Potts stepped menacingly up to Jessica. "We'll go to jail for this unless we shut her up."

"And how do you propose to do that?"

"I been to jail once and I ain't going back." He brandished the shotgun. "I say we plant her in the orchard."

Jessica's heart missed a beat. The man looked and sounded deadly serious. But the next moment Spenser stepped forward. He brushed past her, strode up to Potts and twisted the gun from his hands. "Don't be such a damned hillbilly, Potts," he said curtly. He addressed Jessica. "He's harmless, really. Just likes to talk big."

Potts was looking sulky. "We could have scared her into keeping her trap shut."

"I don't think Mrs. Fletcher is the type to be scared into keeping her trap shut."

He looked back at her again. "Mrs. Fletcher, this was a crazy scheme, born of desperation. We would have needed to prove at least one other attack by Teddy, before he would have been destroyed. But now everything's changed: my sister's dead and Teddy's in the sheriff's charge. The scheme is kaput. Potts won't press the matter any further. So, can't you forget it? After all, what real harm have we done?"

Jessica was silent for a few moments. She glanced from Spenser to the still truculent-looking Potts and back to Spenser before answering. "Well, I don't know what the ASPCA would think of your giving Teddy that drug, but it didn't seem to do him any lasting harm. Nonetheless, it *was* a clear attempt at fraud."

"Guilty. I attempted to defraud a dog out of fifteen million bucks."

In spite of herself, Jessica smiled. She said, "I'll compromise. I shall say nothing about Mr. Potts' part in this." She almost felt Potts relax at these words. She continued, addressing Spenser, "And I'll say nothing about your part in it—providing you make no further attempt to overturn the will. If you do, I shall tell Mr. Boswell all I know."

Spenser pursed his lips. "You drive a hard bargain, ma'am."

"Take it or leave it."

He made a gesture of resignation. "Done."

Jessica took a deep breath. "Very well. And now, if you'll excuse me, I'll be getting along."

"I'll excuse you, all right," Potts grunted. "Didn't ask you here in the first place."

"Forgive my friend," Spenser said smoothly. "I assure you that beneath his rough exterior beats a heart of gold. Allow me to escort you to the gate."

They crossed the yard together and he opened the gate. Jessica went through.

"Thank you," she said. "Goodbye."

As she was walking away he called out after her. "Oh, Mrs. Fletcher." She turned. "Yes?"

"You understand, my promise is solely personal. Morgana and Echo had no part in my little scheme, and I have no influence over what they decide to do about contesting the will."

He raised a hand in final salute, turned around and sauntered back across the yard. Jessica watched him for a moment, then continued on her way, beset by the sudden vague suspicion that somehow she had been conned.

However, she soon threw off the feeling. Compared with murder, a simple fraud was not very important. It was the murder she had to concentrate on. As long as she cleared Abby, nothing else really mattered.

# Chapter Twenty-three

THE courtroom was packed to overflowing. The bizarre circumstances of Trish Langley's death, coming immediately after that of her father, followed by the arrest of Abby, and finally the knowledge of Jessica's involvement, had aroused tremendous media interest. Neither in the press gallery nor on the public benches was there an empty seat. Certainly in all his years as county coroner, Charles Harrington had never known an inquest like it.

The clock showed eleven A.M. He banged with his gavel on the desk, and a hush settled on the courtroom. He made a few preliminary remarks, formally stating the purpose of the proceedings. Official evidence of identification was given, and then the medical examiner was called to stipulate the cause of death. After this a fingerprint expert testified to having visited the security room with Barnes, finding Teddy there alone, locked in, and to his discovery of the dog's paw print on the gate button. He produced the actual button, still set in its mounting, which had been removed from the security room.

When he had stepped down, the coroner said, "This hearing is now going to take rather an unusual turn. I have been informed that a lady who was staying on the Langley estate at the time of the tragedy believes she can, by means of a demonstration, throw light on how it came to occur. Somewhat against my better judgment I have agreed to let her present this demonstration, in the capacity of *amicus curiae*. I've also decided it better be gotten out of the way at the outset, as it may affect the entire course of the hearing. I just hope it isn't going to turn out to be a mare's nest; if so, certain people will have a great deal of explaining to do."

He glared pointedly at Tom Cassidy, who raised a hand to his mouth to conceal a smile.

"Mrs. Fletcher," Harrington said.

Jessica rose and stepped forward. "Thank you, sir."

She coughed nervously. "As you know—as probably everybody knows

—Abigail Freestone has been charged with the murder of Trish Langley, the accusation being that she trained the dog, Teddy, to press the button which operated the gate and so killed Trish. Apart from the fact that Abigail Freestone is an experienced animal trainer, the only real evidence against her is that a whistle belonging to her was found by the sheriff's men, lying in the grass near the intercom at the gate where Trish Langley was killed."

She crossed to a table where the various exhibits, neatly labeled, were laid out, picked up the whistle and held it in the air. "This is it. Sheriff Millard believes this was used to give Teddy the signal to press the button. I now wish to call my only witness—and that is Teddy."

She made a sign to Will Roxie, who was standing by the door. He went out and reappeared a moment later, leading Teddy on a leash. In his other hand Will was carrying a small loudspeaker, from which trailed a long electric wire. The other end of it remained outside the courtroom. He placed the loudspeaker on the table, then looked down at the dog and said, "Sit."

Teddy sat down and looked around expectantly.

"I think we'll dispense with a swearing-in," Harrington said. A titter was heard throughout the room.

Jessica addressed the coroner. "This loudspeaker has been supplied by the company that installed the security system at Langley Manor. It is identical to the ones used in the intercoms there."

She handed the whistle to Will. "Would you blow into this, please?"

Will complied. Teddy's ears instantly pricked, his head jerked up and he gave a bark.

"Of course," Jessica went on, "that is an ultrasonic whistle, audible only to a dog. And there can be no question but that Teddy heard it. Now, Will, I'd like you to go outside into the room on the far side of the corridor. Make sure both doors are closed, speak into the mike that's hooked up to this speaker—and then blow the whistle again."

Will gave a nod and went out. The tension in the room could almost be tasted during the few seconds' silence that ensued before Will's voice came over the intercom.

"I'm ready, ma'am. Going to blow now."

There was a pause. Every eye was fixed on Teddy. But the dog reacted not at all. He was in fact beginning to look rather bored. Then Will spoke again.

"That's it. I gave a long, hard blow."

Jessica turned to the coroner. "You see, sir, even Teddy couldn't hear it this time."

Harrington frowned. "Why not?"

"Because that whistle is above the range of any loudspeaker. The chief electronic engineer of the company is in court and will testify to that effect, if required. The whistle *couldn't* have been the killer's signal. Therefore, the main piece of evidence against Abigail Freestone is quite worthless."

In her seat, Abby was smiling with relief and joy. Boswell gave her a delighted thumbs-up sign. The sheriff's expression was sour, while the faces of Spenser, Morgana and Echo showed no expression at all.

"Well, that's quite remarkable," Harrington said. "You suggesting that whistle was planted in order to incriminate your cousin, Mrs. Fletcher?"

Jessica shrugged. "Obviously it *could* have been. I'm not claiming it *was*. It might have been pure coincidence."

"Hm. Mighty farfetched one. Do you have any idea as to what the signal actually was?"

"I think so. Mr. Barnes—the security guard—and Morgana Cramer have both described something that sounded like a bird call: Mr. Barnes told me it was a mockingbird, Mrs. Cramer described it as 'crying like a mourning dove.' That, I believe, was the signal. This could perhaps be proved by having someone imitate that call and seeing if Teddy reacts."

The coroner considered. "I think we'll skip that for now."

"I believe it's important," Jessica persisted.

"No, I don't see it, Mrs. Fletcher. We know a signal *was* given—the paw print on the button proves that—and if it wasn't the whistle, the exact nature of it is irrelevant. Moreover, anyone could learn to imitate a mockingbird."

He signaled to the bailiff. "Take the dog out, please."

The bailiff complied, and Harrington addressed Jessica again. "Well, thank you very much, Mrs. Fletcher. You've not, of course, exposed the real murderer, but on the other hand—"

Jessica interrupted. "I think I can, sir."

He stared at her. "You saying you know who killed Trish Langley?"

"I believe the evidence all points in one direction. May I proceed?"

"Yes, Mrs. Fletcher, do. Irregular this may be, and I daresay I'll be criticized, but if there's a chance to clear this business up, I say let's try. You turned up trumps over the whistle, so the floor's yours."

"Thank you, Mr. Coroner." Jessica looked around the court. "I was very much confused immediately after Trish Langley's death, because it seemed obviously linked with other attempts by certain, er, interested parties, to have Teddy destroyed, thereby upsetting Denton Langley's will."

She looked hard at Spenser. He was sweating, but his face remained expressionless. Jessica let him worry for a few more moments, then went on: "Actually, the murder of Trish was unconnected with the attempts on Teddy's reputation—unconnected except insofar as the latter provided a perfect cover for Trish's killer.

"Now, why was Trish Langley killed? Not for money. *Denton* Langley was killed for money. His horse was doped to make it bolt. And the person who doped it was"—Jessica paused—"Trish Langley."

She stopped to let this sink in, then continued: "Trish, however, had an accomplice—someone who probably put her up to doping Sawdust, and who then killed her to prevent her talking and revealing her accomplice's identity, perhaps even blackmailing that accomplice. For, after all, fifteen million dollars was at stake."

"But, Mrs. Fletcher," the coroner said, "Trish only inherited fifty thousand dollars under Denton's will."

"Yes, sir, but she had expected to get millions. Instead, she saw practically all her father's money go to Teddy. One can imagine the shock, and the furious anger when she learned the truth. She was bitter, revengeful and almost constantly drunk. She'd been drinking the night she was murdered. She was a dangerous woman who had to be silenced. The murderer's scheme was highly ingenious, and very complex. Everything had to be timed, almost to the second. Barnes had to be lured from the security room. Nobody had to be near. The road had to be clear. And it was that thought that really led me to the truth."

"You're losing me, Mrs. Fletcher," Harrington said.

"I'm sorry. Perhaps I'm not expressing myself clearly. I'll try to explain." She thought for a moment. "The night of the murder, something rather fortunate happened." She smiled. "Mr. Boswell came to my cousin's cottage, and I happened to notice that he had grease on his trousers. I pointed it out to him, and as a result he told me something he would otherwise never have bothered to mention: he'd had a flat tire on his way over and had had to change a wheel. I immediately suggested that the puncture may have been deliberately caused—that the killer might have strewn tacks or something similar in the road to make sure it remained free of traffic at the time of the murder.

"Mr. Boswell didn't think a lot of the idea, but he agreed to come with me to the spot he'd had his flat, and search for something which may have caused it. After we'd been examining the road surface for a few minutes, I was able to show him three large tacks. Mr. Boswell took one of them, and I'm sure he'd agree it could easily have caused a puncture."

She glanced at Boswell and he gave a brief nod. Jessica went on.

"Unfortunately, we weren't able to examine the punctured tire there and then, as Mr. Boswell explained it was at home in his garage, waiting to be taken in for repair."

Jessica gave a signal to Will Roxie, who had reentered the courtroom several minutes earlier. He came forward, producing from his pocket a small pillbox, which he handed to her. She opened it and took from it a small shiny object, which she held up. "And this is, in fact, the very tack that later that day the mechanic at Wilson's garage removed from Mr. Boswell's tire in the presence of Deputy Roxie."

The coroner was looking keenly interested. He leaned forward. "Mrs. Fletcher, it's evident that whoever put those tacks on the road is the killer. Are you saying you know who that person was?"

"Yes, sir."

"Do you have proof?"

"Better than that, I think. I have a confession."

"A confession?" The coroner stared. "Then for heaven's sake, Mrs. Fletcher, don't keep us in suspense. Tell us who did it."

Once more Jessica's eyes swept the room. They alighted finally on Tom Cassidy. Then she looked back at the coroner.

"I did," she said.

A buzz of mystified excitement ran through the courtroom at Jessica's words. The faces of most of the principals were blank with bafflement, but Marcus Boswell was looking extremely angry.

Charles Harrington silenced the room with a further bang of his gavel. Then he looked sternly at Jessica.

"Is this a joke, Mrs. Fletcher?"

"No, sir."

"I take it that you are not confessing to the murder of Trish Langley?"

"No, I'm not."

"I think you had better explain." The coroner's voice was edged with ice.

"Certainly." She held up the tack again. "This is one of three tacks, taken by me from the tool closet at the Langley Manor stables. It can be positively identified, because I scratched my initials on the underside of the head. The lettering is naturally very small, but it can be clearly seen with a magnifying glass. I marked it before dropping it on the road at approximately the spot that Mr. Boswell identified as the place where he'd had his puncture."

She paused. "And that, Mr. Coroner, is really very strange. Because, you see, I'd dropped these tacks just a few seconds before pretending to find them there—twelve hours *after* Mr. Boswell's supposed puncture."

There was absolute hush in the courtroom. It was Marcus Boswell himself who eventually broke it. His face was livid as he jumped to his feet.

"Mr. Coroner, I must protest! I—"

"Please sit down, Mr. Boswell. You'll have a chance to speak later. Continue, Mrs. Fletcher."

Jessica collected her thoughts. "The truth," she said, "is that Mr. Boswell did *not* have a flat. He made that up on the spur of the moment, in order to account for the grease marks on his trouser leg. However, when I showed such an interest in his story, he had to carry on with it. Even to the extent of deliberately puncturing one of his tires. When he and I were out together, I looked at the tires on his car. They all showed a virtually identical amount of wear—a pretty clear indication that none of them was the usual spare, and that a wheel had *not* been changed. I asked to see the tire that had received the puncture, but Mr. Boswell claimed it was back in his garage. He obviously couldn't allow me to see the spare wheel—untouched and intact—in the trunk."

Again Boswell was on his feet, shouting. "Mr. Coroner, this is irrelevant, immaterial, and just plain inane!"

The coroner hesitated. "Well, Mrs. Fletcher: is it? You are certainly attributing strange behavior to Mr. Boswell. But if a man wants to puncture his own tire, I can't see it's evidence of any crime."

"Not *evidence,* I agree," Jessica said. "But when someone does all that to cover up his true actions on the night of a murder, it is surely suspicious. The fact is, as soon as I saw the grease on Mr. Boswell's trouser leg, I recognized it for what it was: the *mark left by a bicycle chain.* Mr. Boswell had been riding a bike that night—and he didn't want anybody to know it."

"And why do you say that was?"

Jessica spoke very deliberately. "Because he used the bike to get away from the scene of the murder after killing Trish Langley."

Once more Boswell leapt up. His face was now convulsed with fury. "This is monstrous!" he yelled. "It's character assassination!"

"It's certainly a very grave accusation," Harrington said. "Do you have anything to support it, Mrs. Fletcher? Anything concrete?"

Jessica went back to the table and picked up one of the exhibits. "This is a bicycle clip. Now, marks such as those on Mr. Boswell's trousers are only made when clips are not worn. This clip was found in the long grass by the sheriff's men during their routine search of the area around the main gate of the Langley estate."

"But . . . but absolutely anybody could have dropped that!" Boswell spluttered.

Jessica looked at him. "But you do own a bicycle?"

"Sure I do. So do millions of other people." He turned to Harrington. "Mr. Coroner, how much longer do we have to put up with this—this comedy routine?"

"And when," Jessica asked, "is Mr. Boswell going to explain why he deliberately punctured his own tire?"

Boswell threw up his hands in a gesture of surrender. "All right. I'll explain. I *did* have to change a wheel that night. But not on *my* car. I was out with a lady—in her car. We had a flat. I lied to Mrs. Fletcher about it because the lady I was with is married. And before anybody asks, I have no intention of revealing her name."

There was silence. Harrington drummed with his fingers on the desk. He looked from the flushed and breathless Boswell to Jessica.

"Well, Mrs. Fletcher, do you have anything else to substantiate your claim? Because that seems a pretty reasonable explanation to me."

Jessica nodded. "It is. I congratulate Mr. Boswell on thinking of it. But, of course, it's completely untrue."

Boswell opened his mouth for an angry retort, but before he could speak Jessica went on.

"Mr. Coroner, I think this could be settled once and for all. Earlier, I asked to be allowed to conduct a further experiment with Teddy. You refused to allow it. May I respectfully repeat my request? It will only take a matter of a minute or two."

There was what seemed a very long pause while Harrington considered. Although she was outwardly calm, Jessica's heart was in her mouth. This was her last ace. If the coroner refused to let her play it, or Boswell trumped it, she was finished—and heaven only knew what sort of slander charges she had laid herself open to.

At last Harrington spoke. "All right, Mrs. Fletcher, I will give you just a little more latitude. But I warn you, this is the end. Prove your case now, or that's it as far as this court is concerned." He spoke to the bailiff. "Bring the dog back."

Jessica drew a deep breath. Now, if only Teddy cooperated. This was about the longest long shot she had ever played in her life.

She went across to the witness table, picked up the gate button in its mounting and moved it to a position clear of the other exhibits. Next she pulled a chair up to the table, so that it was just a foot or so from the button.

The bailiff had returned, leading Teddy. "Unclip his leash and lift him on to the chair, please," Jessica said.

The bailiff glanced at the coroner, and on receiving a brief nod, complied. Jessica picked up the button, held it out for the dog to sniff and replaced it. Teddy, highly alert, gave a little whine and fixed his eyes on it.

Jessica stepped back and looked at Barnes, seated in the witness benches. "Now, please, Mr. Barnes."

Barnes cleared his throat, pursed his lips, and the next moment a passable imitation of the distinctive call of the mockingbird rang out.

Teddy stood up. He placed his front paws on the table. His head on one side, his ears pricked, he gazed down at it. Then he deliberately lifted his right paw and pressed it firmly onto the button.

A communal sigh, like wind in the trees, was heard in the courtroom as the breath was slowly expelled from a hundred pairs of lungs.

But Teddy had not finished his performance. Suddenly he jumped down from the chair. The bailiff made as if to grab him, but Jessica quickly checked him with a raised hand. Teddy trotted across the courtroom to the spectator benches. He stopped, sat down, then raised his front legs and begged. He gazed up trustingly straight into the face of Marcus Boswell.

Jessica's voice rang out triumphantly. "Why don't you feed him his reward, Mr. Boswell? After all, he learned to expect it when you were training him to help you murder Trish."

For a full ten seconds Marcus Boswell stared mutely down. Then he slowly bent forward and fondled the dog's ears.

"Sorry, boy," he said huskily, "I just don't have any treats on me right now."

He straightened up, leaned back and covered his face with his hands.

# Chapter Twenty-four

"JESS, I don't understand," Abby said plaintively.

"Must admit I'm a bit flummoxed, too," Tom Cassidy added.

They both gazed hopefully at her. Even Teddy's limpid eyes seemed to be entreating her for something, though in his case it was no doubt for another piece of chocolate cake.

Jessica smiled. "You want an explanation?"

"Yes, please." Abby and Tom spoke in unison.

"Very well." She settled back in Abby's easy chair. "I suppose the first important thing to grasp, which really nobody did at first, is that in leaving the bulk of his estate to Teddy and appointing Marcus Boswell executor, Denton Langley was in effect leaving the money to his attorney —putting him in virtual control of fifteen million dollars. I'm sure Boswell would have found a hundred clever ways to rake off all he wanted. He must have realized the potential as soon as Denton told him of his intention. The trouble then was that Denton might easily live for another fifteen years, or even longer—and Boswell needed money urgently."

"How do you know that?" Abby asked. "He always seemed very prosperous."

"I suppose I don't *know* it. It may have been just greed that drove him. But do you remember the day you and I visited him, his secretary told him that somebody named Bob Hawkins had tried three times to contact him and that it was vital. I asked you afterwards if you knew who Hawkins was, and you said you only knew that a man by that name had been Denton's broker. It was, then, quite likely he was Boswell's broker, too. Now, I don't know a lot about the brokerage business, but I don't imagine brokers often ring up just to ask how you're feeling. If a broker calls a client three times in one day, and says it's vital, then it's a pretty safe bet he's not phoning to tell him that his stocks are all doing very nicely. That sort of urgency usually means he wants money—and fast."

Tom said, "And so that was one of the things you wanted me to have Will Roxie check out for you."

"Well, it's very much easier for someone with a badge to ask that sort of question. Anyway, Will later got it confirmed by Mr. Hawkins that Boswell *had* suffered a disastrous loss, through some highly speculative stock he'd bought—against Hawkins' advice. So it was a fair guess he was badly off, in spite of his outward appearance of prosperity."

"But surely you weren't suspicious of him from that day we called there, were you?" Abby asked.

"No, I wouldn't say really suspicious. But something else you'd told me earlier had already made me, er, Boswell-conscious, shall we say. You'd mentioned that at the will-reading Trish was furious with him, swore she would never forgive him, was going to get even, and so on."

Tom Cassidy nodded thoughtfully. "Yes, I remember. I thought it was odd. Granted, she was bitterly disappointed; but it wasn't Boswell's fault. Denton was his own man. Boswell could never have talked him into making that will. You think she was really mad because Boswell had told her she was going to inherit a lot of money?"

"Well, I'm certain she wouldn't have tried to kill her father for a mere fifty thousand dollars. That would be chicken feed to a girl like her."

"Can you be sure it was Trish who doped Sawdust?" Tom asked.

"It's not a mathematical certainty, but I can't see any other explanation that fits all the facts. After all, if Boswell were going to do it himself, he had no need to involve Trish at all. I think the *method* was Boswell's idea. It has his touch."

Abby frowned. "How do you mean?"

"He's a gambler. We know that from his stock dealings. This was a gamble. There was a fair chance Denton would be killed, but it was far from certain. Like the murder of Trish herself—so much could have gone wrong with that, from his point of view. I think he got a kick from that uncertainty."

"I still don't see how, if she doped Sawdust, she could be a threat to Boswell," Tom said. "She couldn't talk about what they'd done. So why did he have to kill her?"

Jessica smiled. "You're looking at it from a very cool, rational, sober—and masculine—point of view. Trish was bitter, revengeful, a woman—and, above all, a drunk. She could have easily worked herself into such a state that she didn't care how much she incriminated herself, just so she got even. No, she clearly had to go."

"When did you first suspect Boswell of her murder?" Abby asked.

"I think when he lied about the grease on his trousers. You see, I've been cycling all my life, and I knew instantly what that mark was. It's so characteristic. I've stained my own slacks in exactly the same way. So I was staggered when he came out with that story about changing a wheel. Why should he lie? I knew I had to dig deeper. But I didn't want him to realize I was suspicious; I needed a pretext for questioning him more closely about it. So I made up that ridiculous suggestion that the killer had sprinkled tacks on the road to keep it free from traffic."

Abby stared. "You never really thought that had happened?"

"Not for a moment. But then I decided to make use of the idea. Before Boswell and I went out together the next day, I initialed those three tacks and then pretended to find them on the road. It really shook him. He didn't know what to make of it. It gave me an opportunity to look closely at his tires, to satisfy myself they were all evenly worn, and that therefore a wheel had almost certainly *not* been changed. I asked to see the so-called flat tire—but he had to pretend he'd left it at home.

"Why should he go to such lengths to conceal the fact that he'd been riding a bike? And then it came to me. I'd already worked out how the murder had been done—the killer donning Trish's mink, lying down in the path of the gate, and so on. I realized that he must have had some silent and fairly rapid means of getting away from the scene of the crime. A bike would have been ideal—either carried in the trunk or concealed in the bushes in advance. He could have cycled to wherever he'd parked his car and driven home just in time to take Barnes' phone call.

"It all slotted into place. Teddy knew Boswell, who'd given him to Denton in the first place. Boswell had the opportunity to teach him that business with the gate button. I bet all those so-called walks he took Teddy on were actually spent in the security room."

Abby looked surprised. "Surely Barnes wasn't in on it?"

"Oh no. I expect it was during Smedley's shifts. No doubt he was just told to go off duty and leave Boswell alone there with the dog. I expect Boswell made it well worth his while to keep quiet about it."

Tom raised his eyebrows. "Rather putting himself in Smedley's power, wasn't he?"

Jessica shrugged. "If you decide to commit any crimes, there's the possibility of that risk. In this case the risk wasn't too great. Smedley wouldn't have any concrete evidence against him; he could only threaten to tell the sheriff that Boswell had spent time in the security room with the dog. Boswell could buy his silence for a while, and then I'm sure he could have contrived some equally ingenious way to dispose of Smedley. Or, on the other hand, we don't know that—as an attorney—he didn't have some hold over Smedley to ensure his silence."

"All right," Abby said, "you'd decided Boswell was the murderer and worked out nearly all the details of how he'd done it. What next?"

"I really wanted confirmation and clarification. First of all, I knew that Boswell, having started on this flat-tire story, would have to go through with it to the end. He couldn't risk the fact that he *hadn't* taken any tire in for repair coming to light. He'd have to give one of his tires a puncture. And, as he'd kept one of my tacks, it was an odds-on bet he'd use that to do it."

Tom Cassidy nodded. "Which explains the first commission you had me give Will: find out what garage Boswell used and take possession of anything they discovered embedded in his tire."

"Correct. I knew that however well Boswell had covered his tracks, he'd have a tough job explaining the deliberate puncturing of his own tire. Actually, in the event, he fought back brilliantly—though obviously it would have been almost impossible for him to maintain that story about the married woman indefinitely."

Tom said, "You also had me ask Will if they'd found a bicycle clip near the scene of the murder. You even anticipated that!"

"It wasn't vitally important. But cyclists usually keep a pair of clips handy—sometimes in a saddlebag or basket. If Boswell had been cycling without clips, or with only one, it was in the cards he'd dropped one in the dark and hadn't had time to search for it. It was another point confirming my theory. But I couldn't think of any way to prove it. Remember that my primary purpose was to clear Abby. I realized that a demonstration of some kind would be the best way to achieve both ends. The only time and place at which I knew all the necessary persons and things would be brought together—Boswell, Teddy, the exhibits, witnesses—was the inquest."

"And that's when you came to me," Tom said.

"That's right, and you helped no end. You were also able to assist me in clearing up the problem of the remaining Langleys."

"How was that?"

"Well, there was just a possibility one of them was involved in some way. Could one of them have been in cahoots with Boswell—perhaps in helping to overpower Trish, or carrying her unconscious body? There was no obvious motive, but Boswell *might* have promised one of them a share in the estate for helping to dispose of her. I knew Abby's opinion of the Langleys. But you had known them much longer—since they were children. You largely confirmed her opinion of them. But you added a little. First, you said that Spenser had never been violent and that he lacked the guts to be. But there remained the matter of the attempt to frame Teddy. Somebody had been responsible for that. I went over to Potts' farm, and by a stroke of luck got proof that his claim of being bitten was a lie. I also ran into Spenser, learned that he had been behind the scheme, and that it was true he wasn't of a violent nature. I was convinced then that the doping of Teddy and the murder of Trish were unconnected—and I mentally cleared Spenser of any involvement in his sister's death. There remained the enigmatic figure of Morgana. And there again you helped me. Do you remember what you said about her?"

He thought. "Only that as a girl she was very intelligent."

"That's it. You see, all along I'd been puzzled by Morgana's statement about what she'd seen from her window. I could think of no conceivable reason she should invent such a story. On the other hand, could even the most dedicated believer in the supernatural really imagine that what she'd seen was a ghost? She'd watched an actual flesh-and-blood person standing up and walking away—not a spirit materializing and leaving the body behind. But after what you said, Tom, I realized Morgana's vagueness and eccentricity might be a façade. It occurred to me that perhaps she had understood fully what she'd seen, and that describing it in those terms had been her means of obliquely giving a clue to the sheriff and yet not getting too involved. That way her statement made much better sense. And it virtually ruled out the possibility of Morgana being involved in the murder."

"It didn't rule out Echo, though," Abby said.

"True. But it meant that if she *was* involved, Morgana didn't have the slightest suspicion of it. She would never've mentioned what she'd seen if she thought she might be incriminating her daughter. Morgana, of course, might not have known if Echo was involved. But I didn't really see Boswell seeking the help of a girl like Echo. It was just a possibility, but a very slight one, and there was nothing much I could do about it, anyway.

"Then, as I had Will Roxie's reports—on Boswell's stock-market losses, the finding of the tack in the tire, and the bicycle clip—I became absolutely certain that he was the killer, and that he'd played a lone hand. I knew he was the one I had to concentrate on."

"But you really concentrated on Millard first, didn't you?" Abby said. "On demolishing his case against *me.*"

"That didn't entail a lot of work. I just called on the chief engineer of the security company and learned your whistle couldn't have been used to signal to Teddy over the loudspeaker, borrowed some of their equipment, and got the engineer's promise to testify at the inquest, if necessary. I wasn't worried about that part of the demonstration. I knew it had to work. But the second one involving Teddy—that was a different matter. I didn't even know Teddy would react to the button in the same way in such a different environment. And then, the mockingbird's call was going to be slightly different from the original—though I had spoken to Barnes and asked him to practice imitating the call he had heard as closely as possible, and be prepared to reproduce it at the inquest. But even if Teddy did press the button in the courtroom, that would really prove nothing. It was what he did after that which was vitally important. I don't think I've ever been so nervous in my life as in those few seconds."

"What gave you the idea the dog might go across to Boswell like that?" Tom asked.

"Abby did—when she said how it was necessary to reward an animal when he got something right. What really terrified me was that he might forget who had taught him that particular trick—and beg in front of Abby!"

Abby and Tom laughed, and they all looked down at Teddy, who was now fast asleep.

"It's apt, isn't it," Abby said, "that in the end he should play so important a part in nailing the man who planned his master's death?"

"You going to miss him, Abby?" Jessica asked.

"Of course I am. But I think he's a man's dog, really, and I know he'll have a fine home with Tom."

"I've only got temporary custody so far," Tom reminded her.

Jessica said, "Oh, I'm sure it'll be confirmed when the courts appoint a new executor, or whatever the procedure is."

"Hope so. First millionaire I've ever had to look after. But I promise you this. There's not going to be any special treatment. With me he'll have a real dog's life—in the best sense of the term."

"I wonder what's going to happen to the estate generally," Abby said.

He shrugged. "Only the lawyers can say. If you ask me, the Langleys might have a good case if they claimed Boswell unduly influenced Denton in the making of that will."

"I don't think Spenser will be lodging any claim," Jessica said. "But if Morgana and Echo got a bit more out of the estate, I for one wouldn't begrudge it them."

Tom looked at Abby. "And you're off back home to Kent."

She nodded. "Yes, in a couple of weeks—with Silver King. I'm going to concentrate on making the next Olympics."

"You'll be missed here."

"Thanks. There's an awful lot I'll miss. I was very happy here. But I don't think I ever could be again, after all that's happened."

"And you're off home to Maine," he said to Jessica.

"That's right."

"Well, be sure and come back and see us again. Me and Teddy, I mean."

"I'll certainly try," she promised. "It's nice to know I've made two friends here, at least."

"One thing I've got to ask you before you leave," he said. "Jessica, how the heck do you think up your plots?"

# Epilogue

"WELL," Ethan Cragg asked, "did you have a good time?"

Jessica considered. "In some ways."

He raised his eyebrows. "You don't seem very sure. Weren't the lectures a success?"

"They were very well received, as a matter of fact."

"What about the horseback-riding?"

"I managed to stay on."

"And those were the two things you were worried about. I told you you'd be fine."

"You did, Ethan, and you were quite right."

"I suppose, knowing you, you'll be starting a new book right away?"

"No."

"Oh? Why's that?"

"Because frankly, what I want most of all after my vacation is a good long rest."